See Through My Eyes

A Ghost Mystery Anthology

Edited by Amber M. Simpson and Madeline L. Stout

Fantasia Divinity Magazine

Table of Contents

SEE THROUGH MY EYES

Presented by Fantasia Divinity

MUSIC OF THE WILD

By Victor H. Rodriguez

Music is the coordination between man and time. – *Igor Stravinsky*

Now came the subtle sounds of dawn – a soft caress of wind through a healthy crop of barley, the beating of tiny wings from a darting lark or swallow.

Jagged peaks rose into the heavens, protecting and isolating the valley like a vast cradle of thorns. A golden sunrise peeked over the eastern mountains and touched the village below, illuminating the front doors of two dozen humble wood-and-stone buildings.

The tall new master gazed down at the valley's expanse from the battlements of the black tower, the highest point of Feder Schloss. The entirety of that crumbling medieval fortress was now – thanks to a surprise inheritance from a dwindling bloodline on the European side of his family – his.

One by one, the villagers emerged from houses below, making their way across the dark soil to tend another day of farming. It had been another high-yield year, with field crops, meat and dairy all abundant and of the highest quality.

The master turned his attention to the portable phonograph on the stone table next to him. He reached down and carefully operated the brass-handled crank. The cylinder spun beneath the stylus. Through the amplifying horn came eerie echoes of flutes

6

and violins, the first few bars of the *Morning Mood* prelude by Grieg. Far less resonant than hearing it performed by live players, of course, though it was the next best thing to having an orchestra up there with him. The music suited the scene, and brought a rare, warm smile to the master's lean face.

The gentle melody abruptly stopped. The phonograph's mechanism caught on an imperfection on the cylinder... or perhaps it was simply the morning frost. The music being cut short angered him. He tried to force the crank, yet it stubbornly refused to give.

"Damn," he muttered. These days, he had no patience for machines that didn't work properly. He stuffed his hands into the warm pockets of his deep-pile camel-hair coat and thought briefly of hurling the phonograph from the battlements onto the circular driveway below.

He closed his eyes, took in a deep breath of air that chilled his throat, held it, then exhaled steam out into the morning sky. He knew that if he didn't keep his temper in check, no one here would take him seriously, an American stepping into the local lord's oversized shoes. What was that anti-stress trick his alienist had taught him? Breathe in for four seconds... hold it for seven... exhale for eight. He did it, and after two rounds of measured breathing, his composure returned. *Damn my temper. I'll deal with this later*, he grumbled to himself, picking up the heavy phonograph.

With the angular machine resting heavily in his arms, he

navigated a narrow, spiral staircase that led back inside. Compared to the sunny glow at the battlements, the interior of the castle was an icy gray-green. It was poorly illuminated by the candle-like flames of an outdated gaslight pipe system, and its high ceilings drew the gaze into the darkness. The corridors were always coldest – isolated arteries through the old stone castle, separated from the fireplaces on every floor by closed doors to keep the rooms warm.

In this particular hallway, there was an oval mirror with a brass frame he made a point of avoiding. When he had first moved in, after each morning constitutional, he would check his handsome appearance in the incalculably old, burnished glass. On one occasion, he had been startled by a shadowy shape that suggested a hulking man looming over his left shoulder. He snapped his head around to address Johann the butler – or whomever it was that had been lurking there – yet there had been only air.

It hadn't been the first weird event he had encountered in the gloomy castle, either. There were paintings and tapestries that shifted positions with their brethren overnight. In the library, he sometimes found himself re-shelving certain leather-bound volumes that he had no memory of reading. One of those wayward tomes had caught his attention before he put it away – *Natural Histories of the Celtic Peoples of Austria*. The book described a local archaeological site where a pillar dedicated around 300 A.D. to the old god Nodens Silvianus, the Green Man, had been found.

Then there were the sounds. Creaking, knocking, unexplained thuds. Some of this was to be expected in such an ancient structure, yet such an obscene amount! The disturbing noises robbed him of much-needed sleep. Odd, also, that on the same nights, the servants never noticed or reported anything unusual.

The inherent damp of the Austrian weather penetrated the stone walls. Greenish mold frequently appeared amongst the stones on the first floor, and needed to be scrubbed away before it spread. He hated getting a nose full of the sharp, pungent scent – it reminded him of rot and decay.

He quickened his pace through the hallway, opened an iron-bound oak door, and descended another, more luxuriously-appointed staircase – this one draped in crimson carpet – that welcomed him to the main suite of rooms.

The foyer had splendid frescoes and a black-and-white checkerboard marble floor. Waiting to attend him there, slightly reminiscent of chess pieces awaiting his next move, were two servants: a tall, white-haired man with a deeply-lined face, and his plump, brown-haired daughter. The morning sun shone through the segmented windows behind them, and illuminated the gloss of several oil paintings depicting the master's moustache-sporting ancestors upon the walls. A comforting heat radiated from the fifteen-foot-wide stone fireplace. This was one of the brightest rooms in the castle, and he was comfortable here.

"Good morning." His voice rolled out, deep and soft.

The father and daughter bowed formally in response. The daughter spoke first: "Master Federer, will you require breakfast?"

"Thanks, Eva, yes. Please bring it to the library." He had been practicing the line earlier. His German showed signs of improvement, he hoped.

Her father: "We received a note from Horst, the town innkeeper, sir – a package arrived for you. Shall I retrieve it, or…?"

Unlike his daughter, the old man was not able, or perhaps willing, to drop the formal "sir," despite Federer's insistence. Like everything lately, it set him on edge. *Give it time*, Federer thought. *Ways change.* "Thanks for the offer, Johann. I think I'll go into town myself."

Still carrying the uncomfortable phonograph, he looked out the windows. The sky was relatively clear. "First day the sun's been out in over a week. They'll be practicing for Fasching on the village green." Then, frowning at the horizon, he added, "I'd have to be an idiot not to ride myself while I have the chance. Looks like the next thunderstorm will be rolling in tonight."

"Good for the harvest, my lord, bad for keeping oneself dry."

"Thanks, Johann." Federer tromped off to the library. *Good old Johann is being protective.* I'm *the one who should be making more of an effort to fit in*, he thought. *It would be one thing if I were merely a guest. I'm here to stay, though, and to them – bizarre as it sounds – I represent the old aristocracy, proud traditions that preceded the Great War. Spending hours sequestered in my library, writing... well, listening to my phonographs if I'm being perfectly honest... probably isn't helping. Johann and Eva are my bridge to the people. After a year, I don't know why I'm still uncomfortable around them. They're my servants, for God's sake!*

Europe is changing. Lots of new, liberal thinking in Vienna, lots of exciting new art... am I going to shut myself away and hope that tide of new thinking makes its way out here to the eastern fringe, or am I going to do something to bring it here? We must get out of the nineteenth century... yet how can I do something like usher in the future unless I first win their hearts?

His thoughts shifted to more immediate, practical matters. The round trip could take a couple of hours, more if he became distracted by something in town. The woods that shaded the road on the way down to the village were quiet and pretty, though treacherous after nightfall – on more than one occasion there, he had glimpsed the flash of reflective wolf-eyes.

He reached the wood-paneled library; his sanctum, and the first place to which he had turned his attentions when he arrived. Federer gave his arms a rest by putting the malfunctioning machine on the worktable.

Solitude, and a change of scenery, he had thought, were

exactly the formula he needed to finally get some work done. Back home, in Boston, he had won a poetry contest as a young man, and published new work every year thereafter for a time, though the last time had been years ago.

Things had gone wrong with the move, and the energy spent managing the gang of persistent, related problems sapped his drive for creativity, and conspired to keep him unhappy. Crates containing the neat, black notebooks in which he did his writing had ended up in Hungary. He had brought only one notebook with him on the train, though his misery over the missing ones had been for naught. It took him far longer than he liked to fill one with ideas (bad ones at that – except perhaps one inspired piece about the Sultan of Indies, after *The Arabian Nights*).

Back in Boston, his work had been distracted by family and friends. Here, he was distracted by the movers damaging one of his prized phonographs, and his conversation with a soft-spoken engineer who had advised him about the three thousand dollars of repairs the crumbling castle urgently needed.

After he had tracked down the missing crates, he rewarded himself with his favorite pastime – listening to music. He now had five phonographs – two semi-portables, one standing cabinet model fashioned in Edison cement, a brass-appointed Amberola, and a Berliner gramophone that played shellac discs instead of cylinders.

Federer pulled off his gloves and tinkered with the ailing

machine. He gently lifted the amplifying horn, moved it aside, then unlocked and removed the gleaming cylinder. He approached the window to examine it more closely in the light – flawless. He reverently filed it back in its bookcase alongside its brothers – neatly arranged, like scrolls in an ancient library.

With a magnifying lens, he examined the delicate, oiled gears, and the spindle. He spotted the problem. *Some kind of dirt… a leaf or seed-pod from a local plant must have found its way into the mechanism somehow….*

With long tweezers, he removed the offending plant matter, then dabbed the mechanism clean and applied a fine oil where the plant mass had been. He manually moved the machinery and listened with pleasure to the soft, unobstructed clicking of the parts.

How shall I test it? He went over to the bookcase and picked out another recording – Dvorak's *Slavonic Dances* – loaded it in the phonograph, and turned the crank. It played flawlessly, and he savored the sound – pretty, swirling melodies, cut with a touch of sadness, filled the room with the energy and echoes of traditions long past. His mind was completely immersed in the music, spellbound.

When the cylinder finished, it occurred to him that he should start the journey into town. He wished he could have gone on listening, yet he was growing impatient with himself – the so-called new lord – for thinking of putting his responsibility second to his pleasure.

He emerged from the library in a serious mood, and encountered Eva in the hallway, bringing in breakfast on a covered silver tray.

As he breezed by, he said, "Change of plan, Eva, I'll ride into town now."

"Master Federer," she said, "you must eat!"

He stopped and turned on his heel. "I'll have something at the inn – that will kill two flies with one swat," he said coldly. "And don't tell me what I *must* do."

She stood there holding the breakfast tray, cheeks flushed with embarrassment. "I... I'm sorry, I only meant...."

He broke off and walked on, immediately regretting his outburst, yet too self-conscious to apologize. Oh, for a good night's sleep! With all the weird events plaguing him lately, he was on edge, yet that was no excuse to snap at poor Eva. He cloaked himself in silence, thinking of ways he could make it up to her: a more sizeable bonus at Christmas, a trip to Schoppernau to visit her cousins... he would think of something.

***

At the stables, he donned his black riding gear, mounted his favorite horse, and thundered past the iron gate, down a stretch of rough mountain road.

The woods were dim and sweet-smelling, with verdant holly shrubs bearing bright red fruit, and huge, gnarled oak trees

14

that rose high, lining a path littered with fallen leaves of yellow and red.

He was distracted by a howl, a low keening that made the hairs on the back of his neck and arms stand erect. *Wolves in the middle of the day?* It didn't really sound like wolves. His body nevertheless told him primal danger was near.

Shadowed tree trunks encroached further upon the path the deeper he plunged into the woods. Out of the corner of his eye, he thought he spied a tall man, dressed in black, standing amongst the trees. Yet there was no time for Federer to direct his attention – he was suddenly aware of a man in the center of the road, face contorted in a silent scream of horror, waving him down.

He reeled his horse violently to one side, avoiding the man – barely – and stopped.

When he looked back: nothing. Silence.

He steadied his horse's nervous snorting by patting the massive neck reassuringly. A hallucination? Like the mirror? It was so vivid! The man was dressed in black clothes with a priest's collar. How could he have possibly imagined a detail like that? What on earth was happening to him? First, the dark figure in the looking-glass that made no sound… now that awful keening sound connected to… nothing.

His heart was racing. He repeated the breathing exercise. *Four… seven… eight.* After calming himself, he rode on.

The woods parted to reveal sunlit fields and farmers.

People waved while his horse trotted by, welcoming him, and Federer regarded each round, pink face. In truth, he still had trouble telling most of them apart.

He was thinking how he could make a better effort to get to know the people, when he heard the distant sound of a violin. He followed it over a nearby hill, to the clearing of the village green. Several musicians were seated there, playing together in practice for the upcoming festival.

What new music was this? The violins and celli played violent, rhythmic notes that stabbed at the air, gathered volume... then suddenly stopped. Next, a beautiful melody pushed its way through... only to be swallowed up again by more musical stabs. This was chaos, madness... yet thrilling – music that attracted and repelled him in equal measure. He stayed mounted and did his best to project a calm exterior.

The players finished the performance with a final "boom" of the bass drum. Federer dismounted and clapped enthusiastically, approaching the stout, gray-haired conductor, and extended his hand.

"Monsieur...?" Federer said.

"Rott," the man said. He was going bald, with a white goatee that accentuated his face's satyr-like qualities. "Heinrch Rott... from Vienna."

"Superb performance, Rott. What was it?"

"Stravinsky, my lord Federer... *le Sacre du printemps – the*

Rite of Spring."

"And that… violent rhythm – that's the way it was intended to be played?"

Rott took a deep breath. "I hope my lord is not too put off by the piece. It's been a difficult rehearsal, getting the players to represent it properly."

"Put off? Heavens, no! It was quite… remarkable. I'm remarking on it right now, in fact," he said, jokingly.

"Ah, good," said Rott, straight-faced. "Then you know more about music than the Parisians."

Federer looked at him quizzically.

"There was a riot in Paris about ten years ago, when they first played this," Rott said. "The performance was booed, brought to a halt. The composer was devastated, of course. The people were not ready. A few years later, the Parisians came around. One or two critics wrote of the beauty of it – the truth – then a few more, and now it is known to be what it is – a work of genius."

Federer imagined the heavily-cultured Parisians in their tuxedos and evening dresses outraged to the point that they dropped their façades, transforming into an angry mob. *Pitchforks and torches, a second French Revolution demanding the head of the composer.* "Maestro, I know you're busy," he said. "I won't burden you now. After the festival, though, I hope you and your players will join me for lunch."

Rott bowed. "We would be honored, my lord."

Two violinists who had been eavesdropping clapped at that. A heartbeat later, a handful of others joined in the applause.

This group display of appreciation touched Federer's heart in a way he did not anticipate. His chest tightened and he swallowed in a dry throat. At last! He would not be alone! He would share an afternoon with these talented musicians, and he would make it a lunch to remember. He kept his feelings restrained, trying not to express his emotion to the players, however much he liked them.

"Carry on," he said, then put his boot in the stirrup, and swung up into the saddle.

He rode into town, a collection of tall, peak-roofed old houses with vibrant gardens. He neared the center, acknowledging whoever regarded him, making his way down the cobbles to the two-story inn that doubled as a post office. The business was run by a couple he knew by name.

Federer couldn't help but notice an elegant, dark-brown carriage parked in front. The village didn't often have visitors. His curiosity was kindled.

While he hitched the horse, a black-bearded man with massive forearms threw open the front door, grinning broadly. "My lord, what a pleasant surprise!"

I dare not tell him about that horrid apparition in the woods. The townsfolk think I'm strange enough already. Federer took off his riding gloves to shake the innkeeper's rough hand.

"Good morning, Horst. I received your note. A package?"

"Ah, yes! Please come in! We have guests. Perhaps you'd like to join them for lunch?"

"Lunch already? Is it that late?"

"It's afternoon! In any case, please come in and have tea. Mirella is brewing some."

"Horst?"

"Yes, my lord?"

"Please don't call me 'my lord' – it doesn't suit me. Call me 'Federer,' or use my first name, 'Rainer.'"

"As you wish... ah...."

"All men are created equal, Horst. Social class is quickly becoming a thing of the past."

"As you wish... Mr. Federer! You've been here over a year now, after all! I have no wish to make you uncomfortable."

They entered the rustic, warmly-decorated main room. The front desk was of polished mahogany, and the air carried a faint scent of burnt sage. Christian objects were placed upon the walls, tiny guardians against some ancient, forgotten dread.

Horst led him across the hardwood to his best table. "Mr. Federer," Horst said in a low voice. "You must meet our new guest. She is most... ah... interesting."

"She?"

"Oh yes." Horst spoke dreamily. "Lady Dianthe – I believe she's Greek."

"Married?"

Horst winked in response. "I don't believe so."

A door closed upstairs. A solid-looking man with eyes a size too small for his meat-slab of a face lumbered down, causing the stairs to protest audibly.

Horst politely excused himself.

At that moment, Horst's wife, conservatively dressed to the chin beneath a crisp, white apron, emerged from the kitchen bearing a pot of steaming tea.

After one or two words with the stranger, Horst went back behind the front desk, rummaging through the latest mail delivery. "Here it is! From Hallstadt!"

Mirella poured the sweet-smelling brew into a cup right under Federer's nose.

"Hello, Mirella. Thank you." He was especially appreciative, being chilled from his ride. The tea was hot and delicious. Horst approached Federer's table with a shipping crate the size of a suitcase, and put it down on one of the empty chairs.

Federer glanced over to the small-eyed man, who was peering curiously over the top of a newspaper back at him, then turned his attention to the crate, puzzling over who might have sent it. He knew he had distant relations in Hallstadt, though no one with whom he had ever spoken or written. Yet another mystery. The rain-soaked postage indicated the crate had passed through Hungary on the way from its point of origin in Germany. He carefully removed the wrappings.

Horst assisted him in prying open the lid. Mirella hovered close, slowly pouring fresh tea into Federer's cup. The men worked the lid free.

Federer carefully examined the crate's contents. Nestled securely in packing straw were a smooth teakwood box, and a rather old-fashioned sword sheathed in a brown leather scabbard.

He brought the sword out first. It looked Roman – a one-handed sword, like the centurions used to carry – or was it more of a Viking make? A straight, simple blade, in any case, so well-cared for that it looked no more than a hundred years old. The scabbard was decorated with a few early Christian symbols of polished silver.

He gripped the bright pommel and drew the blade in a single, careful motion. He could smell the weapon oil; the metal gleamed in the light. Closely examining the edge with his thumb, Federer drew a painless bead of blood. The tiny drop ran down the length of the blade, and settled at the handguard. He produced a white silk handkerchief and blotted it.

He sheathed the weapon and placed it to one side of the open crate, then took out its traveling companion, the box. Roughly the size of a baguette, the box's smooth-grained exterior had an iron hinge. The lid was emblazoned with his own family's heraldic shield: the great Mesobalanus oak tree. Opening it, he beheld a brilliantly-polished bronze medallion with the same image.

When he handled the medallion, he had an odd sensation, like someone was tugging at an invisible string attached to his forehead. Horst and Mirella stared at him like there had been some unusual change in his face. "Incredible." He rustled through the package for an accompanying letter. It was empty, leaving him mystified. Who might have sent it, and why?

"They suit you, my lord," Mirella said.

Federer looked at her blankly, his mind preoccupied by the contents of the crate. "Thank you."

Mirella pulled Horst off to the kitchen.

Federer held the medallion at eye-level, then raised the chain over his head and put it on, tucking the medallion under his shirt. The metal was cold against the flesh of his neck, and he was overcome by an odd sensation of déjà vu. He looked around, calm, comfortable. He was more alert than the first day he had arrived in Austria. His social anxiety took a backseat to his newfound confidence. He *belonged*.

The small-eyed man put down the newspaper and stood, looking to the top of the stairs, where a slender, woman in a dark-green velvet-and-lace dress had appeared. She glided down the staircase slowly. The small-eyed man stiffly bowed and pulled out her chair. She took a seat without even acknowledging the man's presence.

Federer found it difficult not to stare. He was usually shy

around women; not now. He approached, and she met his gaze with amazing light-hazel-colored eyes, the color of tree leaves in autumn.

The small-eyed man defensively interposed himself between the two of them. The lady gracefully rose, extending a supple hand. Federer took it, and touched his lips to her knuckle. Her hair was a beautiful mane of thick, black curls, and her scent was of the outdoors: mint, lavender, sandalwood, and something spicy he couldn't quite place.

"Enchanted," was all Federer could say.

She glanced him over. "Don't you look dashing."

"Allow me to introduce the Lady Dianthe," said another man's voice. This one was black-haired, with a thick moustache. He stepped off the bottom stair and approached the table.

"My bodyguards," Dianthe said. "Why don't you join us for lunch? You're the new owner of the castle, are you not?"

Her boldness surprised him. She must have been a photographer's model, or perhaps an actress. "Indeed I am," he said.

"Ah, Lord Federer, then. Splendid."

Her manner was well-practiced. Was she a young flapper, intelligent beyond her years... or an ancient creature who somehow still possessed the blush of youth? "Please... call me Rainer."

"All right, Rainer," she purred. "Then you must call me

Dianthe. I'm passing through on my way to Prague. Have you heard the wonderful music they're going to play at Fasching?"

"I have." *She loves music. Perhaps I can play her something from my collection.* "Rott, the conductor, seems like a good man."

"That music, Rainer…" she closed her eyes, savoring the thought. "That is the sound of truth."

"Indeed. So… you're passing through? I've only recently arrived myself. Been here barely a year." He tried his best to conceal his Yankee accent.

"Originally from the United States?"

"Boston," he said.

"An American." She smirked. "You *are* aware of the history behind your new house, aren't you?"

"I understand one of my ancestors, Duke Feder, oversaw the construction in the thirteenth century," he said cautiously. "I'm not exactly sure when the extra –er was added to the name, or when the title was lost and we became mere 'lords,' sometime in the eighteenth, I believe."

"For which?"

"Both." A few years ago, writing a history paper, he had been disturbed to learn that Duke Feder was one of Western Europe's most bloodthirsty tyrants. The morbid life of the nobleman-warlord had been partially recounted in László Turóczi's 1729 work, *Tragica Historia.*

Federer found it fascinating the native Austrians didn't share the same negative picture of the Duke. Horst lionized the man, describing him a distinguished leader of heroic character, a protector of the realm. Who knew what form of history they taught the children here.

"Would you… like to see the castle?" he said.

"I'm afraid I'll be leaving tomorrow," she sighed.

He pressed the point. "Tonight, perhaps?"

"Rainer, I've heard that wolves run in the woods near here, gods protect us all! Would that not be unsafe for a lady?"

Gods? "Bring your bodyguards. Between the three of us, I'm sure we can get you there in one piece. The fortress is at the base of the mountain."

Dianthe hesitated, said: "I would only agree if you could prepare guest rooms for us. It would be far too late to return to the inn after you've taken me on a proper tour of your beautiful house." She leaned back in her chair, letting Federer get a good look.

Was this the result she was angling for all along? He hoped so. "I'd be honored," he said.

Her lips curved into a smile.

***

They lingered at the inn after lunch, consuming measures of tea and polite conversation. At sundown, Dianthe's bodyguards put on riding gear and sabers, and followed Federer up to the castle.

When they entered the darkened woods, Federer cast wary glances all around, yet noticed no wolfish predators – or mysterious, clerical apparitions – lying in wait.

He escorted the carriage through the woods, past the black entry gate, and onto the circular driveway. When they trotted up, the sky gave birth to a terrific thundershower.

Federer shielded her with his cloak. He led his guest and her entourage through the castle's double-doors, and onto the black-and-white marble floor of the foyer. Johann and Eva were waiting to attend them.

"*Mister Federer*, it's good to see you," said Johann. "And we have guests."

At last! "Good evening, Johann. Thank you. I'm afraid we got a bit drenched."

"Very good, sir." The servants busied themselves gathering cloaks and wet riding gear, then joined the guests by the huge, crackling fireplace.

Dianthe said, "My bodyguards will stay here, if you don't mind, Johann. Mister Federer and I have a castle to see."

Federer offered his arm and happily guided Dianthe through his ancestral home's vaulted passageways.

Soon, they reached the library. When they entered, he said, "Would you like to hear some music?" He placed the ancient sword on his desk.

"Certainly." She moved from one phonograph to the next, curiously examining each one.

With care, he retrieved a music cylinder from the bookshelf and loaded it into a portable phonograph.

He turned the crank handle and the beautiful music came forth – *Die Fledermaus* by Strauss. When the waltz swept in, she danced, miming for herself an invisible partner about his size.

Her movements were graceful. He wished he could abandon the crank and join her.

With a change in the rhythm, she adjusted the gait of her whirls and steps, showing off her skill. His desire grew with each phrase of the music, and he couldn't stop himself from laughing. The graceful way she moved her body pushed everything else out of his mind except a singular need to be with her.

He imagined her lying next to him, soft skin illuminated by candlelight. In his thoughts, she stroked the lean surface of his chest with delicate fingers. Her beauty was intoxicating.

"Dianthe? May I... join you?" He stood up, letting go of the machine. The music slowed to a stop.

His heartbeat thrummed in his ears, yet his courage was unflagging. When he came close, he again noticed her unusual scent. He placed one large hand on her delicate one and the other upon her waist. He knew the basic steps of ballroom, though he hadn't practiced in years.

His desire for her was... growing. He tried distracting

himself with unpleasant things – his father's death, the chaos of the move, clumsy social encounters with the locals....

Her palm was warm against his, He led her in the odd, quiet dance, shoes whispering on the faded Oriental rug. He held her close, and she stared into his eyes, enigmatic, unbearable. He had to know what she was thinking.

She finally whispered, "The resemblance... is really quite... incredible."

He had no idea what she was talking about. "Resemblance?"

"The portraits," she said, gesturing casually to the wall behind them – a medieval painting of the Duke, and another of a priest, no doubt a more recent relation. A priest! Also, something in the image of the Duke... his disapproving look, broad shoulders, reminded him of the dark figure he had seen lurking in the upstairs mirror.

He glanced back to her. "You... think we look alike, eh?" He found it hard to look at the paintings, or anywhere other than her beautiful face.

She lifted her hand and interposed it between them, placing her fingertips below his collarbone, over his clothes, on the medallion he wore. She traced a line down his shirt to his stomach.

He leaned to her and she let him taste her lips.

The sensation was searing, delicate. She slowly pulled away. When he leaned in again, she tilted her head to one side and kissed his throat. Her soft lips and warm tongue wetted his skin.

He closed his eyes, savoring it. Electric pleasure buzzed in his extremities, and for a moment, the world faded like he was about to faint. This was wonderful, comfortable, like sinking into warm water. He glanced up for a moment, and gazed at their reflections in the window.

He was leaning backwards. He might have fallen, yet the diminutive woman was supporting his weight, keeping him upright with ease. He was lost in a euphoric whirl, like he had taken a draught of nepenthe, the drug of which the poets of old had written. Yet her disproportionate strength bothered him. *Another mystery*. He would ask her. The words formed slowly in his mind.

Her teeth tore into his throat.

She tore off a bite of his flesh and wolfed it down. Blood welled up and spurted from the wound. She pressed her mouth to it again, sucking greedily.

The shock of pain gave way to the will to survive. He strained against her impossible iron grip with all his might, trying to push her away, and failed. *How is she so strong...!?*

His blood was on one of her hands where she held his wrist. He tried to twist out of her grasp, slipped free and stumbled backwards, hand defensively covering his neck-wound. He crashed into a heavy bookcase filled with music cylinders, and they tumbled down around him.

She shot him an unbearable stare, a lioness caught feeding

– mouth, chin and cheeks smeared with gore.

"Dianthe!" He kept blinking to dispel the image of the predator that had bitten off a piece of him, not wanting to accept what he could plainly see.

"Rainer, Rainer," she said, head angled down. "You are of the Duke's blood. For years, my people, the True Believers, have patiently awaited their next sacrifice. It is the will of Nodens Silvianus and the gods of old that your family will always fall prey to mine.

"You carry the sword, you wear the medallion. You've had your year of glorification and now your blood must return to the Wild."

"Fertility rite…?" he choked.

"Your family may have mingled its blood with the New World, yet the men of your line always return here… threatening to cut down the Wild and put up the gray buildings and machines of civilization in its place."

"What the hell are you talking about!? Who doesn't want the comforts of civilization?"

"The Wild is a single, living, breathing force. The human mind wasn't meant to comprehend it – do the blood cells of a man comprehend the man? Yet there are certain revelations… ancient rites that open the eyes of one who is willing. My people fight against the gray tide, for the Wild – with every muscle, every fiber of ourselves, we fight.

"We've always been here, visible only to the perceptive. We've been called many things: Maenads, Bacchantes, werewolves, vampires... what you would call *monsters*, striding through the ages, giving shape to the fear of the time. The True Believers have been warriors against your kind, and the gray disease you have brought to this land since the Dark Ages.

"The fight has been costly, though. Thousands on both sides have died. After many battles, our families came to an accord. With a sacrifice, once per generation – the heir to this castle – the land would continue to thrive without any further spilling of blood."

She moved in to finish him.

Federer had been edging along the wall while she spoke, one hand clamped tightly over his throat-wound. He snatched up the sword and bolted through the open doorway. *Flight!* He ran toward the main hall.

She ripped her skirt at the hem to give her greater ease of movement, and laughed out loud, loping after him, quick, strong legs overtaking him with ease. Getting closer... almost upon him.

He spun around, whipping the ancient sword from its sheath. *Fight!* He struck Dianthe across the neck with enough force to behead her, yet the blade's edge was deflected by her flesh like it was the bark of a great, old tree. The cut was surprisingly slight, though there was blood. It stopped her, momentarily.

They both had their hands to their necks now. She steadied

herself against the opposite wall and grinned at him with wet, red teeth. Federer's blade had glanced off her skin and lodged itself in the stone of the wall. He desperately pulled at the imbedded sword once, twice, and on the third try, yanked it free.

Screams came from the foyer. *Johann and Eva! No!* He ran fast as he could to the sound.

He stumbled into the room in time to see Dianthe's bodyguards hacking at the dying bodies of the butler and his daughter. Federer's strength ebbed and his body reacted slowly, though his mind was still clear. His rage was keeping him sharp. This time, he didn't resist the anger – he rode it like a wild horse. He stalked toward the murderers, sword weightless in his hand.

Dianthe's bodyguards faced him with bloodied sabers. He surprised Small-eyes with a fast, low sword-stroke that opened his belly and spilled his guts like water. Moustache turned his weapon on its side and ran Federer through the chest, yet the pain was not enough to stop him.

His opponent pulled the weapon free, and readied himself for another attack. Federer struck first, slashing upward across his opponent's face.

Moustache's weapon clattered on the black-and-white tiles, and he crumpled with palms pressed to his blood-filled eyes, screaming.

Two strokes, two dying opponents. It was like the old warrior Duke had returned. Federer staggered over to the fireplace, struggling to remain conscious. Rain showered the windows. Moustache's screams grew softer and less frequent. He thought of covering his ears....

Suddenly, Dianthe burst out of the darkened hallway, bloody teeth bared.

She lunged, and Federer turned to face her, back braced against the stone mantelpiece. He let the sword drop and grasped the fireplace poker with both hands, holding it out in front of him like a spear. She slammed into him, and the back of his head banged against the stone. Everything went bright white. The last thing he perceived was her hot, bloody breath on his neck.

***

When he regained consciousness, shapes danced before his eyes, dark and blurry. His body lurched, yet there was no pain. The iron-tipped mahogany poker was through Dianthe's ribcage, transfixing her heart. His face, his lips were spattered with her blood. His sense of taste was vividly alive. Tiny droplets of her burned his tongue and sizzled, sweet and spicy, down his throat when he swallowed.

He pushed her limp body off to one side. Johann's bloody corpse was draped over Eva's, arms raised – the butler's last, desperate acts had been trying to protect his only daughter. Looking at their corpses, and those of Dianthe and her guards, realization came. He had chosen violence instead of sacrifice. In that moment, his mind grasped enough truth of the awful cycle to give him his first fleeting glimpse of the Wild.

***

Federer turned the crank of the phonograph and listened. Nothing too dissonant or modern these days. Modern composers like Stravinsky reminded him too much of Dianthe and the killings. The old symphonies from the Baroque and Classical periods were now what suited him best: the heavenly beauty of Bach, the passionate, contrasting melodies of Vivaldi, the brilliant mathematics of Mozart.

By defeating Dianthe, he suspected he had destroyed the pact with the True Believers. For a time, he lived in a constant state of fear that others would one day appear on his doorstep, demanding their sacrifice, or simply out of revenge for Dianthe. No one came.

He had failed to protect Eva and Johann, his bridge to the people of the village. Life for the townspeople grew harder. After that year, there were good harvests and bad, like any other rural place on earth.

The horror he could not shake was that by surviving the savage bite – or perhaps by drinking the blood of his attackers – he had become more like them. His body and mind were changed, infinitely more alert to the nuances of the Wild.

Ensconced in the castle, the sensation was controllable. He could see the apparitions whenever he wished now – the Duke, the Priest; the shades of his ancestors. They had been trying to warn him, trying to get him to abandon his inheritance, and he had been too stubborn to see it.

One spring afternoon, he journeyed back into the woods, and perceived *different* things beneath the shade of those trees... things that would haunt him until the end of his days. It started with a simple feeling. The quiet Wild was busily humming all around him. A recent lightning-strike had cracked and blackened an old oak, incinerating the colony of leafcutter ants that had made their home in the trunk.

Everywhere he cast his gaze, he took in desolation. The poor remains of a hare with brown-and-white fur, its throat ripped open, forever frozen in its last, agonal throes.

His ears directed him to the cries of violated female larks, driven by terrible instinct against their own need to feed, laboring to build the strongest nests. Countless hours gathering dried twigs and leaves, so their bastard offspring – the ones who hadn't already been murdered in their eggs by opportunistic avian predators – would have a chance of survival in the coming weeks.

Brutality in all its infinite forms rose up around his senses like a churning, charnel wind. The smell of death was everywhere. He found it impossible to shut out – the truth of it filled him, permeated him, whistled all around him, and chilled him to the bone.

After that, he never lingered long outside the walls of his ancestral home.

Much like himself, Feder Schloss fell into disuse. He kept mostly to the master bedroom and library, shunning the company of others, and the other parts of the castle.

In the years that followed, fear of other True Believers gave way to a fear of himself. He had seen the results of his rage, and its bottomless potential. He would rather die than kill again, so he did whatever he could to avoid any conflict. He refused to become a monster, and if that meant avoiding all human contact, so be it.

From time to time, he would receive visitors. Constable Mitteregger checked in on him about once a month for the first year, then once per year, at Christmas time, thereafter. "The woman and her cronies were obviously mad," the constable had said, and that was that.

Live music still called to him; a siren's song to a sailor lost at sea. Even from far away, the sustained gossamer melody of a violin or flute caused his heart to stir, reminding him too well of that afternoon when he had experienced the *Sacre du printemps* for the first time… and the evening he understood it, or rather, what it represented. Was Stravinsky a True Believer, too? Probably.

These days, Federer could have been another ghost haunting the castle. Perhaps, in a way, they had succeeded in making their sacrifice after all.

About the Author

Victor H. Rodriguez is a talent manager, novelist and short story writer. He's been a scriptwriter for HBO and published short fiction with Murder of Storytellers, Jaded Books and White Wolf. He also has short stories in the upcoming anthologies *Tales of the Once and Future King* from Superversive SF, and *Hyperion and Theia* from Radiant Crown.

CHARRED MEMORIES

By R.A. Goli

Gina walked carefully, not wanting to stumble on the uneven ground. She swept the torchlight from side to side, illuminating her path as she approached the building. Flowers, cards, teddy bears and photos had been left on the front lawn, tributes for those that were gone. She took a deep breath, her chest expanding, head held high in a false bravado, and walked up the blackened steps.

Stepping over the pile of ashes that had once been the front door, she swung her torch around, noting the broken beams and charred walls. The carpet was destroyed, still wet and spongy from the firefighters' hose. She kept moving, convinced she would find the clues that the police had missed. The bodies of twelve people had been found, but Gina hadn't heard from Kyle for over a week. Initially, she had felt hope, but as days passed, it had turned to dread. She didn't want to believe he was dead, but if not, where the hell was he?

She kicked something in the dark. Aiming the torchlight, she saw a stuffed bear roll to a stop and wondered if it had blown in from the shrine outside. She too had left items at that altar. Their wedding photo and the Eiffel Tower key chain he'd bought her in Paris.

Gina let the torch shine in every room, searching the scorched remains of her neighbors' lives. Not sure what she was looking for exactly, she felt compelled to investigate. She was anxious about heading upstairs, worried the stairs wouldn't hold or that a beam would fall on her head. She climbed at a snail's pace, imagining her foot plunging through a weakened floorboard. Testing each step before ascending, she used the wall to guide her, convinced that what remained of the banister would collapse from the slightest touch.

Relieved she made it up the stairs safely, she headed towards her apartment. Walking through the darkened hall gave her the creeps. Every shadow caused her to stiffen and her heart to thump loudly. She reached her home, stepping over the door that had been ripped from its hinges. Though she had expected it, she wasn't prepared for the mess. Her treasured memories, furniture, everything they had owned, burnt to a pile of ash or blackened and unsalvageable. She bit back tears and forged ahead, passing the kitchen, and on to the bedroom. While she knew she wouldn't find Kyle's body rotting in the corner, the police having somehow missed it, she still hoped to discover some hint as to his whereabouts.

A movement outside caught her attention and she peered out the window. *Was that someone ducking into the building?* She stood very still and listened. After a few minutes of silence, she continued her search. As she walked back through the kitchen she saw a flash of white. She gasped and shone the light around the living area.

"Hello?" She called, her voice barely a whisper. There was no answer. She slowly edged her way pass the bench and towards the front door. As she neared the sofa, she froze. In the corner of the room, in a soot-covered dress, was a little girl.

"Oh my God, what are you doing here?" She said as she rushed over. The girl was facing the wall and Gina was worried she would startle her. She spoke softly, placing a hand gently on her shoulder. "It's all right sweetheart, but you can't be here. It's dangerous."

When the little girl turned, Gina screamed.

The skin on her face and body was charred, the flesh underneath weeping pus through open gashes and sores. Gina felt the bile rise in her throat and cupped a hand over her mouth as she gagged. She dropped the torch and backed away from the hideous child. The girl let out a high-pitched, ear splitting wail, then ran out of the room calling for her mother.

Gina's heart thudded, the pulse causing her head to ache. She swore and bent down to pick up the torch, flinching as cold skeletal fingers gripped her wrist. She screamed, shaking it off and swept the beam across the floor, seeing only a broken chair leg.

That must have been what touched my arm. Now she wondered if her mind was playing tricks on her. Was the girl a figment of her imagination too? Caused by her lack of sleep and the stress of the last few days?

Cautiously, she stuck her head through what was left of the doorframe, glancing left and right for any spectral children or other apparitions. Satisfied that the coast was clear, she entered the hall and headed for the staircase, abandoning her search. She wasn't going to find anything here but memories and ghosts. Then she heard it. *Tap, scrape, tap scrape.* Coming from somewhere behind her.

She swung around, arm outstretched, the torchlight shaking in her unsteady grasp. Frozen to the spot, her feet as heavy as led, she realized she was holding her breath, as the noise grew louder. Closer. *Tap, scrape, tap, scrape.* Her mouth dropped open as the thing rounded the corner and a warbled cry escaped her throat. It walked slowly towards her, dragging one leg behind, its clothes in tatters and covered in soot. The hair was gone and the parts of its face that weren't blackened by fire were red and oozing. Where the eyes should have been, were two soulless, empty holes.

When the thing was almost upon her, she stepped back against the wall, clutching the torch to her chest and closed her eyes. She listened as it shuffled closer. When it didn't attack, she opened her eyes and saw the thing walk into the apartment opposite hers. She frowned, and then brought the beam up again.

"Mr. Phillips?" She asked. He turned his head slightly and nodded, then continued walking.

"Oh my God, oh my God, oh my God," Gina muttered, shaking her head vigorously, as though that would disperse the images. The flames had left him a monster. "This place is haunted by the dead!"

She rushed down the hallway, no longer caring if the floor collapsed beneath her, but when she reached the landing, she was confronted by another horrifying figure. She didn't know the woman that trudged up the stairs towards her, only that she lived on the third floor. Half of her face was caved in, and she held the rest of her head at a lopsided angle as she stared up at Gina with one good eye. Gina didn't wait to get a closer look, instead bolting back to her apartment and into the bedroom. The door, though charred was intact, so she gently pushed it closed then sat down, her back against the dirty wall, and brought her knees up to her chest.

She stayed there for what felt like hours, listening to the moaning and wailing, and the sounds of footsteps and dragging limbs. No one came to her room. She rested her head on her knees and covered her ears with her hands, wondering if she would see Kyle. Worried that he was one of the ghosts weeping on the other side of her door, but too frightened to check.

***

She woke slowly; the sun's glare assaulting her weary eyes. Her back ached and she stood and stretched, then moved to look out the window. She gasped. Kyle was down there, kneeling in front of the shrine. She banged her fist against the window and called out but he didn't hear her. Racing downstairs, forgetting the ghosts that had haunted her the night before, she bolted through the front door and threw her arms around him. Somehow, she misjudged the embrace, falling awkwardly onto the grass. She turned around, frowning at the back of his head as he crouched in front of the mementos.

Watching his body shake with sobs, she moved closer, squatting down to peer over his shoulder. He was holding their photo, his fingers gently caressing her face. When he moved his hand away she cried out, stumbling backwards.

"No," she said. "It can't be."

She had seen her own reflection in the glass. A hairless, tattered, scorched reflection, hardly recognizable as the woman she had once been. Now she understood. It was not she who had placed the key ring and photo in this sanctum of memories. It was Kyle who had laid the tribute, in honor of her. She knelt beside him as he wept, resting her hands in her lap. Only then did she notice her charred flesh and blackened fingers, her wedding ring hanging loosely off raw bone, nestled on the scorched material that was once her favorite summer dress. And then she wept too.

About the Author

R.A. Goli is an Australian reader, writer, gamer and sometime hiker. She writes fantasy and horror short stories and occasionally erotic horror and sci-fi. Due to her varying attention span, she has an ever increasing fondness for the short story, both the reading and the writing of.

She has been published by Deadman's Tome, Whortleberry Press, Fantasia Divinity and Grivante Press. Check out her website https://ragolifiction.wordpress.com/ or stalk her on https://www.facebook.com/ragolifiction.

GET THE DOOR FOR ME, WILL YOU, EDGAR?

By Ken Goldman

The thunderstorm increased ferocity tenfold, thick veins of white light fracturing skies too ominous for an early spring morning. Outside, in the Wednesday world beyond Carver High's eighty-seven yammering instructors, nature's bass drum hootenanny rumbled in the distance. But a good teacher was industrious, and if the flittering lightshow proved distracting, then it created also an effective backdrop to Josh Hooper's lesson. While reading aloud the raven's first immortal utterance of "Nevermore" from Edgar Allan Poe's most famous poem, the sky went *Ka-Boom!* and the lights inside Hooper's classroom flickered. The wind, coupled with the erratic strobing, established a respectable film noir effect, a genuine Poe moment any English teacher worth his spit would have relished.

"Wooooooooooo ..." ghost-wailed Raphael Jones from the back row, appropriating yet another teacher-baiting opportunity. Whatever didn't come from a boom box Jones wasn't interested hearing, and whatever came from the mouth of a teacher immediately turned the kid stone deaf. Hooper knew that Mr. Poe was no match for the likes of Heavy D and Lil' Kim, but that only meant he would have to try harder.

"Quoth the wise-ass, hopefully nevermore," Josh offered

Raphael as his rejoinder, and the teacher's clever comeback seemed to win over the class enough to shut Jones' mouth for a moment. Once Carmella Caparelli laughed, several others followed her lead. Among Hooper's students the girl seemed the most capable of thinking outside the X-Box, a rare circumstance considering her body could open doors for her even if she were brain dead. Since Carmella's intelligence impressed Hooper as much as her ample tits percolated the testosterone of every boy in class, he counted the girl's approval as a win for this round.

A teacher was only as good as his last successful minute, especially with seniors. Upperclassmen felt above anything their middle-aged instructors offered, so Hooper readied himself for those moment-to-moment improvisations whenever he needed to keep yawning students from completely zoning out. In the adolescent world of iPod people, an educator did more than educate; he entertained with the in-your-face aplomb of a Richard Pryor. Teaching had become a daily stand-up in a room of persistent hecklers who, whenever you didn't deliver the goods, might decide to trash your Toyota that same hour. Last semester that had happened three times, and some industrious prick had balls enough to scratch POE SUCKS into Hooper's paint job. That hurt, and not so much because of the vandalism. Excepting a good blow job, American Lit was Hooper's passion.

The Scarlet Letter? Adultery aside, maybe Nat Hawthorne didn't quite make the cut. Fitzgerald's less-than-*Great Gatsby?*

Okay, a little heavy for George Washington Carver High's pimpled party animals. Ditto those more modern clowns Steinbeck and Hemingway. But Edgar Allan Poe? The creator of so many tales of terror? Poe ... *sucks?* What alien breed of cretins occupied these seats?

Bullets of windswept rain pelted the windows. Still reading aloud, Josh peeked down at the courtyard. This morning even the cutters had sought shelter from the downpour. No one liked to fuck with thunder and lightning. No one, of course, except ol' Edgar.

"'And the silken sad uncertain rustling of each purple curtain ...' Hear it? Do you hear those rustling curtains going *SSSSSSSSSSSS?"*

Nothing. Nada. Not so much as a changed expression to demonstrate these kids shared oxygen with him, although Carmella Caparelli's eyes remained clearly fixed on his while she grinned her little half smile. Finally kiss-ass Billy Silverman spoke.

"The hissing sound of the curtains ... It's called a-little-ration, right?" Billy probably required detailed instructions just to put on his socks, but for some reason Hooper liked the kid's die-hard attitude.

"'Alliteration,' ass hole!" some teacher's helper from the back row called out.

"Alliteration, that's just what it is," Hooper said, not missing a beat. "A literary device that works like a sound effect. It's like that thunder and lightning out there. It sets the poem's tone nicely,

Poe's use of alliteration, don't you think? *'Silken sad uncertain ...'* *HISSSSSSSSSSSSSSSS*. Hear it?"

Sensing another opportunity, Raphael rejoined the game with his finest shuck and jive impersonation. "Like 'Big bulging busty boobs.' That's 'literation, ain't that right, Missy Carmella?"

During moments like this, Hooper considered cutting out the kid's heart and placing it beneath the floorboards where it could beat tell-tale hip hop for all eternity. Still, like any good narrator of Poe's words, Hooper offered a cynical smile.

"Right, Rafe. Except boobs don't make much sound. Not unless they're going for a cheap laugh."

Raphael smiled too, offering his toothy grin while completely missing the irony of Hooper's absolute sincerity. That was good. Cracking jokes had become a tough call in an age of political correctness when one misspoken word could earn a teacher his walking papers before the final bell. But Hooper had made Poe's point, and that earned him one more minute of acceptance by the most demanding audience on earth.

"Like all of us, Poe questioned death. He hoped there was something more than 'Nevermore,' something beyond the finality of the grave. As he pines for his lost Lenore, Poe's raven outside his narrator's door might well have been a manifestation of just that. '... *Deep into that darkness peering, long I stood there wondering, fearing ...*'"

Ka-BOOM-BOOM!!!

Thunder sent the lights flickering wildly, seeming almost to glow. They went out. For a moment, there was quiet in the darkness, an absolute surreal silence, especially infrequent occurring in a class of thirty very vocal kids. It didn't last long.

"Wooooooooooooooooooo ..." This new howl came from Kenny Greene.

"Oh my God! They've killed Kenny!" from the back. The inevitable laughs followed.

"Can't read much in the dark, can we, Mr. Hooper? We'll have to wait for power to come back, huh?" The fat fuck Sam Peterson spoke fluent wise-ass.

"Not to worry, Sam. I have the poem memorized. It sounds even better in the dark."

Carmella lit up. "Do you really, Mr. Hooper? You memorized the whole poem?"

Thank God for you, Carmella. Hooper took that as his cue.

"'*So that now, to still the beating of my heart, I stood repeating,*

'Tis some visitor entreating entrance at my chamber door-

Some late visitor entreating entrance at my chamber door...'"

"Nah, Mr. Hooper," from the fat fuck. "It don't sound no better in the dark."

Another crash of thunder. A knock at the door. Then another two. And a third round.

Knock ... knock-knock ... knock-knock-knock ...

Hooper smiled at the perfect timing.

"Who dat knockin' at my chamber door?" from Raphael.

"Who dat who say 'who dat?'" Jeff Lynch, whose classroom of honor students sat next door, entered. Hooper hoped he wasn't going to complain about the noise again. "Just got the call from the office, Josh. Power's out all over the neighborhood. Looks like it's going to stay that way for a while, too. So no one leaves class when the period's over, and no piss breaks either, not while school's dark like this. Security reasons, yada yada yada. Okay?" He turned to the rest of the class. "You okay with that, Poe-philes?"

Some kid proficient in both ventriloquism and the look of innocence muttered "Okay, you big fag."

"I'll take that to mean 'yes.'" Lynch left to spread the news down the corridor. Hooper turned towards his young prodigies and waited for the groaning to die down.

"Looks like it's just us and Edgar for a while, gang. So let's see how that raven is doing. We'll take it from the top, okay? Listen and you can almost feel the narrator nodding off. '... weak and weary ... nodded nearly napping.' Kind of like you guys right now. Listen closely to Poe's words." He shut his eyes to recall them.

"Once upon a midnight dreary, while I pondered, weak and weary,

Over many a quaint and curious volume of forgotten lore,

While I nodded, nearly napping, suddenly there came a tapping,

As of someone gently rapping, rapping at my chamber door..."

Three rapid knocks again at the door, more urgent than Jeff's the last time.

"'Literation again, right?" Raphael asked. Laughs all around encouraged his toothy grin to widen.

"Woooooooooooooo ..." Someone else had picked up Raphael's mantel. Half the class joined in, even some girls. Fucking Lynch really knew how to kill a mood. Hooper went to the door.

Darkness there ... and nothing more ...

Hooper looked down the corridor, expecting to discover some pimply gremlin scurrying around the corner, maybe ducking into another classroom. But the hallways remained dark and empty.

"See any ravens out there?" from Peterson.

"No ravens, Sam. No pits. No pendulums. No lost Lenores." He shut the door hoping to return his class to some semblance of order.

Carmella voiced her take on the matter. "Maybe it's Poe himself. His spirit, I mean."

"Woooooooooo! Carmella, the Ghost Whisperer."

The girl wasn't the type to capitalize on the occasional lapse into chaos so common among high school kids. She sounded damned serious, in fact. Carmella's comment recalled a moment last semester during this very lesson on another rainy day, but not quite this morning's gully washer. Hooper decided he could go off the lesson plan a little. What was the harm of a colorful anecdote, some enrichment to goose his Poe lecture a bit during this extended class period when the kids' attention spans were likely to wane anyway?

Hooper paused for dramatic effect.

"Funny you should mention that, Carmella."

He waited for someone, *any*one to bite. Denise Daniels, the skinny sad-eyed girl who sat in the back and was the least likely to utter a syllable in class, spoke first. That she had decided to speak at all startled him along with half the class.

"My sister was in your class last year, Mr. Hooper. She told me all about that lesson you did. She told me she couldn't sleep for a week."

The girl's remark roused every kid's attention. Anything suggesting the macabre became catnip to a kid.

Denise, you may have just earned yourself an 'A' ...

Hooper faked brief indecision as if hesitant to share some forbidden tale. "All right, then. But what I tell you doesn't leave this room. Okay?" Playing his disciples with the precision of a concert maestro he waited for the telling cue of kids leaning forward in their seats. Locking eyes with the stragglers, he waited until he had them all.

"Last semester I was teaching this same lesson, reading 'The Raven' aloud just like today. There was a knock at the door, like just now." He knocked on his desk for effect. "... and when I looked no one was there. I didn't make much of it; kids are always looking to make trouble in the halls. But it happened again at the same moment I read the line. Just like this." Slipping into Vincent Price mode, Hooper enunciated the stanza. *"As of someone gently rapping, rapping at my chamber door ..."*

KNOCK! KNOCK! KNOCK!!!

The class froze. All eyes went to the doorway. Probably Lynch was again playing hall monitor, or maybe another ass hole kid was capitalizing on the darkened corridors. But that was okay if it set the desired mood.

"Who's there?" Hooper called out.

Nothing.

"Yeah, it happened just like that. So I'm figuring either someone is playing one hell of an elaborate joke, or maybe... maybe there's something else going on. So I say in front of my class, 'Get the door for me, will you Edgar?' Just like that, calm and cool. 'Get the door, Edgar.' And do you know what happened?"

Silence. He expected it. This time he enunciated the words slowly.

"'Get-the-door-for-me-Edgar.' That's what I said. 'Get the door for me' ..."

All eyes returned to the door. Nothing happened. No one said a word. Everyone waited. Waited some more.

Again nothing.

Hooper looked embarrassed. "Guess sometimes the magic just doesn't happen. Anyway-"

The door creaked open.

"Dude, how the hell did you do that?" from Raphael.

"I didn't." A look of skepticism from just about everyone. "Hey, really. Swear. And I'd prefer you not call me 'Dude,' okay?"

All eyes returned to the door.

"Close the door for me, Edgar!" Hooper seemed more insistent this time.

The door shut slowly.

Several gasps from around the classroom. Hooper felt an odd satisfaction, as if he had performed some inexplicable magic trick even he didn't understand. But he had them now, and he wasn't about to relinquish the moment.

Voila, gang! And for your amusement, here comes Mr. Poe to say howdy!

"See, I think what I'd done last time was managed to channel Edgar because of this poem we were reading together. But last year that's as far as it went, just the door opening and closing. I didn't think it could happen so easily a second time. Which means ..."

"He's inside the room with us right now!" from Carmella.

Hooper's eyes darted about the classroom. He knew a dramatic moment when he saw one. "Is that true, Edgar, old pal? Are you in here with us as I speak? You feel like giving us a sign or something?"

"Hokey," said Peterson. "Very hokey."

Raphael spoke in an uncharacteristic undertone. "Think maybe you can get Selena in here too?"

"So now what?" from Carmella.

An answer came quickly with relentless successions of death knell gongs, a harsh and persistent sound of thick metal reverberating inside everyone's brain with painful thuds. Several students pushed fists to their ears but the echoes persisted. Hooper recognized the sound.

"Christ. Can it be ...?"

(... *the tintinnabulation that so musically wells ...*)

"Mr. Hooper, what's ...?"

"'The Bells,' Carmella. Poe's poem. We read it last week."

(... *from the bells bells bells bells bells bells bells ...*)

Here was a literary illusion - and an *allusion* too - from the dead poet himself. But as quickly as it began, the clanging stopped. An uneasy stillness hung over the class. Kids looked at each other as if searching for answers, but no one moved or said a word. The silence didn't last long.

Something scratching, some creature clawing, trying to get out from behind ...

"The wall! Look at the chalkboard on the wall!" Raphael's voice had lost its wise ass edge while the kid pointed with shaking fingers. Heads turned towards the board behind Hooper, eyes bugged, and in a gesture from a bad B-movie, Sondra Winograd threw a hand to her mouth. Hooper looked at the board behind him and felt his jaw go slack.

Any Poe-phile knew about Edgar's fixation concerning walls. The man had this claustrophobia thing going during his entire life, and wall symbols popped up all over his writing. It was the kind of detail only a teacher would notice or even care about, but Hooper sensed Poe's wall obsession was about to assume some big-time significance during these next few minutes.

The shadowy image of a large cat appeared on the board, a bloated creature struggling upon hind legs to scrape its way out as if the chalkboard were made of smoked glass. But the terrified animal wasn't really *on* the board. The feline seemed trapped *behind* it, dates of Mr. Poe's birth and death with a listing of his works superimposed upon the cat's writhing torso. The animal screeched in fright loud enough to chill the blood of everyone in the room.

Poe's famous cat. Black. And here it was, the poor entrapped creature screaming for its life inside Josh Hooper's classroom. If the idea hadn't frightened the bejeezus out of him, it might have given the teacher a genuine sense of celebrity.

EEEEeeeeeeeeeeeeeeeeeeeeeeeee!

EEEEEeeeeeeeeeeeeeeeeeeeeeeee!

The cat was not alone in her screaming. Several of the girls took up the shrieking chorus, but it seemed the screeching performed during a good funhouse ride, not of terror, at least not yet, while pieces of this puzzle remained to be put together. Carmella Caparelli remained silently stoic, staring at the proceedings with curiosity and mild bemusement. The creature disappeared in the next instant, but Hooper knew The Poe Show was far from over.

"Rafe! Holy shit, man! Look at Rafe!"

The fun house ride ended that instant. Mr. Poe's theatrics now took an ugly turn.

Raphael's face leaked bubbles of blood from open wounds that appeared from nowhere. His flesh had turned crimson, seeming almost plum colored upon his dark skin, but the kid seemed unaware any transformation had taken place. His classmates' expressions indicated to him that something had gone seriously gonzo.

"What you mean? Ain't nothing wrong with--" Raphael put his hand to his cheek. Thick lunch meat shavings of flesh peeled off into his fingers. "Oh fuck ... *Fuck, man!*" Raphael reached for his ear. The appendage slipped from its cavity like a sliced cheese, plopping upon his desk in a bloody pool. The boy stared at it for a moment. Then he gagged.

"'And then was known the presence of the Red Death,'" quoted Carmella, as if the girl were reciting text for Brownie points. "You know what you got there is The Red Death, don't you, Raphael? You would if you'd done your homework." But Raphael Jones was not up to playing Twenty Questions while rotting skin flaps hung from each cheek. The boy was decomposing in his seat.

"I gotta get outta this room, man! There ain't gonna be nothing left of me but balls and hair!" Raphael took to his feet. A rat the size of a small dog nipped at his Nike. Several more plump rodents appeared on the floor, squirming throughout the classroom in furry heaps. Raphael stumbled back to his desk, trying to keep his nose attached to his face. Mutters filled the room, but not a peep from Carmella.

A clap of thunder from outside. A burst of lightning speckled the room.

Carmella's voice remained steady. "I don't think Mr. Poe wants us out of our seats. Look up there." She pointed towards the ceiling where a huge pendulum swung, its sharp metal blade catching flickers of storm light. As if having its own mind that determined its tracking and movement, the razor edge descended for a sudden moment, the gleaming blade nearly slicing full into Raphael's head while managing to knick a thick wedge of his remaining ear.

"Shit, man ... Oh shit ..."

The rats of a pit below. The pendulum above. Mr. Poe was playing hardball.

The kids were frozen in their seats. On his feet, Hooper did not move either. One thing was for certain. On this stormy morning, his students were witness to the best Poe lesson in the history of the world.

Someone asked, "Mr. Hooper, can you do something? Can you stop this?"

A single word, whispered from somewhere in the shadows, yet heard by every kid in the room.

"Nevermore ..."

A cawing raven fluttered across the room, then vanished like a dark ghost.

"I don't know. Yes. Maybe." In the midst of Mr. Poe's signature terrors, Hooper struggled to think.

The relentless tattoo of a beating heart from the floorboards below. Twelve beats, then gone.

From somewhere a man moaned.

"Unnghh ..."

The rattle of chains, the death moan of an imprisoned man dying behind the wall who never did find that cask of Amontillado...

Hacking and wheezing, Denise Daniels' lips had gone blue, her skin pale. She was shivering as if the classroom had suddenly fallen into a deep freeze. A wind that affected only where she sat blew through her hair. Her reed thin body shook in a burst of spasms.

"I'm cold ... so cold ..."

Killing and chilling my Annabel Lee ...

"I'm outta here!" from Sam Peterson, already on his feet and headed for the door. He managed a few steps before the floor opened beneath him, a giant maw exposing a darkened pit that seemed impossibly to go on forever.

"Sam, get back to your seat, get back now!" from Hooper, but too late. Fat Fuck fell into the abyss like a dead weight, his screams echoing the whole way down until they abruptly broke off with a thick thud. This no longer was a day in the fun house. Several girls screamed and their shrieks were the real thing.

"Mr. Hooper. Do something for him! Please, do something!"

"Mr. Hooper, please ..."

"It's not real," Carmella tried explaining. "None of it is real. Can't you see that? Mr. Hooper, tell them how he's trying to fool us! Poe is trying to trick us!"

From Raphael, still leaking blood gobs from every pore, "Forget Peterson, man. *All* of us in deep shit now!"

"I'm so cold..."

"*Do* something!"

Hooper understood it was his move. For some unfathomable reason, Poe had selected his classroom to reveal himself, and

Hooper was in charge. It had come time to act like he was. Taking a seat behind his desk, folding his hands as if he were about to deliver some elaborate speech, he looked every bit the teacher in complete control, even if it took a great effort to create the effect. Eyes circling the room, he kept his voice steady, calm.

"I know you're in here with us, Edgar. And I know what you're trying to do. It's all about the fear, isn't it? The terror? It's what brings you here, and it's what keeps you going, isn't it, pal? And it's my job to keep that terror alive, right? Because as long as your words and memory live, in that sense so do you. It's your claim to immortality. Death is what you fear the most, isn't that right? And you know full well it's what we *all* fear."

The pendulum reappeared, swung right at Hooper's throat. The teacher did not budge. The blade whooshed past him, went for a second hit, missed again. It disappeared.

"Nice try, Edgar, but no cigar. '*True! - nervous - very, very dreadfully nervous I had been and am; but why* will *you say that I am mad*?' I know all about that tell-tale heart trick of yours, Mr. Poe. All about the illusion you try to create from our worst fears. I've been teaching your own words to kids for years!"

The piercing scream of a woman buried alive, Madeline Usher's death shriek.

"Oh, I can't say I don't admire your work, but I don't really buy into it either. It's illusion, my friend, smoke and mirrors masking as reality, just like this little show you're putting on for us this morning. But it's not real, none of it, is it? I'll give you an 'A' for the special effects, my friend. Because death IS real and it doesn't matter if you don't personally care for the grave. Because you're dead, and despite your little display here, you're going to remain dead. As dead and buried as your gal pals Annabel Lee, Lenore, Madeline Usher, and Ligeia. Have I left anyone out?"

A plump rat nibbled at Hooper's shoe. He kicked it aside.

"No one wants to face death, Mr. Poe. But we really don't have that choice, not even those whose words live after them. Dead you are and dead you must remain. Your lost Lenore will have to remain lost, and so will you. Your own utterance says it all. That word says everything you need to know..." The teacher allowed the moment to sink in for his unseen audience of one, and when he spoke again he whispered. "So, 'Nevermore,' my good friend."

Hooper had had his say. While his little speech had satisfied him, it had also distracted him from noticing the event occurring before his eyes. His class had grown strangely silent and now Hooper understood why. Peterson had somehow returned to his seat, and Raphael Jones' face showed no indication of a lingering Red Death. But each boy's expression seemed vacant, their eyes cold as moonstones. Looking around the classroom, Hooper saw the same look on every kid's face, as if each student had gone into some trance-like state. Only Carmella Caparelli's eyes remained alert and fixed on Hooper, her knowing half smile firmly in place.

"You know what Mr. Poe has done to our class, Mr. Hooper,

don't you? I mean, what he's done to everyone else but us?"

It didn't take very much brain work for a man familiar with Poe's tales to figure out. The renowned author was pulling from quite an impressive literary arsenal.

"'The Facts in the Case of M. Valdemar.' Mesmerism. Or more modernly, group hypnosis. But the story wasn't on your reading list, Carmella."

The girl smiled. "You know me better than that, Mr. Hooper." She looked around at her classmates. "They won't remember any of this, will they?"

"I doubt it. At least not consciously. But they'll sure think twice next time anyone tells them Poe sucks." He turned his attention to the door. For a moment, he had to focus just to be certain he saw what he did.

A dark figure stood by the entryway. It seemed a cloudy image, a murky semblance of a man whose somber expression could not be mistaken.

Hooper turned to Carmella. "You see him too?"

The girl could only nod her head.

Hooper approached the doorway, kept his voice low and properly respectful. "I'll see to it that your words will be kept alive, Edgar. I can promise that much. You have *my* word on that. Close the door on your way out, will you?"

Perhaps the man smiled. Hooper could not really tell. He knew the shadowy figure did not require opening the door to take his leave, but he did so anyway before fading into the darkness of the school corridor. A class act, no doubt about it, even if the late poet's methods of communication were a bit unconventional. Hooper and Carmella exchanged knowing smiles.

When the door again sprang open, both teacher and student flinched. Jeff Lynch stood in the entryway, noticing Hooper's class staring dead ahead like zombies. The lights came back on that same moment, as did the bell signaling the end of the class period.

"Thought it was getting a little noisy in here, Josh, but I can see I was wrong. Hey! Wake up, people! This is still school, you know! Chop chop! Looks like this period's over!"

Raphael spoke first.

"What happened, man? Feels like I've been zoning for a week."

The other kids laughed right on cue, but Billy Silverman sat scratching his head. "Did Edgar ever get the door for you, Mr. Hooper?"

Hooper and Carmella exchanged glances.

"Nope, Billy," he said. "Sorry. No magic this time around." He turned his attention to the rest. "Pack up your books and move on out, gang. Fun time is over."

His students shuffled out of the room, but conversation among them seemed noticeably absent. Outside, the rain had stopped and the sun made a valiant attempt to come out from behind the remaining dark clouds.

Lingering behind her classmates, Carmella was the last to leave. "Can't wait to see what you do with your lesson on Shakespeare, Mr. Hooper." The teacher had to laugh.

Alone, he opened the window to allow the sun's warmth on his face. The rain made everything outside smell fresh and clean, no mean feat for an inner city public school. The instructor waited a few minutes before heading down the corridor for the teachers' lounge.

Hooper hoped he could find someone in there who smoked. He felt certain he would be needing a cigarette.

About the Author

Ken Goldman, former Philadelphia teacher of English and Film Studies, is an affiliate member of the Horror Writers Association. He has homes on the Main Line in Pennsylvania and at the Jersey shore. His stories have appeared in over 865 independent press publications in the U.S., Canada, the UK, and Australia with over thirty due for publication in 2017-18. Since 1993 Ken's tales have received seven honorable mentions in The Year's Best Fantasy & Horror. He has written five books: three anthologies of short stories, YOU HAD ME AT ARRGH!! (Sam's Dot Publishers), DONNY DOESN'T LIVE HERE ANYMORE (A/A Productions) and STAR-CROSSED (Vampires 2); and a novella, DESIREE, (Damnation Books and recently re-released in Kindle by eXcessica Publishers). His first novel OF A FEATHER (Horrific Tales Publishing) was released in January 2014. SINKHOLE, his second novel, will be published by Bloodshot Books late summer 2017. Ken isn't yet famous. He expects that to happen posthumously.

EXILED

By Paul Stansbury

Tamara's tears had dried by the time she poured half of her large cup of Quik Cola down the sink, replacing it with a half pint of cheap vodka.

This should make it easier. She downed almost a third in a single gulp, then climbed into the tub. Warm water rose to her chin as she slid down. Grime and mold lurked in the seam where the wall met the porcelain. *When was the last time the housemaid cleaned this? What does it matter?*

She drank down another third of her vodka-cola, waiting for her stomach to accept it before taking a breath. The box cutter, taken from her husband's workbench, lay in the soap dish. The tip of the blade was broken.

Should have changed it. Would have made a cleaner cut. Alcohol coursed through her body. *Soon.*

Noise seeped through the wall. People noise, raised voices. Nothing distinguishable, maybe Spanish, maybe not. The alcohol was now in full control of her head.

Better finish up. She sucked down the remaining vodka-cola, letting the cup fall to the floor. The noise grew less distinguishable. *Wait just a bit more for the vodka to do its job.* She watched the faucet drip until her eyes couldn't stay focused. *Get the knife and do it. Quickly.* She reached out. *Do it before you pass out. Do it!* She grabbed the box cutter and raked it across her wrist.

Red tendrils of blood swirled out into the water as she was whisked down into the whirlpool of her alcohol induced dreams. Images floated in and out from the black confines of her mind.

***

The garbled intercom blared at her.

Why am I here? The hallways were empty. The classrooms were empty. No one was to be found in the office. *My children! I'm here for them.* Tamara ran through the deserted building calling for them, but no reply came. She followed the drops of blood that spattered the white tile floors, each leading to an empty room . . .

. . . Her mother writhed on a gurney as it rolled lazily down a sterile white corridor.

Where are they taking her? Tamara ran behind it, her feet slipping on the polished red tile floor. The harder she ran, the deeper her feet sank into the shiny red surface. The thick, coagulating blood, sucked her down . . .

. . . Her husband ran up the stairs from his workshop in the basement. He lunged, slashing at her with his box cutter.

Why are you doing this? She held up her hands to fend him off. Searing pain stabbed her wrists. Blood spewed from the gaping wounds . . .

. . . She ambled through a dark concourse. She had the sense that unfriendly, hungry things lingered in the deepest shadows along indistinct walls.

Where am I? Why are they reaching out for me? As she moved forward, the space around her narrowed. Ahead, she saw a glimmer of light. *An opening! I must reach it.*

She felt the hungry things' boney hands touching her, ever so lightly, ever so inquisitively.

Go! Now, before they take me. Go! Just as she reached the opening, a revenant raised up directly in front of her. She looked into its pale eyes. They held only despair. The light was just beyond. *If I could only reach it!* The revenant bolted straight ahead. Her soul withered under the blast of frigid desolation as it passed.

***

Tamara opened her eyes, glad to be awake. Her night had turned out to be an endless loop of troubling dreams.

She was lying on a freshly made bed. The door to her room was open and the curtains were pulled back. She knew it was light outside, but darkness surrounded her. Everything was cast in the grey pallor of dusk. It was unusually quiet.

Something's not right. Why is my room open, why is the bed made up? Why am I here? She stood, just as the housemaid entered with an armful of bath towels.

"What's going on here?" Tamara called out, stepping forward toward the young woman. The housemaid continued moving toward the bath. "Listen to me!" she shouted, grabbing the housemaid's forearm. As her hand reached the young woman's arm, brilliant sunlight flooded Tamara's senses. Vibrant colors replaced the gray pallet. The robin's egg blue of the housemaid's uniform shimmered and the deep red of the roses in the floral wallpaper pulsed. Sounds assaulted her ears. The morning traffic roared while a TV broadcast from the room next door flowed through the wall. The odor of starched laundry, mixed with the scents of musky perfume and pine cleaner filled her head. She quickly withdrew her hand and everything sank back into twilight and silence. *What's happening?*

The young woman gave no acknowledgement. Tamara moved directly in front of her. She held up her hands to stop her and force a response. The woman did not flinch. She did not stop. Once again, the dreary twilight evaporated as the woman reached Tamara's hands. She passed through Tamara like a warm breeze blows through a lake house on a summer's afternoon.

Instantly, Tamara knew all there was to know about the woman. She was twenty-three, sixth child of a migrant. At age six, she fell from a truck, breaking her arm. For want of medical treatment, it never healed properly. Raped at thirteen by a neighbor, she never told anyone because he threatened to tell the INS her father was an illegal. After earning her nursing degree, she will marry her beautiful fireman. She carries his child. Most of all, Tamara sensed the woman's hope and belief that her life would be happy despite her painful past.

Then, she was gone and the twilight dullness returned. Tamara looked into the mirror hanging over the dented chest of drawers. She saw a pale, desolate caricature of herself. It reminded her of the revenant in her dream. .

Panic seized Tamara. *I must get home to my family. I've got to tell them how much I love them. I've got to tell them how this is all a horrible mistake.* She looked around the room for her suitcase. It was gone. She went to the closet to retrieve her clothes but it was empty. She rushed out to the parking lot to find her car was missing as well.

She stood for some time on the crumbling sidewalk outside the dingy motel, watching the business of the ordinary world go on silently in the dim twilight.

What's going on?

People trudged up and down the sidewalk while cars arrived and departed from the parking lot shared with the liquor store. At first, Tamara called out to every person she saw. Not one of them so much as looked in her direction.

Can't anyone hear me?

She even tried standing in front of a few. Just like the housemaid, each passed through her. Every time, she was instantly imbued with their memories and emotions. Some were happy, some sad. Most were content with their lives. Once, she stepped in the path of an oncoming car. It passed through her without any noticeable effect.

In her twilight world, Tamara had no sense of time; but the clock on the bank across the street marked the hours as the day wound down.

I must get home. Maybe all I need is to make contact with someone I know. Everything will be OK if I can get to my family. That's all it will take.

Home was only a couple of miles down the road. The day still had several hours of sunlight left and she felt it would be better to arrive before it got dark. She was careful to avoid contact with people, not wanting to take on any new memories or emotions. Soon, she turned onto her street.

Her car was in the driveway.

How did that get here? As she got closer, she could see her husband on the porch watching the girls play. She called out, waving her hand. No one looked. She broke into a run up the sidewalk, calling to them. No response. *Can't they hear me? Why aren't they looking for me? Am I so meaningless to them that they haven't noticed I was gone? Do they just not care?*

***

The new Tamara put the finishing touches on the pot roast and looked out the window. She saw the revenant standing at the front gate. She knew sooner or later that it would show up in desperation. She put a large bowl of potatoes on the table, then joined her husband on the front porch.

"Time for supper. Lauren, you and Leslie go set the table," she said, as she gathered her husband in her arms and gave him a kiss. "Jerry, go on, I'll be there in a minute." She waited until they were inside to step down from the porch and walk out to the front gate to meet the revenant.

"I knew you would come back. Every exile does," she said calmly. "At first, I tried to go back. I can tell you it's quite impossible. I know this will be painful for you to accept, but this life is no longer yours. You lost it when you gave up last night. You are a revenant now - an exile. I was like you. I too had given up. That's when my life was captured. Exiles seek out the weak and vulnerable who have given up on lives that can still be fulfilled. They capture those lives just as theirs were captured and leave the revenant exiled, wandering in the shadows. I wandered a long time before I found you."

"Did I die?"

"No, but you wanted to, and that's all that mattered. You wanted to die. You tried to die. You had given in to despair. That was all the opening I needed. It only took a small push, then you were out. I took your place. Now you are a revenant, exiled. Don't waste your time here. You can't come back. Once you accept that, you can start looking. Hang around bus stations and seedy apartment buildings. Old motels are good hunting grounds too.

Don't waste time following happy people and stay away from dopers and drunks."

She turned, walked up the steps and through the front door. She looked back out through the living room window. An evening breeze rolled down the street, sweeping the leaves and the revenant out of sight.

About the Author

Paul Stansbury is a life long native of Kentucky. He is the author of *Down By the Creek – Ripples and Reflections* and a novelette: *Little Green Men?* His speculative fiction stories have appeared in a number of print anthologies as well as a variety of online publications. Now retired, he lives in Danville, Kentucky.

COMMEDIA DELL'ARTE

By Anna Shane

Shelley and Shannon's friends politely referred to their marriage as "failed," although when the murder of one spouse by the other is involved, "failed" may not be quite the right word. Of course, their friends insisted emphatically that it was not murder. But their zealous protests were only an effort to dislodge the bothersome weight at the back of their minds that there was no other way to see it; Shelley had killed Shannon. They all knew perfectly well that he had never intended it, but being in the same room with a man who had murdered his wife, however accidentally, was not pleasant, and they avoided him more and more.

***

"There are things," Shannon had told Maggie, a few days before her death, as she sat in Maggie's living room crying, "that one ought never to tease someone about."

Maggie felt as if a gaping hole had opened in the middle of her comfortable flat where Shannon sat, bundled into her armchair in a shapeless heap of limbs and clothes, her hair covering her face. It seemed the void around Shannon was stretching ever-wider to swallow Maggie as well. Shannon had become a black, impenetrable, hungry darkness, pouring terror onto Maggie's well-polished parquet floor. The very fact that her fear was out of proportion to the occasion made Maggie shrink from her still more.

77

It seemed as if Shannon was living half in another world, one haunted by creatures that Maggie could not see. Maggie felt a palpable lack, as though part of her mind was frozen, or as if she had lost an eye, and could not see the terrible danger that was creeping along her blind side, but could hear it breathing. Shannon's terror was infectious. Maggie shook herself and looked out the window at the clear light of day.

"I can't explain," Shannon whimpered, "I *can't* explain."

"I'll make you some tea," Maggie said.

***

There are many different sorts of fear, most of them illogical. More people are oppressed by violent fears of spiders or insects, which are unlikely to harm them, than by thinking they'll be run over by a car or city train, which is far more likely to happen. Children are never scared that they will fall out of a tree and break their neck, but are almost always frightened that something is lurking in a dark corner, of which there is no evidence in the light of day. Shannon was suffering from a fear that was supremely illogical, since the object of her terror was not meant to be frightening, and was not even real.

From a very early age, she had been terrified of Pierrots, the seventeenth-century version of mimes, sometimes referred to as French clowns. Many illustrators of children's books regarded them as endearing figures to put in the backgrounds of pictures, with their sad white-painted faces and loose white costumes, and her terror must have grown from that. Before she could read, Shannon would leaf through picture books and find the white, odd-faced figures appear again and again. At first, she took no notice of them, but then she began to realise that they appeared in stories with no connection to one another, and no explanation for their presence.

When she learned to read, she sought carefully for any mention of the Pierrots in the text, but always found none. They existed only in the illustrations, tucked away in the background, and because of the similarity of the figures, she could never be sure whether they were one and the same or different every time. The discovery of this pattern frightened her. They were intruders, they were not invited, they crept into the pictures while the author was not looking.

Shannon began to dread looking at new illustrations, as one could never be sure whether the figure would make an appearance in that particular picture or not. The Pierrots showed up seemingly at their own whim, regardless of the story. She felt that they were haunting her, but believed them confined between the covers of books, which she could slam shut, imprisoning them inside. She made a nightly ritual of doing so, shutting every cover with a decisive, military efficiency. She would check at least three times that she had indeed shut them all before standing something heavy on them so the Pierrots could not escape.

When she was seven, her parents took her with them to a picture gallery, where they walked through seemingly endless halls stuffed with pictures that looked exactly the same to Shannon, until she wilted with boredom. Eventually, her parents left her in a gallery of rococo art to wait for them with a book, rather than dragging her after them. Looking idly around the walls and wondering what grown-ups could possibly find of interest in these nearly-identical paintings, Shannon saw, in the background of one, an unmistakable white-clothed, white-faced figure, playing a guitar. She could not move, but sat paralyzed. She thought that she had imprisoned the dreadful things in her books. Had she left one open for the figure to climb out and go roaming about? Where would it not pursue her?

Shannon squeezed her eyes shut. She scarcely dared look around her, for fear that she would see a Pierrot in the room with her. Looking back at the picture was out of the question. She was sure that the Pierrot would be gone, or standing elsewhere. With the utmost caution, her eyes fixed on the floor, she crept from the room. She was convinced that she had released the unexplained figure into the world and it would now never leave her alone. Her fear was so great that she could not even tell her parents about it. She would burst into tears, unable to explain what frightened her, because to say it might make it so real that the world would slide away from her completely and leave her tumbling into an abyss of nothingness.

Shannon's mother at last discovered the object of her dread when Shannon begged her to destroy certain books that had Pierrots in the illustrations. By coaxing and assuring, she got Shannon to point to what was frightening her, and exclaimed to her husband, laughing,

"Oh, she's afraid of the Pierrots!"

Instead of making her feel safe, her mother's amused and dismissive tone made Shannon even more afraid. Clearly, her parents did not understand, and would therefore make no effort to protect her or themselves. When they attempted to question her as to why the figures should frighten her so, she simply cried, because she could not give a simple reason, or any reason at all. That made the Pierrots all the more horrible, as if they were preventing her from speaking through the exercise of some terrible power.

Shannon could explain why she was afraid of heights and large dogs; one could fall off a height and be bitten by a dog. Her fear of Pierrots was of an entirely different order, and her childish vocabulary could not provide an explanation, even if her childish mind could have formed it. It was a disgustingly intimate fear, like the horrible sensation aroused by the countless tiny legs of a centipede in movement on the skin, but magnified a thousand-fold.

The Pierrot faces, fixed in the unchanging expression of bland sadness, hinted to her of some monstrous expression of cruelty and fiendishness hidden beneath the chalky powder. The spotless whiteness of their clothes seemed ready to be stained with splashes of blood. The sack-like ill fit of their garments made her think of misshapen bodies concealed beneath, perhaps inhuman. Everything about them alluded to untold outrages committed upon ordinary human beings. They seemed to her bizarrely hungry, as if they had a swallowing, enormous maw hidden somewhere, which could at any second break through the fragile masquerade of paint and powder to devour the whole world. She found their sneaking, seemingly benign and unobtrusive lurking in the background to be menacing. She imagined them deliberating over whom to devour next.

Every night, she was kept awake by an agony of terror, her heart beating in unsteady rushes, hardly daring to breathe, sure that she would see the repulsive white form emerging from the darkness. Her eyes would strain to keep account of every shape in the room, until, after hours of torment, she would fall asleep from sheer exhaustion. Shannon's parents soon grew exasperated with her fear, and deciding they would not cater to it by humouring her any more, refused to let her have a light on in her room, despite her desperate pleading. She learned, therefore, that to confide her fear was useless. She could expect no sympathy. So she spent her nights in unsleeping horror, eyes aching from peering into the darkness, and body stiff from long hours of continuous, unmitigated fearful paralysis.

The fear could not continue at this intensity without killing her. Had it gone on, it would have burned her up from within. But children, with their quick minds and changeable bodies, soon forget, and slowly, even her fear of Pierrots was forgotten, like the dropping of a bad habit. She outgrew specific books with illustrations that frightened her, and they remained unopened on the shelves. She learned to lull herself to sleep by thoughts of other things. Her parents congratulated themselves on dealing so wisely with her ridiculous fear. Soon, the rare sights of the white-clad forms did not stay with her, she simply shuddered as if they were something slimy and gross, and dismissed them from her mind. She was no longer at the mercy of the irrational ideas her brain chose to throw up, but could direct and instruct her thoughts however she wanted.

She grew older, finished school, went to university where she met and married Shelley, and the two of them settled down to a comfortable existence in Leeds. Shannon worked in an estate agent's office and Shelley in a bank. It did not seem that anything out of the ordinary would happen to Shannon again for the duration of her life.

She and Shelley were invited to a costume party, known as a masquerade ball, a semi-official event at a friend's workplace. It was supposed to be an affair 'with style' (which meant, it must be presumed, a degree of decency often absent from costume parties), and everyone was told to come in a costume from art, literature or myth. Shelley and Shannon decided that they would keep their costumes secret from one another, arrive separately, and try to find each other.

Shannon, dressed as a Valkyrie, wandered around, talking to friends and looking for Shelley. Then, in a clump of people close to her, she saw someone dressed as a Pierrot. She flinched involuntarily, and made a mental note to avoid that person. However, white is a very difficult colour to ignore, and she kept seeing the figure in the corner of her eye, her attention snagged repeatedly by the glare of bright whiteness. She could not attend properly to anything that was being said, and made distracted answers when spoken to, almost at random. Soon, she hardly knew what she was saying, so much of her attention was devoted to not looking at the Pierrot. She wished Shelley would turn up, so she could tell him she was ill and had to leave. She knew it was stupid, but she could not stay there with that figure bobbing around just on the edge of her vision, and her almost-superstitious avoidance of looking at it. It reminded her of the elaborate ceremonies and taboos of her childhood which were supposed to guard her from the Pierrots.

"Hey, you alright?" Maggie asked, looking at her intently.

"Yes, I mean, no," Shannon said. "Not feeling the best, I think I need to leave. Have you seen Shelley? I haven't been able to find him."

Maggie laughed. "There he is," she said, pointing. "He's been trying to see how close he can get to you without your recognising him for ages."

Shannon slowly turned to look where Maggie was pointing and realised that the person in the Pierrot costume was her husband.

Her heart clenched sickeningly in her chest as the forgotten fear resurged with all its former strength. In an instant, she was transformed into a small, defenceless child with no power or control. It seemed to her that her husband had been swallowed, and now something else was pretending to be him. She could never, ever let it near her. She backed away instinctively, slowly, like an animal retreating in tense caution before a predator, terrified of making any sudden moves that would provoke an attack.

"Did you really not know it was me?" Shelley said, coming towards her. His movement was predatory, like a lion stalking his prey. He was going to do something terrible to her, she could feel it.

"Don't!" she cried, shrinking against the nearest wall.

"Shan, what's wrong?" he asked, hurrying forward with concern.

The revival of the long-abandoned fear shook her to the core. All she could see was the terrible white thing advancing on her, speaking in Shelley's voice, making Shelley's gestures, but it *was not* Shelley, of that she was sure. How could it possibly think to deceive her in that? Every thought in her head was drowned beneath the feeling that it *must not* touch her. Like a tiny trapped animal, she could not see the spaces around her properly, she did not know where the door was, how large the room was, how long the wall went on for.

She had never told Shelley about her fear, it had seemed both too insignificant and too enormous to mention. She was sure he would just laugh, he would never understand. She was completely alone with her terror. No one would ever do anything to assuage it. She was doomed to live with it, isolated from the rest of the world, just her and the dreadful Pierrots, locked together forever in the dark chamber of her mind.

***

Three days later, Maggie was woken up by knocking at the door of her flat. She found Shannon outside, wrapped up in her coat like a bundle about to fall apart, shaking with cold and misery.

"Shan, what's the matter?" Maggie cried, ushering her inside.

Shannon dropped into an armchair, covered her face with her hands, and rocked herself slowly, rhythmically, as if trying to hypnotise herself into some primal sensation of comfort. Maggie knelt by the chair.

"Talk to me, Shan, come on," she urged.

After a few seconds, Shannon slowly lifted her face from her hands. It was the face of pure terror. Her eyes seemed to look straight through Maggie, to something beyond her, with such a fixed and abject expression that Maggie turned to see what was behind her and found only her ordinary room. Shannon's eyes were huge, the pupils dilated, the whites cracked with the red of sleeplessness and tears. Her skin looked yellow, worn and haggard, her lips red and swollen with being bitten, and deep lines were engraved between her eyes and around her mouth, compressed to hold in a scream. All this framed by dishevelled, scattered hair, snarled up like the roots of a tree.

"It's Shelley," she said, in a cracked, dry voice, which sounded like the rasp of withered grass. "I can't bear to have him touch me, I can't bear to have him *near* me, I will *die* if he touches me!" she gasped, and clutched her hands against her mouth, breathing rapidly, as if her very words frightened her still more. She froze again, sitting fixed in utter stillness. Her eyes seemed the only living thing about her, staring up at Maggie in a wordless pleading for help.

"What happened?" Maggie said, trying to keep her voice steady, to inject every bit of reason and calmness she possessed into her expression, but it wobbled in her own ears.

It was at least a minute before Shannon was recovered enough from her paroxysm of panicked immobility to answer.

"Ever since the masquerade ball," she said. "I can't be near him after I saw him in – in that costume. I've always been so scared – "

"Of Pierrots?" Maggie finished for her.

Shannon draw her entire body into a knot around itself, and nodded frantically.

Maggie got her to drink some tea and to stay with her for the night, promising to talk to Shelley the next day and explain.

Maggie and Shelley met at a cafe at noon the next day. Shelley looked worried, and like he hadn't slept all night.

"What on earth's going on?" he asked. "Is Shannon alright? What've I done?"

"It isn't your fault," Maggie said, studying her coffee. "You see, apparently she has some bizarre childhood fear of Pierrots."

"That's what she said, but, come on, that's absurd! To be frightened to *that* extent! Maggie, she wouldn't let me *touch* her, she started screaming. I must have done something."

"It's a phobia, or something of the sort, you know, they can be really bad. She ought to see someone."

"She ought to see *me*! I'm her husband!"

"I meant a doctor. She was in a proper state."

"You're telling me! It's ridiculous, it couldn't be just this weird childhood fear. And if it is, she ought to just confront it, and then she'll forget about it."

"I'm not sure this whole "confronting it" idea is a good one."

"Look, let's go back and talk to her and get her to come home, yeah?"

Maggie and Shelley talked long and soothingly to Shannon, and finally convinced her to go home with Shelley. With the removal of Shannon from her house, Maggie felt as though the vast abyss of horror into which her life was draining had been closed as suddenly as it had opened. Steady daylight reigned over a peaceful and soothingly unremarkable world. It was much easier, when not confronted with a half-crazed Shannon, to consider her problem in scientific, quantifiable terms. A question of balance and understanding of some strange twists and quirks of the mind. It was no longer the unstoppable onrush of some primal horror forcing its way through her friend's body.

But the very next evening, Shannon was dead.

Maggie got a call at around nine in the evening.

"Oh God, Maggie, you've got to come."

"Shelley? What is it, what's wrong?"

"It's Shannon, she's – Maggie, I think she's dead."

"What?"

"I think I've killed her, Maggie. I think she's dead and I've killed her, please come, please –"

"Shelley, that's rubbish, you couldn't have killed her, just tell me what's happened."

"Just come, please, Maggie, please, I'm – I'm too scared to touch her, I think she's dead, I think she's – she's really dead."

"Alright, I'm coming, just – just stay calm. I'm sure it's a – a misunderstanding," Maggie said, using the only word she could come up with. Catching the frantic mood of Shelley's voice on the phone, she began to laugh hysterically as she struggled on her coat, at the ridiculous inadequacy of the word. "Misunderstanding – misunderstanding," she gasped, her side seizing up with uncontrollable hilarity that was monstrously out of place, horrible in its utter unsuitability to the situation. She could not stop the laughter, the harder she tried to press her lips together, the more insistently they burst apart, like the broken zipper on an overflowing bag, and gusts of laughter racked her body. She could barely breathe through the pressure of it, and she had to sit slumped in the corner of the taxi she hailed, trying to inhale steadily and calm herself. Even so, she kept bursting into wild little convulsions of laughter, which caused the driver to look at her oddly.

When she got to Shannon and Shelley's house, she ran up to the door and pushed it open, not bothering to knock or ring. The lights were on in the living room, and she rushed directly there. Once inside the door, she stopped dead.

On the carpet lay Shannon, motionless, her face covered by her hair. Above her stood Shelley in his Pierrot costume.

"What the hell were you doing?" Maggie demanded, staring at him.

"I – I thought she was being ridiculous and she ought to just face it, so I – dressed up like this again to try to sort of – shake her back into her senses, you know. Oh God, Maggie, oh God, I'm such a bloody idiot. She was sitting in here, I think she was asleep, she hasn't been sleeping well at night and she must have dropped off. All the lights were off and I stood near the door and called her, I thought she'd have a bit of a scare and then we'd both laugh it off and forget about it, I thought – "

He broke off, staring at Shannon's inert body on the floor.

"Well, what happened?" Maggie demanded.

"She sort of started awake and looked towards me, there was just enough light from the street for her to see me, especially with the white clothes, but not enough light for her to recognise me. She jumped up and gave the most horrible scream I've ever heard, it was –"

He broke off and stared around the room, as if seeing Shannon's last scream bouncing between the walls, following its progress with his eyes.

"She jumped forward, I think she wanted to run, but she just fell and – well, that was all."

Slowly, Maggie walked forward and knelt over Shannon. She moved the hair away from her face. The look of absolute horror there, even in death, was such that Maggie's heart gave a sickening lurch, and the blood beat furiously in her head. Transfixed, her sickened fascination suspended her instinct to jerk away, and she remained bent over Shannon, unable to tear her eyes away from her friend's distorted, agonized face. Her eyes were wide, her mouth lopsided, every muscle in her face immobilised in unbearable tension. The stark, naked terror was chiselled forever into the hard stone of Shannon's face.

As if turned to stone herself, Maggie remained on her knees, bent over and staring at every fixed feature. With cold ripples cascading down her spine, Maggie realized that no one could understand the depth of fear Shannon had suffered, because to understand it fully would kill. Looking at Shannon's face and hearing Shelley's story, she felt the clutch of a cold hand squeezing her heart, stifling her breathing. And this was just the faint echo of what Shannon must have felt when she saw that white figure standing in the doorway, ambiguous and uninvited. Its face shrouded in anonymity, no identity save that of the recurring figure she had instinctively and unreasonably conceived a terror of in early childhood.

A strange thought flashed through Maggie's mind. Perhaps this was exactly what Shannon had been afraid of all her life, this death, the moment of seeing that figure in the doorway. Perhaps her fear had been driven by the unexplained foreknowledge that this was how her life would end, like those self-fulfilling prophecies in Greek myths, that come true by the very action of trying to prevent them. Perhaps all her life, an echo of that final apogee of terror in her future flashed across her whenever she saw one of the figures, the memory of something that had not yet happened.

Maggie was not sure how long she stayed, staring down at that face, until, by long study, it grew familiar. Shannon's face, or rather the face that had been Shannon's, seemed to fragment. It no longer had one expression, but fell apart in her eyes into separate features bizarrely wrinkled or twisted, as if Shannon was playing a game. Maggie sat back on her heels.

"Well," she said, looking at Shelley, who was kneeling opposite her and watching for her pronouncement. "She's definitely dead."

Shelley looked down at his dead wife and as she watched, his lower lip began to quiver and his face twitched. Maggie felt a sense of distinct unpleasantness, like she had plunged her hand into some viscous and clinging substance, because she thought he was going to cry. But it was not tears contorting his face, but laughter, the same horrid merriment that had seized her earlier.

The overpowering urge to laugh swept back over her, and she could feel her own lips twitching in response to his. She pressed her mouth closed, compressing her lips, but a little cry of laughter slipped out, and dropped to the floor with a gross, indecent flop, like a massive toad. She clapped her hand to her mouth, too late to stop it, and looked with guilty slyness at Shelley from under her brows, as though inviting him into the joke.

The second their eyes met, he ducked his head and began shaking with laughter, his sides heaving quickly and spasmodically. And then they were clutching one another, howling with laughter over Shannon's dead body, unable to catch their breaths, tears seeping out of their eyes. Their fingers dug into one another's flesh with maniacal strength, and they were powerless against the hilarity that twisted tight knots in their lungs, until they fell forward, against each other, against Shannon's body, utterly spent and weak. They did not heed her cold limbs, they lay on the floor next to each other, gasping with the remnants of laughter. Slowly, their breathing calmed and their heartbeats slowed. There was silence. Neither of them could think of anything to say, and neither of them wanted to be the first to move, to make a decisive action. So they lay there, tangled up with the dead body, until, quite without meaning to, they fell asleep.

Shelley woke Maggie up hours later, still in the dead of night. They did not look at one another, and spoke in short sentences, making no allusion to what had happened between them. They called the police and the ambulance. The medics certified that Shannon had died of a heart attack. Under the glare of the kitchen lights where they spoke to the police, Maggie's and Shelley's swollen faces from laughter and sleep looked blotched and inflamed with prolonged weeping.

"Poor man," one of the medics commented to a policeman, "you can see from his face what a shock it was."

***

Spending time with and speaking to Shelley became a duty that the former couple's friends performed scrupulously at first, with a great effort to overcome their instinctive revulsion that was inaccessible to the cool logic of reason. What had happened was not Shelley's fault, but still, they could not forget it. Slowly, their calls and visits grew more and more infrequent, as soon as they felt they could reasonably justify leaving off. Maggie was the first to desert him completely. She could not bear the weight of guilt at her remembered laughter every time she saw Shelley, their common monstrous secret. One by one, they all dropped off, until Shelley was left completely alone.

It did not matter to him very much, as he did not want to see anyone. He developed an all-absorbing pastime: he began to collect Pierrots. He collected the old picture books that had terrified Shannon; Watteau reproductions, illustrations, figurines, plays. He would leaf through the books and stare at the paintings for hours, unsure why he did so. Perhaps he was trying, by continuous attention, to wash his hands of guilt. To assure himself that no normal person would be frightened of Pierrots, that it was an unpredictable abnormality in Shannon's temperament, and not his own actions, that were responsible for her death. Perhaps he was trying to fathom his dead wife's fear or perhaps to reassure her, from beyond the grave, that there was nothing to be afraid of.

But the more he studied the pictures, the more he found the Pierrots disquieting, their unwavering placidity, their ambiguous, bedraggled, resigned feint at cheerfulness. Their white faces were like something diseased, something that had never seen the sun and was rotting inside. It seemed to him that the second he looked away, their picture-face warped into expressions of aggression, greed, glee at his loss. He imagined inhuman, sharp teeth under grey lips, ghastly smiles of malice. He cultivated this fear, because it was all that remained to him of his wife. The terrified beating of his heart and crawling of his skin was like the miraculous resurrection of her touch, the physical assertion of her presence in the world; as long as he was afraid, she was with him.

He was found by a neighbour one morning, books spread open all over the floor, all of them to illustrations with Pierrots. Pictures with Pierrots adorned the walls, little figurines and dolls encircled him, all standing so that their white, sadly cheerful faces were turned towards him. He had been dead for over a day, had taken an overdose of sleeping pills. His former friends felt that the manner of his death, surrounded by Pierrots, was in decidedly bad taste, and all secretly suspected that it was one last, horrible joke on them all, and on the fate that had taken away his wife.

About the Author

Anna Shane declined to provide a biography.

THE OUIJA BOARD

By Vaggelis Sarantopoulus

Where to start? Oh yes. The game. Julia's idea. We were supposed to have a relaxing weekend; Julia, Peter, Sam, Helen, and myself. Julia's parents had bought an old manor a few years back, outside a small town called Conway up in North Wales, a place to go for holidays to relax.

After their deaths seven months ago, Julia inherited the place, but she didn't have the heart to visit it alone, having spent so many weekends and holidays there with them before they both died in that terrible can accident; an accident that left only one survivor.

Julia herself.

We all felt that we had to go when she asked us to spend the weekend with her at the manor. She was handling her loss pretty well, but we thought maybe she needed us to help her put some of the ghosts that haunted her life to rest.

Ha! Ghosts. If I only knew back then how real those ghosts were going to be!

Anyway, we agreed to go, although I think Peter's motives were not so pure, as he was trying to get into Julia's pants for quite a while.

The house was totally impressive, one of those really old residencies that have been reconstructed to fit in the modern era. Two floors, twelve bedrooms, three bathrooms, a library, two studies, a huge kitchen, a beautiful hallway decorated with paintings, a living room with three big sofas and a plasma TV, and an old-style dining room with a large wooden table. It was what I'd imagine my dream house to be.

Too bad I had to burn it to the ground.

We settled down quickly and having arrived around half past one, we had lunch in the living room watching TV. We chatted a bit and then the guys and I went for a walk around the surrounding areas of the house while Julia and Helen stayed in to have their girl talk.

Did I mention the garden? It surrounded the whole house and it was full of trees and flower plants. It even had a pond with a small fountain. It was there that I had the bad feeling. It felt like something was about to go terribly wrong and suddenly the place didn't look so idyllic anymore.

"Hey, Mark! Are you alright, mate?"

It was Sam. Apparently, they had noticed the change in my mood.

"Yeah, I'm fine. Just a little dizzy from the trip. What about you guys? What do you think about the place?"

"It's all right," Sam said. "Peter here thinks it's perfect."

"Perfect for what?"

"Nothing," Peter said, looking a little uncomfortable. "Cut it out, Sam."

"Why? Mark is a very cool guy. He will understand."

"OK, guys. What's going on?"

Peter opened his mouth to answer but Sam beat him to it.

"He is going to make a move on Julia."

Peter's face turned red.

"Sam! Shut up!"

"No, it's OK," I said calmly.

"It is?"

"Yeah, mate. It's fine."

"See?" Sam said to him. "I told you Mark would be cool about it."

"Oh, God!" Peter said, obviously relieved. "I just didn't know how you would react, man. You and Julia had this thing not long ago."

"Yeah, but it's over now. It's time for both of us to move on."

After that, Peter was all smiles. But how did I really feel about it? Actually, I was feeling pretty good. After the accident, we were not the same, Julia and I. She changed, which was normal if you think all the things she went through, but even so, there were times where she acted like a completely different person.

The sun was down and we were all sitting in the living room, when Julia asked if we wanted to play a game.

"Yeah, why not?" Helen said.

"What kind of game?" Peter asked.

Julia went upstairs and came back holding a large wooden

box. She placed it on the table, opened it, and took out a Ouija board.

"You are joking, right?" That was Sam. He was obviously as shocked as we all were.

"Why? Come on. It will be fun."

We all looked at each other. So that was the reason Julia brought us here. She was hoping to communicate with her parents. I didn't really know if I actually believed in that kind of thing, but if it helped to bring her some closure, then I was in. Apparently, the others thought so too, because after a couple of minutes, we all agreed.

We switched off the lights, placed a bunch of small candles on the floor around the board, and sat down in a circle.

"Which spirit shall we summon first?" I asked. I was sure that she would want to talk to her mother first, because they were very close.

I was wrong.

"Mr. Gripo."

"Who the hell is Mr. Gripo?" Sam asked, while the rest of us exchanged glances of surprise.

"He was a nice old man living next door to us when I was a kid," Julia replied.

"Why him?" asked Helen.

"Why not? We have to start somewhere. Come on! Let's hold hands!"

And so we did, closing our eyes and waiting for Julia to begin. It was in the darkness behind my eyelids that I felt the same thing as before. A sense of dread that something was very, very wrong, and when Julia started chanting, I felt a cold grip around my hand.

"Mr. Gripo, Mr. Gripo, come to us. Hear our summoning and come to us!"

I could hear the others trying to suppress a laugh, but it didn't seem like a joke to me anymore. I opened my eyes and looked at Julia. Her eyes were shut and she was smiling in a way that made her look like another person entirely.

It wasn't a nice smile.

"Open your eyes," she said, and I immediately closed mine and opened them again so she wouldn't know I'd opened them already.

"Is he here?" Helen asked.

"Let's find out," came Julia's answer. She touched the planchette with both hands and asked in a low voice, "Mr. Gripo, are you here?"

Her hands moved to YES.

Everybody smiled, except for me.

"Do you remember me?"

Again, YES.

"Do you guys want to ask anything?"

"Why would we?" Sam asked. "We didn't know the guy.

You did."

"Let's call someone else, then." Julia said. "Goodbye, Mr. Gripo."

The planchette moved to GOODBYE.

Julia was obviously having fun and so were Sam, Peter and Helen, but I wasn't so sure about all this. Something was off.

Next was a Claudia Perkings, again someone from Julia's childhood. Then it was John Stone, a kid who died when she was little, and after him came Mr. Grey.

"Who's Mr. Grey?" I asked. I didn't like that name. It sounded ominous.

Julia looked at me and I saw something in her eyes that made me feel uneasy.

"My third-grade teacher," she told me and instantly I knew that she was lying.

"Can I ask something?" I asked next.

"Yeah, sure," came the answer, but she seemed uncertain.

"OK, Mr. Grey," I said. "Here it goes." I took a big breath before asking. "What is your first name?"

Everybody looked at Julia, but she was looking at me. Then, slowly, her hands moved.

M-A-R-T-I-N.

"Martin Grey, then," Peter said. "Useless, but good to know."

"We should stop now," Julia said. "I'm tired and I think we

had too many spirits for one night."

"Are you sure? Don't you want to speak to someone else?" Helen asked, surprised.

"No, why would I? Come on! Let's make dinner!"

The dinner was roast beef with potatoes, and fruit salad with ice cream for dessert. After we finished, we all went to our bedrooms. I was putting on my pajamas when I suddenly felt sleepy and a very strange thought crossed my mind.

She drugged us.

Now, why would I think that? It was a very paranoid thought but it stuck with me and I felt better only when I locked my door.

Sleep took me immediately. Sometime in the night, I thought I heard someone trying the door handle, but I couldn't be certain.

When I woke up in the morning, I felt worse. Something had happened during the night. I was sure of it. I went downstairs and found them having breakfast, talking to each other and laughing. Everything seemed normal. Was I getting paranoid? Julia saw me first.

"Hey, Mark! Good morning. Come, join us."

The others greeted me with smiles. Sam even gave me his seat at Julia's side. Another thought came to me, more paranoid than the one I had the previous night.

These are not my friends.

Enough! I thought to myself. *You are acting crazy. Everything is fine.*

I ate my breakfast and joined their conversation, something about old houses and spirits. After a while, I felt sleepy again, the same way I had the night before and suddenly I couldn't keep my eyes open. Seconds before I passed out I thought, *she drugged me again.*

In my dream I was naked, in a place full of colors. It was like I was inside a rainbow. Two people approached me, dressed in white, a woman and a boy. The woman was Julia.

"Hey, Mark," she said, and I felt tears coming to my eyes.

"Hey, Jules. You look amazing."

"You know it's not me back there, don't you?"

"I had my suspicions, but I wasn't sure. How is it possible?"

Her smile faded away and I saw pain in her eyes.

"I died, Mark. I died in that accident along with my parents. The thing that came out of that car wasn't me."

"Who is she, then?"

"She is old, very old, and she wanted to live again. She assumed my life and her goal was to bring more of her kind into the world. And she succeeded."

It suddenly hit me like a wave.

"The Ouija board!"

"Yes," the boy said, speaking for the first time. "She summoned the evil spirits and then she drugged you, all of you.

She went to each of your friend's bedrooms while they were sleeping and used a very old ritual to possess their bodies with those evil beings."

"Mr. Gripo and the others."

"Yes. Fake names, of course. You were only spared from that fate because you locked your door. The others weren't so lucky. Dark fiends inhabit their souls now."

"How did locking the door save me? And what are we talking about here? Spirits? Ghosts? Demons?"

It was Julia that answered my question.

"She didn't want to make any noise by breaking into your room, and she didn't want to force anything on you, as any kind of resistance could spoil the ritual. As for what they are, all of those things you mentioned and more."

"And then she drugged me again this morning. Right?"

"Yes. Right now, as we speak, she is doing the ritual again, with the help of her new friends. She wanted you for last, because you will be the vessel for their leader."

"Mr. Grey."

"Not his real name, of course."

"So, what now, Julia? I'm screwed, aren't I?"

She smiled at me, putting one hand on the boy's shoulder.

"Not if can help it. That's why Barry is here. He can help."

I turned my eyes to the boy.

"Help? How?"

"Let me in," Barry said.

"Let you in?"

"To your body. Don't worry. You won't even know I'm there."

"Please, Mark." Julia said. "We are running out of time."

"OK, Jules. For your sake. What do I do?"

"Just say my name," Barry said.

"What? Barry?"

"Not that. My real name."

"And what is your real name?"

Julia came close and whispered to my ear the boy's true name.

Suddenly I understood everything and as I said the angel's name out loud, the world exploded in white light.

"BARACHIEL."

I woke up to the sound of voices.

"What happened? Did it work?" Helen's voice.

"It must. He is waking up."

Peter, or more accurately, the thing inside him, "Master?"

I opened my eyes and found myself tied to a chair inside a basement illuminated by the light of candles. The floor was covered in symbols drawn with red paint. Or blood.

"Master," Julia said again, looking into my eyes.

They were all leaning on me, their eyes full of expectation. I looked at them, one by one, my old friends, these evil beings that drugged me and tied me up in the basement. I wasn't paranoid after all. This was really happening.

"Release me," someone said, and it took me a moment to realize that it was my voice that had spoken.

Someone used my body to stand up, as they removed the ropes from my arms and legs.

Someone in my body. Someone else.

Panic filled my mind. Was I Mr. Grey's slave now? Had they succeeded?

"*No,*" said a boy's voice inside my head. Barry. "*Stay calm. Their master doesn't dare enter your body with me inside it, but they don't know that.*"

They made room as I stood up, then all of them fell to their knees.

"Welcome wanderer," Julia said. "The road to this world is open to you."

I felt something inside me then, an anger I hadn't known before. I reached out with one hand and grabbed Peter's shoulder while the other one touched Sam's head.

"Zagan!" I said with a voice that wasn't mine and Peter fell on the floor, unconscious.

"Abraxas!" I said again and Sam fell too.

Julia stood up and started to retreat but Helen wasn't fast enough. I grabbed her by the neck while she was trying to stand and called out the thing that inhabited her soul by saying its name.

"Vapula!"

She hit the floor with an awful sound but I was already turning towards the stairs that led back to the house. Julia was nowhere to be seen. I followed her up in the house and found her in the living room with a gun in her hands.

"You are not him," she said, aiming the gun at my face. "And you are not Mark. Who are you?"

"Tell me your name and I will tell you mine."

"Ha! I don't think so, White Spirit! I saw what you did to the others using their names. But you will not find mine. It is hidden."

"Tell me," I said a second time.

"No!" she screamed and pulled the trigger.

The gun roared in her hands and I heard something break behind me, but I didn't move. I felt no fear, only a sense of purpose.

"TELL ME YOUR NAME!" I cried out and an invisible force came out of my body and hit her like a wave.

"Bushyasta!" she screamed, unable to conceal her name from my divine voice and fired the gun again and again until it was empty.

"Bushyasta," the creature inside me said and she lowered the gun and was still.

"Reveal yourself."

Her skin started to burn and under it I saw yellow flesh and small, pointy bones like thorns. Her eyes turned black and her mouth opened to reveal big sharp teeth.

"What now, creature of the light?"

"Now you go back where you came from. Be gone!"

And with that, the flames took her. I went back to the basement to see how the others were doing. Fortunately, they were waking up. We didn't have a lot of time.

I helped them get out of the house and we watched it burn while waiting for help to arrive. The others didn't remember much, so I did the talking and the conclusion by the police and the fire department was, "fire by accident."

I didn't go to the funeral. I knew that it wasn't Julia in that coffin. She died long before that.

I see her sometimes in my dreams. I can't say that I understand everything that happened, but I do know this: Julia saved me. She reached out from the other side and saved my life.

I don't talk to the others much these days and I think it's better that way. We are all trying to forget. As for me, my life will never be the same again, but that's OK, because I know that when my journey comes to an end, there will be someone waiting for me at the end of the road.

About the Author

Vaggelis Sarantopoulos is a Greek writer living in the UK. He's been writing in Greek for many years and now he is making his debut in the English language with the short story "Ouija Board." In 2012, Universe Pathways magazine of Greece awarded him with the Second Larry Niven Fantasy Award for his novelette "Sunrise Deep Under The Earth". The Author lives with his wife and his cat in Wales.

EVP

By Jeff C. Stevenson

"Good news!" the property manager said. "The house on Warwick Avenue is rented!"

"Wonderful," the owner replied. He hung up the phone, relieved.

***

"Mary?"

She was in the kitchen drying dishes the first time she heard the voice. She lived alone. Startled, Mary set the plate down and peered over the pass-through counter into the living room.

"Hello?"

The drapes were open. She saw that the early evening sunlight had started to push itself in. Shadows were just beginning to lightly caress the furniture; the two easy chairs were already stained in sunset red. The coffee table and sofa would soon turn amber. Off to the left was the short hallway that led to the master and guest bedrooms, the passageway already clothed in the gloom of near dusk. The front door was closed.

I imagined the voice, Mary told herself firmly. *New house, new neighborhood, new noises. Bound to be some unfamiliar sounds.*

She moved the plate from the counter to the cupboard, not liking the way her heart was pounding; not liking it at all. Her hands were shaking. The silverware clattered a bit as she put the pieces away; sharp, shrill sounds in the silent house.

She closed the drawer. Her name was called again. She was certain it came from the living room. She didn't bother to check. Instead, with three frightened leaps, she was out the back door. Almost before she knew it, she stood in the weeds of her yard, nervously looking at her home. She dialed John, swallowed several times as she waited for him to answer.

"Hey, babe, what's up?" His voice was solid, friendly, sure of itself and certain of their relationship. She immediately doubted all she was about to say to him, felt like a silly, frightened child.

"Someone called my name. Twice."

"What?"

She told him what had happened. "And I know it sounds ridiculous, but I heard it. Twice."

"I'll be right over. Stay outside, in the front of the house. Wait for me there. Don't go back inside."

***

John arrived ten minutes later. Mary was trembling, her voice muffled against his shoulder. "I was so scared," he heard her say.

"I'm going to check it out. You stay here."

Once inside, John clicked on a lamp. He hesitated. He looked from the entryway into the kitchen. He'd been to the house several times, had helped Mary move in, but hadn't yet spent the night. He was waiting for an invite. Mary was special, worth being patient with. He wondered if someone was in the house, messing with her. He listened. Behind him on the front porch, he sensed Mary watching over his shoulder.

Out of the silence, John heard a rustle, then a short, muffled noise from the kitchen. A common sound, a familiar one. A drawer being pulled open? Then there came a loud BANG! Something solid, metal, heavy, had landed on the floor. He flinched, startled by the noise. Mary gasped behind him. She
grabbed his arm.

"What was that?" she whispered into his right ear.

"Dunno." He took a couple breaths to steady himself. He gestured for Mary to wait by the front door; he didn't want her to see how nervous he was. He felt like he was playing the role of the father or the fearless boyfriend, but there was no courage in his movements. It was all instinct, like immediately feeling for the light switch when encountering a dark room.

"Hello? Who's there?"

He wanted to shout, *I have a gun*! but didn't want to escalate the situation. The house swallowed up his words, gulped them down like he hadn't spoken. He made himself walk quickly toward the pass-through. He felt for the wall switch. Light burst out against the gathering shadows. He didn't enter the kitchen; instead, he rose up on his toes to see in. It was empty. He was both relieved and unnerved by the vacant space.

Once the kitchen light was on, he cautiously walked onto the white tile. He froze. A counter drawer was open. On the floor, he spotted a silver tool, about twelve inches in length. Impulsively, he darted forward, grabbed the object, dashed out of the house.

"It looks like a wood filing tool," he said, safely on the front porch. "You rub it back and forth to smooth out rough areas."

"Where did it come from?" Mary asked

"A drawer in the kitchen was open. I guess it…fell out?"

Outside, three shades of illumination covered them: Moonlight, porch light, and the subdued glow of the lamp in the living room. He looked at Mary. Her eyes were wide with uncertainty and bewilderment. He could see how frightened she was, how much she needed to be cared for.

"I didn't leave any drawers open," she said, her words shaky, uncertain. Had she?

"I think I heard it open," he said.

She leaned in, needed to be in closer contact with him. "Someone took it out of the drawer?"

"Don't worry, no one is in the kitchen," he quickly said. He was certain her heart was beating as hard and fast as his. He squeezed her hand.

Mary asked, "So who opened the drawer?"

John ignored her question; he had no answer. Instead, he asked, "Is this tool yours?"

Mary shook her head, shrugged. "I haven't cleaned out all the stuff from the previous tenants. They left all their junk behind when they skipped out on their rent."

"John?"

They both stiffened, turned to face the empty area where the voice had originated. Mary fell into John's arms with a cry. He pulled her close.

The voice called out his name again.

***

They went to dinner, decided on a plan. First, they would return to Mary's to collect clothing and whatever other items she needed, then she would spend the night with John. While they ate, they made a list of all she would retrieve.

"We'll go in together," John said.

"You got that right."

"Then we'll lock the house up, see about getting help."

"What kind of help? And what do we tell them, that we're hearing voices?" She finished her wine and wanted another, but thought it best she didn't overindulge after all she had just been through.

"And objects are moving. Something is going on in your house, we've both experienced it."

"Any idea who to contact?"

"There's a parapsychology department at the university," John said.

"How do you know that?"

"There was an article about them a few months ago during Halloween. It was all about how universities are closing these departments down due to lack of funding and the inability to provide concrete evidence. I remember reading that there were once thirteen prominent universities that funded this stuff. Duke, Stanford, Princeton, big name schools."

They declined dessert. He shook his head in response to Mary's offer to pay.

"I know this whole thing was a just a sexy ruse to get me to take you to dinner and have you move in with me," he said, smiling.

"I'm only staying with you until we get this figured out." She took his hand as they left the restaurant.

"And then?"

"And then we'll see…"

***

It was a week before they could schedule time to meet with Professor Attila Bayless. His basement office gave clear evidence as to the university's opinion and value of his studies. Located under the engineering building, as soon as the elevator doors opened, all they saw was a dimly lit hallway that ran in two directions. Arrows pointed to the right and left. Faded lettering indicated the two departments, either Anomalies Research in one direction or the Crawfield Imaging Center in the other.

"'Anomalies'?" Mary said. "Really?"

"Before I called, I looked up this fellow, Professor Bayless," John said. "He's all about human consciousness and its role in the establishment of physical reality. Or anomalies."

"Whatever that means."

Their shoes click clacked quietly on the worn tiled floor. There was a musty smell, undercut by the too-sweet lemon scent of floor polish. They passed a silver drinking fountain that hummed and gurgled. Overhead, the fluorescent lights didn't so much flicker as seem to pulsate slowly, from dimly lit to sepia tone.

Mary said, "He should study up on the physical reality and benefits of bright corridors. Seriously, is he trying to make this hallway as creepy as he can?"

"He's got nothing to do with it. The university set him up down here."

"And forgot about him. I don't think his department is long for this world."

The only office at the end of the passage was Professor Bayless's. The door was open, a yellow glow spilled out along with the sounds of Steely Dan's song "Do It Again".

John called out before they entered. The response was a hearty "Come in! Come in!" With a click, the music was cut off.

Professor Bayless stood behind his massive oak desk, gestured for them to enter his chaotic office. He was thin to the point of being gaunt with tightly cropped white hair, a faint, pink complexion, bright blue eyes, and a wide, engaging smile. A frayed black-and-red patterned sweater vest clung loosely to his chest. A pale blue, long-sleeve shirt covered his arms.

"You must be John and Mary. Please, dig through until you find something to sit on. I'd offer you a drink but you've already passed the fountain, so I hope you helped yourself if you were thirsty. The little office fridge I had died years ago. I tend to become literally buried in my work as you can see, so I forget that others enjoy eating, drinking, sunlight, and so forth…"

The disarray reminded Mary of a snow globe that had just been violently shaken; everything seemed to be in the process of settling. They gingerly set aside mounds of paper, folders, books with multi-colored sticky notes slotted between pages, and thick files with their insides overflowing due to the busted rubber bands that no longer restrained their contents. John located an empty metal trashcan he turned over and sat on while Mary managed to pry open a folding chair. Once they were seated, the professor leaned forward.

"So. You've heard voices calling out your names?"

Mary was surprised he started right in. She had expected some chitchat.

"Yes," John confirmed. "First Mary's name was called when she was alone at the house, then we both heard my name, along with a drawer opening and a tool being dropped to the floor."

"Did you see the drawer open?" Professor Bayless asked, straightening up, a flicker of excitement in his eyes.

"No," Mary admitted, wanting to be part of the conversation. After all, it was her house where the occurrences were happening.

"And then?"

"We left. Came back later, got Mary's things, haven't returned since."

The professor nodded thoughtfully. "It's best to leave. Especially if it knows your name. Was it a male or female voice?"

They said it seemed to be a masculine voice.

Bayless asked more questions, jotted on the crumpled yellow pad in front of him, nodded a great deal. Then he went silent, seemed to be deep into his own thoughts.

"So...?" John finally prompted.

Shaken from his private considerations, the professor said, "I think that seeking out EVP would be the best way to proceed. It doesn't put you at risk
and sometimes this method can produce some helpful information."

Having no idea what the professor was talking about, John and Mary waited expectantly. Bayless rummaged around one of the desk drawers, pulled out what looked like a slim remote control for a TV set. He held it up like it was an award he had been given. "I just got this a few months ago. It's exceptional. Can continuously record for up to a thousand hours and it plugs right into the computer for fast file transfer and evaluation. Just ask your questions, leave it running, pick it up the next day, and we'll see what it captures."

"What is it?" Mary asked. She had been leaning closer to Bayless trying to figure out what the gadget did.

"It's an EVP recorder. EVP stands for Electronic Voice Phenomena. You're familiar with spirit photography, right? Pictures that are taken of ghostly manifestations?"

Mary and John nodded slowly in unison, uncertain where this was all headed. Bayless's voice took on the tone of a lecturing professor. "This is the same thing as spirit pictures, but it involves capturing the utterances entities or beings from other realms say. Whatever it is that has contacted you has spoken your names. It knows you, wants to get your attention, has something to tell you. Or show you. So you'll use the EVP machine to ask some questions while the recorder is on, then see if we pick up any answers on the playback. At the time of the session, you may not hear or perceive an answer, but when it's played back, we often find there is some audible response." He smiled, then added, "It really can be remarkable."

While Bayless explained the process, Mary had reached for John's hand. The idea terrified her, as did what the professor kept insisting: *It knows your names.*

Not clear he understood, John asked, "So it records...voices?"

Bayless nodded. "We often hear human-like vocal sounds, mixed in with static, room noise and a lot of chatter, cross talk, but sometimes we can pick out a word or two."

"That's it?" John asked. "Just a word or two?"

The professor grinned again, his lips so thin it was almost like a sneer, but a friendly one. "A word or sentence. The very first authenticated EVPs were recorded back in 1956 and included the phrases, 'This is G!,' 'Hot dog, Art!.' and 'Merry Christmas and Happy New Year to you all!'"

After a beat, Mary burst out laughing as the disturbing feelings scattered. John smiled. Bayless nodded, clearly in on the joke. "Yes, it all sounds a bit silly, but there are thousands of EVPs available to listen to; even aliens have participated, but of course, no one knew what they were saying."

"Have the spirits ever had anything of interest to say?" John asked. "Confirm there is life after death or reveal what the secret of the universe is?"

The professor shook his head, still good-natured about the discussion. "No, no, no such luck. I guess it's safe to say that the dead or beings from other dimensions have had very little to say to us. But you never know. You may be the exception."

Mary couldn't help but stare at the contraption in Bayless's hand. Whatever was in her house already knew their names. What would happen if they gave it a chance to say more to them?

"So we can borrow it?" she asked, jutting her chin at the object.

The professor looked down at the recorder as if he wasn't aware he was holding it. "Oh! Of course, yes! It's simple to use, let me show you."

They huddled close together. The scent of Old Spice, Mary's late father's cologne, lingered around Bayless. She felt a surge of affection for this kind man locked away in a deserted basement, trying so desperately to talk to ghosts and spirits with no apparent success. She thought of her dad, his great sense of humor, his delight in pranks, love of children, toys, all things make believe. How he would have loved to be part of whatever was going on. He might even have enjoyed conversing with the professor.

Once she and John were confident how to use the EVP recorder, they
all stood at once, releasing a flurry of dust particles. "Maid's day off," the professor apologized with a smile. He winked at Mary.

They wanted to do the EVP session in the daylight for obvious reasons.

"It would be scarier at night," Mary said.

Bayless chuckled. "But it really makes no difference. The spirit world doesn't distinguish night or day or seasons or even time. And yet it *is* more frightening at night, so of course go when you are comfortable, ask the questions we discussed, leave several seconds of silence between them, and then leave the machine running."

***

Mary and John arrived at her house Saturday morning at 10:30. Their goal was to quickly complete the EVP session and be on their way to brunch by eleven.

They stood outside her rental for a few seconds. Like every other home on Warwick Avenue, it was generic in appearance. The large front window, the yellow door set off to the right with the square front porch, the short roof over the entryway, the longer one that extended over the living room. All very cookie cutter, nothing threatening or out-of-the-ordinary about it. Just a tract house built in the late 1990s.

"Let's go," John said. "Brunch awaits."

They hurried to Mary's bedroom. She quickly packed some clothes, makeup, and other items that she kept reaching for at John's but couldn't find. She stashed everything into her overnight bag. For some reason, they completed the tasks without speaking, as if they didn't want the house to know they were there.

The kitchen drawer was still open. The shaving tool was on the counter where John had returned it. But it was close to the edge, near the stove burners. He knew he had left it next to the backsplash, right by the faucet handles. Had someone been in the house, moved it? Or…?

He didn't mention this to Mary. "Come on." He took her hand, led her to the sofa. From out of her jeans she pulled the paper with the questions. John set the EVP recorder on the coffee table. He looked at Mary. She nodded. John tapped the record button. A tiny red light appeared. Since it was her home, the professor suggested she be the one to ask the questions.

Mary took a breath. Began.

"Is there anyone here who would like to speak with us?"

John watched her count silently to thirty before she asked the next question.

"Can you make a sound to show us you're here?"

"What is your name?"

"How old are you?"

"Are   you   here   alone?"

"If not, who is with you?"

"Is this your home?"

"What is your favorite room in this house?"

"Is there anything in particular that you would like us to know?"

Each time she spoke, they could feel the atmosphere around them tighten. It felt like the house was holding its breath. The stillness became heavier as if it wanted to smother the woman who was speaking, silence her voice.

After the last question, they immediately walked toward the front door. Their hearts were beating hard even though nothing out of the ordinary had occurred. John's hand was sweaty on the doorknob. He gently pushed Mary out onto the front porch. He pulled the door closed behind him and was about to let out a huge sigh of relief when Mary screamed.

"What?" he cried, as she backed roughly into him.

On the lawn in front of them were two large dead birds.

***

"A dead bird is not an omen of death or doom," Bayless said, trying to calm them over the phone.

"But it must be a sign of *something*," Mary insisted, still unnerved by the encounter.

"Mary, dead birds are typically a *good* sign, indicating that an end to turmoil or pain is occurring. They can even represent the conclusion to your search or struggle. It may mean that a new beginning is just around the corner." When they didn't respond, he said lightly, "Or it may be just two dead birds, right? Let's not read too much into this, okay? We'll listen to what's on the recorder before we try to figure this out. It's probably nothing at all."

Mary knew he was trying to reassure her that everything was all right, and that meant a lot to her. Even over the phone, she sensed his warmth, his desire for her to find the answers but also do it in an orderly, scholarly fashion. There was something so giving and compassionate about the man; she trusted his insights and was thankful he was helping them.

"Too much emotion in this business," he said dismissively. "Too many ghost hunter organizations, bad movies, and TV shows about the supernatural. They never get it right. I don't care what people *think* they see, I want to find out what is *real*, and let *that* be the experience we investigate. If there is anything going on at your house, you'll both find out, but we'll do it my way, if that's all right. Slow and steady, we'll find the evidence. I have my own methods and they *work*."

Talking with Bayless, she thought again of her father, wished he were there with her. What would he have said or done? Probably the same as the professor. *Trust him*, her gut said. Relieved after the conversation, she handed the phone back to John, grateful that he and the professor were there with her for whatever was going on.

***

Sunday morning, John stopped by the house to fetch the EVP recorder. It had been on for about twenty-four hours. He wondered if anything had been captured. Such a thin, sleek machine, warm to the touch but not hot. He was told not to turn it off until he had left the property. He pocketed it, was about to leave, but found he couldn't resist checking on the position of the wood shaving tool. He crept into the kitchen, not sure why he was trying to be so silent. The floorboards under the tiles creaked just a bit.

The drawer was closed. The counter was empty. He glanced around, didn't spot the tool anywhere. Again, he felt the thickening of the atmosphere, then an uneasy sense that someone was watching him. He noticed the EVP recorder felt warmer in his pocket.

He hurried out of the kitchen. Behind him, he heard a rustle of movement, then a dry sound of resistance. Without looking back, he knew

the drawer was being pulled slowly open.

***

"I just plug the flash drive into the computer. It automatically scans the file for any sounds," the professor said. They were in his office, crowded around his desk. "It filters out any room noise or static, then provides us with the edited source material. In the old days, you'd have to listen to the entire tape, locate any sound spikes and then decipher the source and determine if it was an EVP, or some external noise or the machinery itself."

Within five minutes, they had an edited digital version. Bayless clicked some keyboards. A visual sound file appeared, with the lines spiking and shrinking in response to what Mary had said. The images, like mountain ranges, were elevated when her voice was recorded, then ran flat during the silent stretches before the next question was asked.

"Is there anyone here who would like to speak with us?"

Jagged vertical images represented her voice. They were immediately followed by a horizontal line.

"Can you make a sound to show us you're here?"

"What   is   your   name?"

"How old are you?"

"Are you here alone?"

"If not, who is with you?"

"Is this your home?"

"What is your favorite room in the house?"

A spike, taller than Mary's voice, suddenly shot up and a harsh, garbled sound or word was heard: *"BELLOW!"*

"Is there anything in particular that you would like us to know?"

Again: *"BELLOW!"*

The playback ended. No other sounds on the file. The only audible responses occurred when Mary had asked the last two questions. They played that section over several times.

"What does 'bellow' even mean?" Mary asked.

"Sadly, most of the EVPs we get are these random, nonsense words," Bayless said. He sighed. "Remember, the first verified communication was simply the phrase, 'This is G!' No one ever figured out what that meant."

"I still don't really understand this. We didn't hear anything when we asked the questions," John said. "Where did that voice come from?"

"And what does it mean?" Mary asked again.

"It's not always what it means," the professor said. "We can't be too literal with this. Think of it like your name. When you say 'Mary', it can be your name or the word to marry someone or to be merry. Sometimes the spirits or entities seem confused or have a difficult time saying what they mean."

"But we didn't hear anything when we were in the room," John insisted. "How did it get on the tape?"

"Lots of explanations. If it wasn't a true EVP, it could have been the result of interference from cell towers or cell phones or cable boxes or radio or TV signals, even baby monitors. Most EVPs are simply one or two garbled word statements that make no sense." The professor shrugged. "I have to admit, I was expecting greater results since it already knew your names."

John and the professor continued to talk about EVPs while Mary found herself drifting with her own thoughts. If bellow was the word the machine had picked up, it had to mean something. She grabbed one of Bayless's worn notepads, wrote the word bellow on it, wondering if it was possibly an anagram. She wrote each letter down, rearranged them, crossed them out, formed words. *Blew. Bell. Bowel. Well. Web. Woe.* Under her breath she muttered bellow, bellow, below, bellow, below.

Wrote *below.*

"Below?" she said. John and the professor looked at her. "Maybe we didn't hear it correctly. Could the word be 'below?'"

They played the file back, isolated the word, replayed it at a slower speed.

"The questions!" Mary cried, pointing at the screen. "I think it *is* the word below! Look what I asked it!"

"What is your favorite room in the house?"

"BELOW!"

"Is there anything in particular that you would like us to know?"

"BELOW!"

The professor looked at her, smiled his thin, friendly grin. "I think you're right, Mary. Its favorite room in the house is *below*, and there's something important he wants you to find out, and it's *below*. I'm guessing your house has a basement, right?"

Mary nodded.

"Then that's where I think you'll find the answers."

***

"Have you ever been down here?" John asked. The overhead, dirty gray bulb was turned on with a pull string. The light by the stairs pushed back the darkness for about ten feet, just enough to make it safely to the foot of the basement stairs.

"No," Mary said nervously, following close behind John.

Bold, aggressive shadows and heavy dark patches crowded around them. Cardboard boxes, heavy pieces of furniture, and items covered in filthy sheets filled the space. John turned on his bright, blue-white cell phone light. They were able to see dirty crates, piles of clothes, stacks of dusty containers, and a woodworking area in the corner.

"This must be where the wood shaving tool came from," he said. "It must mean something." He lit up the area. The shadows bent and swayed in response.

"What are those?" Mary asked, pointing. They moved closer to the table. Two simple, crudely made birdhouses were exposed under the glow of John's phone. Both were solidly built, generic in design. They appeared to be recently made. The wood smelled fresh and there was a slight dampness to it. A hole in the front allowed entrance for the bird with a perch below. The sides, base, and the slanted roof were all solid and fit tightly together.

"Is someone coming down here to build...*these*?" Mary whispered uneasily. She glanced around at the thick shadows that surrounded them. Were they alone or being watched? John set his phone on the counter.

"Feel above the hole," he said after a moment in a hushed tone. "I have something carved on this one. Feels like some straight lines. You have anything on yours?"

"Just one line. With a curve to it." She felt like she was reading Braille.

"Let me see." He handed Mary his birdhouse, took hers.

She realized the markings formed the letter *M*.

"The one you're holding is a *J*," she said dully, her mind spinning, feeling as if she was about to lose consciousness.

"What?"

"Mine is a *M*. The carvings form the letter *M*. For Mary. Yours is a *J*. For John." He held his light up to the wood structure to confirm what she had said.

Suddenly, there was a loud squeal and splintering grunt. To the left of the workbench a shelf abruptly collapsed, followed by the clanging of paint cans as they fell and rolled on the cement floor. Then the entire wall sounded like it was being violently torn away from its foundation. Mary screamed and dropped her birdhouse onto the workbench. John flashed his light and exposed the rotten planks on the floor. He aimed the beam up. They saw a decayed entryway that had been hidden behind the shelving.

"Let's get out of here!" Mary cried, pulling frantically at John even as she squeezed her eyes closed, not wanting to see what was being revealed to them.

"No, I want to find out what's in that room," John insisted, his voice
oddly calm. "It tore down the shelving. It's trying to show us something, right? That's why we're here isn't it? To find out? Come on."

"No, I don't want to know, I don't want to find out," she protested.

He tugged at her hand gently. She resisted.

"Please, John." Close to tears, she felt like a lost little girl.

"We'll just look, really fast. Then we're out of here. I promise."

She shook her head, felt like screaming, pouting, throwing a tantrum, anything to get her way. John shushed her, held her close, murmured to her. She didn't understand what he was saying. He tightened his embrace, continued to speak to her in a low, quiet tone.

Mary clung to him as he whispered in her ear. She cast about for safe images and memories. She thought of her dad, how he loved playing games with her, hide and seek, blind man's bluff. Running and darting about the house, outside in the backyard, at the park. There was always a slight sense of risk to the games, having your eyesight blocked or the exciting, giddy terror of hiding when someone was looking for you. But that was all outweighed by the promise of joyful discovery, a big hug, ice cream, and walking home hand in hand.

"Please, John." She begged him to stay with her, but he pulled free. She squinted into the darkness and saw him step over the paint cans, broken shelving and rubble. He raised his light. She heard him grunt, then push open the decrepit door. It creaked, then squealed like a living thing in agony. She wondered how long it had been since anyone had entered that place. He coughed, gagged from the uproar of dust.

"No," she whispered, but didn't move any closer, only watched helplessly as he moved farther into the shadows. She could see the illumination of his phone peek through the slats of the old room. She heard him choke on the filth that permeated the air. The floorboards responded to his presence as if in pain.

Then, nothing. No cellphone light. No coughs or gasps.

Mary called out softly. "John?"

She stepped closer to the darkness where he had disappeared. She encountered a paint can. It rolled on and on endlessly, like train wheels gone off the track. She pulled out her phone, flicked on the beam, flinched. She was closer than she had imagined to where John had vanished. There were strange markings on the wooden planks that made up the old door, circles, cross hatches, symbols that appeared to shimmer and vibrate as she examined them. She flashed her light into the pitch-black room.

"John?"

Mary cautiously forced herself forward, her phone in front of her like a
torch. It was a cluttered space, piled with discarded, broken pieces of wood of all shapes and sizes. There was the thick smell of rot and decay and mildew. She looked closer. Disorder became order. She gasped.

Birdhouses were everywhere. The structures were stacked and piled high, collapsing into one another, many becoming one. It reminded her of photos she had seen from the Dust Bowl or nuclear test sights or overcrowded tenement buildings, places where the dwellings blurred into one another as if they had fused together or were frozen in a moment of intense destruction.

There had to be hundreds of them; the area was packed. It made no sense, why were they here in this room, for what purpose? She stepped closer, aimed her light at one house that was eye level. Something fluttered. She pushed in closer. She screamed when she saw the small human figure at the hole, frantically gesturing at her.

Mary fell backward, couldn't stop shrieking. She had fallen onto a stack of the miniature homes. Her light flashed madly about at the small wooden dwellings. For a second, she saw the tight mesh netting that covered each of the holes above the perches. In that one eternal instant, she had witnessed dozens of imprisoned men and women silently pleading with her, their tiny arms and hands in supplication, their eyes wide in fear or insanity, their mouths open in high-pitched cries that she refused to hear.

She crawled out of the hidden room on her hands and knees, scraping her phone on the floor as she moved. The ground tore at her palms, bloodied her legs. She didn't want to form a thought, or process what had occurred. She only knew she needed to keep moving, to get out of the basement. She held her phone up to see where she was. She located the workbench. Now only one birdhouse remained; she was certain it had the initial *M* above the hole.

Looking for a safe mental place before all was lost, Mary desperately reached for thoughts of her father, of playing red light, green light, and how she always managed to tag him. Maybe he cheated a bit, made it easy for her, but the game always ended in a big hug and ice cream.

She tried to muster her father's image, but it was fuzzy, bland, out of focus. It never again became clear to her. What was happening? Where was he?

"Daddy," she sobbed.

Then the professor's smiling face rose up before her, and Mary immediately sensed a calm serenity envelope her. It held her close, rocked her gently as if she was an infant. The panic subsided. She was going to be okay—she would be all right—if she concentrated solely on the professor.

Trembling, she stood up. She walked over to the workbench, picked up
her birdhouse, recalled the professor had said, *"If there is anything going on at your house, you'll both find out."*

John had already found out. Now it was her turn.

With her wooden structure in hand like an offering, Mary returned to the small room, envisioned the kind face of Professor Attila Bayless.

"I have my own methods."

Once inside, she pushed the door closed. She walked deeper into the darkness. Transfixed and focused, Mary held tight to the vision of the smiling professor until the very last instant when his thin lips and wide mouth opened wide and devoured her whole.

***

The property manager had good news: After two weeks of vacancy, the home on Warwick Avenue had just been rented.

"Wonderful," Professor Bayless said. He hung up the phone, relieved. All his properties were now occupied. So many new beginnings were just around the corner.

For Mitch Baum

About the Author

Dean Koontz has praised the writing of **Jeff C. Stevenson** as "unique and compelling," while Jonathan Kellerman calls it "fascinating and disturbing." Stevenson is a professional member of Pen America and an active member of the Horror Writers Association. He is the author of *FORTNEY ROAD*: The True Story of Life, Death and Deception in a Christian Cult and more than two dozen dark fiction short stories. Jeff is finishing a two-part, supernatural suspense novel and he also writes mainstream fiction under the pen name of Mary Saliger. Film rights to all stories are represented by Steve Fischer of the Agency for the Performing Arts in Los Angeles.

MAYA'S LAST DANCE

By Anusha VR

Over the years, it had become a habit of sorts for him to wander into the ruins of the school. It was situated on the banks of a muddy river. The roof of the school had caved in during the fire. Some of the walls had collapsed as well, but it retained its rustic charm. The quietude of the place soothed him. For the few hours he spent between its precariously balanced pillars and charred walls, he felt closer to her. His life had become a void of which there was no escaping. The ruined dance school provided a degree of respite. He was well aware that the place would resurrect memories that should stay buried. But that was a price he was willing to pay. This place was all he had left of her.

One gloomy afternoon, he was staring absentmindedly at the moss-covered sandstones and the delicate blades of grass powering through the crevices, brooding over the fateful events that had transpired years ago.

If only he had made it in time, he could have saved his Maya. He owed everything to her. She had believed in him when no one else had. He was the one-armed clown of the village. But she saw him for who he really was. She saved him when he thought he could no longer be saved. She gave him a job. A purpose. A haven where he felt welcomed.

And in return, he couldn't save her. He didn't notice it at first. She had been good at hiding it. But when the bruises got too evident, she stopped performing. She'd say she wanted her students to get more time on stage, but he could see through the charade.

Her husband had always loathed the very idea of her opening the dance school. She was the Zamindar's daughter-in-law and it was about time she started acting like it, her husband felt. It's a job fit for a whore, he had screamed one evening before storming out of the hall. But she loved the stage, the rhythm of the beats, the costumes. All she wanted was to pass on the love she had for the arts to the rest of the people in the village. She wouldn't let a petty man deter her, not even her husband.

And like a mute spectator, he had watched the woman who had given him the respect no one else gave him, the woman he knew he was undoubtedly in love with, be beaten and scorned by her own husband.

On the night of the fire, Maya had told him that she would be leaving her husband. She said he had taken it more calmly than she had expected him to. There was a lightness in the way she spoke, a genuine smile graced her lips. It was almost unheard of for a woman to leave her husband in rural India. But Maya had made up her mind. She wasn't a woman who waited to be saved.

He'd left early that night. There was a fair being held in the village and he wanted to buy her something pretty. He'd made up his mind to tell her how he felt. Social strata be damned, she wouldn't be a married woman anymore. He'd made it halfway to the fair when he remembered he'd left his wallet back at the school.

As he made his way back, he saw the flames. He assumed it was a bonfire some of the kids had started. When he did reach the school gates, it took him a minute to register what was happening. He looked around, dead sure Maya would have long gone home by now, when he saw someone inside beating the window panes with their fists, trying to break the glass. The doors had been locked from the outside. By the time he found a rock to break the locks on the door, it was too late.

His train of thought broke abruptly when he heard the faint jingle of anklets. He tore his eyes away from the ground with alarming speed but the place was as deserted as it had always been. He chided himself for letting his mind wander.

He heard it again. This time it was slightly louder than before. The jingle seemed to be getting closer and closer to where he was seated. He stood up and looked all around trying to locate the source, but the sound began receding till silence was restored to the ruins. He frantically searched every corner, only to find the empty walls staring back at him, reaffirming his initial thoughts that perhaps he was flirting with insanity. He gave up and went back to the spot where he was seated earlier, when he saw her.

His blood ran cold and a lump began forming in his throat which seemed to grow larger by the second, threatening to suffocate him.

He didn't know how long he stood there watching her. She had her back to him as she walked in the backyard which ran amok with weeds. She was draped in her white sari with blood red pleats and borders. The delicate golden embroidery glistened as it caught the dying sun-rays. Jasmines were braided into her thick mane. Henna adorned her hands. She was dressed in the traditional costume she donned when she was going to perform.

He didn't question any of it. He had seen the flames engulf her. He had heard the blood curdling cry. He'd watched from a distance, when the man who had no right to call himself her husband, set her funeral pyre on fire. Yet, not a single rational thought plagued his mind. All he knew was that she was back. He didn't want to know how or why. All he wanted was to apologize to her for not being there for her. For not showing up that wretched night on time. For not mustering up the courage sooner to tell her that he loved her.

He stumbled over a few charred blocks of stone in his haste to reach her. He didn't want to let her out of his sight, even for a second, afraid she might disappear at any moment; that perhaps all of this was just an illusion, a coping mechanism to deal with his loss. He ran into the back yard and a sense of relief flooded him when he saw she was still there. She was looking out at the river which had now turned into an expanse of liquid rose-gold due to the drowning sun. He was merely a few feet away from her now. His hand hovered over her shoulder with hesitance.

She must have heard the crunch of dead leaves and overgrown grass behind her and turned around.

"Maya..."

Before he could finish his sentence, her face turned a sickly grey. Her lips parted as if to let out a scream, but no sound came.

***

She ran as fast as her legs could carry her, not daring to look back. She couldn't look at that vile man.

His face was burnt beyond recognition. Beneath the tattered remains of his clothes, the exposed pinkish-grey rotting flesh was visible.

***

She forced herself not to think about what she had witnessed a few hours ago while she performed at her recital. At first Tina was hesitant. Even as her aunt came to congratulate her on her performance, her mind kept replaying the terrifying being reaching out to her. Almost as if he was asking for something.

The only reason she had even been to that godforsaken place was to get some quiet before the show. When she'd first moved into her aunt's house a few months ago, she'd heard the story of the dance school. No one paid much attention to it. There were no rumors of hauntings attached to it. Just a long drawn out legal battle between relatives as to who gets to inherit the property. She had figured what better place to still her jittery pre-recital nerves than a dance school which had been way ahead of it's time. But she could no longer write it off as a trick her mind had played. The nagging feeling drove her to open her laptop. It was easy to track down the article she was looking for.

On 7th September, 1966 a fire had broken out in the local dance school in the neighboring village. The local *panchayat* and the police declared that the source of the fire could not be ascertained. The casualties had been the dance teacher and the groundskeeper.

She shut her laptop and absent-mindedly turned to the window to draw her curtains. She saw him standing right outside her window.

"Maya, let me in."

About the Author

Anusha VR is a Chartered Accountant and Company Secretary residing in India. She has a penchant for traveling and reading novels. Her short stories have appeared in several anthologies such as Monsoon Winds, Carol of the Spells, and Spectral Book of Horror Stories among others.

DARK INHERITANCE

By Victoria Dalpe

The driver arrived. He was thin as a bone and dressed in a fine black suit. His car gleamed like a beetle's carapace. The driver didn't react at all to the strange sight of a newly orphaned girl, jumping excitedly into the backseat of the car. Emeline didn't look back at her old home. In her mind, she was already gone.

As the miles fell away, Emeline felt lighter and even a little happy. She was separated from her old life. Her future was as wide open as the gray sky overhead. She was as free as the blackbirds that circled above the car. She was free of *It*.

For as long as she could remember, *It* had followed her, dogged as her very own shadow. *It* was the feel of air moving on her skin when there was no wind. *It* was the whisper of breath on the back of her neck when she was alone.

As a child, *It* kept her awake at night. Branches at her window became claws; creaks of the old house became *Its* footsteps drawing near. Every night was a symphony of small tortures, tiny paper cuts of fear, slowly draining her.

The worst thing? Every night ended the same. She would wake at dawn with the weight of *It* on her chest, its invisible mouth latched to her own. Not in a kiss – it was sucking up her breath.

By the time she'd entered her teens, she was unstable and perpetually exhausted. Her grades were poor, her attendance lacking, and her friendships non-existent. She wandered the halls of her school, eyes wide and feverish, dark circles under them like make-up.

To her peers and to Mrs. Johnson, her grandmotherly looking homeroom teacher, her trauma appeared an affectation. Mrs. Johnson derisively referred to her as an Edward Gorey drawing come to life. Poor Emeline, so dramatic, as if she wanted to look like a ghost made flesh. They laughed and thought she was *trying* to be haunted.

Then when Emeline was fifteen, her parents died. Her mother first, succumbing to her mysterious illness, and then her father, driven mad with grief, taking his life right after. Leaving her all alone.

"Chronic Withering Disease," is what the doctor called it, *It*. Emeline knew he had no idea what he was talking about. But she didn't press for more information; the medical community could not help her. All that mattered was that they were dead and *It* was still haunting her every night. Worse still, *Its* attentions doubled after her mother was gone.

Like the Victorian orphan she appeared to be, Emeline was to be shipped North. She had a great Aunt there, her only living relative. The aunt's name was Bernadette. Emeline had never seen her, let alone spoken to her.

Emeline hoped that *It* would not follow her North. That *It* would be content to have taken her parents. She thought, surely, *surely*, the spirit would stay tethered to her home. That was how hauntings worked, right?

The driver was silent, so in tune with his car as to seem a simple organic extension of it. He had no name that he gave, nor any offer of condolence for the orphaned girl. Emeline didn't mind though, the simple peace of being out of her house, and free of *It* was all she needed. She closed her eyes and slept.

Hours later, they arrived at the old manor house. Emeline gazed up at it as she exited the car. It was taller than it was wide. A flight of rickety stone steps led up from the road to its ornate wooden doors. Though it embodied every gothic fantasy and nightmare, the sight of the house still made Emeline hopeful.

She started up the stone steps into her new life.

***

Aunt Bernadette sat in a wheelchair by the fire. The light and heat from it vainly chased the chill and the gloom but failed to catch either. Bernadette was a small hunched woman, with large eyes and a pinched mouth. Her hair was piled, tall and elaborate, on top of her head, reminding Emeline of an exotic bird's nest.

Emeline sat beside her, her valise by her feet. Her aunt appraised her slowly, seeming cautious. Finally, she nodded and sat back in her chair, arthritic hands interlaced on her blanketed lap.

"You've got it. When I heard about your parents, I thought you might." Her voice croaked, somewhere between a whisper and a groan.

Emeline's entire body instantly covered in gooseflesh. She leaned in closer, to be sure she heard her clearly. "Got what?"

"Mara."

"My name is Emeline, Aunt Bernadette. Not Mara."

Bernadette's mouth broke into a sardonic smile. Yellowed teeth caught the glint of the firelight. "I know your name. Emeline was my mother's name," the old lady fixed her rheumy eyes on her. "A *Mara* is what you've got. It's trailing you. I'm close enough to death that I can almost see it." She cocked her head. Sniffed the air. "It's not as pretty as I thought it'd be."

"I don't know what you mean, Aunt." But even as she said it, Emeline knew it wasn't true. She knew exactly what her aunt was talking about. *It.*

It was still with her, floating just above her.

The unseen was dancing in the shadows with the firelight. Whispering in words no one could hear or understand. If anything, *It* felt stronger now that her parents were gone. If anything, *It* seemed happy to be in a new place. Emeline nearly sobbed.

Bernadette saw the emotions and the realization cross the girl's face. "Runs in our family, unfortunately. They attach themselves to babies in the womb. Cause a lot of miscarriages. Me and my brother, your grandfather, were the only two of ten that lived to adulthood. Don't know why our mother kept at it, the silly cow, but she did."

Bernadette smiled ruefully, and Emeline could see the pain

in her aunt as she continued. "She just kept popping out the cursed and   the   damned."

As her aunt spoke, Emeline could feel *It* more and more, the Mara, perched on her shoulder, playing with her hair, fluttering her skirts. *Its* mouth under her shirt, on her skin, the prick of its sucking. Taunting her. Making her feel ashamed that she'd ever dared   hope.

It had a name now. *It* was real. Mara.

"I was lucky, if you consider being alive lucky. My brother had one, your Grandfather, that is. It killed him, killed his wife, killed most of his children. 'Cept your mother. But it got her too, eventually."

Emeline had never considered this. Never considered that perhaps her mother had suffered as she suffered. Perhaps she should have tried speaking to her mother when she had the chance.

"What   is   it?   The   Mara?"

"Precisely? I'm not sure. Consider it a parasite; a leech. A sucking   thing."

"Can I get rid of it?"

Her aunt pulled a chain from around her neck. At the end hung dozens of pendants and satchels. She fingered through them like   they   were   some   strange   alchemical   rosary.

"We can burn some sage, get you some charms, even say some prayers. But honestly, it won't do a lick of good. Some families have cancer or diabetes. We have this. My father spent his life researching how to rid himself, with no luck. He never found a cure for it." She was so emotionless and matter of fact about it. Emeline's face darkened, angry. Her whole life she thought she was insane. Now this old woman was telling her that wasn't the case, but it was still hopeless. She was slowly dying no matter what.

"What about you, then? Why not you?"

The old woman's smile turned sad. "I was sickly-- all my life, really-- and weak. I guess the Mara didn't want me. It saw what was on the menu and sent it back to the kitchen."

***

Emeline's new bedroom was a tiny servant's room in a drafty eave at the top of the house. She sat on the narrow cot and unpacked her things. All her worldly possessions lay on the mattress before her; a few outfits, a photo of her parents, and some old books.

She took stock of herself. Yes, she *was* cursed. But the Mara, now that it had a name, was almost a comfort. At least she wasn't crazy, and neither had her mother been. And at least she wasn't Aunt Bernadette, stuck in a drafty house surrounded by empty memories of those she'd lost. Yet.

Emeline crawled into bed and pretended that she was trying to sleep. Of course, the Mara's attentions were on her instantly. The pressure on her chest. The suck on her mouth. Stealing all her breaths.

She lay there, as she had every night of her life. But on this night, its attentions were more intense, taking more of her than ever before. But that made sense now, didn't it? She was the last of her family line. The last of those afflicted by the Mara's kiss. As it sucked her breath away, it filled her with something new: resolve.

She would not go the way of her family. She was going to beat this.

***

By anemic dawn light, she explored the musty, elaborate old   house.

The library was two stories, almost as full of books as it was of dust. She spent hours, obsessively looking for some clue of the Mara. Her aunt was right, her great-great grandfather had been quite a scholar. His collection was full of texts that dealt with the fantastic, with possessions, with spirits and hauntings. As she retraced his investigative steps, she felt a glimmer of hope that with time she could discover something he had missed. She could find the clue, the antidote, the ritual, the *anything* that would relieve   her.

That first day passed in a blur. The sky darkened. She stumbled out of the library, her aunt nowhere in sight, and tumbled into bed. Her dust covered fingers gripped the pillow as the Mara perched   on   her.

Days passed, and much like the first, she spent her time in the library poring over the pages and pages of arcane law and folklore. She learned of every beast and ghoul that had tormented the earth at one point or another, but never more than a whisper of the Mara. Every turn through the maze of books was a dead end.

One day, she looked up to see Bernadette. She'd wheeled her chair into the doorway and was staring at Emeline.

"You ready to return to school?"

"I'm looking for an answer," Emeline said.

Bernadette nodded, sagely. "I admire your will to live, girl. My father had that will, too. I loved that about him. He spent his life in this library, searching and searching. All he ever managed to find was the thing's name. And he still ended up dead."

Bernadette started to wheel herself away then stopped. Looked back at Emeline. "Give up your search, child. Do not fear death. It is sometimes better than the alternative."

Emeline continued her hunt. That night, the Mara was so voracious that her mouth bled from its incessant sucking.

***

"But how did they get to be this way?" Emeline was sitting at the dinner table, a steamy brown broth in front of her. She had no appetite and even lifting the spoon tired her. Bernadette stared at her across the table.

"Surely there must have been a source. An originator of this… affliction."

Bernadette narrowed her eyes and sighed.

"It's just a story, one that my father used to tell me about his own father. He was an important man, a landowner and a businessman. I'm sure he had some good traits but generosity wasn't among them." Bernadette stopped to slurp her soup.

"There was a drought. Nature's not known for its generosity either. Many of the farmers were unable to pay their rent. There was one family, an old and respected family, that allegedly practiced local magicks..." she trailed off for a moment as if not sure what to say about them.

"My grandfather was a modern man. He was a man of dwindling Christianity and fancied himself a man of science. A great lover of Darwin and reason. He was warned, but he didn't listen. He evicted the family." Emeline listened to all of this, rapt.

"They cursed him?"

"If that's the word you feel comfortable with, yes. I don't know what process they used, what god they implored, what favor they called in. But that was the moment when the Mara became our family's burden. Our punishment. Since then, we've all withered. We've all wasted. And so it will be... well, until you die. You are the last, after all."

Bernadette stopped speaking then. Again, it seemed to Emeline like the old woman was holding back a piece of information. Emeline watched her face, waiting for some final word, some clue to aid her search, some signpost to lead her out from under the Mara's shadow.

"How's your soup?" was the next thing out of Bernadette's mouth.

***

Another week of scouring the library, another week of no answers. She started to get the impression that the Mara was laughing at her. Her dresses hung off her shoulders as the weight fell off her. And each night, the three-story hike to her attic room became   more   and   more   of   a   challenge.

She decided she needed to expand her search. Her grandfather had failed to find an answer in these books. She needed   new   ones.

She found the driver, still bone thin, still dressed in black, sitting   in   the   kitchen,   eating   a   sandwich.

"I need to go out," she said. He turned and looked at her. Even he appeared shocked by how wan she looked. "Can you take me to some place that sells old, rare books? Like the ones in the library   here."

He swallowed his bite of food and nodded.

***

It became clear rather quickly that the driver had a specific place in mind. He drove her away from the house, through a hilly and pastoral countryside and finally into a quaint village. He drove her down small, nameless roads. Then he stopped the car in front of a rundown shop with a sign that simply read: "Books". She got out   of   the   car.   The   driver   waited.

Emeline was so weak from the Mara's nightly feasting that it took her two tries to push in the old door.

The room inside was narrow and long, crammed floor to ceiling, wall to wall, every inch, with books. There was no system whatsoever. Cookbooks and children's books, maps and ledgers, pulp ghost stories, and field guides mingled together. Not even alphabetized.

A sickly ray of daylight struggled its way through the windows and she had to squint to make out the spines on the old faded books. She was halfway through the first shelf on the left when a man cleared his throat behind her.

She spun around. He was an old man, half her height, bald pate shining, glasses so thick as to hide his eyes.

"I was looking for something, maybe you could help me?" she said timidly, the old man watchful behind his foggy lenses. "I can't seem to navigate your... system here."

"What're you looking for?"

"Occult books. Specifically..." she hesitated, not sure exactly how to say it. "...banishments. How to banish malevolent spirits."

The old man scratched his chin and looked down the line of the shop. "What kinda spirits?" he asked.

"A Mara," she said.

He nodded, like maybe he'd expected this. "We've got a book on that topic – only one. Highly specific, it is. Been here for a number of years. You'll find it in the back. You'll have to look yourself though-" He took his glasses off revealing two eyes clouded with cataracts, milky white. "I never find what I'm looking for anymore."

She went to the back. Shelf by shelf, the hours passed, her eyes throbbing. She was going through the last shelf in the last row, when she shoved the book on mysticism she was holding with more force than was necessary. The entire case shook and a smaller book fell to the floor. With a sigh, she knelt, the movement making her dizzy, and noticed a book tucked underneath the massive bottom shelf. She reached under, prying it free.

What she pulled out was an old book, older than Darwin or the United States itself. As she opened its worn cover, she could feel the Mara's intake of breath on her ear. She must be close to something.

It was an old grimoire, written in sprawling, ornate English. It was indeed full of rituals, spells, incantations and, yes, even banishments.

Her heart fluttered when she realized what she had stumbled across. It had an entire chapter of spells devoted to Maras.

She brought the book to the old man, fearing its cost, knowing she would steal if the price was too steep. "How much is this?" she asked as the Mara scratched at her neck. She ignored the tugging on the book by invisible hands. "I believe it already belongs with you. Just take it and go."

***

At home, Emeline went right up to her room with the book, ignoring dinner, ignoring her aunt. By the time she reached her bed, she was so weak and exhausted by the Mara, that she could barely read the book by the brightest light.

It was hard work to parse the meaning, but by deep night, she had uncovered something she doubted even her Grandfather knew about the Mara.

The more she read, the more active the Mara became. Its movements fluttered the curtains, her wardrobe door opened and closed, and the floorboards sporadically moaned. When Emeline saw the indentation of weight on the quilt beside her, she knew she must be close to something. She had never seen it so animated while she was fully awake before.

Her entire body crawled with excitement when she found the passage that she sought. The language was ornate but it boiled down to one simple truth: *The Mara cannot be banished. It can only be absorbed.*

Absorbed. Into herself. As hard as she looked, she could find no information on what that actually meant. What happened when one absorbed a spirit?

That next morning at breakfast, Emeline could barely contain herself.

"Did your father ever talk about the ritual of Absorption?" Emeline   asked.

Aunt Bernadette gave her an odd look. She sniffed, and said "No." She was so clipped that Emeline thought she was lying. "Why? What nonsense do you have in your head now?"

"Nothing... just found a mention of it in one of his texts." Emeline didn't tell her aunt about the book. She had a theory the old woman was not an ally at all.

"Nonsense," Bernadette said, then went on forcefully. "There's no mention of absorption in any book in that library. Ritual magic is messy business. It is powerful and extremely dangerous."

***

What does danger mean to someone who is already doomed? That thought pounded into Emeline's head that night as the Mara laid atop her, mouth to mouth. She felt her muscles dwindling, and she yearned for sleep, any sleep at all. What she would give for a single moment of unmolested rest. She hated the way *It* felt clinging to her. Hated how fat *It* must be off her life force. She imagined a fat gray tick riding along on her back.

No. She would not allow the Mara to slowly drain her of life. She would not follow in her parents' footsteps. She would not die as three generations had died. She was stronger. She would live.

She spent the entire next day gathering the materials

needed for the spell. They were not as obscure as she expected: simple herbs, a cup of salt, three links of silver chain. The bird feather was the hardest and in the end, she pulled a pheasant feather off an old hat in her aunt's closet.

The blood was the easiest - she'd use her own.

That night, she set about drawing the sigils in salt and herbs on the floor. When it came time to gather the blood for the internal sigils and binding circle, she paused, hand poised above her wrist, razor touching the pale skin there. Could she do this?

Yes.

Yes, she could. And with a hiss, she cut, the sharp razor tracing over her flesh, parting it with ease. She filled the cup and bound the wound.

All the while, the Mara struggled with her. Her skin bruised where *Its* invisible fists struck her. *It* ripped a hunk of her hair out and tossed it to the floor. She ignored it as best she could and stayed strong, but her hands shook as she stared from the book to the floor. Her fear of botching the ritual grew stronger as she triple checked each symbol and made sure she followed the pages exactly. She would get only one chance to do this. She knew the Mara would never let her try again.

Emeline trembled as she started to drip her blood into the shape of a circle. Her eyes welled with tears as she got closer and closer to completing it. Once the circle was complete, the ritual would   begin.

The blood dripped, dripped, dripped onto the floor. The Mara screamed in her ear, she felts its mouth open in front of her, felt it trying to consume her, to end her. But she did not flinch. A lifetime of its nightly attacks had hardened her more than she'd even   realized.

And then, finally, the lines of the circle met.

And the attacks just… stopped. As if a door had been slammed, as if the sun had finally set. Inside the circle, the Mara could not touch her. Laughter burst out of Emeline. So this was what   the   rest   of   humanity   felt   like!

But of course, the ritual wasn't done. It had only just begun. She pulled the book to her lap and began to chant the words written   there.

At first, she said them timidly. But soon the chant began to take on a life of its own. She said the words over and over, louder and louder. The words opened her up, pushing through her, inflating   her.

She started to scream the words, her lungs filling with oxygen and exploding the words out. Her body felt like it was being unmade, like it was being torn apart at the seams.

Then, the candles went out. The only sound was her voice.

The darkness began to waver and undulate. There was something out there, in the dark. And still she chanted.

The   salt   line   burst   into   flame.

She lost herself in the fire and the words. She was being inflated with air, being filled with hot sand. She was going to explode, she was too full, she was stretched too thin.

The fire circle dimmed to a low flickering and she saw something on the other side of the flame. Something watching her.

It was more insect than human. Its eyes glistened blackly, looking in all directions at once. Mandibles clicked above a strangely human mouth. It smiled and revealed rows of sharp, needle-like teeth. Its neck was long, like a praying mantis. Its chest lined with breasts, its legs covered with sharp porcupine quills. It circled the ring, hunched on all fours, trying to find a way in. Upright it was huge, tall, with long lethal limbs, utterly inhuman and strangely feminine. It breathed loudly in the silence. This was the thing that slept on top of her, the terrible mouth that had been to hers, the breath she had felt on her skin a thousand times. It was horrible.   It   was   beautiful.

It   was   The   Mara.   Her   Mara.

Emeline's hand moved of its own accord, reached out and broke the circle of salt and fire.

The Mara charged in.

***

When she woke, the sky was orange and purple with dawn.

She stretched and stood, noting that the blood boundary was gone and the salt circle was now a black ring, burnt into the floor.

Emeline timidly crossed the line and waited. She could not sense the Mara anywhere. It had worked! She was finally alone. Truly   alone.

It was on her second step outside of the circle that she felt it. Her insides were *off*. The movement in her limbs, the air in her lungs, the taste in her mouth, all foreign and strange.

She rushed to the vanity mirror, brought herself nose to nose   with   her   own   reflection.

Her eyes had changed color. No longer pale brown, they were black as onyx, as ink. She pulled back her lips and saw her teeth, blunt, regular, as was her tongue. All looked normal.

But those eyes. Those were NOT her eyes. As she stared out of them into them, her skin tingled. Then itched. A sound began, inside her head, like a swarm of insects. Inside and out, her body   revolted   against   her.

Emeline fled the horror of the mirror. Raced down the twisting stairs. Burst into her aunt's bedroom. The old woman was awake, propped up in bed. Emeline didn't have to say anything; Bernadette   saw   her   eyes.

"What have you done?" she whispered, fearful, unsympathetic.

"I thought it would vanish. I thought the ritual was supposed   to   make   it   go   away-"

"What   ritual?"

Emeline's breath was short, her insides twisted into knots

of pain and fear. "The ritual of Absorption. I found a rare book, one from a shop - one that had a ritual of absorption in it. And I used   it."

Bernadette frowned, her face falling. "The shop? You fool. You poor, young fool. I told you there was no cure. That book was nothing but false hope and evil. That is why I got rid of it all those years ago. To stop my damned father from doing that ritual. And you   found   it.   I   should   have   burnt   it."

Emeline's dark eyes stretched wide. "What have I done?"

Bernadette laughed humorlessly. "The Mara is pure spiritual emptiness. That can't be destroyed. You can't smother a black hole, or fill it in." The old woman spat the words, her voice caught between anger and sadness. "The void remains, girl. The hole always hungers. You didn't defeat it, you absorbed it into yourself."

"What does that mean?" Emeline's question was whispered in a voice that she no longer recognized as her own. Her head swarmed, her skin crawled, her heart thumped fast and hard.

Emeline fell into her aunt's arms, squeezing her fragile old body   tight.   She   sobbed.

Whatever   it   meant,   it   was   happening.

Awareness bloomed inside of Emeline. And with it, an appetite stirred. An indescribable emptiness awoke in her. The black hole, the hunger that was never sated. The Mara, now inside her, now part of her, flared to life. It pushed her. She could sense the   life   inside   her   aunt.

Her aunt was old. She was weak. She could not fight.

Emeline pressed her mouth to her struggling aunt's. Sucking, starving, desperate. The old woman's fists beat feebly against her embrace.

Frustrated, her jaw opened impossibly wide, it snapped and jointed, rows and rows of razor sharp needles pushed out of her gums. Emeline took her aunt's whole head into her mouth. The old woman was too frail to fight back. But she did scream.

Emeline bit down. The skin and tendons parted below the chin, the skull bones cracked like thin ice, and a fount of blood erupted, spraying her face, soaking her nightgown.

Emeline moaned and gulped, filled herself with the meager life   force.

The old woman tasted sour. Her myriad cancers and ailments provided little nourishment. The Mara had, of course, been right to ignore the old woman all these years.

Emeline was now the Mara and the Mara was now Emeline. They were intertwined into one mind. And they were very   hungry.

She visited the driver's room next. He opened his mouth to beg, but he did not get the chance. His screams, like his blood, sated her. The Mara was no longer a creature of spirit, but one of flesh,   and   its   hunger   had   changed   accordingly.

Emeline/Mara crawled up the stairs to the attic bed and

curled up, full and sated. At least, for the time being. And for the first time in years, Emeline slept.

Peacefully.

About the Author

Victoria Dalpe is a writer/visual artist based out of Providence, RI where she lives with her husband, writer and filmmaker Philip Gelatt, and their young son. She has been published in various anthologies and her novel *Parasite Life* with ChiZine Press is due out in 2017. Visit http://victoriadalpe.blogspot.com/ for more details.

GWISINS OF THE NEW MOON'S EVE

By Russell Hemmell

We walk out of the subway - the first train of the day has left us in a Gangnam still asleep. The last party-goers stumble back to their dormitories in the freezing haze of the morning. The pervasive smell of yakiniku reminds me I had no dinner last night. I look around with a deep sense of disorientation. *This is something Miyumi is familiar to- not me, never me.* At 5.30 AM, I'd be in my deepest slumber, while my roommate thrived and reveled.

But not today. Today we're together in the twilight hours before dawn, when everything is possible, and the world doesn't watch.

I look at Miyumi's cheeks, reddened by the cold breeze. It's windy - spring is coming, but nights remain chilling, and the only way to warm up is to drink soju - gallons of it. I can't wait.

"Christie, look at this."

She takes my hand and points it at the Samsung Tower's glittering roof. It's imposing as always, even scarier in the crepuscular sky.

"What?"

"Do you see it?" She says, and her green irises are like cold flames. She scares me sometimes. "The reflection of a gwisin's face."

I try to focus, following her stare, but I can't see anything. "No."

"That's good news -only victims can see gwisins. It means they're not coming for you," she says. "Not yet."

"What about you, then –why do you see it?"

"Me? I was a victim once. Now I'm part of the family."

Only a glint in her eyes suggests she's making fun of me. Her hair dancing on her face, an empty bottle of soju thrown away, Miyumi touches my nose and laughs - and I feel a shiver run down my spine.

***

It was during my first year at Yonsei Uni that I heard about the infamous gwisins of Gangnam, or the Gangnam's Ghosts, as everybody called them. In a hush-hush way, of course, because nobody in Seoul would admit they existed for real. Not the population of the city, the sprawling 24-million people capital of a fast-rising country; not the police that every month had to deal with them and with the souls the gwisins grabbed away. And certainly not the area's inhabitants themselves. There were no ghosts in Gangnam, period. You would find the Samsung Research Centre headquarters, ubiquitous shopping malls, a couple of streets full of fancy restaurants, and nightclubs with the best of the best of the K-Pop. All the rest? Just rumors to attract morbid tourist attention.

What were you saying, Christie-yang?

My enquiries always ended up in this rather inglorious way - in irony, laughter, or denial. Not one single person would to talk to me or take me seriously, making me even more determined in my quest. *Maybe because I'm not one of them*, I repeated to myself. *I'm not allowed to know and lift the veil of mystery that wraps these ghosts. But to know I do want – now more than ever.*

The story itself was simple. Every fourth New Moon's Eve, someone was killed in the fancy neighborhood of Gangnam. Presumed dead, at least, since they disappeared altogether from the bustling face of the city without a trace. This was what Miyumi told me when I asked her about that weird story, in between two bottles of soju, in a drunk night out. No pattern existed in those deaths from what I had been able to find out; that or my Korean was not good enough to detect one.

Miyumi was the first one to openly acknowledge their existence: still is. And whatever the truth about the gwisins, my knowledge has not substantially increased since that day - I still ignore a lot of details. One thing, however, has become clearer to me: the souls of the murdered come back as gwisins to where they've been killed, haunting the living and trying to drag them down. For eating their flesh, people say. For company, Miyumi explains. They are lonely, sad souls searching for comfort.

How frightening. How fascinating.

Curiosity gnawing at me, I decided to crack the mystery and that's why I ended up befriending Miyumi, a Japanese that's lived in Seoul for most of her life.

And that's how I'm finding myself with her now, in this scaring New Moon's Eve, in a freezing, almost desert Gangnam street.

Waiting for a gwisin to grab me and take me away.

***

Miyumi insisted we should head back, saying that nothing interesting was going to happen to us.

The gwisins weren't getting after us; no gwisins, no fun.

I wasn't afraid, but I never had the strength to say no to her. And when she came, white and cold and naked, to sleep in my bed that morning, I didn't send her away. I guess that was what I had wanted too since the beginning; in that case as in many others, letting people get the initiative is a way not to ask yourself embarrassing questions. You might not like the answer.

But I soon found out I had mistaken her intentions.

"Don't worry, Christie, I'm not searching for anything… impure."

"You're not?"

"No. Only want to sleep by your side. Have company. Keep warm."

"Oh."

I was vaguely deluded, but also relieved. I took her close to me, and we fell asleep.

***

Since that moment, Miyumi regularly visited me in bed – even when she was going out and getting back in the first hours of the morning. White, cold, and silent, she would slip in, put her head on my shoulder and fall asleep immediately.

In the morning, I would never find her, and only a faint scent of soju would remain to remind me I had not dreamt her.

***

It's New Moon's Eve again, and it's gwisin night again.

I'm thrilled and ready.

It's not yet dusk, but I'm already in Gangnam, fluttering around like a crazed butterfly. Someone's going to be killed tonight, so I'd better be there before it gets dark -this is what I told myself in the morning, trying to play down my excitement. Maybe a gwisin will show up, and I'll see its face.

Miyumi has come with me.

She doesn't want to leave me alone in this night. "Not safe for you, Christie-yang, if you head to Gangnam all by yourself," she says.

I laugh.

"Let's get some soju," she says.

We go to a small restaurant with wooden panels and iron braziers at the entrance, not far away from where we dined last

174

time. There are only a few people sitting inside - because it's still early, I guess.

And yet, tonight I feel there's something different in the air. There's an eerie calm in what I expected to be a lively tavern. Everybody is drinking in silence, raising glasses and cups in slow motion.

Everybody but one, a young man that glances around like a scared rabbit.

Miyumi's eyes are cat's eyes – green and round and wide-open – and there's a slight smile on her face.

"You see that one?"

Her regard stops on the frightened youth that eats alone in a corner, the one I've already noticed.

"What about him?"

"He's going to be dead. Soon," she says.

"How do you know?"

"You'll see." She drinks her soju. It occurs to me she never eats – only drinks, bottle after bottle. And she never gets drunk, either.

"Will you kill him?"

I'm not sure why I've asked this question. This is not something you're supposed to say to a friend, is it? But my words have their own way out of the mouth that is meant to control them. They scorch my lips and hang suspended in the air like splinters of dark light.

Miyumi raises her hands like she could touch and feel their quality, caress their roughness.

"No, not this one," she says. "I would if I had to, yes -to protect you." Her mouth curls in an open smile and shows something I haven't oddly ever noticed before – feline white fangs, minute and sharp. "But it won't be necessary."

"Why have you taken me here?"

"Can't you imagine?"

"No." The moment I say it, I confusedly realize the reason. This night I'm seeing a city I didn't know, with a person I've just discovered I ignore. I'm not scared, though – I'm simply beyond fear.

"You told me you wanted to see a killing – see gwisins in action."

"These people-"

"Yes."

I look outside the window that gives on the alley. There's nobody around, even though by now it should be teeming with life. Like if we were entangled in a warped space-time, ones where the living are for grab and sacrifice and the gwisins reign unchallenged.

There are streetlights all around, but their red glimpses are of a ghostly quality – flickering like candles in the wind.

A green mist seeps into the restaurant from the semi-closed door and through the small fissures of the wooden walls, while the temperature drops by many degrees.

I shudder and brace for what is going to happen.

The young guy snaps on his feet, in a sudden realization that electrifies his body even before reaching his mind. Too late for him – it has been too late since he arrived here, in this place, in this city, in this New Moon's Eve.

They get up and walk toward him, slowly and inexorably.

His eyes search mine, while he opens his mouth to scream with a voice that comes out no longer. I taste his terror like sour kimchi – with the same appetite and much of the same mixed, uncertain pleasure.

Miyumi takes my hand. "You're safe. They won't come for you tonight."

"I know."

Why should they, when they're going to be sated soon? The crowd has surrounded him, carnivore ants on a wriggling prey. I can see neither his table now, nor the meal of blood and flesh they're enjoying, suddenly awaken from their slumber, hands and arms that swivel around like raven's wings.

Feasting. Relishing.

Or so I imagine – because, when they finally disband and get back to their seats, there's nothing left. No man, no blood, not the shreds of flesh I've pictured in my head.

There's a void, like a white hole in the fabric of the universe, or a magic mirror that reflects an imaginary space.

"Is this the way you do it?"

"No." She smiles. "I like being alone in my feeding."

"Killings."

"Killings."

"Since when?"

"Since I met you."

***

It is dawn when we go out of the restaurant, which has reclaimed its space in the Gangnam I used to know. One I will never look at with the same eyes again.

Visitors come and go, ghosts of a different quality, unaware of what happened here in a dimension that escapes their eyes. They laugh, but their voices reach me like laments from the underworld.

We take the subway and head back home, without saying a word, but holding hands like little children at their first walk in the adults' precinct.

At the entrance of our dormitory, I stop and look up, at the crown of buildings that encircles us in a cuddling embrace. And in a moment, I see the bloated face of the restaurant's victim appearing everywhere.

I can see his spirited eyes chasing me from the window glasses – each window a face – I see his reflection on the metallic doors. He's in my house too, on the TV screen switched off, on the computer's aluminum cover, in the mirror on the shelf. Even the yolk of my eggs grimaces at me from the frying pan.

Yes, he will come for me – in one of the hundred New Moon's Eves after this one, not to punish me for having let him die, but to have somebody to keep him company.

One night -not just. Not until Miyumi needs me as her companion, a living being to feel alive again, a warm creature to curl against in the cold night. Not until that moment.

I take her in my arms, and we lie down in bed, her face on my stomach, my mouth on her forehead and rivers of soju to keep us warm in our warped universe.

About the Author

Russell Hemmell is a statistician and social scientist from the U.K, passionate about astrophysics and speculative fiction. Stories in Not One of Us, Perihelion SF, SQ Mag, Strangelet, and others. He can be reached at: @SPBianchini.

SOMETHING OLD

By Benjamin Langley

As the bride released the bouquet, Amelia raised her hand. The trajectory was perfect and it sailed into her palm. When she closed her hand, a pain forced her whole body to spasm and without thinking, she released the bouquet. It was swallowed up by a sea of bodies at her feet.

A bead of blood formed on her finger tip, ran down and around to the back of her hand, then fell onto one of the bodies writhing on the floor in competition for the bouquet.

Briefly, she was taken back to the moment that she'd last dripped blood.

"No wedding for us, then."

Stephen stood in front of her, his hair held by excess gel and his jacket as crease-free as when taken from the hanger. Once an attractive feature, his impeccable presentation now made Amelia think of a mannequin.

"What have you done?" Stephen gently held Amelia's hand and looked at the small cut.

"I caught the bouquet, but… there must've been a thorn." Amelia looked around to see a girl in a vintage-style red dress burying her face in the bouquet, her rivals for the prize standing around her admiringly. If there was a thorn, surely the girl would have felt it? Amelia looked at her stick-thin legs. How had *she* gotten the bouquet? She was practically anorexic. Every one of the girls around her was at least twice her size.

The girl lowered the bouquet and Amelia jumped back. Her face! It was as if she was suffering from a wasting disease. The skin was tight across her forehead, almost translucent; her cheekbones so prominent they looked implanted; and her lips were almost entirely devoid of colour, yet there was something familiar about her. Amelia recalled looking through family photographs and seeing a particular picture of her great-grandmother standing next to her sister. What was her name? Edna? Elsa? That's who this woman looked like. Perhaps she was somehow related. There were bound to be plenty of distant relatives at a family wedding.

Her parents had drummed into her the importance of family, but she was an only child, and none of her cousins were her age, so visits to family as a child had always bored her. Leanne, the bride, was closest in age, but Amelia remembered her as a child obsessed with Barbie and Day-Glo pink. They had nothing in common. Her parents and grandparents were the only family she was ever close to, and she wasn't thrilled with the idea of catching up with the rest.

"You okay?" said Stephen.

Amelia shuddered then looked at her finger. No more blood. It must have been a tiny scratch. "Shall we get a drink?"

Stephen had been so protective when Amelia first told him she was pregnant. He'd given up drinking too, in support of her, which only made Amelia feel worse when she'd slipped out with colleagues at work and had a few glasses of wine too many. Stephen was so sympathetic when she got home, buying her stories about weird cravings for prawns which had made her feel queasy. It was after that when the wedding talk started. He didn't come out and propose, but suggested it might be best for the child. He was old-fashioned like that. But after the miscarriage, he'd been drinking more than ever, and the marriage talk was forgotten.

Amelia and Stephen snaked through the crowd towards the bar. Amelia was surprised to find how few people she recognised. It was as if they'd wandered into the wrong party. It was a shame her parents had had to leave. At least there would have been someone they knew to sit with, but when her dad complained of heartburn, her mother had decided to get him home. The only reason Amelia had gone was because her mother insisted, and in the last few months she'd entirely lost the will to fight with her. Would she have turned into her mother had she not lost the baby? Instantly, she hated herself for thinking that maybe one of them had had a lucky escape.

Amelia looked again at the outfits of those around her. They looked like they'd been worn to her parents' wedding. Amelia cringed as she brushed past the moth-eaten and musty suits, imagining plumes of dust bursting off them when touched.

Stephen held a twenty pound note between two fingers. "Could you get the drinks in? I need the loo."

Amelia nodded and took the money.

The barman looked similar to a boy that Amelia had gone to primary school with. He had died when he was hit by a car one morning while crossing the road. She remembered his photograph, distorted on the overhead projector, shining on the wall as they said hymns at a special school memorial service.

Amelia ordered the drinks and as the barman turned his back she added, "And a glass of water."

He filled a glass for Amelia. "There you go."

When Amelia went to thank him, she could see that his face had changed into something vile and repulsive. His hair was matted together with dried blood, and his face grazed and peppered with gravel. She gasped and when he glared at her she saw that his face was clean. She'd not thought about that boy for years.

An elderly man propped himself at the bar beside her. "Young Amelia, is it?"

Amelia nodded. He'd definitely had his suit for generations. The huge lapels had faded at the edges, and in one of the button-holes was a wilted yellow rose.

Amelia struggled for breath. She gulped at her water.

"Got a kiss for your Great Uncle Jeff?" He leant towards her, and the thin hair he'd combed over his balding head flopped in front of his face. He turned his cheek fractionally then remained still, waiting for her kiss.

Amelia scanned the room. No one was looking her way. She glanced towards the toilets, but Stephen was not on his way back. The song that was playing came to an end, and the chatter around them ceased. All Amelia could hear was the breath rattling in the old man's lungs. She had to either kiss him or run, but what was she so afraid of? She pushed her cold lips together and leant towards Great Uncle Jeff. She couldn't part them to complete the kiss. The thought revolted her, but neither could she stay there forever, so she pulled back having only pressed against him. Her lips felt like they were coated in ash. She grabbed the water and downed it, then choked back a bitter taste that rose in her throat.

"So," said Great Uncle Jeff, bouncing a little, as if revived by that pathetic kiss, "You got a fella?"

"Not at the moment," said Amelia and felt terrible. How could she deny Stephen when he'd been so good to her?

"Someone should have snatched up a pretty young girl like you by now."

Trying to change the subject, Amelia racked her brain to think of what Jeff's wife was called, and whether she was still alive. She thought she'd been to a funeral for someone from that generation. Part of her was sure it was Jeff's funeral, but it couldn't have been.

"I thought you would have been married before Leanne," he said, nodding over to the bride and groom's table. As he did so, flakes of dust drifted off him. How old was he?

"You can land yourself a dishy fella like that." He pointed at Andy, the groom, and a memory popped into Amelia's head, the night she *had* landed a fella *exactly* like that, only a few months ago.

"Who's this?" Stephen was back. He quickly homed in on his pint then stood between Amelia and Jeff.

"My Great Uncle Jeff," said Amelia.

Jeff turned to shake hands with Stephen and Amelia caught sight of the spot on his cheek where she had kissed him. A grey imprint of two lips remained on his face.

"And you said you didn't have a fancy-man!" said Jeff.

Amelia picked up her wine and took Stephen by the hand and led him away from the bar.

"Where are we going?" asked Stephen.

"Away."

"Told him you were single, hey? Trying to hook up with him?" Stephen giggled.

Amelia slapped Stephen on the arm, a slap that would have been playful a few weeks ago, but she felt herself put more force into it than was needed.

"He's my uncle!"

"If not, you would have been in there, right?" Stephen flashed his impeccably white teeth. "However old is he?"

"Looks about one-hundred-and-two. I thought he was dead."

"Maybe he is." Stephen chuckled then gulped at his pint. "He didn't smell too fresh."

Amelia thought back to the feel of his cheek. A shudder went down her spine. Was it his funeral she'd attended? It couldn't have been. She sipped at her wine and thought she'd better make it last if she was to avoid wandering back into Jeff's territory again in a hurry.

The band played a song that Amelia remembered from her first date with Stephen. He'd taken her for dinner, but after the meal they'd ended up at a run-down place with torn seats and a sticky floor, where a band was playing.

"Shall we dance?" Amelia asked and they placed their drinks on a table and headed for the dance floor. The smoke machine had pumped out a thick fog. It was barely possible to see the faces of the other dancers. Amelia welcomed the smell of synthetic smoke which finally overpowered the musty smell that had clung to her since her encounter with Uncle Jeff.

They danced through fast songs and slow, and for a while it was like the last couple of months had never happened. When Stephen held her, Amelia felt safe, far from that night when she woke to cramps so strong it was like something trying to cut its way out of her with a rusty razorblade. She'd managed to clamber out of bed and saw the trickle of blood running down the inside of her leg, forming a tiny maroon stain on the blue carpet. She'd looked at the bed, touched the warm stain there, and realised what had happened. She was alone, and barely able to function. The pain was so great she begged for it to stop, and somehow she managed to reach into her bag for her phone. It was Stephen's number that she'd dialled. Stephen who dashed over and comforted her. Stephen who drove her to the hospital and stayed with her the whole night. Of course, he felt like he'd lost something too, but he hadn't.

The memories came back to Amelia as she felt a tap on her shoulder. It was Andy.

"Mind if I cut in?" he asked Stephen.

This was his test. Amelia willed Stephen to refuse, to stay with her, to claim her as his for eternity. But Andy was the groom who wouldn't be denied a dance on his wedding day, and Stephen slipped off into the fog without so much as a word.

"Where's your wife?" asked Amelia as Andy took hold of her hand.

"Bathroom. Freshening up before we hit the road."

"You're going?"

"Staying at a hotel near the airport. We fly out tomorrow morning."

"Anywhere nice?" Amelia felt ridiculous making such small talk with Andy. They used to be close. That was until the night he came over, drunk, saying he was having doubts about the wedding. Amelia had always joked about how she didn't understand that phrase, 'one thing led to another' but that's how she remembered it. He said he'd leave Leanne, which he never did, and she didn't think about Stephen. She never told Andy about the baby. She had planned to, one day, but before the opportunity arose, it was gone. What could telling Andy about it now possibly achieve?

She broke away from him and backed up from the dance floor until she felt something against the back of her legs. It was too sudden to do anything to regain her balance and she felt herself falling. Instead of hitting the floor, she was lifted and a childhood memory washed over her: she was at her grandparents' house, jumping on their bed when her grandfather snuck in and grabbed her in a bear hug.

"Thank you," said Amelia, as she was placed back on her feet. She'd been dazzled by the disco lights on the way down. Everything was a blur. There was a smell that was almost intoxicating, an aftershave she hadn't smelled in many years. That's why she'd been reminded of her grandparent's house. Her saviour wore the same scent. She shook her head and it started to settle. The figure before her came into focus and this time she was certain that the man before her was dead. It *was* her grandfather. He'd died when she was fifteen years old. She'd wept for a week. Her parents had to carry her from the crematorium.

"How's my little doll?" he asked. As always.

Amelia couldn't speak.

"Cat got your tongue?" He reached towards her and tweaked her nose, then showed her the fleshy part of his thumb. "Got your nose."

Amelia turned around. There was an unoccupied chair, which, as long as he didn't say another word, she was sure she could make it to without vomiting. She trudged towards the seat, each step an incredible effort. She sat down, then realised he'd followed her.

"Saw you dancing with Andy," he said. "You'd have made a lovely couple." The way that he was standing over her, looking down, reminded her of the time she'd smashed a pane of glass in his greenhouse with a Frisbee, and then tried to hide it. He stood over her and told her that he wasn't angry; no, he was disappointed. That was much worse.

"You've danced with him before," he said. "Haven't you?"

Amelia tried to avoid his eyes.

"The horizontal dance." He thrust his hips forward and laughed with his mouth open. His dentures came away from his gums and from the pink cavernous opening a thick streak of drool ebbed out and dripped to the floor.

This was not the grandfather she remembered.

Over his shoulder, Uncle Jeff had appeared. He was laughing at Amelia and the sick-looking woman was there too, holding the bouquet tightly in her hands. Streams of blood ran down her fingers and were splashing onto her thickly coated shoes.

"Hey," said Stephen. His hands were on her shoulders. "You okay?"

Amelia looked past him to see that her grandfather, uncle, and the wasting woman had gone.

"You were totally zonked out."

Amelia wanted to speak, but her mouth was too dry.

"You missed the send-off," said Stephen. "I thought you were right behind me."

"Oh," murmured Amelia.

"You didn't miss much. Tin cans on the wedding car, 'Just Married' painted on the back window, the usual."

"I saw my granddad."

"You'll have to introduce me."

Amelia tilted her head to one side and stared deep into Stephen's eyes. "He's dead."

Stephen rubbed Amelia's shoulders. "Do you think we should go?"

"Home?" asked Amelia, her brow furrowed as if the very concept was difficult to understand.

"Yes."

"But you booked a room."

"I'll call a taxi. You don't seem well."

"Let's go up to our room." Amelia nodded like a child.

"No." Stephen placed his hands on Amelia's shoulders. "You're not yourself tonight. Let's get you home."

Some of the fog that had formed in Amelia's brain departed. She was able to stand, and with a little help from Stephen, wandered out of the hotel's banqueting hall into the foyer. There must have been something wrong with the fog machine, thought Amelia, it was pulsing out a fog so thick that she had not been able to see a thing. It couldn't be healthy. Maybe that's why she was feeling so strange.

Stephen sat her down in the foyer while he went to reception. He wandered back and puffed out his cheeks. "All fully booked."

"Shall we get another drink, then?" Amelia couldn't believe the words that came out of her mouth. Why would she want to go back in there? And yet some impulse told her it was where she should be.

"We'll go up to the room, maybe order a bottle of wine?"

Looking at the fog that drifted out of the banqueting hall and swirled around the heels of the guests who were standing outside the door, Amelia nodded.

As Stephen helped her up the stairs with a comforting and steady arm around her waist, she thought of how lucky she was. When they reached the top of the stairs and the electronic door slid open, the smooth tiled floor gave way to thick carpet, causing Amelia's heels to sink and put her off balance. She leant against one of the pillars between the doors to remove her shoes. When she started to walk again, it was like walking on marshmallows.

The carpet had an odd pattern: golden ribbons crossing over each other on an aubergine background. The shapes left by the ribbons were like large kidney beans which Amelia tried to avoid walking on. Stephen must have thought she was very drunk, the way she was wobbling along the corridor, but there was something wrong with those shapes, and Amelia couldn't bear to step on them. But if the carpet in the hall made her feel uncomfortable, the one in the bedroom made her feel utterly queasy. As the lights flickered on, the deep maroon swirls on the carpet seemed to be moving. They had an intense deepness, and looked like you could fall into them and keep going forever. They reflected off the stark white wardrobes and table, so Amelia hurried to the bed and pulled her feet up as far away from them as possible. No sooner was she on the bed than an overpowering tiredness hit her. She slipped off her dress and before Stephen had even taken his shoes off, she was out.

***

Stabbing pains snatched Amelia from sleep. She yelled and put a hand on her midriff. There was something beneath her hand, fighting to escape. As she scrambled out of bed and switched on the side lamp, Stephen stirred. Another sharp pain hit her and she gasped for air. She covered her mouth to stifle a scream. With her arms wrapped tightly around herself, as if to stop herself from being wrenched apart, Amelia struggled to the bathroom.

Under the fluorescent light her skin looked like ash. She checked herself, expecting to see a gory mess below, but there was nothing. The pains eased away.

Maybe it was a shadow of the past, haunting her after the events of the wedding party.

She tiptoed back into the bedroom and carefully pulled back the covers, and what she saw sent a shudder through her body. Where she had been lying, glistening in the light, was a thick blood stain. As she screamed, Stephen sat upright.

"What's the matter?" he said. His breathing was sharp and his eyes wide. He twitched as he adjusted to being forced awake.

"There's blood," said Amelia, "On the bed."

Stephen looked down, his head darting around, rodent-like. He stared at Amelia, confused. "Where?"

Amelia looked down again and the bed was clean.

Stephen pushed a hand through his hair, causing it to look dishevelled. "You're not well."

"I'm fine." Amelia let her hands rest over her belly.

"I thought you were okay, but we can get help." Stephen arched his back and his neck cracked.

"It was my fault," said Amelia.

Stephen scooted across the bed to the side where Amelia was standing and stroked her arm. "Don't say that."

"It's true. I didn't want it. I didn't look after it. I killed it."

"It wasn't your fault. It could have happened to anyone. Get back into bed." Amelia climbed in and lay on Stephen's chest. He kissed her gently on the face and stroked her soft hair.

"It wasn't yours," whispered Amelia.

Stephen stopped stroking for a second, as if he was taking it in, but then continued.

Maybe he hadn't heard. She could feel his heart beating, the volume and pace increasing, until its ferocity forced Amelia to jerk away from him.

She straightened up. "I need some air."

"Open a window." His voice was low and slow, like a child's toy with worn batteries.

"I'm going to go downstairs for a minute... to stretch my legs."

"Do you want me to come with you?" he asked without making eye-contact.

"No."

Stephen rolled onto his side, away from her. "Make sure you take the room card to get back in."

Amelia slipped on her casual clothes and left the room. The fog that had filled the banqueting hall had drifted all the way up to the first floor. The machine must have been really broken. She edged along the corridor and then became aware that the smell wasn't like the synthetic smoke she'd smelled downstairs. It was dirtier, like mould spores, thick and musty. She walked along the corridor for several minutes until she hit a second corner and thought she must have missed the doors to the stairs. She turned back, but with the first step she took, she heard a tiny cry coming from beneath her. She looked down, but the fog was too thick. She turned back the other way and kept moving. With every step, there was a cry.

She checked the room numbers. They weren't in order, jumping from 103 to 237, then back down to 113. Despite not turning another corner she soon found herself back outside room 107, her room. She slipped the card into the door and when the light blinked she pushed it open. The fog dispersed a little and she was able to see the carpet again. Those kidney bean shapes had formed faces and were crying out, like tiny, deformed foetuses. She quickly slammed the door and shut herself inside. She went to the bed but it was empty. She scanned the room. Stephen's things were gone.

She was again consumed by tiredness and it was as much as she could do to pull back the bedding. The blood stain was there again. It didn't matter. Amelia climbed into bed and hugged the sheets. She was certain that as the wetness of the blood clung to her body, the sheets were hugging her back.

***

Sun shone through a gap in the curtains. Amelia stretched and climbed out of bed, went over to the curtains, and threw them open to let the light pour in. She caught a glimpse of herself in the mirror. She didn't remember changing back into her dress before falling asleep. Where was Stephen? Why had he left? She remembered going into the corridor and feeling lost, and when she came back he had gone. Not only had his things disappeared, but her bag was gone too. All she was left with was the dress. She suddenly felt uncomfortable in the room and wanted nothing more than to be out of the hotel.

Standing by the door, she paused for a moment, afraid of what she would see when she opened it. She took three deep breaths, closed her eyes, and opened the door. The first thing she noticed was the smell, or lack thereof, so she opened her eyes. As she walked down the corridor, she noticed that the room numbers were in order, with evens on the right, and odds on the left. After turning one corner she was at the stairs. But as she headed down, a troubling realisation hit her. Something was wrong. Light should have been pouring into the foyer, given the glass-front of the hotel, but with each step it only got darker.

When she reached the bottom of the stairs she hurried over to the reception desk.

"Hi, I was in room 107. I don't know if my partner settled the bill...?"

"But you can't leave, Amelia." The receptionist smiled. "There are so many people who have been waiting to see you."

Amelia turned around to see her grandfather standing before her, his grey skin flaking away from his face. He reached out a skeletal hand. This was where she was supposed to be, with her family. Amelia put her hand in his and let him lead her back to the party.

As they walked through the double doors, Amelia saw that the room had been reverted to ceremony layout, with rows of chairs on either side of a carpeted aisle. Skeletal people turned to look at her, some with flesh still hanging from their faces, others without. Amelia realised she was holding the bouquet again. She could feel the thorns digging into her palms but she couldn't let go as the blood dripped down onto her dress. Her wedding dress. When had she put that on?

Her grandfather continued to lead her down the aisle towards the man waiting at the front. Was that where Stephen had slipped off to? It didn't look like Stephen from behind, but not much looked like it should to Amelia as she glanced around the room.

She hadn't noticed the crackle of an old record player until it stopped and an uneven wedding march played, which led to even more of the guests turning around. A tiny cry sounded out. Amelia's stomach cramped.

As she was almost at the makeshift altar, the groom turned around and Amelia felt as though she was covered in insects and her body spasmed. It was Andy. Once. His face was caved in, with one eye hanging loose and the other somehow hidden behind a flap of flesh.

"We had him brought back here for you." Uncle Jeff smiled, showing his greening teeth.

"But... Leanne," said Amelia.

"She wasn't badly injured, don't you worry about her, pet. This is your big day."

"No," said Amelia.

"The family must be reunited," said a weak female voice.

Amelia turned to see the wasting woman. She was holding a blood-soaked blanket and from within, a cry.

"My baby..." Amelia took half a step away before her granddad pulled her back.

"Once it's all official, you can all be together."

Amelia stepped back into her position. She looked at Andy, who may have wanted to speak, but given the abyss where his mouth should have been, she doubted whether it would even have been possible.

"Shall I begin?" asked the wedding official. He was short and grey and his head seemed to get wider towards the top. He had enormous insect-like eyes.

"No, I don't want this," said Amelia.

"You must put this right. Unite the family," said Granddad.

"No. Andy was a mistake."

Andy's head drooped and his one eye was glassy.

"You know it, too," said Amelia. She stroked Andy's hand and then stepped away.

"You can't go," said Granddad.

"And what about baby? You can't leave baby behind!" cried the wasting woman. She held the bundle of blankets forward.

"I have to."

"Stephen won't have you back; he knows what a tramp you are," said Jeff. "You've got no choice."

"I have," said Amelia, and she tossed the bouquet over her head. As she heard people scramble out of chairs, she darted for the fire exit.

When she leant on the push bar of the fire exit, it moved so quickly that she almost fell out into the gravel car park. The sun shone off the large puddles that consumed much of the car park and came almost all the way to the door. Clumps of wet confetti had formed and framed the pathway across the water which led back towards the main road. It would be a long and lonely walk to the train station. Her feet would be soaked. Whatever would people think of her?

She heard an infant's cry come from the room behind her. Maybe it would be easier to turn back, to accept her mistakes and live with them forever. It was the right thing to do. It's what her family would expect.

A cramp doubled her over. Her breasts felt suddenly swollen, heavy with milk. She could feel wetness leak from her nipples as the hungry baby summoned her. She had to go back.

Together, with Andy, they could be a family. It was her motherly duty.

But she wasn't a mother. That had already been taken away from her and she'd suffered ever since.

She folded her arms across her stomach to ease the pain of the cramp, took a deep breath, and stepped into the puddle.

About the Author

Benjamin Langley has had over a dozen pieces published online and in print including at Flash Fiction Magazine, Litro and The Manchester Review. Benjamin is currently working on a supernatural novel set in the Cambridgeshire Fens. He lives, writes and teaches in Cambridgeshire, England.

A DAY IN ANTARCTICA

By Paul A. Freeman

London, 1921

When the art collector Josiah Wilson died in his study from a massive heart attack, a curious watercolour came onto the market. Interest in the painting was partly due to the fact that Wilson was examining it at the moment he died. Even before Wilson's death, the picture in question, titled *A Day in Antarctica*, had a somewhat lurid history, as Mrs. Wilson explained to us at the pre-auction viewing of her husband's art collection.

"Josiah is the fourth owner of this painting to have died in mysterious circumstances," she said, perhaps erroneously hoping the picture's infamy might raise its value.

Harold Bagley, my friend and a fellow art enthusiast, rather tactlessly pointed out that Josiah's sedentary lifestyle and fondness for port and red meat may equally have been responsible for his demise.

Mrs. Wilson was adamant though. "Josiah developed a superstitious dread of the painting, as did its three previous owners. All three of them met their end on a bitter winter's day with snow lying on the ground. So, Josiah made it his business to learn what happened to them. One died in a car crash on an icy road. Another fell through the surface of a frozen lake. The third slipped in the snow on a country walk, broke his leg and had frozen solid before help arrived."

"Mere coincidence," insisted Bagley, adding crassly, "I believe the coroner attributed Josiah's death to natural causes."

Mrs. Wilson gave my friend a baleful look. "Then how do you explain the paw prints in the snow outside Josiah's study?"

"Paw prints?" said I, my interest piqued by the revelations unfolding about a fellow art lover's death.

"Aye. Paw prints of a gigantic beast – the gigantic beast that scared my husband to death."

We had both heard rumours about the terrified expression etched on Josiah Wilson's lifeless face, as had the crowd of art dealers who, drawn by the widow's discourse, listened spellbound.

It took but a moment however, for Bagley to break that spell.

"What did the police reckon to your gigantic beast theory?" he asked.

"They said the paw prints probably belonged to a large dog," Mrs. Wilson conceded, her anticlimactic admission causing the audience to dissipate. "But I know differently. It's that painting that's responsible. It disturbed Josiah. He was never a happy man once it came into his possession. Yet, I couldn't convince him to get rid of it."

Bagley saw this superstitious talk as a test of his rational, rather unimaginative mind. So, looping his arm in mine, he guided me over to the painting in question – *A Day in Antarctica*, by Patrick Garrett.

The watercolour was quite remarkable, showing a polar landscape enveloped in a blizzard. The swirling snow scintillated as if composed from flecks of silver, nearly obscuring the emperor penguins huddled together for warmth and protection on the left hand side of the picture. But what was that pushing through the blizzard towards its penguin prey, its fur as brilliant as the eddying snowflakes, its maw a red, angry slash?

"A polar bear!" I exclaimed.

At first Bagley did not understand the significance of my outburst, but Mrs. Wilson was on hand to explain.

"Patrick Garrett was a self-taught artist with little education," she said. "He loved nature and spent his days at the London Zoological Gardens painting the animals. However, the surrealism of his work went against the movement towards anatomical realism which was dominating the art world at the time."

"What did the establishment make of Garrett?" I asked.

"They were torn. Some considered him a frustrated genius. Others dismissed him as a gifted amateur, deriding him because of his humble origins. His fate was decided by the picture before you – the picture that ultimately killed my husband."

"Decided how?" asked Bagley, thoroughly engrossed by the anecdote.

Mrs. Wilson hesitated, but perhaps because of Bagley's previous bluntness over the likely cause of her husband's death, she continued. "As your friend has already noticed Mr. Bagley, *A Day in Antarctica* features a group of penguins cowering before a prowling polar bear."

"So?" said Bagley.

"So, there *are* no polar bears in Antarctica. They live in the northern polar regions, whereas penguins are creatures exclusively of the southern hemisphere. Garrett's mistake turned his masterpiece into nothing more than an oddity, a joke, thereby giving ammunition to his detractors. Art critics pilloried him; holding him up to public ridicule. His career as a serious artist was effectively over."

These last comments sobered Bagley. "What happened to Garrett afterwards?" he asked.

"He was found dead one snowy winter's day at the zoo he loved so much, frozen to death on a bench facing the polar bear enclosure. Since then, everyone who's owned Garrett's *A Day in Antarctica* has died before their time, *always* when there's snow on the ground."

"Then why sell the painting if it's so lethal?" Bagley enquired, not unreasonably.

I honestly believe Mrs. Wilson was considering withdrawing the picture from the auction sale, but my friend's belligerence, coupled with her need for financial security now that she was widowed, must have decided her against such action. With a dismissive shrug she moved off to engage other art enthusiasts in conversation, leaving Bagley to make the fateful decision to bid on the picture.

Suffice to say, the notoriety surrounding *A Day in Antarctica* put many buyers off, thus ensuring that Bagley secured the painting at a very reasonable price.

Once the auction was concluded, I thought no more of Garrett's flawed masterpiece until a fortnight later when I received an urgent call from Bagley. We met that evening at the Constable Club, a place where artists, critics and collectors gathered to lounge about in leather armchairs, smoke cigars and opine on the latest fads of the art world.

"You look terrible," I said without preamble. My friend was haggard, pale, with dark rings under his eyes. I noticed, too, his dishevelled, unkempt appearance. "Are you sick?"

"Oh that I were," said Bagley before relating a tale so bizarre, I found it difficult to credit.

"It's that painting," he confided. "I was such a cynical prig the day I bid on it. Yet, once I mounted the picture on my wall, I realised what a fool I'd been, for I saw that the polar bear had moved, diverting its course away from the penguins it was previously intent on aggrieving and instead heading towards the viewer."

"The viewer being you?"

Bagley nodded. "The bear's dislocation was more pronounced the following day," he continued, "and even more so the day after that. It's as though Garrett put part of himself into the picture. Through the painting he haunts those of the same ilk who ridiculed him and his work."

I was tempted to laugh at my friend's superstitious fancies, but the sight of him and his earnestness precluded this. Instead, I accompanied him home to examine the allegedly possessed watercolour painting.

Bagley had placed it face down on the kitchen table of his London tenement to avoid inadvertently catching a glimpse of the ever-altering picture. However, he told me that on a daily basis an irresistible urge gripped him, forcing him to turn the painting over to see how far into the foreground the polar bear had moved. With trepidation and trembling hands, he took hold of the frame and flipped the picture over.

"I see no difference between this and the watercolour we viewed at pre-auction," I told my friend.

Bagley's expression was a cross between relief and anxiety - relief because the phantom polar bear had proven to be nothing of the sort, and anxiety because perhaps he felt he was suffering hallucinations or some other aberration of the mind.

"If the painting's causing you such distress," I said, "why not donate it to a gallery?"

At this suggestion Bagley's agitation increased and brought forth his innate nobility of character. "I cannot imperil others," he said. "If I transfer ownership, I may be handing some innocent bystander a death sentence."

"Then perhaps you should destroy the painting," I said, even though such a scenario went against everything we believed in as art collectors.

Bagley was horrified. "That would be like throwing acid in the face of an angel."

Instead, he decided to loan the painting to the *Graff Gallery* on Tottenham Court Road.

***

After that bizarre evening at Bagley's home, I forgot all about my friend's assertion that the polar bear in Patrick Garrett's *A Day in Antarctica* had somehow come to life. Assuming Bagley had loaned the picture to the *Graff Gallery*, I carried on with the day-to-day goings on of my humdrum life. Then, in the midst of a cold snap, I received a call from Bagley begging me to come to his home.

On arrival at his tenement, I noted that my friend was even more dishevelled and agitated than the last time we met. I also observed that Garrett's painting was nowhere to be seen.

"Did you loan the picture to the *Graff Gallery*?" I enquired.

"I did," he said. "But giving it up hasn't proven easy. Inquisitiveness gets the best of me, and on occasion I'm obliged to sneak off to Tottenham Court Road, pass by the gallery and view the painting."

"Is the polar bear still advancing on you?"

Bagley shook his head. However, the haunted look in his

eyes told me something more sinister had occurred.

"The creature is no longer *in* the picture," he said. "It's on the prowl, following me, stalking me."

I wanted to make light of my friend's absurd assertion, but realised his very sanity was on a knife edge.

"Put your coat on," I said. "Let's take a stroll to the gallery."

The night was bitter, and as we headed towards Tottenham Court Road sleet began falling from the sky. I pulled my coat tight about me and watched from the corner of my eye as the once confident Bagley scurried along beside me. Every now and again he looked over his shoulder, as if expecting to catch sight of some imaginary fiend.

The *Graff Gallery* had closed by the time we got there, but *A day in Antarctica* was on view in the front window. I put my nose to the glass and squinted into the darkened studio. The huddle of penguins was there, as were the swirling snowflakes of the blizzard. As for the predatory polar bear, there was no sign of the beast.

Nonplussed, I turned to consult Bagley, only to find him transfixed. Wide-eyed, he was staring at something rearing up before him - something invisible to my eyes. His lower lip trembled and without warning he swivelled on his heels and fled.

As I made to follow, something barged past me, pushing me into the snow that had accumulated on the paving slabs. By the time I got to my feet Bagley was a good fifty yards ahead of me, and when I finally began my pursuit in earnest, the chase was effectively over, for in his panicked flight, my friend had run into the main road, directly into the path of oncoming traffic.

A single blood curdling scream emerged from Bagley's lips ere he fell beneath the wheels of an omnibus.

By the time I got to the scene, there was nothing that could be done for Bagley. His chest was crushed and he had breathed his last. When the police arrived I held back, pretending to be a curious bystander, for what kind of a story could I relate to the constable taking statements?

While I stood watching in craven silence, I noticed a trail of huge paw prints in the snow, just like the marks Mrs. Wilson had discovered outside her husband's study on the night he died.

I followed the tracks back along the pavement, all the way to the *Graff Gallery's* front window where they abruptly stopped. Putting my nose to the glass, I peered into the gloom, focussing my attention on *A Day in Antarctica*. The polar bear had returned to its original position in the painting, emerging from a snowstorm in search of prey.

About the Author

Paul A. Freeman is the author of Rumours of Ophir, a novel which was taught in Zimbabwean high schools and has been translated into German.

In addition to having two crime novels, a children's book and an 18,000-word narrative poem commercially published, he is also the author over a hundred published short stories, articles and poems.

Paul currently works in Abu Dhabi, where he lives with his wife and three children.

THE DEAL

By Joni Chng

If we were classmates in school, I would be the last person you would want to be friends with. I was that loner who stared at the wall or out the window during lessons, lost in my own little world. Sometimes you may catch me smiling to myself, which would probably make you think what a weirdo I was. Being the only child to an overprotective single mother who had to juggle the roles of breadwinner and caretaker really didn't help my early social skills. We lived in a modest flat in a middle-class neighborhood in Tsim Sha Tsui, where community spirit was rife. People looked out for one another and news of every kind grew legs and travelled across the block at the speed of light. I never knew my father. Ma maintained that he drowned at sea before I was born – she never spoke about him besides that.

By the time I was seven, Ma decided I was independent enough to stay at home alone, so she dismissed the babysitter to save money and made me a copy of the house keys. She had a caterer on the fifth floor deliver warm cooked meals to me when I came home from school. Auntie Pui next door was tasked with checking up on me between 2pm and 3pm, which she always did like clockwork. In case of an emergency, Ma left specific instructions of the people I should run to and numbers to call. She was meticulous like that.

Home was where my imagination had free reign. I had a lot of friends here – boys and girls of various ages – whom I conjured up as my imagination fancied. My only real friend was Lula, a girl who lived two apartment blocks away.

Lula was my age, always had her hair in two high pigtails, and wore the same pink dress and white shoes whenever she came over. She never brought any toys with her, nor allowed me to follow her home. Our play dates only happened at my flat, where we played with my stuffed dolls, which she never wanted to touch and would only watch me handle. But whenever she was over, we always had fun. Sometimes we played hide-and-seek and chased each other around.

Lula would show up at my doorstep at 4pm sharp after Auntie Pui left, and would leave at 6pm on the dot, before Ma came home from work. She never came over when there were other people with me in the flat. I once asked her why, and she made me promise not to tell anyone that we were friends. If I did, she said, she would stop being my friend. I wondered if she was scared of Ma. My mother was very stern.

One time, I accidentally knocked over the sugar canister and couldn't clean up the mess on time before Ma was home. Desperate to save myself, I said it was Lula who did it, because she was trying to make us tea before she left. Ma was furious, but not because of the sugar. She sat me down and interrogated me about Lula.

I told her she was my friend from block D. I would never forget the mortified look on Ma's face, followed by her firm warning to never talk to Lula or let my friend into the flat again. I did not understand why Ma was so angry, but it nevertheless upset me. The next day, I tip-toed past Auntie Pui's front door and ventured over to block D to find Lula. I wanted to apologize to her for breaking my promise, and hopefully she would still be my friend. She never told me which unit she lived in, so I loitered about the elevator area before 4pm, hoping to catch her when she would be heading to my place. Time passed and there were no signs of her. I thought she must have found out. I ran home and cried myself to sleep that night – I had lost my only friend.

Lula never showed up again, and the only solace left for me was having more imaginary friends. One time, Ma came home and caught be in the midst of my pretend plays. Since then, I would receive a tirade of scolding whenever she saw me talking to myself. Perhaps out of resentment towards Ma for making Lula go away, I made sure my invisible friends never left me.

***

Ma worked as a clerk at a private language school where locals went to study English and expatriates learned Mandarin and Cantonese. She got the job because of her solid command of the English language. There, she met George – the man I would eventually call dad. George was Canadian of German descent. He was a visiting professor of psychology at Hong Kong University, and was studying Mandarin at the language school.

How their romance really developed remained a mystery, but I did remember when I started my second year in primary school, George became a frequent visitor at our flat. He would sometimes bring along his son from his late wife, Steve, who was four years older than me. Despite our parents' best efforts, Steve and I never bonded until many years later, when we were adults.

Shortly after my eighth birthday, George officially became my stepfather and we moved to Guelph, Ontario to be a family. Dad had a nice house with a big garden and a study full of books. Ma became a full-time homemaker after the marriage, while I had to get used to speaking English at school every day and being called a different name. In this new country, I answered to Sylvia Mung instead of Mung Ka Wai. Dad chose it, or else my name would be Ka Wai Mung, according to the western naming custom. He also decided I would not be taking his last name, because it would save me the trouble of having to explain my name in the future. It was a decision I was eternally grateful for. Ma, meanwhile, could never stop calling me Wai Wai.

Dad had been the only paternal figure in my life. He was the first person to take notice of and encourage my tendency for make-believe. Sometimes he even played along, asking me to tell him more about my imaginary clique. Having invisible friends, he once said, is a sign that a child has a healthy and active imagination. He was so convinced that I would grow up to be a writer, since I had a knack for creating characters. That never quite sat well with Ma. But much to her delight, it didn't take long for me to integrate with my new world, and gradually, I began making real friends at school to replace the imaginary ones.

***

It was a mid-November Friday, close to the winter holidays. I was making my way home on foot as usual after school. Steve attended the middle school a little farther down the road. He had told me this morning to go home on my own and not wait for him, because he would be playing video games at a friend's house.

The school was just a five-minute walk from home, but it felt like an eternity in the harsh winter air. I dug my hands into the pockets of my thick coat when I realized, feeling the pockets of my pants underneath, that my purse was not there. I stopped in my tracks and quickly rummaged through my bag and couldn't find it either.

I turned and walked back to the school as fast as my freezing legs could carry me across the thick snow on the ground. In my head, a mental movie of Ma scolding me for being absent-minded and threatening to reduce my allowance, began to play. I blocked it out and started mentally retracing my whereabouts for the day, trying to figure out where I might have misplaced my purse. The only time I'd taken it out of my pocket was during gym class that morning, so it should've been in a gymnasium locker. I quickened my pace to a jog, hoping my purse would still be there in the same locker that I left it, and the custodian had not locked the doors yet.

I arrived back at the near-empty school and made a dash for the gymnasium. Thankfully, the doors were still unlocked. I snuck in and ran across the basketball court to the changing room beside the stage, and located the locker I used earlier. There it was, the purse I left behind. I inspected the contents to make sure the remaining lunch money was still there. *What a relief! Time to go home.*

As I turned to leave, I was startled to find that I was not alone. A girl stood guarding the door, staring straight at me. She looked to be my age, had straight dark hair tied up in two high pigtails, and wore a fuchsia dress that ended above the knees with an elbow length red cloak draped over. Her high white socks went all the way under her skirt and her white loafers looked worn. I knew her.

"Hello," she said with a small wave as I took a few steps forward.

"Hi," I said. "Are...aren't you going home?" She said nothing and shook her head, sending her pigtails swishing side to side around her face.

"My name is Lula. Don't you remember me, Sylvia?" she said.

"Lula? It's...it's you!" I really did not recall ever seeing her around school. With such peculiar clothing, she would have stuck out like a sore thumb.

"Would you stay here for a while and play with me, Sylvia? I missed you." It was rather odd speaking English to Lula and hear her address me by my new name.

"I need to go home. We shouldn't be staying here. Come with me! You can meet my parents, and we can go play at my house, like we used to." I wasn't sure whether to be glad or uneasy at having found my long-lost friend here, on the other side of the world, in the same school. But at the mention of my mother, her face scrunched in anger.

"You told your mother about me!"

"I'm...I'm sorry...I didn't mean to. Why won't you want to meet my mother?"

"She doesn't like me!" I was taken aback by her anger, and then her gentle demeanor returned immediately as she said, "I promise I'll be your best friend again, if you will keep it a secret from her."

"Uh...okay. I'll see you again on Monday, then. I need to get going now." Lula gave a light giggle and dashed out the door, letting it slam shut before I could follow. When I stepped out of the changing room, she was nowhere to be seen. *That's odd.* The whole gymnasium was in plain sight, with the basketball court between the entrance and the locker room. There was no way anyone could make it across so fast.

"Lula?!" I called out from the middle of the gymnasium. No answer, except the echo of my own voice.

"Over here!" I heard Lula's giggle and spun around to see her running across the stage, loud footsteps thudding on the wooden floor, before disappearing out of sight behind a door at the corner that led to a backstage dressing room. There was something uncanny about this whole scenario, but curiosity got the better of me, so I got up on the stage and proceeded cautiously towards the backstage door that Lula left ajar.

"Lula?" I called, as I descended a small flight of steps into the dressing room. Besides boxes of colorful stage costumes and foam props, there was nothing else there and definitely no sign of anyone. There was a ventilation shaft and two high rectangular shuttered windows in the small space, with no other exit besides the door. Before I could search under the dressers and behind boxes, I heard a banging noise and a hint of keys rattling from the direction of the gymnasium main entrance. *No...!*

I spun around and ran, hopped down the stage, and sprinted across the basketball court towards the closed doors. With both arms outstretched, I pushed the heavy doors, only to stumble backwards and land on my back. I got up immediately and ran to a side door that would open to the soccer field, frantically cranking the handle. It was locked from outside and so were the other two exits. I returned to the main entrance and pounded on it, hoping someone walking by the hallway outside would hear me.

"I'm inside! Open up!" I screamed and pounded until my throat was sore and my fists hurt. Finally, I gave up and slumped down against the gymnasium doors, sobbing with my head to my knees. I didn't know how long I sat there crying. When I looked up, I could tell from the high windows it was getting dark outside and the air was chillier. The central heating system must have been turned off and everyone had left for the weekend. Ma must be worried sick, and I wondered if she knew how to find me here.

"Don't' cry, Sylvia. I'm here for you," I wiped away tears that blurred my vision and looked up to see Lula smiling at me.

"Lula? We're locked inside!" I said. "Don't you have to be home?"

"I live nearby. Besides, I don't want to leave you here alone, Sylvia." There was hardly a hint of worry, or any emotion for that matter, in her voice. "It's been awhile since we've seen each other. But Sylvia, you have to promise me that you will not tell anyone in school we're friends."

"Why not?" Something didn't feel right.

"I can't tell you why, but if you do, something bad will happen."

"O-okay...I promise."

"I'm so happy!" she said gleefully. "Come! Let's go play with the props backstage! We can while away the hours until someone finds us." I got up and followed her towards the stage. We went to the backstage dressing room and Lula pointed at one of the boxes there. "Let's start with that one."

"Okay." I walked over and began fumbling through its contents.

"Tell me what you find in there," she urged. As I picked up a pair of foam swords, I heard my name being called from outside the gymnasium.

"Ma?" I dropped everything and rushed out of the room. "Ma! Dad! I'm in here!" The gymnasium entrance door burst opened, and I ran into Ma's arms, with Dad and Steve right behind her.

"Wai Wai! Are you alright? What are you doing here after school?" Ma asked in Cantonese as she brushed off strands of hair from my tear-stained face.

"I left my purse behind in the changing room, so I came back to get it," I confessed.

"How could you be so careless with your belongings? Let's go home." She took my hand as Dad thanked the custodian for letting them in to find me. As we were about to leave, I looked in the direction of the stage. I wanted to call for Lula and ask her to come along, but before I could utter a word, I heard her disembodied voice whispering in my ear, *Remember! No one must know we're friends, Sylvia. Or bad things will happen...to you.*

I kept quiet.

$$***$$

As expected, I got a mouthful from Ma when we got home. Turned out she called the school when I did not come back home on time, and made a few calls to my schoolmates' houses that were nearby. Luckily, one of my classmates told her mother she saw me running back to school.

After everyone retired for the night, I lay in bed and thought of Lula. Did she and her family migrate here last year? That would explain her sudden disappearance. What a coincidence that we would find each other here, in the same school. But that promise she kept holding me to…

Sylvia…Sylvia…!

I sat up in bed. I was certain I heard my name being called. It was unmistakably Lula's voice and it was coming from the backyard, which I could see from my bedroom window. I walked over and peeked out from behind the curtain. There, standing in the snow in our backyard, was Lula, in the same outfit I saw her in earlier. She met my eyes and waved, even though she was not supposed to see me. *What is she doing here?!* I ran downstairs to the kitchen and opened the door to the backyard. There was not a single soul there, not even footprints in the immaculate snow that blanketed the ground.

Don't tell anyone, or something bad will happen…to them!

I felt a sudden chill overtake me and it wasn't from the winter.

I ran back upstairs and buried myself underneath the covers, eyeing every corner of my room in the dim lighting, before pressing my eyes shut. I had never been so desperate to fall asleep. One thing I knew for certain – I didn't want to be friends with Lula anymore.

***

The weekend went by as usual, but on my way to school the following Monday morning, Lula was smiling and waving at me from across the street. I looked away and kept walking. When I was in class, I caught a glimpse of her outside the window. During lunch time, she was there among the crowd, watching me. When school was over for the day, she stood waiting for me in the hallway, while everyone walked by her on their way out. I lowered my gaze and quickly headed for the exit, my heart pounding violently in my chest.

Just when I thought I'd be safe from her at home, there she was standing in the garden when no one was around, holding a finger to her lips as a warning sign for me to be quiet. At night, I wouldn't dare look out the window, because I could sense her standing outside. I wanted to run to Ma and Dad and tell them. As if reading my thoughts, I could hear her voice echoing in my head; *Don't tell anyone, Sylvia, or something bad will happen...to you and them!*

I barely remembered how long it took before sleep arrived, but I woke up to Ma's worry-stricken voice, calling my name. My head felt heavy as I had come down with a high fever.

***

The whole trip back to Hong Kong was fuzzy to me as I could barely stay awake. According to Ma, I was having persistent nightmares and kept muttering indistinctly in my sleep. Since the fever started, I never stopped seeing Lula whenever I closed my eyes. In those vivid dreams – if they were dreams at all – she kept calling my name and beckoning me to follow her into some sort of abyss. When I tried to run away, she would seize me by the arm or neck, pulling me into the darkness against my will.

Ma knew a spiritual medium at a temple nearby where we used to live, whom she insisted on taking me to. My condition, she believed, was caused by the negative *chi* of a ghost, sapping away at my life force. Being an agnostic with a respect for the unknown, Dad agreed that we needed some kind of spiritual intervention, especially since I was getting worse after being on antibiotics for a week.

For almost half a year since we left Hong Kong, I was back in my old bedroom at the apartment I practically grew up in with all my imaginary friends, and where I had first welcomed Lula into my life. The following afternoon, my folks welcomed an elderly gentleman into the living room. He was a thin fellow, with grey hair and a long beard, dressed in black traditional Chinese attire.

They talked for a while before coming into my room. Ma introduced him as Chin *Sifu* (master).

The old master squinted at me briefly, as if looking for something unseen around my person. He then concluded that I had attracted the attention of a restless spirit. Such spirits, Chin Sifu explained, were not necessarily evil. Their lives were taken too soon, causing their spirit to be stuck in purgatory, and thus they were in search of a substitute – someone to die and take their place in the spirit realm, so they could go into the light and be reincarnated once more. They would often appear to vulnerable and unsuspecting individuals, who would be unaware they were not of the living. Eventually, their victim would either be lured to their death or would slowly waste away as their life force depleted. Thankfully – Chin Sifu further explained – since I had rejected the spirit's attachment to me, my link to it had gradually weakened and would be easy to sever. All that was left for him to do was cleanse the negative vibes the ghost had rubbed off on me and I should get better.

Chin Sifu had me go through an exorcism ritual where I knelt on the floor and he pressed a palm against my forehead, while making hand signs and chanting an incantation I couldn't understand. There were joss sticks and talisman papers burned, and rice grains scattered around me, with my parents watching from the side. By the time it was done, though, I felt as if a dark veil casted over me had been lifted.

***

The day following Chin Sifu's ritual, my fever subsided and my vitality returned. Lula didn't visit me in my dreams anymore. Chin Sifu gave me a big round bead made of black gold, tied to a yellow string. It was a talisman that could ward off evil spirits, as he believed – based on reading my aura and birthday numerology – I was one of those psychically sensitive individuals that spirits trying to get in touch with the living would cling to. He also warned me of my own imagination, saying if I were not careful enough, I could unknowingly allow spirits to form attachments to me, and in fact I a hand in drawing a ghost to me.

We stayed in Hong Kong for a few more days to make sure I was well enough to endure a twenty-three hour flight. By the time we were back in snowy Canada, the holiday season rolled around and I was looking forward to my first of many Christmases. My normal routine resumed, and I made sure I was never alone in the school gymnasium again for the entirety of my elementary school years. But my old friend was far from done with me.

***

One winter's day, in my first year of middle school, I was walking home with a group of friends when I saw a familiar figure, clear as day, standing at the cross junction. My heart almost leaped out of my chest as I stopped dead in my tracks. I recognized the unmistakable pale skin and dark piercing eyes. It had been four years since I last saw her and she now appeared to be my age of twelve. She wore a red dress, white shoes and hair tied in two high pigtails. This time, however, she said nothing to me, like a bitter old friend who felt abandoned and betrayed. I paid her no heed, hoping she would never show herself to me again, but that was not to be the case.

Since my old friend's return, the food I ate wasn't digesting properly, my heart rate would fluctuate randomly, and I would break out in a cold sweat although we were having a particularly harsh winter.

Whenever I found myself alone, I could feel her presence, watching my every move in the shadows. Sometimes, I caught glimpses of red in my peripheral vision. At moments when I could work up enough courage to glance over my shoulder, she would be standing there, at a distance. It was as if a protective circle kept her from moving any closer. This must have had something to do with the black gold amulet. Since it was given to me, I made sure to carry it with me wherever I went.

After a week, I couldn't take it anymore. I waited for Dad to come home from work and sat my parents down to tell them my old friend had returned, recounting almost every sighting and the anxiety attacks that were slowly taking over my life. The color drained out of Ma's face as she began going over hypothetical worst-case-scenarios. Chin Sifu had passed away a couple of years ago; it never crossed our minds to keep handy the emergency contact information of a medium in Hong Kong, in case an incident which needed a Taoist style exorcism should occur again. Dad, who was always the voice of reason, calmly assured us we would find a solution, like we did before. He then proceeded to talk to me about some anxiety management techniques.

***

Turned out Dad really knew what he was talking about when he said we would find a solution, because when I got home from school two days after our dreadful conversation, an unlikely guest was waiting for me.

"Sylvia, this is Samantha. She's here to help us with the thing that's been haunting you," Dad introduced us. Samantha seemed like the unlikeliest person you would seek to solve a haunting. She was a rather tall, lanky oriental woman in her early 30s, with a short bob, pale skin and dressed entirely in black. She spoke in a husky voice that was oddly comforting, urging me to relate my entire paranormal experience. I later learned that she was a renowned spiritual medium based in the States, referred to us by one of Dad's colleagues.

I told her the entire story, starting from what happened at our Tsim Sha Tsui home to the exorcism done by Chin Sifu four years ago. I finished up by recounting the recent haunting and how the ghost had grown up as I had. Dad filled in some of the details from his observations which I missed, but Ma remained oddly quiet. She didn't say a word and I caught her staring into space a few times. After I was done, a tense silence descended upon all of us in the living room, until Samantha spoke up.

"This entity haunting Sylvia is a malevolent spirit that has been following her around since she was a child, maybe even since birth, and only first showed itself when she was seven. The fact that it keeps returning means that it wasn't a chance encounter. Entities like these are beings of lower vibrations, usually spirits of those who died a violent death. They are ritually summoned and held captive by a person to accomplish a task," Samantha explained.

"Are you saying someone sent this thing to harm Sylvia?" Dad asked.

"In short, yes. But I believe it's not that simple in this case. These entities do not act out on their own and try to harm the living unless there is incentive for them to do so, which is a life in exchange."

"So, this spirit wants Sylvia to die and take its place?"

Samantha gave a nod, "Precisely. The old master you went to was only half right, and had it not been for that black gold charm he gave you, and Sylvia's strong will, it would have already accomplished that," she pointed to Chin Sifu's amulet around my neck.

"But why her?" Dad asked the question that had been burning in my mind all along.

"You see, there are black magic practitioners in the Borneo region of Southeast Asia who keep spirits, known as *saka*. People would seek out the services of these shamans when they needed something accomplished that ordinary means would land one in jail – to steal something, to exact revenge, to eliminate an enemy. Those shamans then send out their *saka* to do the work. Of course, when you make a deal with something that is not of this world, there is a hefty price to be paid and I'm not talking about money. Sylvia obviously has no mortal enemies who would wish death upon her by enlisting the help of the dark arts. So, that can only mean that she has become part of the payment," she gave a lengthy pause because of the puzzled looks on our faces, "What I'm getting at is that…someone made some sort of deal with an evil spirit, whether willingly or not, with Sylvia's soul as the payment."

At that, Ma broke her silence with a soft sob and all eyes turned to her. What she confessed next made my heart sink and forever changed the way I saw her.

***

Linda Mung was told by more than a few fortune tellers that she had exceptional luck in love. It was hardly a surprise to everyone when she married the man who swept her off her feet at a young age of twenty. He was a prominent Bruneian businessman. Their courtship lasted for only three months, while he was going back and forth on business trips to Hong Kong, and then he proposed. With the material comfort and stability he could provide her, and a seemingly good character to go along, her parents were willing to overlook the fact that he was sixteen years her senior and twice divorced. She passed up a college education and left her homeland for his, where they live in a luxurious bungalow, complete with servants waiting on her hand and foot.

Perhaps signs of trouble were already present in her marriage; his short temper, the angry outbursts and his tendency to throw objects when things didn't go his way. Linda was just too deep in love to see the red flags. But after a month of marital bliss and a two-week honeymoon around Europe, he made his true colors known.

In Brunei, away from her friends and family, Linda would only eat the foods and wear the clothes that he dictated. Even the social circles she was allowed to be a part of needed his approval. On the rare occasions in which she spoke up to make her displeasure known, his retorts would make her question her memories and sanity. The time she finally had enough and raised her voice at him was the first of many times she received his palm and fist to her face.

Less than half a year into the marriage, Linda knew she needed to get out, but she was already carrying his child. Not that he cared; his only response to the news of her pregnancy was that it better be a son, because there were plenty of women lining up to bear him an heir. He didn't stop with the beatings either, which he would often follow up with sweet talks and gifts. In the opulent prison she called home, Linda's only confidante was Yasmin, the Indonesian maid assigned to attend to her. Yasmin was always there to nurse her bruises after her husband laid his hands on her and took care of her morning sicknesses. Unlike the other household staff, Yasmin spoke fluent English, and had briefly attended college before poverty forced her into her present circumstances.

As the child in Linda grew, so did her hatred for its father. Just when she thought things could not get any worse, her first ultrasound revealed she was expecting a daughter. When she told her husband the news, he stopped laying hands on her and made her move to a separate bedroom, so she could bear witness to him bringing home a slew of women. She could no longer hide her disdain for him, and that was when Yasmin nonchalantly told her about a curse that could bring death upon a person. Normally, Linda would not be one to buy into the idea of spells and hexes, but each passing day with that man was driving her to the brink of suicide.

Yasmin told Linda about a *dukun* (shaman) in Kalimantan who could weave spells so powerful, even the dead can be revived. She offered to take Linda there for nothing in return. At that point, Linda would willingly give a few years of her lifespan in exchange for being free from her predicament for good. With some money stashed away in a secret bank account unknown to her husband, and her pregnancy entering the second trimester, Linda made a trip to Indonesia with Yasmin on the pretense of accompanying the maid to visit her family. She followed Yasmin's lead into a remote village on the outskirts of a Kalimantan jungle, and with the help of a local guide, they located an old hut nestled among banana trees.

The *dukun* – a heavyset woman in her sixties, dressed in black from head to toe, with gray hair peeking out underneath her headscarf – sat cross-legged on the floor inside the minimally furnished hut. Laid out before her were small dishes of unknown ingredients and a burning sandalwood cone, filling up the small space with a heady aroma. As soon as the two women entered, she said something in a language Linda did not understand before gesturing her guests to sit before her on the floor. It then occurred to Linda that the shaman woman was blind. The *dukun* said something at length to them, to which Yasmin translated to Linda, saying the *dukun* already had a premonition of their visit.

After a few words were exchanged, with Yasmin as the interpreter, Linda took out a stack of cash notes tied up with a rubber band, and placed it in the only empty bowl among the dukun's strange ingredients. The blind shaman handed her a black cloth bag containing a glass bottle of clear water, capped with a cork. She gave instructions that Linda must place the bottle somewhere near her husband's sleeping place, but make sure it was out of sight to anyone. Once her wishes had been granted, she was to pour the contents of the bottle into a stream far away from where she lived, and walk away without as much as glancing over her shoulder.

Whatever spell was in that bottle of water, it did the job. On the third day after Linda secretly placed the bottle under the bed she once shared with her child's father, she heard a terrified scream coming from his room shortly past midnight. A terror-stricken young woman in her twenties, clad in fishnet stockings and a red mini dress that was hastily slipped on, stumbled out of the room with a panicked look on her face. Linda's husband had stopped breathing from being bound and gagged in a kinky sexual game.

For a while, Linda was the talk of the town – that poor pregnant lady whose husband was killed in a tryst with a prostitute. It was a small price to pay for freedom from his abusive clutches. She took care of his estate, got her cut as his spouse, and played the grieving widow until gossip subsided, then planned her move back to Hong Kong before the third trimester of her pregnancy.

Before Yasmin left for Indonesia, after her service was discontinued following the death of the master, she reminded Linda of the charm given to her and the dukun's words. When Linda went to retrieve the bottle, it was still under the bed exactly where she had left it, right beneath where her husband's head would be when he was lying down. Somehow, it had escaped notice when the police inspected the scene. Now that the dust of her husband's death had settled, and Yasmin had left, the visit to the blind shaman woman's hut felt like a fleeting dream. What was she thinking back then, in the midst of despair and desperation? She held up the bottle of water in her hands, tilting it side to side and watched its contents swish around. Did the blind woman's magic really kill her husband or was everything purely coincidental? It didn't matter, now that the bastard was dead. Linda pulled out the cork and poured the water down the sink, then left the empty bottle to dry on the dish rack.

***

"You were supposed to set that thing free after it had done your bidding, and send it far away from you, into the wild. Instead, you let it linger around and it followed you. Now it's calling you on the deal," Samantha said. Ma said nothing else. The uncomfortable silence returned to hang over us. I was sure it was not Ma's intention to tell me the truth about my biological father that soon. She might have waited a few years more, until I was eighteen, though she'd have probably omitted the part about her killing him with black magic.

"So, what can we do now?" Dad broke the silence.

"We have to banish this thing and send it somewhere it can't reach Sylvia," said Samantha. There was calmness in her demeanor and indifference in her voice. She must have been too accustomed to dealing with such situations, perhaps she'd seen worse. I couldn't help but wonder for a moment what sort of interesting career a spiritual medium must have.

"And how can we do that?"

Samantha appeared contemplative for a moment, and then finally said, "We need to act fast. If you can do precisely as I say, we can get rid of it tonight." She then turned to Ma, "But I need to have a word with Linda in private, if I may."

***

I lay in bed, fighting to stay awake, though my eyelids seemed to weigh a ton. The only illumination from the street lamps outside prevented my room from being in absolute darkness. The glowing digital numbers of the clock on my nightstand indicated it was 2:56am. I didn't see the strip of light underneath my door, which meant all lights were off in the house and everyone was sitting in the dark, waiting for my cue.

I had kept the black gold talisman in a drawer, away from me as the medium instructed, making me feel very vulnerable. I had never wanted a night to be over with so badly. My only consolation was that after tonight, the ghostly entity that had been following me, waiting to lay claim on my soul since I was born, would be gone for good.

As if it could sense my fears and read my thoughts, I suddenly felt its unseen presence in the room. My heart was threatening to pound its way out of my chest, but I sat up slowly, and braced myself for the confrontation.

"Lula?" I called into the darkness.

Nothing but dead silence at first, followed by a sudden temperature dip so extreme, I could see my breath when I exhaled.

And then, I saw it, standing in the shadows by the window – a familiar face looking back at me.

"Go away," I took a deep breath to steady my trembling voice. "Go…leave me alone!" I yelled at the top of my lungs. The entity in red stood there in the corner, silent and unmoving. Before I could yell again, an unseen force hurled me off the bed and against the wall, almost knocking me unconscious.

I tried to shake off the concussion to my head and stood back up. When I got to my feet, the entity was already standing before me. It grabbed me by the neck with both hands, and though it appeared to be a girl of my age and stature, it was able to render me helpless. I looked square into those menacing eyes as the grip on my neck tightened, squeezing the air out of me. The last thing I recalled was a dark mist seeping into my nose and mouth. I let out a scream, though I couldn't hear my own voice. In a matter of seconds, it was as if a black veil had been wrapped over my face, suffocating me until darkness took over.

***

I didn't know how long I was out. According to Dad, they rushed into the room as soon as they heard me scream. All I remember was by the time I regained consciousness – my vision still blurry – I was lying on the floor and Samantha was kneeling over me with her thumb pressed into my forehead, between my brows.

As my awareness gradually returned to the room, I felt a painful rumbling in my stomach, like a gerbil trying to crawl its way up my esophagus and out my mouth. I gagged and sprang up into a seated position, lurching forward and spewing out some foul-tasting slimy liquid into the wide-mouth glass jar Samantha held to my lips. As soon as she stepped aside, Ma and Dad rushed over to help me to the bed.

When I fully regained my senses, I saw Samantha holding the glass jar I'd vomited into, but it was full of clear water, like the kind that ran out of a filtered faucet. Nothing near what I imagined came out of me moments ago. A cork cover was secured over the mouth of the jar and Samantha slid it into a black cloth bag.

***

More than twenty years have passed since the evil that haunted me was banished. Although I didn't become a writer as Dad speculated, he is nonetheless proud that I followed in his footsteps and became a professor of psychology. My stepbrother never showed any interest in academics, and now lives with his family in Kingston where they own a diner. Ma never lived to see this day though; she lost a two-year battle to lung cancer the same year I graduated high school, despite never having smoked a cigarette in her life.

I recalled clearly the morning following the medium's visit; Dad left for work as usual, while Ma prepared Steve and me for school as she would any ordinary day. That was a cue to bury the events of the night before from my conscience, to treat it like a conveniently omitted chapter in my life. But things weren't the same with Ma. She became more distant towards me than ever. No one in our family ever spoke of our paranormal experience again, though. It was as if everything had simply been one long nightmare that never actually happened.

Shortly after Ma's passing, I was going through the things she had carefully boxed and stashed away in the attic. Ever the meticulous organizer, she had left us specific written instructions as to where her possessions were and to whom they should go. In a dusty box filled with old paperback novels that she wanted disposed, I found a black cloth bag containing a glass jar of crystal clear water. Dad somehow didn't know that cursed thing was with us all those years, and I didn't want to burden him with that knowledge, so I took it with me when I moved out on my own to attend college. I managed to track down the medium, Samantha, for answers and that was when I discovered the secret Ma took to the grave.

A *saka* – the medium explained – needed a living master from whom it could draw energy for sustenance in exchange for servitude, until it could find a soul to take its place. Keepers would normally set their ghostly slaves free to somewhere remote, as far from them as possible, hoping that an unfortunate individual would cross paths with the entity and become its substitute. However, if no victims were claimed, a *saka* would always make its way back to the master. In order to set me free from it and to prevent it from harming others, Ma had agreed to take ownership of the *saka*, letting it feed away at her life force until her health suffered. But with her gone, the *saka* once again would seek a master.

I needn't ask any further. I took out the black gold amulet from an old trinket box I'd almost forgotten about, and tied it around the neck of the jar before placing it in a small locked chest in a corner of my storeroom. Hopefully, this would do the trick. But who knows, perhaps a day would come when I would need to call upon my old friend Lula to do my bidding.

About the Author

Joni Chng is a writer and photographer by profession. In her spare time, she reads and draws. But in between writing scripts for choose-your-own-adventure online games, doing photo shoots, urban sketching and interviewing some professional for magazine articles, she continues building and expanding her own imaginary universe – one story at a time. You can follow her on Facebook, Twitter and Instagram under the handle jonichng.

THUNDER AND LIGHTNING

By DJ Tyrer

The air was cold enough that her breath slipped out as a fog and there was a hint of frost on the bus windows. Sally hadn't expected it to be cold. Of course, people had mentioned winter, but she'd taken it to mean 'not as hot'. After all, when you thought of the Middle East, you thought of a blazing sun overhead baking the desert sands. But Syria, this part of Syria, at least, was nothing like that at all. Despite the drought and the shelling, olive trees still covered the district.

The bus rattled awkwardly along the churned and rutted road. She was going to be sore when they finally reached their destination.

Sally was one of five passengers on the bus, which was provided by Medicines Sans Frontières to bring them to the hospital where they would be working. She'd been surprised to discover that as dirty and rusty as it was, it was no worse than the one she used to take to and from work every day. She'd been expecting worse.

The driver was a local who'd introduced himself as Ahmed and seemed unable to resist the lure of the road's many potholes and shell holes. Sally's fellow passengers consisted of a Swede called Olav, an American named Jessica, a Briton called Roger, and Phillip. Phillip was the reason she was here.

Sally had offered her services as a general volunteer to the charity because Phillip had decided that, as a recently-qualified doctor, he had a duty to help out in the warzone. Personally, Sally would've preferred to stick with her job as an administrative assistant and cheer Phillip on at a picket line in London. But, if he wasn't there, she couldn't bear to remain without him, even if the alternative consisted of danger and disease.

Like Jessica, a doctor offering help, Sally wore an ankle-length, long-sleeved dress and a headscarf; appropriately-demure clothing for travelling through the region. Although she'd chafed at the idea – assuming Phillip and the other men would be in shorts and tee-shirts – she was finding herself grateful for the extra warmth the outfit provided. Instead of the clothing she'd predicted, Phillip wore a sweater and sturdy khaki trousers with a dark-blue parka over them. Roger was dressed in a similar fashion, save that his coat was a patchwork of brighter colours. Olav, on the other hand, perhaps more acclimated to such a chill, was wearing shorts and a tee-shirt, in his case celebrating some obscure Scandinavian death metal band. He seemed perfectly comfortable.

Indeed, Olav didn't even seem bothered by the repeated bumps, almost snoozing. He was a nurse. Roger was a general volunteer, like her, and much less at ease with the way they were being tossed about.

They all sat bunched together, ignoring the space that would've let them spread out. Jessica appeared to Sally to be something of a seasoned traveller, while she and the others stood out as new to the experience.

"How long till we're there?" Sally asked. Outside, the fig trees were thinning out. She craned her neck. Ahead, she could see the dusty outline of a village on a hill.

Phillip glanced at his watch. "Still another hour."

"I wish this thing could go faster," she said as it bounced across another crater.

Roger started to say something, but there was a sudden flash and a thunderous crash.

There were screams as Ahmed fought to control the bus.

"What the hell was that?" Sally gasped, looking around.

"I thought it was a bomb!" cried Jessica.

The bus appeared to be undamaged and they all seemed okay. Ahmed was still trying to control the bus, and they all clutched at the seat frames to hold on.

"Must've been lightning," said Roger. "The bus was struck. It was the flash of the lightning and the crash of thunder."

Phillip gave a nervous chuckle. "You're probably right. Man, it gave me a fright." He turned to the front of the bus, where Ahmed was still fighting with the wheel, and shouted, "Get a grip!"

"I'm trying!"

Suddenly, the vehicle was careening down a slope.

"Hang on!" shouted Ahmed, then he shrieked in Arabic.

"Phillip!" Sally grabbed for him.

A bounce threw them all into the air. They screamed.

Jessica shrieked, "Help!"

Then, they were flying... and there was a sudden flash and a thunderous crash.

There were screams as Ahmed fought to control the bus.

"What the hell was that?" Sally gasped, looking around.

"I thought it was a bomb!" cried Jessica.

The bus appeared to be undamaged and they all seemed okay. Ahmed was still trying to control the bus, and they all clutched at the seat frames to hold on.

"Must've been lightning," said Roger. "The bus was struck. It was the flash of the lightning and the crash of thunder."

Phillip gave a nervous chuckle. "You're probably right. Man, it gave me a fright." He turned to the front of the bus, where Ahmed was still fighting with the wheel, and shouted, "Get a grip!"

"I'm trying!"

Suddenly, the vehicle was careening down a slope.

"Hang on!" shouted Ahmed, then he shrieked in Arabic.

"Phillip!" Sally grabbed for him.

A bounce threw them all into the air. They screamed.

Jessica shrieked, "Help!"

Then, they were flying... and there was a sudden flash and a thunderous crash.

"What the hell was that?" Sally gasped, looking around.

"I thought it was a bomb!" cried Jessica.

"What?" exclaimed Sally as Roger started to suggest lightning. "You just said that!"

"What?" asked Phillip, eyes wide.

"We did this already!"

"Did what?"

"*This*: the flash – the conversation – everything – it's repeating. Why's it repeating?"

Phillip rubbed his temples and looked at her, confused. "What do you mean, repeating?"

"Happening over and over."

Phillip turned to the front of the bus. "Get a grip!"

"I'm trying!"

Suddenly, the vehicle was careening down a slope.

"Hang on!" shouted Ahmed, then shrieked in Arabic.

Sally swore.

Then, the bounce and the screams.

Jessica shrieked, "Help!"

Then, they were flying... and there was a sudden flash and a thunderous crash.

"What the hell was that?" Sally gasped, looking around, then exclaimed, "It's happening again!"

"I thought it was –"

"– a bomb," interrupted Sally. "You keep saying that."

"I do?" Jessica looked at her, confusion and fear in her eyes.

"Everything keeps repeating! The flash, our conversation... I don't understand! What's happening? Why?"

"What?" asked Phillip. He looked to the front of the bus and shouted, "Get a grip!"

"I'm trying!"

Suddenly, the bus was careening down a slope.

"Hang on!" shouted Ahmed, then he shrieked in Arabic.

"It's going to –" Sally started to say as the bus bounced and they all screamed. "–happen again!"

Jessica shrieked. "Help!" And then, they were flying.

A moment later, there was the flash and the crash.

Sally looked around and started to ask what was happening. "It's happening again. Didn't any of you notice? This keeps happening again and again."

"What are you talking about?" Phillip asked.

"This. We're living the same moment over and over and I don't know why."

Phillip looked confused.

"I'm trying!" Ahmed cried in response to an unasked question. As the bus was careening down a slope, he shouted, "Hang on!" Then, he shrieked in Arabic.

"Not again! Not again!"

Phillip tried to say something, but Jessica shrieked, "Help!" and a moment later, they were flying.

Then came the flash and the accompanying crash.

Sally looked around and started to ask what was happening. "Again! Why is it happening again? Why don't any of you seem to notice?"

"What are you...?" Phillip started to ask, then trailed off. "I..." He looked confused.

"You remember, don't you?"

He nodded.

"I'm trying!" Ahmed cried, the shout trailing off into a confused sound. Then, the bus was careening down a slope. "Hang on!" he shouted uncertainly, then he muttered something in Arabic.

"It's happening again."

Phillip nodded.

Jessica shrieked, "Help!" and then, they were flying.

The flash and the crash weren't a surprise this time and Sally barely looked about in confusion. She felt oddly calm.

"This has already happened," she said loudly, to ensure their attention. "This is, um, the fifth... sixth time it's happened."

Phillip was nodding at her words. "It has."

"Why does it keep happening?" she asked them.

Even with the rising sense of terror, she had their attention.

"I recall..." Olav mumbled.

"We have to understand what is happening..."

The bus began to careen down a slope.

"Hang –" Ahmed didn't finish. He muttered something in Arabic.

"If we can work this out, we can stop it..."

"How? How do we?" asked Phillip.

"Help," Jessica said, looking at Sally with pleading eyes.

Then, they were flying.

"An explosion!" shouted Sally as once more there was light and sound. "It was an explosion." She looked at Jessica. "It *was* a bomb."

Jessica looked wildly about. "But –"

"But... the bus isn't damaged. We aren't hurt." That was the flaw in her thinking.

"It's happening again," muttered Phillip.

"I remember..." mumbled Olav.

"I'm confused," said Roger.

"My head hurts," said Phillip.

"Hang on!" shouted Ahmed as the vehicle began to careen down a slope. Then, he asked, "What's going on?"

"We're repeating the same moment over and over."

"We need to stop it," said Phillip.

"How?" asked Ahmed.

Jessica leapt to her feet and staggered to the door, then yanked it open and threw herself out, screaming "Hel-!" The cry was cut short as the bus took flight and she was swept away. Then came the explosion.

"An explosion," said Sally, no longer fazed by the blast. "But, the bus is okay and we're okay..." Then, she saw Jessica was sitting back in her seat. "You're..."

"I –" Jessica replied, then shook her head.

"We're reliving this over and over," said Phillip. "Why?" Then, he added, "My head hurts."

"We need to understand it," said Sally.

"I'm trying!" Ahmed cried. "Understand what?"

Then, the bus was careening down a slope.

"We haven't long!" he shouted.

Sally swore. "We need to understand. We're trapped until we do." Then, she added, "Why was I the first? What do I know?"

"Help us," said Jessica, staring at her, tears in her eyes.

Then, the bus was flying and the explosion came again.

"An explosion," said Sally, "but the bus is okay, and we're okay... and I was the first to notice..."

"We're reliving this over and over," said Phillip. "Why?" Then, he added, "My head hurts."

"Your head hurts!"

"Yes. This is all so confusing."

"It is!" shouted Ahmed as the bus began to career.

"I think I understand now. But..."

"We haven't long!" Ahmed shouted.

"I don't know if..."

"Help us," sobbed Jessica, staring at her.

"I will."

Then, the bus was flying and the explosion came again.

"An explosion!" shouted Sally. "There was an explosion, but the bus *wasn't* okay. And, we weren't okay. Shrapnel hit you in the head, Phillip."

"My head hurts," he said.

"Yes. Shrapnel. The rest of you... I don't know. But, I think you all died first."

Ahmed shouted in Arabic as the bus began to careen down a slope once more.

"Then, you, Ahmed. I'm sorry."

"We haven't long," the driver replied, a sob in his voice.

"Then, Phillip died, I guess. And..."

"And...?" asked Phillip.

"I guess I died, too," she said, slowly. "And, now, we're living out that moment over..."

"Help us," sobbed Jessica, staring at her.

"I don't think I can."

Then, the bus was flying.

There was a sudden flash and a thunderous crash, cutting off Roger's comment. There were screams and she heard Jessica shrieking, "Help!"

"What the hell –" Sally cried.

The bus was slewing wildly across the track.

She thought she heard Ahmed shout, "I'm trying!" his voice slurred and weak.

It was almost as if time stood still and she took her surroundings in with amazing clarity. There was a hole in the side of the vehicle and blood. So much blood. They were all dead. Except Phillip. He was slumped over beside her, a shard of metal buried in his head, blood pouring from the wound. She heard his breath rattle away to nothing and screamed his name, desperate to save him.

Somehow, it seemed she was unhurt.

Then, the bus was flying and turning over sideways. For a moment, Sally felt weightless; as if she were in a dream. When the roof rushed up to meet her, she felt a momentary pain.

Then, nothing at all.

About the Author

DJ Tyrer is the person behind Atlantean Publishing and has been widely published in anthologies and magazines around the world, such as Chilling Horror Short Stories (Flame Tree), State of Horror: Illinois (Charon Coin Press), Steampunk Cthulhu (Chaosium), Tales of the Black Arts (Hazardous Press), Ill-considered Expeditions (April Moon Books), and Sorcery & Sanctity: A Homage to Arthur Machen (Hieroglyphics Press), and in addition, has a novella available in paperback and on the Kindle, The Yellow House (Dunhams Manor).

WHAT MEETS IN THE DARK AND RAIN

By Darren Todd

The storm began after my parents left for the evening. This was a trial, they told me. To see if I could handle myself alone. If anything went wrong, it'd be right back to babysitters.

I'd turned twelve a few weeks earlier after starting sixth grade at my new school. Too old for babysitters.

The house still felt strange. The living room alone was the size of our old place in the city. Our tiny couch and chair sat in the middle of the huge room like kid-sized versions of regular furniture.

I never minded the sitter at our old place. If I stayed out of trouble, she'd let me watch TV or play games. I could tell her I had no homework and she believed me.

My sitter for the last few weeks never let me do anything. She took control of the TV and mom's laptop. She made me do all my homework, even checked it and piled on more if I finished early. She'd have people over and make me promise to keep it secret.

But that night would begin my freedom. I was fine with my folks going out all the time if that meant I could stay home and do my own thing. From what I could tell at my new school, no kids my age had sitters anymore. They'd been driving tractors and working the fields and staying at home by themselves for years.

I never told any of them about my sitter, but none of that mattered anymore. All I had to do was not mess up.

Then the storm came. What started as a drizzle grew louder and stronger, until gusts of wind threw droplets against the windows in the living room so hard I barely heard the television.

With a house that size, I could find someplace quiet, away from the storm. I considered my bedroom. My mom had found me a TV/VCR on Craigslist, and we'd bought a bunch of tapes at a local yard sale for a quarter apiece, movies I hadn't seen in years.

I craned my neck to look up the stairs at the glow pouring from my room. I could just make out the sound of the TV, which I must have left playing. Unfortunately, my bed sat against a huge window. The storm would be just as loud up there, so I stayed downstairs.

My back faced the living room windows. I kept turning to watch the sheets of rain ripple and the sky going dark. I couldn't focus on the TV show. While I stared out the window, the first bolt of lightning flashed. It shone so bright, I shielded my eyes, since they'd adjusted to the dim.

Only a moment later, a crack of thunder ripped through the air, and the power went out. With the sound from the TV gone, the storm seemed to double in volume. Light filled the living room with each bolt.

Who knows how far the outage spread? We lived a long way from our neighbors. I could see one or two other houses during the day, but couldn't make out much of anything though the window now. I finally spotted the big house up the road when another bolt struck. Their lights seemed to flicker, but stayed on.

Somewhere upstairs, in the few boxes still left unpacked, sat my flashlight, a nice metal one I'd gotten the Christmas before. Or maybe we'd lost it during the move, like a bunch of my stuff. Candles would have to do.

I felt my way into the kitchen, waiting for strobes of lightning to guide me. Shadows danced around like ghosts darting between hiding places. Before my imagination took hold, I started talking to myself.

"Should be matches in the junk drawer," I announced.

Mom used some candles only for decoration, so I'd have to make sure not to light any of those. Dad picked up matches from wherever they went in the evenings, so I found plenty of books full. He never did anything with them, so I figured he wouldn't mind.

I gathered a few candles, the kind set inside a glass jar, and lined them up on the dining room table. I struck a match and leaned over each one to look for a wick blackened from use. I found one, touched the match to it, and the light swelled.

When I held the candle up, it only lit a small area around me. Not enough light to do much in. Even if I lit more, with no electricity, what could I do? Time seemed to slow, like I had days to kill instead of hours. I would have gone to bed, but I wasn't tired. The thunder would have kept me awake anyway.

On a shelf in my room sat about a dozen unread books. I read a lot before, but since the move it made me feel isolated. Now I mostly played online games with friends from my old neighborhood. But without power, reading seemed my only option. Solve a puzzle, maybe. Homework? Yeah, right.

But when I thought about it, the walk upstairs and down the hall to my room seemed farther in the darkness, even with the candle for light. Maybe I should just make dinner. I had to eat something cold with no way to nuke one of the frozen meals my parents kept stocked for me. Cereal might work.

I ended up grabbing chips and munching on them while flipping through a gaming magazine. The storm kept up, but something about having the only light around made me feel safe, like I was tricking the storm. It had knocked out the power, but I was still winning, safe inside my bubble of light. The thought made me smile through crispy bites of chip.

A sudden bang of thunder hid another noise behind it, something closer. I tilted my head and listened, the magazine and chips forgotten.

The sound came again, more apparent now without thunder to mask it. Someone was knocking on the front door.

My bubble of light seemed to pop. Now, holding a candle when all the windows shone black, made me imagine things staring in at me that I couldn't see. I shook off the fear, got up, and walked toward the door. I meant to yell something over the pelting rain. "Hold on!" or "Just a minute!" but when I opened my mouth, nothing came out.

The lightning flashed again and silhouetted a figure staring in through the glass. My heart jumped, though what did I expect? Of course someone was there, only now he must have seen me by the candlelight. So much for ignoring it, though back in the city my parents said never to answer the door. Don't even look out the peephole without them around.

A moment later, the knock came again, the banging almost as loud as the thunder, but along with another sound. Not quite yelling, more rhythmic somehow.

Our house was only new to *us*. It was an older home, and all the doors still used a skeleton key, though my dad had installed deadbolts on most of them. I crept behind the door and dropped to my knees. I peered through the keyhole to see my uninvited guest.

The darkness clouded everything, but when the lightning flared again, a distinctly animal face hovered inches from the keyhole. I recoiled at the sight, falling backward and taking the candle with me. Melted wax spilled on the floor and the candle went out. It hadn't burned me, but I still screamed out of shock.

"Hello?" a voice called. "Is anyone there?"

It sounded small and female. A moment later came the noise I had heard earlier, the unmistakable bleat of a sheep.

I righted the candle, stood, and twisted the deadbolt, my fear replaced by curiosity. I opened the door and on the stoop stood a girl my age with a lamb cradled in her arms. Even in the darkness, I saw both were drenched. She bobbed up and down, either from the chill or to comfort the lamb.

"Thank you," she said, dipping her shoulders. "Please can we come in?"

I stepped to the side and then closed the door on the storm.

The girl looked at me and sighed. "You're not going to believe this," she said.

"Hold on." I'd put the matches in my pocket, so I struck another and relit the overturned candle. The low light showed the numerous drops and small pool of wax congealing on the wood. My panic only grew when I noticed the dark patch forming beneath the girl's feet. The water dimmed the wood, soaking in.

"Wait, let me get you towels first." I hurried to the downstairs hall closet, found the most threadbare towels, the ones Mom used for cleaning, and brought them back.

"That's so nice of you," she said. "I'm pretty cold, and so is Belle." She wrapped the lamb first and then managed to drape a towel around her shoulders with one hand. I meant to help, but only held the candle up for light.

"Do you... need a blanket or anything? The power's out or I'd turn on the heat."

"Can you start a fire?" she asked. Long, straight hair, light brown or even red, framed her lean and beautiful face. Freckles stood out on her cheeks like she spent a lot of time in the sun. Some girls my age wore make-up, but she either didn't or the storm had washed it away.

"I... I don't really know how to use the fireplace." I turned around and shone the light on the stone hearth. My dad had made several fires in it since the warm weather broke. I'd seen him do it, but I'd also seen my mom fix lasagna, and I'd be *no* help in the kitchen.

"If I could just..." she said and held out the lamb.

I realized she meant for me to take Belle. I hadn't so much as pet a dog in the city. Some kids had fish, maybe a hamster, nothing else. I put the candle on the floor and held open my arms as far away from my body as possible.

She slid the lamb into my arms and pushed it up against my chest. "Hold her like a baby," she said.

"I don't have any babies. I mean, I don't have brothers or sisters."

Her hands moved over my bare arms, and they felt cold as stone. Still, they sent heat through me. Her long fingers moved with a confidence mine only managed when holding a video game controller.

"You'll do fine," she said. Her teeth chattered, as if the lamb had been keeping her warm. She wore a long-sleeve cotton shirt so wet it clung to her. Even the denim vest she wore over it looked black in the light, also soaked. Same with her blue jeans. Her feet squished inside cowboy boots as she danced from foot to foot.

"Do you want to change?" The thought of her putting on dry clothes meant her taking off her wet clothes and my brain short-circuited. "I mean, do you want dry clothes? My mom has clothes."

She smiled. "You're really nice. The fire's better, though. Just gimme a minute."

And she meant it. In a single minute, she had set the kindling and stacked up the logs. She held out a hand for the matches, but my arms were still wrapped around Belle. "I can't...."

"Which pocket?" she asked.

"Um, right front."

My stomach dropped when she came over and fished for the matches. I squirmed without meaning to, never ticklish before. I held back my laughter and stood at an angle to help her.

She caught the kindling with a single match and added to it over several minutes until the sticks ignited. She placed a single log on top and moved the others closer, like little soldiers waiting to carry out orders.

"Bring her over here, please," she said. She took the towel from her back and doubled it over on the stone floor in front of the fire. After freeing Belle from the folds of her damp towel, she did the same with it. The lamb seemed pleased. It bleated twice, folded its legs under itself, and settling down, shut its eyes.

"I wish I could dry your clothes, but the power's out." I felt like an idiot saying this, but she smiled up at me like she knew I meant well.

"It's okay. Let me warm up and we'll check the breakers."

"The breakers?" I asked.

She squinted and smiled like she thought I was teasing her. In the firelight, she looked so cute doing this. I didn't say so, but the image snagged and set itself in my memory. "The circuit breakers. In the basement."

"Right," I said, still not positive what she meant.

"So we can get the power back on," she finished and giggled.

"Gotcha."

The light from the fire grew as one log caught, then another two.

"So what were you guys doing out in the storm?" I asked.

"I heard our momma sheep Henrietta calling out from the shelter, like she'd lost one of her lambs. I can tell when she's worried. It just sounds different."

"So you, like, went looking for Belle in this?" I pointed out the bay window.

"I would've saddled Prissy and taken her. Would've found Belle even faster and Prissy would make her way home in the pitch black or a blizzard, but I knew Daddy would say no, so I just took off on foot."

"I had a hard enough time finding candles," I said.

She laughed, a melodic, genuine sound that made me smile.

We talked for a while, and the house that had — minutes before — felt awkward and even scary, now felt comforting.

I walked back toward the door where the flickering orange glow reflected off the now solid wax.

"Oh no," I said and lowered the candle to look closer. Sure enough, the drops were more flat than rounded, not like I could just pop them up with a fingernail and leave no trace behind. We'd had different wood flooring in the city. It was smooth as glass and felt more like plastic than wood. Dad liked these floors better, but I didn't know why. Right then, I wished for the slick floors of our old home, where I could have scraped up the wax with a butter knife in two seconds.

"Everything okay?" she asked.

"There's wax all over the floor. My parents are gonna kill me. Well, not so much kill me as make sure I have babysitters until I'm eighteen, which is worse."

She walked over and leaned down to inspect the wax. Her hair had gone wavy, which at least meant it was drying. She had taken off her boots and socks, barefoot now, her jeans rolled up. "Yep, let's go ahead and check the basement. Now we've got two reasons."

"Two?" I asked.

"The heat for one. But we need to iron out that wax." She held up a hand like she expected me to protest. "I know it sounds crazy, but it works. You put down newspaper and iron over it. It pulls the wax out of anything. I've seen it."

"I don't know if we have any newspaper."

She wrinkled her face. "Your folks don't read the news?"

I nodded, suddenly worried she'd think my parents were dumb or something. "No, they read the news. They do it online."

She kept her forehead crinkled.

"On their tablets, y'know?"

She looked behind her, toward the basement. "Sure. Well, rags work too. You ready?"

No one I knew in the city had a creepy basement. That would mean wasting a bunch of space, so the only basements I'd come across looked like any other room. I'd seen our new basement only once: when we toured the house before closing. Even then, we only glanced into the dark depths, down a slanted set of narrow, wooden stairs where a single bare bulb lit up the stone walls and cobwebs.

Something about going with her made it easier. I just hoped she turned out as cool as she seemed. Even in my own house, other kids might play tricks once they figured out the basement scared me. She seemed cooler than that. After knowing her less than an hour, I felt like I could trust her. She probably had a great sense of humor, but had way better things to do than play pranks or tease someone.

I led the way to the basement entrance, pulled open the door, and lowered the candle. Its circle of light revealed those deathtrap steps.

"Do you want me to go first?" she asked.

I held the candle between us, showing a kind face not at all mocking me. I wanted to lead the way down since this was *my* house, but what came out was: "If you *want* to."

She took the candle and eased down the steps, crouched low so the light fell over the next step. Even being cautious, she soon left me behind, and I rushed to catch up. With no rail to hold, she moved her free hand along the dusty shelves and then the stone walls. The best I managed without getting a serious case of the willies was to put a hand on her back. She didn't seem to mind, so I kept it there against the still-damp fabric of her vest.

"Where's the breaker box?" she asked.

"Uh, I'm not sure. In the regular place, I guess."

She turned around and smiled. "Isn't it cool down here?"

I said yes right away, and once the uneasiness passed, I guessed it was. I would never have gone down there alone, even on a dare. But with her, it felt like an adventure. Right then, I imagined I could go anywhere, do anything, if it meant being with her.

The breaker box came into view along the leftmost wall. The candlelight reflected off the thin pool of water on the basement floor.

"Where's your dehumidifier?" she asked.

"Uh…" I said, which she must have gotten used to by then.

"You have to run a dehumidifier in here all the time, even when it's not raining, or you'll get mold and stuff. Especially now, or the floors will stay wet for weeks."

"I think Dad was getting one," I lied. I cataloged what she said and planned on mentioning it to Dad the following day.

She brushed spider webs from the breaker box and tugged the metal door open. I'd seen too many movies to trust the box myself. To me, it was eager to shock anyone who touched the wrong wire, or something the good guy might kick the villain into, electrocuting him.

Inside, black and brown levers, like fat light switches turned sideways, were flipped to either the left or right. She held the light to the inside panel, where someone with sloppy handwriting had marked several numbered labels.

"We just have to find the main," she said. She scanned the labels, saying each name as her fingertip danced over them. "Kitchen, upstairs bath, master bedroom."

"You can *read* that?"

"Main," she said. "Here it is." She looked back at the switches and found the corresponding number. She turned to me. "Cross your fingers." She pushed it to the left with a sharp whacking sound, and at first I thought nothing had happened. Then I looked up the stairs and saw the glow from the living room light.

"It worked," I said, elated. "Nice job."

Even with more to do, I felt a strange urge to stay in the basement. Like the wonder of her visit would disappear in the electric lights. Down there, we still had unexplored darkness. So long as she stayed with me, I would have mapped every inch; spiders, leaks, and all.

I was blocking the stairs, and she stood there waiting. When she raised her eyebrows, I snapped out of it.

"Sorry," I said, and turned to head up. The light from above cast enough glow across the stairs to see them in all their splintered glory. They were so steep I used my hands to brace myself, like a toddler just learning to climb. As brazen as she had been, the idea of putting my bare hands on the shelves sent shivers through me. I pictured them breaking off in my hands or a family of spiders waiting for that moment to crawl on me all at once.

A few steps higher and I stumbled, miscalculating the depth of the board. My foot slipped down to the plank below, scraping my shin and sending me careening forward. I would have plowed face first into the steps, but a strong hand caught my arm.

"Whoa," she said. "I got ya. You okay?"

I turned toward her. "Yeah, just scraped...." Her grip was icy. "You're still cold," I said.

She let go and pulled her hand to her side. "I'm all right. It'll warm up fast now." She smiled, but it looked different than before.

We turned into the kitchen, and I hit the switch. In the flood of light, I saw her much better. She still looked like she was freezing. Her lips even had a bluish color.

I cranked up the heat on the thermostat. "Do you want hot chocolate?" I asked.

She grinned and it seemed like she was about to say yes, but she went quiet and gazed down for a few seconds. "No, thank you. I'm think I'm fine."

"Okay."

She looked up. "What's that sound?"

I listened. The house seemed noisy compared to a minute ago. The heat was whirring, the fridge, the ceiling fans. The storm kept going, but muffled now. Between rumbles of thunder, the fire crackled in the living room, but then came the distinct sound of my television upstairs.

"Oh, that's my TV. I'll go turn it off."

"Can I see your room?" she asked.

My mind wandered upstairs, to the laundry on the floor and the soda cans on top of my dresser. Maybe I could race up there first and clean before she saw it. "Sure," I said. "Let's go."

I led the way, feeling silly for thinking the house seemed ominous before. Now, bathed in light, it was harmless, especially compared with the storm outside. I only hoped it would keep up so she had to stay. I didn't even care when my parents were coming home. She needed me, and I needed her. I felt more connected to her than with anyone at school in the weeks I'd been there.

I raced ahead and threw my clothes into a pile, chucked soda cans into the trash, and swept an armful of comics into a stack by my computer desk. The television played *Jungle Book*, which seemed childish now, though I'd always liked that story. I toggled the power button on the side to quiet it. I was kicking the clothes into my closet when she came in.

She looked around, but not like I'd hoped, not seeing the cool posters or movie props along the shelves. Not scanning my books or even admiring my new computer. Instead, her eyes moved from place to place with something like suspicion.

"I know this," she said.

"What do you mean?"

"What's going on here?" She grew angry all the sudden. Her hands balled into fists at her sides and she leaned in, as if

271

ready to pounce on me. I would never hit a girl, but right then I was pretty sure she could beat me up whether I hit back or not.

"I don't understand," I said. "What's wrong?" I moved the rest of the laundry into the closet with a foot and closed the door. I kept my hand on the door jamb, like I might need to launch myself across the room if she came at me.

But then she went slack, hands and mouth opening. She stared past me at the closet, her face confused.

I looked down at my hand, along the frame. I'd seen the tick marks before. Dad said he'd paint over them, but I'd asked him not to. Something about the marks I liked.

Melissa, 2, 1995. Melissa, 4, 1997.

Now that I looked again, something clicked. That script. The weird L's and almost cursive E's. I'd studied it for several minutes the first time I'd seen it to figure out the name. It was the same writing as inside the breaker box.

"Melissa," I said aloud.

"What?" the girl said, still confused.

"You're Melissa." Saying the name out loud caused my stomach to sink and my head to feel light.

She stared at me. "How did you know that? I never told you my name."

"This was *your* room." My breath quickened. Still, while I expected fear, I felt only bewilderment.

She looked around again, her face going through several emotions, one after another. "I don't understand. This isn't my house. I... it can't be. If it is, what are *you* doing here?"

I looked back down at the tick marks and followed them up all the way to *Melissa, 12, 2005*. "You haven't lived here in a long time," I said. Despite a dizzying stupor, despite not knowing if she would hit me, I walked over and took her hands. I'd expected as much, but still the cold surprised me. It no longer fit. The house was warm, even stuffy, with the fire burning and heat on full blast.

"That was your dad's handwriting in the breaker box, and here on the door frame."

"What's happening?" she said, her face breaking and tears forming.

I thought about all she'd done since stepping inside. Thought about what sort of twelve-year-old was brave enough to wander through a storm just to get a lamb to safety. I swallowed my own apprehension, and said, "You're all right" and hugged her. Her whole body felt cold and damp, but she settled into my embrace and we stood there for what seemed like minutes.

"I'm scared," she whispered.

"No, you're not," I said. "You're brave. Braver than anyone I've ever known."

I thought about that date: more than ten years since her mom or dad had made that last tick mark. I didn't know much about the previous owners, but Dad had said they were older. If they had kids, they were long gone. Maybe the house had gone through a few people since Melissa lived here. Had she come before now, looking for shelter? Maybe this was her first visit, either the only time someone answered her or the first time she'd found it.

Ten years she'd been wandering, looking for her home in the storm.

"I don't know what to do," she said.

"Just stay," I said into her ear. Her hair smelled like earth and rain.

"I have to go home," she whimpered.

"You're already home, Melissa."

She pulled away from me, her face alight. "Do you hear that?"

I shook my head. "Hear what?"

She turned to listen. "Henrietta's calling out. She must have lost Belle in the storm. I have to find her." She broke away and tore down the stairs.

I followed her. "Wait," I called. "She's here. You saved her already." Over the stairwell, I looked down into the living room. The fire burned on, but nothing but damp towels lay in front of it.

Melissa ran for the front door. "I'll be okay. I'll find her and bring her back. Don't worry about me."

"Stop, please. You don't come back," I said. I all but fell down the last several steps and put my hands on the door. "If you leave, you won't come back." I shook all over, my knees trying to give out.

She seemed to consider this, her breath heaving in and out, cold on my face. "You've been very kind," she said. "But I have to go home." She leaned in and kissed me, the chill of her lips sending a jolt through my body. Then she pushed firmly on my chest, opened the door to the raging storm, and fled into the night.

When I recovered my senses, I flipped on the porch light and threw open the door. I saw nothing but the pelting rain and the impenetrable darkness beyond the glow. I searched the living room. Her boots had vanished along with the lamb. I stepped into the storm and called for her, yelling over the thunder, the cold drops soaking into my clothes. I listened for her, for the lamb, for anything. Nothing came.

***

It's been almost a year since she knocked on my door. After she left, I cleaned everything and used her trick for getting rid of the wax. I even blow dried the damp spots in the wood and got rid of any evidence of the fire. I couldn't have my parents pushing a sitter on me now. That would ruin it. She wouldn't come back if a sitter were here, storm or not.

Ever since, I'd checked the weather reports and insisted my parents go out and enjoy themselves whenever the forecast called for a storm. I prayed for a power outage, even tried flipping the breaker myself when the lightning failed me.

Still, no Melissa.

Tonight will be different. It has to be. I turn thirteen tomorrow, and somehow I know that'll change things. The tumblers won't line up just right anymore after tonight.

My bedroom light is on, the television is playing *Jungle Book*, and I'm watching the downstairs TV. I've hidden every new piece of furniture, the dehumidifier is unplugged, and I'm wearing the same clothes, even if they don't fit as well anymore. My room is lined with dirty laundry and Coke cans (though I've grown sick of soda). The same towels I'd given her wait washed and ready in the downstairs closet.

I check my watch. My feet tap out a nervous rhythm on the hardwood floor. This storm is really going. With every flash, I wait for the thunder, willing the power to go out. One bolt fills the whole house with its luminescence, and I close my eyes. The thunder follows not a second behind; the house goes quiet. I open my eyes to darkness and my heart quickens.

"Please," I whisper. "Please."

About the Author

Darren Todd writes short fiction full time, along with freelance book editing for Evolved Publications and narrating the occasional audiobook for Audible, Inc. His short fiction has appeared in twenty-three publications over the last eleven years. He has had three plays produced and a non-fiction book published.

While many of his works fall under the literary umbrella, he often returns to horror. His style and reading preferences tend toward the psychological, as he enjoys stories that linger in the imagination long after he's closed the book on them.

He lives in Scottsdale, Arizona with his wife and son, and does his best work in coffee shops on a dated Alphasmart word processor.

THE TOWNSHIP

By Cyndie Goins Hoelscher

. I drove through the familiar woods where my father once hunted rabbits. Building rabbit gums and carrying lifeless animal corpses home was not a hobby. As the second eldest in the Appalachian family, he was responsible for putting meat on the table for his mom and six siblings. After he married a woman from the city, he told me – his eldest daughter – the stories about the woods so I would never fear them; I would never be lost.

After I graduated from college, the woods became a nostalgic place where I could reflect on a simpler life. Throughout the years, I continued to be lured back to the shadows of the sentinel pines and the soft clay earth. When the television blared recent events repeatedly, I wanted to withdraw to those woods. They were safer than the television, safer than the newspaper. The woods were a benevolent refuge from a loud, violent world; and each year, I planned my pilgrimage back to the rural home of my ancestors. I drove hours so I could kick off my shoes and run into their embrace.

This day was different, however. The Appalachian piedmont was showing her temperament. The gray skies hovered unreasonably close to the ground, and the fog swirled as if ghosts were walking about. As I drove my black Buick down toward the bog of Little River, I found myself stopping and walking a few feet ahead, so I could judge the distance. I had to convince myself I had not drifted off course – that I was still on the badly maintained county road leading to the speck on the map called Black Ankle.

"Dammit!" I swore softly. The Spring mornings had been splendidly clear every day of the week – except on this morning when I planned to travel deeper into the past.

"I don't think you should be going out to see that Singleton man," my uncle warned me. "There are some places we just shouldn't go. And let me tell you," he paused to point a shaking brown finger at me, his gray eyes misty. "Now, those woods are different."

"Woods are woods! How can they be different? They are only thirty minutes from here." I could not reason with my uncle. He did not care how many years I had been plotting our family's homes from the census records. Old papers did not mean anything to him. With a sixth-grade education, he could read the papers well enough, but he could read the signs better. I understood the gift of sight and how 'feelings' were something that city people no longer believed in. There was a time when survival depended on knowing what could not be learned from a book. It was a knowing that something was out of place, a knowing that pushed our feet backwards instead of forwards when the chill traipsed down the spine and the tongue caught a bitter taste.

At 26 years old, I assured my uncle that I was fine. I wasn't exactly a city-slicker, because my father taught me the secret of the forests. The elderly Mr. Singleton was gracious enough to escort me into the older woods. They were not the woods of my father or my grandfather. They were the woods of my great-grandmother.

The fog lifted as soon as I passed the pottery center at Seagrove. As the fog raised, so did my spirits, because I could see the tall pines. They had not been cut in generations. I rolled down the window to let the fragrant aroma fill my lungs. Soon, I would be deep in the heart of them. I pulled up to my guide's house.

It was not a house as I expected. The small stone-cut building had served as a post office for over 250 years. The heavy wooden door creaked on one antique hinge and a large, stone hearth with an iron kettle dominated the small space. Even smaller was Mr. Singleton, and if I were to guess, I thought he might have been 250 years also. The planes on his face were inscrutable among the deep crevices of wrinkles, and his wild, white hair looked like an avalanche from the ice age.

My uncle would call Mr. Singleton "quare" in his ways, for he spoke what amounted to nonsense to others. The people of the surrounding towns just shook their heads when he spoke of Little River Township, a place decimated in the late 1800's by the repeated floods of Little River.

"Let's get to it," Mr. Singleton said as he pulled on his cap. "Now, who be you again?"

"I'm Ben's grand-daughter," I smiled and took tick spray out of my bag.

"I remember Ben. Yes, ma'am, I do. He was the hardest working man I ever did know."

I saw he could remember a lot more about my grandfather, but was too polite to say in front of a young woman he had just met. A tell-tale grin formed on his lips before he turned to the door.

"I will carry you back there, but we'll have to go now. It's not a good day. We should make this quick and all." He refused my offer of tick spray. "Nah! They won't bite me," he said, shaking his head as he sauntered off in front of me.

The shiver I encountered the moment we stepped off onto the thin red-dirt trace surprised me.

Of course, the woods folded around us as I had anticipated. The colossal pines swallowed the sun's rays before they reached the pungent soil. The smell became musty from decayed leaves and earth. Perhaps the proximity of the bog was what made the stench of decay almost unbearable. Despite my determination to stifle a cough, the hoarse croak escaped like an involuntary convulsion.

Mr. Singleton turned to glare at me and my cheeks flushed scarlet. I was a daughter of the woods. I knew how to walk heel to toe, softly, so as not to leave much of a sound or a footprint. I understood that there was no room for human banter, laughter or coughs in the woods, because it disturbed the order of nature. There are many layers in the woods. I could feel decades of

Autumns past as my feet sank into the deposits of fallen leaves. It was difficult to walk without rustling them, without shuffling them out of their place.

But something was wrong. These woods did not feel right. They did not smell right. These woods were not respite. For once I considered that I shouldn't hunt for the answers to all my questions. The blank hundred years in my family tree were for four or five generations that I could not account for. Now, it seemed that Mr. Singleton was my last chance to find out about the empty lines on the ancestral chart hovering over our family bible in my city apartment.

After a mile of tedious walking, I wondered when we might come upon the township. I wanted to ask Mr. Singleton, but knew that conversation was out of the question. It seemed we had walked more than was necessary, according to the map I had carefully studied the evening before. I noted that the leaves were getting softer and my footsteps heavier, as if the earth was sucking my boots down with each step. I found myself watching my feet instead of my surroundings. I frowned at the change of terrain. I no longer felt the protection of the trees. I did not hear the rustle of the wind, tickling the pine needles above. I did not hear the calling of birds. I only heard my own spongy footsteps, slurping in red clay mud. I collided into Mr. Singleton, before noticing that he had finally ceased walking.

With surprising strength, the old man righted me before I fell into the mud. He looked me over and whispered.

"This is as far as I go these days." He pointed to a section of woods that seemed to be impenetrable.

Thick vines spread over the trees like a contagion. Staring into the greenness, I could extricate human made structures. A stone chimney from a thickly covered home. A steeple from what must have been a church protruded out of the variegated vegetation. A rusted wrought iron gate indicated an abandoned cemetery in the shadow of the church.

Determined to see what I journeyed from my familiar woods to know, I left the old man sitting on a stump. Only briefly did I worry that he might leave me there alone in the menacing dark woods.

But, I was no longer me.

As I stepped into the township, my body shuddered and my young soul died.

I felt the moment my blood froze in my veins, an eternal chill that a fire cannot slake. My green eyes turned a shade of silver – a color of gray with a light behind them. The same distinct color of eyes that my uncle bore. My uncle had warned me, but he did not try to stop me.

Drawn to the cemetery, I saw countless headstones. There must have been people who flourished here, before the woods reclaimed the land. But there were no names inscribed on the headstones. There were only rows of stones, some large and some small. Adults, some. Infants and children, others.

"Non-persons," my great-grandmother whispered to me. I turned to greet her, amazed that she was as real as I was.

Her bronzed skin was three shades darker than mine. Her wavy, black hair fell to her waist. In her arms, she rocked a sleeping baby.

"Surely you have a name?" I had traveled so far. I crossed over the river.

"No longer," she said.

"But there are so many!" I exclaimed as I tried to count the river rocks in the cemetery.

She smiled as I realized that we were not speaking the same language.

"The sun will drop and the woods must sleep. Go home," she said as an adult would instruct a child.

I turned to find the path to the trace, surprised to see Mr. Singleton still perched on the stump. I looked deeply into his face and saw that his eyes too were the eerie gray with the light behind.

He stood, apparently anxious to reach his home before sunset.

"I don't have the answers to my questions," I said aloud, believing that the rules of the woods only applied in the day, when the woods were most alive.

"You are not asking the right questions, then," Mr. Singleton said without looking behind. He kept his quick pace.

The sounds of the woods were returning. The owls thrashing in a mating dance. The roosting birds seeking a safe place for the night. The crickets chirping and the frogs croaking. All the sounds I found comforting as I went to sleep each night were joining in a chorus, serenading my thoughts. The song warmed my blood and I realized that I was the same, but I was also different.

I am the descendent of non-persons.

Back at my apartment, I removed my ancestry chart from the frame. Carefully, I used the white-out to remove my name and my father's name from the chart. It did not make sense to leave myself there with my father's family removed.

As I tried to rehang the elaborate chart, the frame slipped, breaking the glass.

I felt my skin pierce from the fragment of a small overlooked shard.

The slashed skin produced drops of blood – no longer red, but inky black. My hands trembled as my fingers faded before my eyes.

About the Author

Cyndie Goins Hoelscher is of Croatan Native American descent and shares her heritage with her Lumbee cousins in North Carolina. She earned her BA: History at Texas A&M University Kingsville and studied anthropology under Dr. Miguel Latham. Her non-fiction work has been recognized in USA Today; Margaret Walker Creative Writing Awards, College Language Association, Spellman College, Birmingham, Alabama; and Phi Theta Kappa Diversity Hallmark Award, Elizabethtown, Pennsylvania. Her poetry and fiction have been published in the Birmingham Journal for Arts, Cezanne's Carrot and Writer's Digest. She lives with her husband Ronnie and their furbaby, Lady Tiva von Hoelscher in Corpus Christi, Texas.

ANNA'S SECOND CHANCE

By Jonathon Cromack

Anna Crawford gazed over the street below. Glass shop fronts gleamed underneath black and white timber framed and red brick houses. She watched as shoppers ambled by, loaded with shopping bags; suited office workers hurried along clutching sandwiches and coffee, or talking, with arms waving, into mobile phones. In the midst of this hasty, mercantile scene, the timeless spire of Old St Alkmund's Church soared skyward, stabbing blackly into the mottled white sky. Upon it climbed a figure, an ant-like body tentatively scaling the stones. Anna knew that this man was about to fall to his death. She had seen it countless times before. In fact, truth be told, he was already dead.

The figure was a workman clad in buff leather who was hauling himself upwards using metal foot and hand holds set into the stone; he had no scaffolding or safety harness. Every now and then, he would pause and wave down to someone below. Taking a slow, careful grasp on each metal loop, he steadily climbed straight up towards the pinnacle. The narrower and more precarious the spire became, the more care he took with his progress, and the less concerned he was with his comrades on the ground.

As Anna squinted up from her seat on the churchyard bench, the figure reached the very top and, gripping with his knees astride the narrow steeple, he reached up towards a now non-existent weather vane. At this point, things took a bizarre turn. The man's whole body visibly jerked and then froze as though shocked by something. He seemed to stare at something on the brickwork in front of his face. He cowered back and uttered some single fearful cry, and then began to hurry back downward; but this time without his former care and attention. In his haste, he missed his grasp on one of the metal loops which caused him to fall back. He scrabbled desperately, but the angle of his body was now such that he was out of reach of the loops. As though in slow motion, the man plummeted backwards, thrashing wildly into the empty breeze. He cried out in a desperate, echoing scream as he dropped out of view behind pitched rooftops and chimney pots. A sickening wet thud preceded a sound like a shower of heavy raindrops on concrete.

"He saw the Devil's claw marks," Anna mumbled to herself without expression, except for the single teardrop which ran to nothing down her cheek.

***

Anna had once been told that her unique 'gift of sight' had been bestowed on her for a reason, and that one day that reason would be revealed to her. She gradually became secretly obsessed with reports of ghostly phenomena; scouring libraries and small bookshops for rare, obscure books and newspaper cuttings to take home and study meticulously. Within those pages, she hoped to find some path which might lead her to the answers that she craved. The highlight of her year came in the autumn, around Halloween, when she looked forward to attending one of the annual public ghost walks through the old town.

It was a damp November evening when Anna attended her seventh and final ghost walk. She merged unnoticed into the group of tightly clinging couples, giggling teenagers, and retired tourists nursing soggy maps. The tour guide was a tall man dressed eccentrically in a long waxed jacket and matching fedora hat, who introduced himself as Raymond. The group was led along dark, sleepy streets and narrow passageways to peer up at august timber framed buildings and fine Victorian houses.

Anna would occasionally see the subjects of the tour - a shadowy child trapped at an upper window of a burning room; a smoky grey lady waiting sadly and eternally for her suitor at the bottom of a twisting ballroom staircase; or numerous dark, looming figures standing nearby, watching sinisterly from the shadows. Anna never mentioned what she saw - she guessed that most of the group assumed, from her silent nature and the way she would often gaze into space, that she was odd or eccentric and best left to herself.

As the disjointed rainbow of waterproof nylon was gazing up at the spire of St. Alkmunds, the guide took his place on a low wall in front; he paused and took a deep breath to begin the story:

"In 1791, a local steeplejack by the name of Henry Diarimple had been drinking at the Queen's Arms just over the road."

All eyes turned to a narrow street, at a whitewashed pub

bathed in orange light.

"He made a bet with his fellows that he could climb this steeple of 184 feet, and turn the weathercock. Unfortunately, because he was so drunk, he never made it to the top, falling to his death below."

A singular murmur of ill-judged laughter morphed into a self-conscious cough.

"No!" murmured Anna, quietly.

"Some say that, on occasion, his ghost can still be seen making that fateful climb..."

As the faces squinted harder up at the tower, hoping to witness something extraordinary, Anna seized the moment. Her voice seemed loud as it cut through the murky air.

"No! You're wrong. He wasn't drunk." She had to shout above the dripping rain. "That's not what made him fall. It was shock. I've seen him myself, many times. I see these things. He thought he saw the Devil's claw marks on the stonework... you know...? The old legend. He believed!"

Some of the group shifted their weight from one leg to the other, while others looked around, bored. Most of them ignored her completely. The guide removed his hat, inspected the sodden brim, and without looking up, said: "The details of all these accounts are in my book 'Ghostly Tales of a Medieval town'. Please get yourselves a copy. Everything's in there."

The freezing rain had become heavier as the tour ended and

the group split into small, whispering clusters that dispersed like breezy autumn leaves for a drink or for home. Anna waited until she was alone, then she gazed up at the old town-hall clock, oblivious to the persistent rain. She began the long walk home as one of the church bells announced the hour, in its deep sombre tone.

***

After another unremarkable week at work, Anna arrived at the town library on Saturday morning. She headed straight to the Local History section situated within a corner alcove and scanned the shelves. There were two copies of the tour guide Raymond Cunningham's book; she leafed through the pages of one, smelling the newness of the printing. She took the book and seated herself, alone, at one of the study tables.

Though she was well acquainted with the reports and sightings that she read, she came to a section on more recent phenomena - new ground for Anna. She settled herself to read about grey shapes and so-called 'orbs' in dark cellars and old houses...

Same old! Same old!

She scanned her eyes over the pages to see what, in her opinion, had wrongly been written about the ghostly Steeplejack of St. Alkmund's, but her attention was drawn to a chapter cataloguing poltergeist activity - newer accounts of moving objects and lights mysteriously switching on and off during the night.

Then something caught her eye.

She sat bolt upright in the chair, tensed and focused. It was a fresh report which involved the very building in which she worked! She read:

The former Victorian prison house, now Wood and King's Chartered Accountant's, is subject to a recent poltergeist manifestation. Stationery has been seen to walk itself around the offices and corridors. Cups of coffee and tea are reported to have been found upon desks when nobody has made them, and employees have been aware of an invisible presence. The employees feel that this is a friendly and helpful ghost who tries to contribute to the daily grind. Some of them who have been employed for a number of years call the spirit 'Anna', claiming that this is the spirit of their old colleague and clerk, Anna Crawford, who unfortunately died tragically this year. Perhaps 'Anna' is returning to the place of work she liked most...

Anna blinked as the electric lights hummed around her. A floorboard slowly creaked somewhere above. She tried to read the passage again, but the words seemed to hold no meaning.

OH GOD, OH GOD, OH GOD!!

The unthinkable idea hit her like a blow to the head. She flung the book away from her across the table as though it was infected. Raising herself slowly onto weak legs, she wandered around the deserted table, trailing her fingertips over its cool edge. She feared and dreaded what truth might confront her around the corner, though deep within her mind, she already knew.

There were two female librarians standing behind the issuing desk scanning books, making electronic pinging noises. A young man was rotating a rack of DVD's on its revolving unit which squeaked irritatingly. A young mother with a child's pram was standing by a shelf, studying a book. Anna stood close to the girl, craving to be near someone; she pretended to scrutinise the rows of book spines until she felt able to speak. Clearing her throat and in a weak voice which cut into the silence, she simply said: "Excuse me."

The girl made no response.

Anna's stomach tightened. She repeated herself, louder this time, looking up at the girl's face. The girl simply leaned over the pram and fussed over the child inside, oblivious to Anna who scurried over to the issue desk.

"Excuse me."

The two librarians continued with their pinging.

"Hello..."

No response. The women resumed a hushed conversation about last night's Coronation Street.

Anna turned and fled the library to escape the choking heat. As she glanced back towards the building, she saw, through the window panes, blazered schoolboys milling around a blackboard like a swarm of maroon bees - a scene from two hundred years ago when the building had been a school. Their grinning faces looked sinister and cruel. She ran on into the busy streets, among the crowds of shoppers.

A huddle of teenage girls walked towards her joking and teasing happily with each other.

"Hello there..." Anna blurted.

The girls ignored her.

She reached out to grab one of the girl's shoulders as they passed by, but she clutched only a handful of disappointing emptiness. Stepping backwards, shocked, Anna accidentally moved into the path of another one of the girls, into a flurry of dark hair and red check cotton. She flinched and began instinctively to mumble an apology but, impossibly, there was no impact.

Looking back, the girls had passed through and were walking away.

Anna ran along the bustling street shouting out words, phrases, insults; but she may as well have been shouting at a running projection screen. Catching her reflection in a mobile-phone shop window, she stopped dead and stared at the image. *Thank God* - she recognised her familiar petite form, her tweed jacket and dark, tied-back hair. *I'm still here!*

She stumbled forwards into the cold pane, slammed both of her arms onto the glass and rested her head onto them. She choked on sobs as her breath misted the glass. *At least solid objects are real,* she thought, laughing bitterly through her tears.

***

As Anna lay in bed, listening to the drone of passing traffic and the occasional laugh or shout from the street outside, she tried to make some sense of her new existence as a ghost, spirit, or whatever she was. It was as though she had been shifted to some alternative radio wavelength. Perhaps there were thousands, millions of souls - living and dead - existing on earth simultaneously, but on different *wavelengths?* Perhaps there was an infinite number of different wavelengths and sometimes they would touch or overlap so the dead could see others who were dead, or the living could mingle among them – ghosts, as they were called. Did human consciousness ever end? Did her psychic gift have some bearing on this? Her mind swarmed with these questions; questions she could not answer.

She now saw the barrenness of her life stretched out behind her. She had kept so much of herself locked away inside; always living her life in hope of a better future.

She twisted and turned in bed. It wasn't all her fault though; much of her younger life had been devoted to looking after her mother in their tiny Victorian house. Myotonic Dystrophy they had called it. She was only fifteen when she found herself rushing home to cook and clean every day straight from work. Then there was the exhausting ritual of daily exercise sessions bending and stretching her mother's legs where muscles gradually became weaker and joints stiffer. She remembered her mother's refusal to accept the use of a wheelchair as the illness became worse. Those times, she remembered her mother falling to the floor, too weak to use crutches, yet refusing Anna's help to pick her up - flinging her arms out viciously. Anna shuddered at the memory of being woken up at night to the sound of smashing; rushing downstairs to be confronted by the pitiful sight of her mother dragging herself around the kitchen among broken crockery while ranting and sobbing drunkenly.

There had always been shopping or washing to do, carpets to vacuum or cooking. Anna had kept herself busy to stop her mind from wandering. Could she have done more for her mother when she was in those low spells? Was she wrong to have gone against her mother's wishes and insisted on a wheelchair? Should she have accepted the offer of outside help, even though her mother had so vehemently opposed it?

Don't know! Don't know! Had to keep busy! Keep busy!

Anna's eyes followed the ghostly headlights as they moved across the bedroom curtains. She realised that she had had no opportunity for social activities, which over the years had developed into a lack of inclination. Young men from her school and college had shyly asked her out on dates, but it had always been easier to refuse them straight out. After all, there was her mother to think about.

She figured that now at fifty-five, the prospect of finding a partner and perhaps marrying had sailed over the horizon long ago, though there had always been hope. She forced herself to face the unavoidable fact that she had let life slip through her fingers like sand. Now any chance to right this crushing wrong had also fallen away forever.

***

Anna opened up the heavy blue ledger and began marking off expenses. Her well-practiced hands moved with croupier-like dexterity. She had done this routinely for twenty years, but things were different now. She could go anywhere she liked, she was invisible; she could just keep walking in any direction and see where it led - into a stranger's house, across a busy road, even walk off a high building... no. The thought gave her an icy shudder.

She dropped the pen and looked about her, at her colleagues scattered around the spacious office. They had always seemed too wrapped up in themselves to pay any attention to her. She had often passed them silently and awkwardly in the narrow corridors, not daring to lift her eyes from the floor. Anna wheeled back her chair and watched them closely. Some frowned hard at their computers, others typed away, swearing at the screen. She noticed a group of four twenty-something's who were gathered around the water-cooler looking around themselves suspiciously like naughty schoolchildren. Anna left her seat and crept over to eavesdrop. They were talking about the manager, Andrew, how he habitually smoothed his eyebrows, brushing his knuckles over one and then the other. Anna smiled to herself as she pictured him doing this.

"He's a bit stuffy," one of them, a girl with red hair, was saying.

"He's alright," commented the other girl, who had large hooped earrings.

"It's his professional formality. You've got to respect that," agreed one of the men.

"I don't trust him. He's a creep," Red Hair argued.

Anna felt herself bursting to tell them that she had worked with Andrew for twenty years; she had always found him to be a true gentleman. He had been one of the few people in her life that she had felt comfortable around. They had worked together intimately on a daily basis since she had first started all those years ago; their relationship had been strictly professional of course, but she appreciated their shared need for organisation and tidiness. They both had a love of nature - she had often seen him at the office windows watching the autumn squirrels or the spring rabbits as they ran free outside. She had to admit to herself that she had liked him.

"He's been off sick for a while now," commented the second man.

The others nodded.

"I wonder if we'll ever see him again. He's retiring soon, or so I've heard," he said.

A surge of disappointment flooded into Anna; she wanted to learn more of this.

"Good," said Red Hair indignantly, "I'll be glad to be rid of him."

Anna felt an urge to swipe the young woman, but she knew that any action would be futile. She had to concede an unfamiliar feeling welling up inside - a strong loyalty to another human being. Ironically, it made her feel... alive.

She wished that she had some inkling of the nature of her own death and at what point in time she had died. 'Tragically' it had said in Cunningham's book. They say that the mind can block out the most traumatic events from memory, but then, it made no difference now.

***

Some days later as Anna was sorting through a huge stack of letters, she noticed someone enter the single doorway of the small, windowless filing room. It was Adam, an incredibly tall and gawky junior accountant who had not worked long at Wood and King's. As he looked up, he suddenly stopped dead, threw back his head and stared at the envelopes in Anna's hand.

Anna's breath caught in her throat. She surged towards him. "Adam...?"

She waved a hand instinctively in front of his face but he continued to gaze through her, unseeing. Anna stepped back, reached out and flung a few of the letters from the shelf. Adam twitched his head in their direction and watched, open mouthed, as they scattered to the floor.

"Adam. Can you see me?" Hope surged. She picked up another handful of letters and flung them into the air to fall like giant confetti. This was too much for Adam who fled the room, the door slamming behind him as Anna started to call out. She grabbed as many envelopes as she could fit into both hands and hurried from the room. She burst into the sleepy boredom of the office, noticing Adam leaning on a desk, sipping from a plastic cup. With a determined yell, Anna flung the envelopes into the air using all her strength, feeling a surge of freedom in this mad, child-like act. The letters scattered outwards and fluttered down like a flock of doves. She prayed that maybe she was somehow getting through at last, but nobody stirred from the slumber of their work. Even Adam merely continued to sip, mournfully unaware. She looked around, hoping for some relief from this disappointment. She rushed back into the filing room.

The envelopes were back in a stack where she had left them on a table. It was as though she had never taken them away. She shook her head in confusion and then scurried back out again, exhausted.

There were no letters littering the open-plan office. Everything was as it should have been - the hushed voice of someone talking on the telephone some distance away, keyboards tapping, and the monotonous hum of the air conditioning. Anna stood blinking and alone in the centre of the room. The fleeting moment of hope had passed.

***

The turning point for Anna came unexpectedly one morning when she slipped into the office of her former boss, Andrew, to start her routine tidy-up. He was unexpectedly sitting at his desk studying a letter. He looked up as Anna appeared through the doorway, and was on his feet in an instant, flinging the chair back to slam against the wall behind him. With pen in hand, he gawped.

"Anna?"

Anna dropped her armful of letter trays with a horrible plastic clatter and the two stood like mannequins staring blankly at each other over the polished wooden desk.

"Where have you been?" asked Andrew "They said that you'd... died. Months ago?"

"I did." Anna said simply.

He smoothed his knuckles over each eyebrow quickly. His lips moved, trying to form absent words.

Anna bent down to retrieve the letter trays from the floor, trying to think what to say, when a thought occurred to her. "Oh, God!" she said, "Oh, no. Andrew. No." She straightened herself, "Has anyone spoken to you or acknowledged you in any way this morning?" she asked.

"I live alone, Anna. I came straight into the office, so, no.

Why, what're you getting at?"

"Will you go into the office and say hello to the staff? Will you do that for me? Please."

"What... Why... Anna? What's going on?"

He looked perplexed - taken aback by the sudden re-appearance of Anna, her bizarre reaction, and now by the uncharacteristic concern that she was showing. Keeping his eyes fixed on her, he walked around the desk and, straightening himself self-consciously, he left the room, shutting the door softly behind him.

When Andrew eventually returned, his face was pale and gaunt; he stared at the carpet, deep in thought, his hand lingering on the door handle.

"They didn't seem to see me," he said quietly. "It's as though I wasn't there." He turned and looked meaningfully at Anna, "You can see me though, can't you, Anna? This isn't a joke. I mean... I am here!"

Anna nodded gravely but said nothing, keeping her eyes fixed.

"What's going on, Anna? If you know something, please tell me."

He didn't wait for her to answer but went back to his desk, lifted the telephone and punched out some numbers from memory. After a few seconds, he spoke, "Hello Clive, its Andrew. I just wanted to ask... Can you hear me? Hello, Clive... CLIVE...?" he replaced the receiver. He dialed again, this time speaking to someone called Claire, but the result was much the same. He turned again to Anna, standing in the corner wringing her hands - a lonely figure brimming with helpless compassion. The man's eyes looked glassy, "What's happening, Anna?" he asked, his voice beginning to choke.

Anna walked towards the pathetic figure with his head in his hands, and she did something, for her, quite remarkable. Tentatively but assuredly, she placed a comforting hand on the dead man's shoulder.

***

Anna spent the remainder of that day and those of the following weeks at work, watching over Andrew. She felt useful being able to provide words of support to another lonely, lost soul like herself. Of course, he could not accept that he was actually dead at first, but the world around him gave enough cold, constant proof. Anna explained her theory of 'Wavelengths' which seemed to offer some explanation.

She would notice him staring vacantly out of a window, mumbling to himself as he battled angrily with some inner emotion. Other times, he would be away from work for several days only to re-appear looking haunted and tired; he would sometimes be sharp and snappy, rebuking her words of comfort, though he always apologised afterwards for this brusqueness. Anna assumed that everyone coped with trauma in their own way and that this was merely his way.

***

A rare smile crossed the face in the mirror as Anna ran a comb through her ebony hair one spring morning. Perhaps she should ask Andrew to accompany her for a walk on Sunday. They could go anywhere they wanted; sneak into a theatre; wander around a museum after hours. They could secretly watch the world of the living together, unseen, within their own intimate, shared perspective.

Yes. She would ask him. Perhaps, at last, her time had come. She had been given a second chance to live life, even if it was within death.

When Anna arrived at work later that morning, Andrew was shuffling papers at his desk. He smiled shyly as she entered the room and greeted her with genuine pleasure, "There's something I want you to see," he said.

"What's that?" she asked cautiously, trying to conceal her tingling excitement.

He gestured for her to follow him into the open office where workers were draping their coats over chairs, stretching, yawning and leaning over desks to switch on computer screens for the day ahead. None of them were aware as the fleeting pair glided to the far wall where a small brass plaque was fixed. The couple stood together as the morning sun shone warmly through the window. Anna read the engraving on the plaque and felt Andrew's hand gently take her own:

In memory of two long-standing and loyal employees of Wood and King's. Gentle and kind colleagues who shall always be remembered. Both sadly died within only a few months of each other. May they find peace forever, Andrew and Anna.

Anna looked up at Andrew who still held her hand.

The perfect moment to ask had come.

The man's grip was firm. She laughed up at him but his eyes were snake-like and narrow.

"What's wrong, Andrew?" she asked, a little unsure.

"They can't see us, can they?" he asked as he smoothed one eyebrow, then the other.

"No. Of course not..." she forced a laugh. "You know that..." her tone was questioning, unsteady.

"That's good. Don't you think?" He still held her hand tightly, his eyes fixed on her own. "You don't remember, do you?" he asked.

Something wasn't right. Had she misjudged the situation? He was smiling, but his mouth was twisted, mocking.

"What do you mean? Why do you say that?" She wanted to be alone now, to re-group her feelings. "Remember what?"

Andrew continued to smile smugly as he made a grab for Anna's free arm. He pulled her towards him, roughly.

"I always liked you Anna, but you were always such a prude!"

He twisted her wrists making her wince, and then he leered into her face, his nose wrinkled into a sneer.

"We stayed late, working on the Fanshaw account; we *had* to make that deadline - you and I in my office. I had a bottle of Cava, just to be friendly, to pass the time. Of course, you didn't want any. *Don't* you remember?"

Anna frowned and shook her head.

"Things got out of hand, I'll admit that, but you were always such a prig." He laughed. "You had one of your panics and started shouting. I had to slap you a few times to shut you up."

As he threw his head back and laughed, Anna tried to twist away, pleading for him to stop, but his grip was strong. He continued to laugh freely, his confidence surging amidst her powerlessness.

"You fell back into the wall and hit your head. You passed out. I honestly didn't mean to kill you." He smiled with amusement as he remembered. "You went into the river that same night. When they dragged you out, they presumed it was suicide, of course. Well, you were never quite right, were you?"

He was so close to Anna's face now, that she could see the cobwebs of purple blood vessels stretching across his cheeks, and smell his putrid breath. He leaned delicately forward as if to kiss her, but then drew back and released her at the last moment, splaying his arms out widely in a playful show of defenselessness. This caused Anna to fall back to the floor, her head thudding against the edge of a desk.

As shock gave way to terror, she tried to claw up the side of the desk, desperately trying to alert the strong, kindly looking young man talking on the telephone. But of course, he was oblivious to her peril. Andrew loomed over her, kicking her away and back to the floor. He kneeled over her, pinning her arms down to her sides.

"No one can help you, Anna," he sneered. "You're all mine now, and you know what?"

He stood up again, placing the sole of one shoe heavily onto her abdomen. The sadistic smile had returned to his face as he unbuckled his leather belt and snaked it away with one hand.

"We've got all the time in the world."

About the Author

Jonathon Cromack declined to provide a biography.

.

WHAT LIES BELOW

By Amber M. Simpson

Livi's mind slowly swam up from the depths of murky nothingness. She was lying on a hard cement floor, that much she could tell. The first thing she felt was wet; the second was cold. Every inch of her ached.

What the hell happened to me? Livi wondered, struggling to peel her heavy eyelids open and roll over to her hands and knees. *What the fuck have I done this time?*

It was pitch black and there was a strong metallic scent. The last thing she could remember was fighting with Adam in the motel room, then locking herself in the bathroom.

She heard a splash and droplets of warm water rained down on her head and back. Livi's breath caught in her throat and her pulse quickened. She wasn't at the motel's indoor pool, was she?

A memory began to materialize in her mind. Adam had brought her to the pool, tried to coax her into going for a quick dip with him, even though he *knew* she hated the water. She'd refused to get in the pool and had stormed off to their room, shaking. When he followed her, she'd flown at him, screaming, pummeling his chest with tight fists. How dare he take her there, how dare he try to make her swim?! Then she'd locked herself in the bathroom, ignoring his insistent pounding and pleas at the door.

But they *had* gone back to the room. So why was she at the pool? And where were all the lights? She peered through the darkness around her, waiting for her eyes to adjust. Yes, she could see the pool just a few feet to her right, pale fragments of dim light bouncing off the water's surface.

Livi pushed up onto her knees, her mind spinning, trying to make sense of things. Was she sleep walking again? She hadn't sleep walked in over a year, though once there was a time she was doing it almost every night.

Unbidden, a face floated up from her subconscious, a sweet little face with floating yellow braids and wide open eyes of baby blue.

No, no, NO! Livi shook her head and tugged violently at her dark wet hair. She wouldn't think of Jenny now, she *couldn't.*

She took a deep breath and tried to get her bearings. No, she hadn't sleep walked, her head was too fuzzy, too heavy. She must have left the bathroom at some point, wandered down here after partying too hard and passed out. They had brought plenty of liquor with them and a baggy full of the fine white dust Livi had recently grown fond of. That was it. It wasn't the first time in the last few years that she'd numbed herself to ease the pain and woken up in a strange place she had no recollection of going to.

311

Jenny's face popped back up, but Livi shoved it forcefully down.

As she rubbed her temples, thinking, there was another splash in the water, this one huge. An entire wave drenched her. Gasping and sputtering, Livi sprang to her feet, stumbling away from the pool. She found the wall and groped around until she felt a light switch and flicked it up, the sudden burst of bright light blinding her momentarily. Covering her eyes, she turned, pressing her back against the wall and peering between her fingers.

She screamed.

There was the motel pool, sure enough, but it wasn't filled with water. It was filled with blood. She looked down at her arms and body and saw she was covered in it. From the center of the pool a series of dark red bubbles formed on the surface, then popped. Whatever had made that huge splash was still down there.

"What the fuck?!" Livi cried in terrified disbelief, whipping her head around, searching for a way out.

There, at the other end of the room was a set of metal double doors, a neon green exit sign hanging above them. She bolted for them, staying close to the wall, her heart pounding a frantic beat in her ears. She didn't dare look back at the blood pool.

When she heard the wet, gloppy sound of *its* body climbing out of the pool, she choked on another scream. She ran faster, her bare feet slapping painfully against the hard cement.

She was running and running. The doors were right *there,* so why did it feel like she was running in place?

Behind her, the thing from the pool chittered like a strange insect from another planet. She could *smell* it, a mixture of filth, rotted meat, and blood; the sharp metallic scent she'd first detected upon waking.

"Help! Adam!" she screamed, the fear a razor-sharp knife twisting in her gut.

She ran into a beach chair and tumbled over it, skinning her knees on the concrete. Ahead of her, one of the doors slowly clicked open and a wave of relief washed over her.

It was Adam! He'd come looking for her!

But it wasn't Adam with his unruly mop of dark curls and mischievous crooked grin. It was a little girl with yellow braids and eyes of baby blue.

Jenny.

"Get up!" Jenny cupped her hands around her small, pink mouth and shouted. "Don't let it touch you! Run!" She turned and ran, her long blonde braids bouncing on her back.

Livi used every last ounce of strength to push herself from the floor and sprint out into the hallway, the heavy metal door slamming shut behind her with a loud bang. On the other side, the pool monster slammed against it so hard, Livi could feel the vibration rattle her rib cage. But the door did not open. She heard its strange tittering; saw its shadow moving back and forth through the gap at the bottom of the doors. She turned to find Jenny at the end of the long, carpeted hallway, staring at her.

"This can't be real," Livi whispered to the little girl watching her. "You're dead... you... you died."

Jenny raised a finger to her lips in a shushing gesture and shook her head, then disappeared around the corner.

"Wait!" Livi cried, stumbling after her. "Stop, please!" She made it around the corner just in time to see Jenny's braids float around the next. She chased her, the ceiling lights flickering wildly. The hallway tilted and swayed like a ship on rough waters. Livi staggered with the sickening motion, bumping roughly into the walls, knocking a picture frame down here, jarring her shoulder on a wall sconce there. Nauseous, bile rose in the back of her throat. Just as she thought she could take no more, the hallway lights winked out completely, throwing her once again into total darkness.

She could hear the metal doors to the pool crash open, slamming against the walls in a booming wave of sound that washed down the halls. Her ears rang.

Choking back a terror-stricken sob, Livi continued to stagger down the hall. The lights flickered back on and Livi gasped when she saw the walls now dripping with blood. The lights flickered. The blood was gone.

Again and again, as she struggled down the hall, the lights went on and off, the walls bloody then bare, as if they couldn't make up their mind. She felt like she was trapped in some sick, twisted fun house.

The monster was close, its sickening little sounds turning into a full-blown squeal, reminding her of a stuck pig.

Finding a door, she burst inside, desperate to be out of the hall.

She locked the door then backed away, nearly jumping out of her skin when she heard a soft voice say her name. Swinging around with a gasp, she found Jenny sitting on the edge of the bed. Shocked, Livi realized it was the room she had rented with Adam. There was the empty liquor bottle on the dresser, the baggy of coke spilled out all over the night stand. How was that possible? She remembered their room being three floors above the pool.

None of that mattered though, as she crumpled to her knees before Jenny and held her in her arms, sobbing, stroking the long soft braids against her back.

"I'm so sorry," Livi whimpered, holding the little girl - her little sister - and crushing her to her chest. "It's all my fault, I let you die. I'm so sorry, Jenny. I'm sorry."

She leaned back and looked at Jenny, wanting to see the face that had haunted her the past three years. The face she'd last seen when she had run, panicked, into the bathroom, turning her over in the water, but too late. She had been too late. She had left her too long. Pale, so pale, her blue eyes wide open, not peaceful, but terrified, her yellow braids floating around her head. Jenny had slipped trying to get out of the bathtub because Livi had left her for too long.

"It wasn't your fault," Jenny said in the small, sweet voice Livi missed so much.

But it *was* her fault, and Adam's, for dropping by after she'd told him not to. Her parents had left her in charge of Jenny that day and had specifically told her NO Adam. But there he'd been, smiling crookedly at her through the screen door as she'd answered his knock, patting the rolled joint in his shirt pocket.

"Miss me?" he'd teased, stepping into the living room and grabbing her around the waist.

"I told you not to come here! I'm babysitting!" Livi had protested weakly, allowing him to catch her lips with his. Before she knew it, he'd had her pinned to the couch, his lips all over her, making her forget who she was, much less where she was.

Five minutes went by, ten minutes, then fifteen. When she'd finally come up for air, she'd remembered Jenny, and sprang from the couch, her insides clenching sickeningly.

"It was coming for me that day no matter how it happened," Jenny whispered against Livi's neck, bringing her back to the present.

"What was coming for you? What are you talking about, sweetie? *What* was coming?" Livi was aware of her voice growing sharp and shrill but could do nothing to control it.

"It's coming for you now," Jenny said cryptically. "It wants to go back with you."

"Back where? What's coming?" Livi cried.

Jenny reached out and pressed her fingers to Livi's forehead and the memory flooded her brain. The fight with Adam, locking herself in the bathroom, filling the tub and getting in. Watching drowsily as the water around her turned a faint pink then a dark red. Letting her heavy head slip below the surface. Seeing Jenny's face one last time.

Jenny took her hand away from Livi's head and pointed at the bathroom where the door slowly swung open of its own accord. There was the tub, filled with blood, Livi's dark hair floating on the surface.

"No!" Livi cried, clutching at Jenny, pleading. "I don't want to go back! I want to be with you!"

"You will be," Jenny said in a deep and unfamiliar voice. It was no longer the voice of a little girl. It was the voice of a monster.

Livi watched, too horrified to breathe, as Jenny's eyes and ears began to gush blood. The little girl smiled. Her lips began to part and spread across her face, her mouth stretching wider and wider until all Livi could see were two rows of long pointed teeth, jagged and gleaming. Livi screamed just as the pool monster crashed into the room and Jenny struck, tearing into the tender flesh of Livi's neck.

***

Livi splashed up from the bathtub, gasping for air, as Adam burst through the bathroom door, breaking the lock, his eyes wild and frantic.

"Livi!" he screamed, pulling her out of the bloody tub and wrapping a towel around her wrists. "It's OK, baby, it's OK," he murmured in her ear. "I'm here, I've got you, it's OK."

"Jenny," Livi moaned, her neck throbbing. She pushed Adam away to race on shaky legs to the mirror. Her neck was littered with at least a dozen gaping puncture wounds. Staring at her reflection in shock, her vision began to blur and go red as her eyes and ears began to gush blood. By the time Adam came up behind her, holding her and crying into her back, Livi was smiling. Her mouth began to stretch, growing wider and wider, her long pointed teeth gleaming in the bathroom light.

About the Author

Amber M. Simpson has been writing short stories and poetry since the age of ten. Lover of all things horror and fantasy, she writes mainly in these genres, often with a touch of romance thrown in for fun. Amber lives in Kentucky with her husband and their two crazy but loving little boys.

DANIEL'S SCREAM

By Patrick Winters

Some say that after death, the dead stay quiet; they move on. It's not always so. Sometimes, they linger.

They long to be heard. They *need* to be heard. Most will only ever whisper, others speak clearly. But some *scream*. I can attest to that. My name is James Whitfield, and I have heard the dead.

***

Daniel Wilson was the kind of kid that never deserved the terrible things that happened to him.

He was quiet, intelligent, respectful—all the qualities that make one a target to ignorant and brutish bullies in high school. At the age of sixteen, Daniel was dreadfully lanky, pathetically short, and terribly soft-spoken. He had a penchant of looking down at the ground, staring blankly through thick, round glasses, rarely making eye contact with the few who spoke to him. When he walked, he moved swiftly, maneuvering his way through heavy crowds of people like flowing water over rocks in a creek. His hair was always combed neatly, kept very short and proper. His clothes were never colorful or expressive in any way; he typically wore khaki pants and beige or white t-shirts or dress shirts.

If there had ever been a more successful student at Gregory's Bluff High School, no one could rightly confirm the notion. Daniel was a straight A student. If he had ever even received a B minus, the world may have stopped spinning on its axis. Whenever he wasn't in class watching the teacher's every movement like a hawk, Daniel had his nose buried in a book, collecting any and all information he could. For all anyone knew, he could have been a NASA super-computer on legs.

Devoted entirely to his studies – and appearing to be physically incapable of speaking to anyone with an ounce of confidence – Daniel kept to himself, off the radars of the majority of the student body. I was a part of that small minority that did take heed of Daniel's existence. Having known him since elementary school and being neighbors since junior high, I was well aware of him, though I, too, paid little attention. We only spoke in the halls or cafeteria, just long enough to say "hello" before quickly walking away. In retrospect, I wish I'd have said more to him when I had the chance.

So there was Daniel in a nutshell: a brilliant, shy, humble young man that longed for nothing but quiet times to study and read peacefully. On the opposite end of the spectrum was Jason Woodruff, a towering, muscular, and boastful delinquent who loved nothing more than tormenting poor Daniel. At six feet four inches tall, and with a bulky body like a Hummer, Jason was always bad-mouthing someone or something, throwing in curse words and derogatory terms right and left simply for the sake of uttering them. If it wasn't football, alcohol, or nude women, Jason didn't take any interest in it. Except, of course, for Daniel; the one other thing Jason did take interest in.

Jason made sport of ridiculing and tormenting Daniel. The lumbering bully could be seen pushing and shoving him into the lockers multiple times a day. Along with this misguided show of force came other similar, brutish attempts at showing supremacy over the weak and timid Daniel. Foul and insulting names were always in supply; I haven't the heart to repeat any of them.

But worst of all, were the beatings, regular enough that split lips and bruises on his thin, pale cheeks became a typical feature of Daniel's appearance. More than once, I had seen him cowering in a corner of a classroom or the cafeteria, attempting to cover the bruises and cuts on his face with an open book or his tiny hands. Hiding his shame seemed almost pointless; no one was looking anyway.

But nothing compared to that one fateful day in October, a week before Halloween, in Mrs. Carmichael's Literature class.

It was an average day. Mrs. Carmichael was delivering her lesson with more passion than the class had in listening to it. She stood at the front of the room, her graying hair done up in a beehive fashion, writing key-terms on the chalkboard. A fine layer of chalk dust covered her unappealing brown dress.

Jason, of course, was fooling around and flirting with the girls, paying the least attention of all. Daniel was sitting in the back mid-section of the room, his eyes fixed on the textbook in front of him. I sat in the back left corner, silent and out of the way – the perfect vantage point to witness all that was about to occur.

Tired of having her lessons ignored and disregarded by the class, Mrs. Carmichael decided to make an example of someone. That someone just had to be Jason Woodruff.

Jason was called on to answer Mrs. Carmichael's question about who wrote "The Legend of Sleepy Hollow." Not knowing the answer, Jason's face turned bright red as he answered with a mumbled, "Stephen King."

The whole class erupted in laughter while Mrs. Carmichael simply shook her head. For a brief moment, the tables had been turned on the school bully, and I remember taking in the laughter of my classmates with an odd mixture of emotion – partly pleasure, partly baited anxiety. All the while, Jason clenched his fists, glaring down at his desktop with a slanted, angered glance, saying nothing.

Courageously, Daniel raised his hand from the back of the room, breaking that bubble of protection and solitude he always kept around him. Mrs. Carmichael's face switched from a look of stony chastisement to a beaming smile. When she called on him, Daniel looked up slowly, and sheepishly uttered, "Washington Irving." Mrs. Carmichael praised Daniel, affirming his answer.

Jason turned around and glared back at Daniel, who quickly looked down and slumped in his seat. Jason glared at Daniel with that cold, steely stare for several more minutes. When he finally turned back around, he did something he'd never done before – he went the rest of the class period without speaking.

I sat there, trying to ignore what I had just seen in Jason's eyes – an unspoken declaration of war.

And with war come casualties.

***

As I said, Daniel and I lived next to each other. Our homes were in a small cul-de-sac called Silent Meadows, positioned at the edge of town, just on the brink of the countryside. Surrounding the cul-de-sac was a forest full of oak trees, where children went to play and teenagers went to partake in sexual rendezvous. This forest cut our little neighborhood off from the rest of town, making it a quiet, isolated place.

The school was only a mile away, so the teenagers who lived in Silent Meadows usually walked to school. Daniel and I were no exception. The quickest way to get there was straight through the forest, so every Monday through Friday, that was my route, often in a hurry to get to school on time. And every day, walking far enough behind me to prevent any conversation, was Daniel.

The pattern we had in getting to school was followed on the day of Jason Woodruff's embarrassment in Mrs. Carmichael's class. The pattern of going back home, however, was not.

I remember rushing out of the school's front entrance mere moments after the final bell rang, hurrying with the speed of a bullet shot from a gun. I was ready and eager to get myself home and unwind from the stresses and irritations of a high school Wednesday. In my rush, I only barely noticed that Daniel was nowhere in sight as I reached the edge of the woods. I brushed the realization away as quickly as it entered my mind, like a hand swatting at a fly too close to one's face. I entered the forest, the idea of coming home to a comfortable couch and a welcoming television enticing my teenage mind.

The occasional, cool winter breeze wafted through the limbs of the oak trees that surrounded me on every side, causing a faint rustling noise as the bare branches rubbed and scratched together. Like bare bone scraping against bare bone. Their leaves, long since fallen, lay scattered at my feet, brittle and dead. Each step I took found one or two of these leaves, and every time my foot came down, a harsh crunch seemed to echo with force through the stillness of the woods.

As I made my way through the forest, the occasional soft breeze transitioned to more frequent bursts of chilling, biting gusts. My pace quickened with each of these gusts, and soon enough, I found myself at the back door of my house. Quickly, I pulled out my house key, unlocked the door, bolted inside, and slammed it shut behind me.

I did not look to see if Daniel was anywhere in sight.

**

Later that night, after gorging myself on my mother's homemade dinner – a heaping helping of mashed potatoes, peas, freshly-baked rolls, and mouth-watering fried chicken – and after my father and I discussed in exuberance the Pittsburgh Steelers' defeat of the Baltimore Ravens the night before last, I settled into my room for the night, content as could be with no complaints in mind.

I was relaxed, full from a warm meal, and the growing darkness outside my bedroom window signified something to me. It was time to write.

I had always held aspirations of becoming a writer, and cold, dark nights were when I felt my creative juices flowing at their greatest rate. Something about the night soothed and relaxed me and put me in the apt mindset for crafting my "works," as I referred to them, trying to make my young, ignorant self seem already accomplished in writing. These works focused mostly on action and adventure: dragons and knights, spies and gadgets, that sort of thing. I wrote fun, enjoyable stories, their purpose nothing more than creating uproarious explosions and grand fights.

I had never fathomed the idea of writing such a tale as I am trying to spin for you, now.

I sat myself at my computer desk, switched on the small lamp sitting at the corner, pulled up my trusty Microsoft Word Processor, and began typing away, my mind set on crafting the next big bestseller. Ideas flowed from my mind, down to my scurrying fingers, and up onto the computer screen before me. The sound of the night was a symphony of clattering keys, whooshing wind against the window, and the faint voices of my parents sitting in the living room and conversing. It was the perfect soundtrack to my writing.

The only time my concentration broke from my fervent typing was to occasionally look out the window across the room from my writing desk. Sitting dead center in the wall, my 5'x 4' window was a portal of darkness. The sun had set, and with the shades pulled back, sheer black of night was the scene outside.

Staring at the black void served as a screen to my inner thoughts, a blank canvas in which I saw the scenes of my stories depicted in clarity. It helped me to better picture and craft each idea that found a home in my head, and in turn, a place in my stories.

That was how my night went. It became a pattern: type, swivel chair, look out the window, swivel chair back, type, repeat. How long I held close to this pattern, I'm not quite sure, as I didn't keep track of the time – I was on a roll. All I know is that the night continued to stretch on as I wrote my tale of adventure...

...and brandishing his sword, the knight stood defiant before the cave of the dragon. The horrid stench of sulfur and burnt flesh from the beast's victims reached the brave warrior's nose. The sight of discarded bones lying in piles at the cave's entrance did not shake the knight's determination in felling the dreaded creature within. He inched closer to the yawning mouth of the cavern, sword and shield held in steady grasp, ready for

glorious battle. Then, from deep within the cave…

A shrill sound broke the night. A spine-tingling, bone-chilling screech of a sound. I jumped in my seat, hairs standing on end as the noise rang in my ears. I swiveled my chair to face the window, realizing the sound had come from outside. It was not the wind. I knew that much, as the wind had died down as the night had crawled by. Even if the wind *had* been blowing, it surely couldn't make a sound like that.

Filled with such force and raw intensity, I didn't recognize it for what it was. At least, not at first. My breath stuck in my chest as the sound began to die off, trickling slowly to silence.

Wide-eyed, I stared at my window.

Pure darkness stared straight back. It was not until the sound had ceased that I could finally place what it was and where it came from: a scream. From somewhere out in the woods behind the house. A *human* scream.

It came again, more audible, and far more pain-riddled. My fingers ached as I clutched desperately at the arms of my chair, as if that act would defend me in some manner. My spine tingled as a chill crept up to the nape of my neck. That second terrible howl stretched on for what seemed like forever. It echoed in my mind, filling me with fear and amazement at its sheer intensity. Tears welled at the corners of my eyes.

Like its predecessor, the scream trailed off and slowed to a stop. Silence once again reigned. Like a figure carved of stone, I sat there, unmoving, unflinching. Seconds crawled by like the slow movement of a caterpillar, inching by with a measured sluggishness. I waited for yet another horrid scream. But one never came.

The wind began to stir outside, blowing against my window. I heard my parents down in the living room, my father clearly saying, "What the hell was that?"

***

After hearing the screams, my mother called the police in order to report the incident. She was flustered, shaking and speaking quickly, and I could tell my father was as well, though he tried to hide it. I was clearly not the only one affected by the awful screams.

The police informed my mother that a few other people from around the neighborhood had already called in to report hearing the screams. On a possible related note, Daniel Wilson's parents had called them to report that he hadn't come home from school.

An hour later, Daniel Wilson's body was found in the woods.

The police came out to investigate, and with news of Daniel's failure to come home from school, several of the adults from the neighborhood – including my own father – went out to help them.

After two hours of scouring the woods, Daniel was found,

somewhere near the heart of the woods, a short way off from the path we walked each day to get to and from school. According to my father, a police officer literally stumbled over Daniel's body while wading through a pile of dead leaves.

Having listened in on what the police taping off the area said, my father was able to glean some information concerning what had just become a murder case. It seemed that after school released that day, Mr. Cranston, the chemistry teacher, asked Daniel and a few other students to stay behind in order to help him with organizing the chemistry lab. Daniel agreed to help, staying with two other students until five o'clock. Mr. Cranston called the police to inform them of this as soon as he received word of Daniel's disappearance, shortly after the search began. The other two students' families called the police as well, corroborating Mr. Cranston's story, and saying that both students saw Daniel heading in the direction of the woods before they walked home in the opposite direction.

My father told us how badly Daniel's face was bruised, black and blue splotches covering it. The police had murmured that they believed Daniel was beaten to death. It was confirmed the next day that Daniel had indeed been brutally pummeled up until his dying breath. The coroner found that several of Daniel's ribs were broken, a few teeth were missing, and almost every inch of his body was covered in sickening bruises. He determined that Daniel had been hit numerous times with a strong clubbing weapon, possibly a heavy branch, or even a steel pipe. No matter the weapon, it was clearly no accident. Daniel was murdered, and his body was purposefully hidden within the pile of leaves.

According to the police, there was no suspect yet in mind.

After my father told my mother and me about this last little detail, I lumbered slowly to my room, those two words going through my mind over and over. *No suspect. No suspect. No suspect.*

A wave of thought and memory washed over my mind as I made my way sluggishly to the solitude of my room. I remembered how Daniel walked through school so sheepishly, so lonely, so undeserving of his tribulations. I remembered how his eyes would gaze at the floor, no emotion on his face save for a forlorn, blank stare. I remembered that class of Mrs. Carmichaels' – the one that seemed like ages ago, yet was only earlier that day. And with this memory came another: the cold, glaring stare of Jason Woodruff. A stare of utter hatred and unwarranted indignation. And it was this memory that forced those two words to keep flowing through my mind.

No suspect. No suspect. No suspect.

Finally, I remembered those few times – *those all too few times* – when I felt pity for Daniel, yet never said a thing to him in comfort or friendship. Even now, I remained silent. Despite how I was beginning to despise silence, I still clung to it out of some pathetic sense of being powerless to do anything.

When I reached my room and began to shut the door behind me, I could still hear my father and mother talking. My mother was saying how horrible the whole situation was and how no person deserved such a fate. My father agreed, and before my door closed and cut off their quiet voices, he mentioned seeing Daniel's face after the police officer who'd found him brushed the leaves away from his corpse.

Daniel's face was twisted in obvious agony, he said, wide-eyed in terror. And his mouth was agape in a silent, ghastly scream.

***

A week and its events passed by surprisingly quickly. The search for Daniel's killer went on, without much fruition. A few days after his body was discovered, Daniel's funeral took place. Although we did not attend the funeral, my parents and I went to the visitation out of respect. We were neighbors, after all, and it seemed like the right thing to do. I signed the guest book and gave my brief apologies and condolences to Daniel's parents. But I did not – *could not* – go up to Daniel's casket. I shied away from it as much as possible, refusing to even look directly at it. I had it in my head that if I looked at the open casket, Daniel's dead face would stare back at me, and I would hear those dreadful screams once again.

Besides what I'd heard from my father, I knew very little about the investigation of Daniel's murder. No other breaking news or revelations came to light. However, one interesting fact came to my attention through conversation with one of my school friends. Apparently, Jason Woodruff had been questioned as to his whereabouts that fateful Wednesday night. Nothing came of it, however. Jason stated he was at a party with friends at the time of Daniel's death. He named names, and each one corroborated his story. Nevertheless, I found little faith in the validity of Jason's story. I had known him long enough and had seen him do countless dirty-handed deeds to realize that alibis and lies were in constant supply to the vicious bully.

Life at school saw little change. For a place full of people that rarely paid attention to Daniel when he was there, it was no real surprise to see their lack of empathy and concern in his absolute absence. The only concern anyone ever worked up about the situation was the occasional mention of Daniel being the first of a serial killer's killing spree. The teachers did their best to quell any such talk amongst the student body, and even tried to prevent any talk about Daniel, period. The latter was, sadly, an easy enough job.

The school did not change. I, however, did.

I spoke little, even when I was among my friends. I developed a tendency to simply stare up at my teachers, looking, but not really listening. The only time I did listen was in the two classes I had with Jason Woodruff, and I did not listen to the teacher; I listened to Jason. His typical boasting and ignorant remarks continued as they always did. He fooled around in class, whispered insults and curses, and what's more, he seemed utterly at peace and resigned to do so. There was no sign of gnawing regret, no hint of remorse for any misdeed.

I was convinced he was guilty. Still, I said and did nothing.

In light of what happened, the school decided it was best that its students living in Silent Meadows no longer walked to or from school, as it was seen as a possible risk. So instead, I began to ride the school bus. Most of the kids saw it as an inconvenience. I saw it as a blessing. Just thinking of walking through those woods made sweat bead up on my brow and my stomach churn with fear. I'd hear those dying screams of Daniel's in my head, picture myself running through the trees, the screams growing louder and nearer as I desperately tried to get away from them. If I were to never go into those woods again, it would be too soon.

I found some solace in my writing. My practice of writing at night and in the dark, save for the small lamp being on, continued. I drew the shades to where they were almost closed, leaving an open gap no wider than an inch. I could write in the near-dark, but the thought of staring out that large window and seeing only darkness wasn't something I relished.

It had been two weeks since Daniel's untimely end when I finally continued where I had left off in my story.

Night had fallen, dinner was digesting in my stomach, and I sought to write – more so to calm my nerves and relax me than for the desire of writing my hopeful bestseller. Situating myself comfortably in my chair and being mindful to look towards the window as little as possible, I wrote…

Then, from deep within the cave, an ominous rumble echoed outwards, reverberating against the rocky walls. The knight felt the ground at his feet begin to shake. Peering into the wide mouth of the cave, the knight saw a faint red pinpoint of light forming in the darkness within. Heat poured out of the cave, filling the air. The pinpoint became a ball, the ball became the size of a shield, and within seconds, it seemed as if Hell itself were coming to battle the knight as flames spewed out of the cavern. The knight held up his shield to defend himself from the licking fire. He cautiously peered over the top of his shield. And lumbering forth from the darkness and the fire was the dragon.

It was gigantic in size, with blood-red scales covering its body and yellowish-orange covering its underbelly. Boney spines jutted out of its skull, nostrils flared as smoke came out of them, and teeth like knives were brandished in a snarling mouth. With eyes of shining amber, the beast glared at the knight in disgust, angered at the sight of the intruder, but overjoyed to have another meal. Rearing its scaly head and taking a vile breath into its monstrous lungs, the beast launched forward with a thunderous roar…

And then it happened. Like last time, without any warning, a haunting scream pierced the night. I exhaled in a rush of shock.

My hands clenched involuntarily, hovering above my keyboard. My body shook, and I slowly turned in my chair toward the window. I felt compelled to do so, though I'm not sure why – the thought of what I might see beyond the window frightened me incredibly. Nevertheless, I looked.

The horrible howl had ended by the time I was fully situated in front of my window, the small gap in the shades a straight, black line going down the center of the glass. It seemed the darkness was threatening to burst through the window and attack me. Standing at the window, a thought took hold of me: that scream had sounded familiar. It was almost exactly like the first scream I'd heard a week before – the desperate outcry of a dying Daniel Wilson. I say "almost" because it was strung out at the same rate and as high-pitched as the other night, containing just as much agony and defeat. But there was something off about it. It sounded hollow, like an echo or recording. It had what I can only describe as an *inhuman* quality to it.

Something inside me told me to brace myself for another scream, and sure enough, mere seconds later, a second scream rang out from the dark woods. And just like the last time, the second one was even more agonizing than the first. A lump formed in my throat as I held back a cry of fear. My chest heaved as I struggled to breathe. My eyes blinked in an uncontrollable flurry and began to water, tears threatening to burst out like a faulty dam.

As the scream dragged on, I covered my ears with my

hands. I stumbled back to my chair, leaning forward, trying to bury my face in my knees. I rocked back and forth, pathetically incapable of controlling my actions at this point. Madness was something I'd only known of in movies and stories. Looking back on it all, I believe I was on the verge of slipping into it myself. Perhaps being thrown in against my will.

Thankfully, before madness could be reached, the scream trailed off. But no respite came. Unlike the other right, a *third* scream immediately cut through the night.

Even though my hands still covered my ears, muffling this last scream, I realized it was different from the previous two. It shared the same degree of pain and fright, but aside from this, there were no other similarities. The pitch was different. It was deeper, far less shrill. Most notably, this scream had the human quality to it that the other two had lacked.

There was no doubt in my mind that this scream came from a different source than its predecessors.

I kept my head down and my ears covered as I waited for the scream to end. Within seconds after its beginning, it ended, cutting off with a definite finality. I did not move from my chair after its conclusion. Unlike last time, I stayed put, firmly situated in my seat, not needing to run off and ask my parents if they'd heard what I had. I imagined all of Silent Meadows would have heard those horrid cries of suffering. I sat and waited for my parents to come and ask if I'd heard the screams.

Oh, yes. I heard them. By God, I heard them.

***

Within a half hour after the screams, the police were out once more scouring the woods. This time they came with shotguns in hand and attack-dogs on leashes. Within half an hour more, another body was found.

This time, it was the body of Jason Woodruff.

As the week passed by, details became known to the public at large, primarily through gossip, a little from the police. It was all quite peculiar. The word around town was that Jason was found close to where Daniel Wilson was found. No one knew what he was doing out there. None of his fellow slacker friends had seen or heard from him, or so they claimed. His family hadn't spoken to him since he left for school.

Rumors continued to spread that a serial killer was on the loose, though several discrepancies between the two deaths contradicted this idea. First of all, Daniel's body had been hidden – Jason's was left out in the open, with no apparent attempt at concealing it. Also, Daniel was clearly beaten to death. Determining Jason's cause of death was much more difficult. The coroner found no distinguishable bruises, marks, or lacerations on Jason's bulky, muscular body – none whatsoever. Death by physical interaction seemed highly unlikely.

After further inspection and dissection, no foreign substances were found in Jason; no drugs in his system, nor any alcohol. There were no signs of poison or any such thing – not a hint of foul play at all. Cause of death was announced as undetermined. Through word of mouth, however, the coroner's opinion on the situation was revealed. It was, and I quote, "as if the kid died of fright."

I was inclined to agree with this. Deep down, I had a good idea as to what happened out there in those woods, though even I had difficulty believing in it, as impossible and horrific as it seemed.

What do I believe happened out in those woods? In a word: retribution. Others I heard speaking about the night of Jason's death said the three screams came from Jason. I believe only the last was his. The other two were Daniel's. To be more exact, they were Daniel's *ghost's*.

I'll never know why Jason was in those woods, ignorant to what his violent and misguided ways had spawned in the murder he'd thought he'd committed so flawlessly. Perhaps to gloat and revel in the place of his atrocity. But what he found there was none other than the vengeful remnants of someone he had wronged in the worst possible way. What he found was a scene of horror as he stared in disbelief at the ghost of Daniel Wilson, screaming his death-screams to taunt the vicious bully who had tormented him until his dying breath. What Jason Woodruff found was his doom.

Part of me wished to accept this explanation without a second thought. The idea of the meek and powerless Daniel getting payback gave me some sense—be it a sick and depraved one—of justice. Then again, part of me dreaded believing this explanation.

The idea of the dead rising from the grave was by no means a pleasant one. If Daniel could rise from the grave to exact revenge, what would prevent his spirit from coming to others who had wronged him, or perhaps *ignored* him, leaving him to his demise at the hands of a brute like Jason Woodruff? What if his screams would be heard by others just before they, too, were sent screaming into a dark afterlife? What if he came after me? Would I hear those screams yet again, as they followed me to the grave? That nightmarish thought has kept me up on countless nights.

I never ventured into the woods behind my house again, imagining what I might see amidst the tall oak trees. Or what I might hear.

I continued my writing, but in a different fashion then I once practiced. Rather than simply turning on the single, small lamp on my desk, I turn the overhead lights on, illuminating my entire room. I keep the shades of my bedroom window closed, always. My blank slate for imagining and picturing my stories became the wall in front of me.

Darkness is no longer a canvas on which I picture grand ideas for my tales. It's now a menagerie of horrific images that I can never shake: the face of a young man I once knew, his face pale as death, his mouth agape in a gut-wrenching scream.

Silence is no longer a welcomed solitude. Instead, it serves only as a prelude to the enacting of my deepest fear: that whenever silence falls upon my world, those ghastly screams will once again echo through not only the night, but my very soul.

***

Some say that after death, the dead stay quiet; they move on. It's not always so. Sometimes, they linger.

They long to be heard. They *need* to be heard. Most will only ever whisper, others speak clearly. But some *scream*. And when the dead scream, the living scream, too.

About the Author

Patrick Winters is a graduate of Illinois College in Jacksonville, IL, where he earned a degree in English Literature and Creative Writing. He has been published in the likes of Sanitarium Magazine, The Sirens Call, Trysts of Fate, and other such titles. A full list of his previous publications may be found at his author's site, if you are so inclined to know: http://wintersauthor.azurewebsites.net/Pages/Previous%20Publicati ons.

FALSE AWAKENING

By Michael J.P. Whitmer

"Eight… nine… you're feeling refreshed and awake. Ten… open your eyes, Carl."

Carl blinked his eyes open. He lay on a brown leather couch in a white room. His soft blue eyes set on the ceiling fan humming rhythmically above him. Sunlight poured through a window behind him.

"Carl," a gentle male voice said.

Carl turned his head to see an older man in a shirt and tie, staring at him through circular seeing-glasses.

"What did you see, Carl?"

He thought for a moment, but his mind was still hazy. It made it hard to recall what he had dreamed.

"I… there was screaming, blood, fire… death. It all happened so fast." He tried making sense of the images and sounds flashing in his mind's eye.

"Take your time, Carl."

Closing his eyes, he thought hard, hating what he saw. "Eight. Zero. Five… they keep showing up… haunting me."

"These numbers, what do they mean to you?"

"They scare me," he admitted.

The doctor nodded, jotted something down on the notepad in his lap, then looked back to Carl.

"We're getting somewhere, Carl. Perhaps these three numbers can be used as a constant throughout your dreams. Something your subconscious can identify with to distinguish reality from a nightmare."

Carl stared unblinkingly up at the ceiling fan, thinking on what the therapist was suggesting.

"You're making positive strides. You just need a little more time, but unfortunately, that's it for us today."

Carl nodded, sitting up on the couch.

"So, when do you want us to meet again?"

"What about sometime next week?"

The doctor glanced down at the pad in his lap, thumbing through it casually. He looked up once he settled on a particular page.

"It looks like I'm all booked 'til August. How's the fifth for you, instead?"

Carl translated the date to numbers and stared at him nervously. "Eight, zero, five, Doctor?"

The therapist frowned. "I'm afraid so, Carl…"

***

Carl shot up in bed with his heart beating rapidly. He breathed a sigh of relief.

He lay motionless for a moment, long enough for him to realize his wife was not in bed next to him. Crawling from under the covers and off the bed, he slid into his house slippers, then shuffled his way towards the bathroom.

"Morning, Dad!" squealed his daughter, Emily, as he entered the bathroom.

Carl jumped, looking down at her standing on the sink counter where she had been making silly faces in the mirror. He couldn't help but return her enthusiastic smile.

"Morning, kiddo. Where's Mom?"

"Making breakfast!"

"Why don't you go help her with breakfast and let Daddy wake up a bit?"

Emily gave a small frown at the idea. Carl sighed, placed a kiss on her forehead, and helped her down from the counter.

"Go on," he said, watching Emily reluctantly exit the bathroom.

Carl looked to the mirror. Dark half circles ballooned beneath his eyes. His beard was a stubble down to his neck. He turned the faucet on, cupping his hands under the cool running water before splashing his face.

"I need a drink," he groaned at his reflection.

***

Carl entered the kitchen showered and freshly shaved. His daughter sat at the kitchen table, stuffing her face with French toast. She turned to him and tried to say 'hey' with a mouth full of breakfast.

"Hey, kiddo. Is it good?"

Emily nodded excitedly before going back to shoveling food in her face.

"You're up early," Vanessa chimed blankly from the stove, cooking another batch of French toast.

"Yeah, I didn't sleep well," he muttered, making his way over to a portion of the counter dedicated to an assortment of alcohol. Reaching for the handle of scotch, he poured a shot worth and slammed it back, gritting his teeth to pinch off the sting.

"Really?" Vanessa said with disgust.

"What?" he asked, pretending not to know what she was referring to. He poured another drink, this one a bit fuller than the last.

"Are you really going to drink today?" she said, whipping around with a livid stare only to watch Carl take a seat at the table with Emily. He sipped on his scotch, ignoring her. "Seriously, Carl?"

"Yes, seriously, Vanessa," he finally looked up at her. "I'm going to drink today. I had a rough night, and I still have to go into the office for a few hours."

"You have to do what!"

"I have some paperwork that needs to get done," Carl explained, as he turned back to his drink.

"You're a real piece of work, Carl. You knew Emily had her recital tonight!"

"I work sixty hours a week! You don't think you could have reminded me at some point before now?"

"I've mentioned it at least eight times the last five weeks! You've been too drunk to remember, Carl!"

He went still at her words, and his heart started beating with fear, picking up speed like a ball rolling down a hill.

The numbers, he thought.

Slowly, he forced himself to turn towards her. Vanessa lunged at him, screaming an agonizing shriek. Her hair was singed and missing in clumps. A melting mess of flesh dripped and fell from her face like wax burning from a candle. She reached out for him with smoldering arms, littered with bubbling blisters. Her hands went for his throat.

"You did this!" She howled.

The two toppled to the kitchen floor. Vanessa fell on top of him, her skinless fingers tightening around his neck. Gasping, he tried to scream but couldn't find his voice between the horror and her grip.

Wheezing for air, Carl sprung up in his recliner chair. His body was covered in sweat, and his heart was beating faster than he thought possible. He tried calming his breathing, telling himself it was only a nightmare. In his hand, he still held half a glass of scotch, and in one gulp, he downed the drink.

He stood from the chair and moved to the den for the kitchen. It was empty, and the small window over the sink revealed it was nearing dark outside.

How long was I out for? he wondered, as he reached for the bottle of scotch and filled his glass. *Where is everyone?*

As if to answer him, he heard Emily giggling from the living room. Carl made his way through the kitchen, stopping just where the two rooms met. From where he stood, he could see Emily sitting in the center of the floor, her back to him.

"Hey, kiddo… I'm sorry about forgetting your recital," Carl said, moving into the room. "I'm not going into work. We'll be able to make it."

She didn't respond.

"I know you're upset, baby. But sometimes adults argue. It doesn't mean Mommy and I don't love each other."

She said something, but so softly the words weren't distinguishable.

"What, kiddo?" he moved closer, taking a sip of scotch.

She muttered again.

"Emily, what are you doing there?"

She stood and turned to look at him. Carl's eyes went wide as terror flooded his body, ripping at his insides. Shards of glass dotted Emily's face. From each protruding piece, blood ran down her smiling face like tears. Playfully, she began to pluck the glass from her skin, exposing the gashes, allowing more blood to spurt out.

"Eight... Zero... Five..." she said softly as if reciting a nursery rhyme. Carl backed away from her.

"...No," he shook his head.

"Eight... Zero... Five..." she continued, repeating the sequence of numbers. Her voice rose each time until she was yelling it.

"No," he said again, dropping his drink and plugging his ears with his palms.

"Eight! Zero! Five!"

"No!" he screamed, shutting his eyes tightly.

"Yes, you are, Carl! You're drunk. You're not okay to be driving!" Vanessa insisted from the passenger seat.

Carl eased his eyes open. His hands were on the wheel of his car, driving down the highway.

"Are you even listening?"

He glanced in the rearview mirror and saw Emily smiling in the back seat. Her face was normal.

"I'm fine," he said, more for himself.

"You've been drinking all day. You're not fine!"

"Will you shut up," he snapped, turning to her. "You wonder why I drink? It's you, and your intolerable bitching! It never stops!"

"If you were more responsible, maybe I wouldn't need to bitch at you all the time!"

"Responsible? I work—" he started but she cut him short.

"That's the problem! You work, and forget about your responsibilities as a father and a husband! You couldn't even remember a simple recital for your daughter, which," she paused and glanced at the clock and then back to Carl, "we're now late for."

Carl looked from Vanessa to the clock on the radio.

8:05pm.

The neon colored digital numbers glowed tauntingly.

"Carl, look out!"

He looked up in a panic. The car was drifting off the road toward the median. Before Carl could correct the wheel, the car jumped the curb and was heading into oncoming traffic. The moment appeared to come to a standstill. Everything moved as if in slow motion, yet it occurred so fast Carl was incapable of anything but watching.

In a daze, he looked around the car. They were overturned and the smell of gasoline lingered heavily in the air. Smoke and heat filled the compartment.

Smoke, he thought.

"Smoke," saying it aloud brought him back to. He turned to Vanessa. She was unconsciousness and flames stretched from her floorboard to the dash.

He tried to move but was stuck at the legs from where the front end of the car had been initially impacted.

"Vanessa!" he screamed, as the blaze inched closer for her. She didn't respond, not even when the fire caught hold of her.

"Vanessa!" Carl continued to struggle to free himself but it was no use. He was stuck powerless, as the flames ate away at her until she was fully engulfed.

"Oh, God, please!" he screamed with tears in his aching eyes.

"Emily!" He fought to turn to look in the back seat, but his line of sight was limited.

"Emily!" There was no reply – only the sound of the fire as it flooded the compartment, closing in on him.

"Help!"

"Eight..."

"Help," he pleaded.

"Nine... You're feeling refreshed and awake."

"Please!"

"Ten... open your eyes, Carl."

Carl nearly flung himself out of the brown leather couch as he awoke in the white room. His heart pounded like never before, and his body burned as if the fire was still inches from him.

"I know what eight oh five is," he said, crying.

"It was the time of the accident." Carl buried his face in his palms, continuing to sob.

"I killed them. It was my fault," he muttered.

"Carl, it's okay," a soft hand rested on his shoulder.

"We forgive you…"

He looked up to see Vanessa standing over him.

"Let's go, Carl… Emily and I are waiting for you. It's time to come with us..."

"I can't!" He cried.

Carl bolted upright in bed, his breathing heavy and his body drenched in sweat. He felt Vanessa's cool subtle touch against his bare back, trying to calm him.

"You okay, honey?"

"Yeah," he breathed. "Just a nightmare."

She sat up beside him, glancing at the alarm clock, then back to him.

"Go back to bed, Carl. It's only eight oh five..."

About the Author

Michael J.P. Whitmer is a father, husband, and published speculative fiction writer, casting a shadow in his sunny hometown of Jacksonville Beach, FL. His writing has appeared electronically and in print. Follow his ramblings @MJPWhit on twitter or get exclusive content at michaeljpwhitmer.com.

UNLIFE

By Raven McAllister

My work was done in secret, in autumn, on a chill-bitten landscape of leaves. It was done alone. It was only me, the man with the pocked scars along his cheek, clockwork bits scattered across his altar, wife and child in the ground.

But I was known for what I did. The people who had been funding my toils for almost six years, up until this day of lord November 30, 1907, had handled the raw materials of my labors since the inception of my efforts. They provided the bodies, after which I did my work of a clandestine nature. Then it was finished for another year, until the summer days receded and the air was again cool and dry, ideal weather for my task.

My work was painstaking, yet dreadfully simple in summation: circle, star, diamond.

I am a horologist by trade, a craftsman of all things fine and precise in operation. I had apprenticed in and was eventually contracted by the same shop over the course of my adult life. A simple 'watchmaker' I am not, though. My tinkering went far beyond time-pieces. It went where it was never supposed to go. But the challenge and the personal stakes compelled me to immerse myself in proceedings most arcane.

It was the man who represented the group (out of Eastern Europe is all they've ever revealed to me, which I could surmise by his accent, anyhow) who introduced me to a fundamental working knowledge of the human heart. The organ's functioning is not terribly removed from clockwork itself, and I took to manipulating cadaver hearts rather quickly. There was nothing particularly extraordinary about this.

Rather, the extraordinary element was the material from which he had requested me to forge the brass hearts. I knew immediately that this was not 'brass' in the truest sense, as he had informed me. It was slightly less malleable, and its properties allowed for the impossible. With the proper alignment, the metal permitted the existence of perpetual motion, a bastardization of natural laws that opens the door for…well, my work of that secretive nature. But my time for harboring secrets of any kind is over.

Each brass heart was two and half inches wide by two inches long ('top' to 'bottom'), and took me two months each to forge. The movement (inner workings) demanded the longest attention to properly create, set, and calibrate. The case itself, honestly, was little more than an aesthetic touch. This is my profession, after all, and I do take pride in creating a pleasing, symmetrical shape; in this instance, it was the popular St. Valentine's Day representation of the heart. This was the work that was done leading up to the three consecutive autumn days on which I backpacked from town, and headed north into the woods between civilization and the Atlantic coast.

Here was the place I was taken once and only once by another – by the man with the accent representing his esoteric group – and shown the altar in the clearing. The altar itself looked old and worn, chiseled from stone, yet it did not seem to have sat in the clearing for long. I guessed that his group had had it moved here, and he never answered my question about where it originated from (my accented friend mostly ignored inquiries not directly related to the performance of my work). The altar was sized just wide and long enough to accommodate a human being on their back, which may well have been key to denoting a past purpose equally macabre to its present. It stood at waist level, well enough to allow me to do what I came to do.

Most certainly, I never expected anyone to happen upon me during the process. The spot was well tucked away between a rocky coastline a little over a mile out, with several miles of forest on all other sides. And if anyone had ever seen me in this place, I would have simply called them mad. Who would believe the horologist, the watchmaker, was squirreling about the woods performing seemingly occult acts? That poor man, that watchmaker, who'd lost his family ten years ago when they were on the balcony at the Barberry Club in Nolhaft, posing for a photograph, when the whole damn thing collapsed. The whole shoddy, aged, damned excuse for craftsmanship of a balcony.

I digress. That tends to happen when I ruminate on imperfection. There is little room for that in what I do, though it saturates everything else. Life itself is one imperfect decision after another. That truth I have attempted to embrace, and I feel with commendable commitment.

On the first day, left for me on the altar downwind from where I camped some few hundred yards away, was the first body. Usually, I could smell it.

I did not go to it immediately. Rather, I waited until the sun began to lower behind the skeletal treetops. The coloring of the leaves that crinkled beneath my footsteps was still present, but muted; silhouettes would start to dominate on the western side of the clearing. This was the time I had been instructed to perform the work, and I did not deviate even at the very end.

The growing shadows always made the meticulous operation rushed. There were a few times I had to work by lantern light, with the cold numbing my fingers to the point of their feeling like useless icicles dangling from my palms. This made things challenging to say the least, with an already non-existent margin for error.

When I arrived, the bodies were already on the table, on their backs, bare. Beside them were two small satchels. One was a coin purse with my compensation inside. The other contained the final piece to the brass heart. Three days, three bodies, one body per day. It was a solitary, grim half-week to be certain.

Each corpse was not too far removed from their deaths. The bodies were typically in a very preserved fashion, the cause of mortality not ostensibly traumatic to the flesh. Branded upon each chest, at what would become my incision site, was a mark: a circle, a star, or a diamond. There was always just one of each, but their order was randomly presented to me. I opened up the chest cavity, inserted the brass heart, and carefully clamped the valves into their proper places in the device. The last piece – the gear which was of a particular shape and material different from the pseudo-brass – was inserted atop the heart once it was set. I wound this with two clicks, and my movement began to tick imperceptibly away (I could tell only by the slight vibration of the case against the back of my hand).

Then the body was sutured shut (as best as I could manage), and was left to lie in repose. With my tools in tow, I departed back for my makeshift camp. The group would then come in the dead of that night. They would take the corpse away as they left the next subject upon the altar, along with another coin purse and another winding piece. I supposed I was never meant to see the final results of my work, but a true craftsman always finds a way to check in on what he's done.

I've had the most luck (or misfortune) in locating the whereabouts of the circles. Once they had wandered mysteriously and inexplicably back into the lives of their loved ones, there seemed to be a modest window of normalcy. They returned to work, to grammar school. Then the repetitive behaviors came; they were reported to have paced around their own homes, to have disassembled and reassembled objects around their estates repeatedly, to have said the same phrases over and over for a set number of refrains. These behaviors started as mere eccentricities.

What made them easiest to locate were the newspapers. The headline was typically something to the effect of "GIRL THOUGHT DEAD MURDERS FAMILY IN SLEEP," or, "DRIFTER WITH CADAVER SCARS STABS SEVEN." The ones brought back by the circle gears spiraled towards homicide. I've come across five of them. They've all snapped at some point, and began killing indiscriminately. They carried no rhyme or reason. Their repetitive tendencies simply shifted to repetitive killings. They've all been caught, either executed or stashed into an asylum somewhere.

The stars are very difficult to locate—I've only found one. A boy of about twenty I had operated on. His head had been shaved to the scalp, and he looked to have been thin and sickly in life. The following spring, a man came in to my shop with the boy accompanying him. He was dressed in a long-sleeved shirt and beige vest, all tucked and neat. However, he had a simple way about him. His hair had grown out some, but in matted, unkempt curls. He seemed only half-present, preoccupied with something happening within himself. Naïve to the world would be the best way to put it. He smiled at me briefly, though I'm sure he did not recognize me.

When I asked him what his name was, his father spoke up for him. "He doesn't talk much. Not anymore. He...had a horrible accident. It left him touched. The most he ever talks about are his dreams. But his mother and I are just happy to have him with us." He hugged the boy tightly with one arm as he regarded him with appreciation. The boy smiled again shortly, but still seemed distracted. Not once did he speak. The father's gratitude warmed me, but...I had never been confronted by my own work at that point, and I did not sleep well that night. I mostly wondered who the boy had been before he died.

The diamonds sometimes found me. I knew them first by their knowing looks and slim, sinister grins. There is a dark novelty to them, one I can't put a specific label on. I can only speculate that something inhuman was introduced into them through the resurrection process.

It was an encounter with one that led me to the precipice of what I am about to do.

She came on a snowy January night this year. I was the last out of the shop, locking up the cabinets inside and quelling the hearth before I left and locked the main entrance. When I reached the door to leave, two sharp knocks before me stilled my motion. I opened the shop door, and on the street in the snow stood the woman, cloaked in a navy-blue scarf and furs head to toe. She had been probably thirty when I last saw her. I recognized the nature of her expression immediately. It stung me as harshly as the winter breeze I'd let through the entrance.

"I know what you've been thinking, watchmaker," the woman said with a disdainful smile, not bothering to introduce herself.

The expression, as I've said, gave her away. "I'm sorry, ma'am, but we're just closing up," I played off.

"You're right. You know you are," she went on, standing there without taking a step forward. "Go on. How long are you going to make them wait?"

At that point, with a swallow, I decided to skip the charade and ask her what I'd been wondering for some time about the diamond gear recipients. "What are you now?"

She offered neither a verbal response nor a change in expression. I stepped out of the shop, locked the door quickly behind me, and pulled my coat tighter as I faced her in provocation.

"Come on now, out with it! You live and breathe because of me. You owe me an explanation at the very least."

The woman folded her hands, looked to contemplate, then offered the only insight I've ever gotten into the existence of a person who should no longer be alive. "The others like me understand it, even if not completely. They feel it. They know that we are outside of the dead now. Outside of ghosts, and gods. We feel the strings of fate fastening to something else entirely. We feel their every pluck and wane, and we move with them despite those of you who are numb to it."

Her fingers waggled in illustration.

"I am here to urge you to feel it as well, watchmaker."

Her smile broadened before she turned and walked away abruptly into the snowfall. Yes, she had known what I was thinking, in her black, unknowable way. It was her argument that seduced me to this final decision, to come to this moment where I sit now and chronicle the series of events that led here. I did feel the strings move me in this direction, and I stopped resisting, letting them take me toward what I felt was a natural, terribly imperfect choice.

Bradley was thirteen when he passed. Between his head hitting the cobblestone path, and the larger timbers that fell atop him from the splintering balcony ledge, his death most likely came from the multiple fractures of his young skull. Had I been conscious directly after the fall myself, I would have cradled him, regardless of the gore and blood I had been told of. I would have pleaded for him to wake up, despite how obviously fatal his state may have been. I've imagined that scene unendingly, day and night, no matter where I was or at what I toiled. I was not awake at that time, not there for him, or her. I wanted one last chance to apologize for that, to show him how much I loved him. He needed me, and fate didn't allow that.

I was going to be there now.

I spent half of my savings toward my family's unearthing. You might be surprised how easy it is to hire a graverobber; the expense, really, is the only issue.

Upon their secret delivery to me at a predetermined spot in the woods, I braced for the worst as I examined both the bodies of my wife and my son. Athelia, I feared, was too far gone. Decomposition had left little semblance of proper humanity. But, for whatever imperfect reason, the same embalmer who had prepared my wife had executed his craft well enough with my son as to leave only hints of decay after a decade. His cheeks were shallow, much of his muscle mass gone, but his skeleton was still covered with skin and some hair. I decided I would take him with me. Bradley would be the last of my secret work.

The operation would have to happen on the first day, when I had access to all three final winding gears. My strongest intuition told me that the altar played a more important part in the process than it would seem, which meant I had to perform the heart insertion where I always had. There would be no residual blood in the body, no intact veins and arteries to carry it anyway. I had many doubts about my objective, but one sentiment was certain: this would be my last trip to the clearing.

I made the journey come the autumn cold, as I had done year after year. I carried my son on my shoulder the entire way, swaddled in off-white linens with burlap tied around him. I did not bother setting up camp when I arrived late to my usual nesting ground. Instead, I sat alone with him, on an olive blanket spread out on the ground, holding and rocking him in the dark. I spent hours picturing that horrific day again, hoping this would be the last time that it gnawed at my being.

When the proper hour finally broke the next day, I lifted Bradley and carried him the rest of the way to the altar. There sat what I had expected: two bags, one body.

This subject was an older man with a horseshoe of grey hair running around his scalp. He had a pointed nose and narrow visage; he looked to have been a rather dire man during his normal life. Atop his chest was branded a diamond. That seemed fitting. I could easily picture being accosted by this stranger unexpectedly one day, with a grim message to bear and a near-malicious smile on his thin, pallid face. I removed his body from the altar and replaced it with Bradley's.

Here it was, then. My light was dying by the minute. I wanted to finish my work, and leave with Bradley back toward town all on that same eve. Once the brass heart was in place, clamped by faith alone into my son's desiccated chest, I was left with that one last, simple imperfect choice.

The truth, of course, is that I had made the choice at least a year prior to that moment.

It's been a few months since my final trip to the clearing. I assume I am done with my secret work. I have neither heard nor seen anything in the way of repercussion from the group which had employed my talents in that time. I spend fewer hours at the shop now, especially now that I am not forging brass hearts behind the scenes. Instead, I spend that time at home, with my son. It is well-known in this town that he is deceased, hence this bars me from allowing him out and about. This is much to ask of a thirteen-year-old boy who, every day, becomes more and more like the Bradley I knew over a decade ago.

I watch him carefully, both out of adoration and appreciation, and for other reasons. I've asked how much he remembers of the accident, and what he recounts of the ten years after. Nothing, he says. He seems to forget the accident often, asking now and then when his mother is coming home.

But time has grown short. That is the reason we moved into this cabin, in these very same woods where I played god as if tinkering on a timepiece.

I attempt to train him a little in my craft every day. In particular, I have explained the mechanism of the brass heart which keeps him alive. I explained this to him clearly, carefully, and have shown him the place within our home where the very last brass heart is kept. It sits in the satchel with the two unused winding gears.

The old clocks I have him work on for practice he disassembles several times a day, and puts all three back together the exact same way every time. When I tell him to stop practicing, he only ignores me. He seems obsessed. He's breaking one of them down once again, with machine-like precision, even as I write this by candlelight.

This correspondence will soon be left nailed to the exterior of our front door. The door is locked (very well), and the windows are about to be nailed shut. I ask much of you, stranger. I want you to come find my son within, but I do not want you to hurt him. Understand that he, too, will have an imperfect decision to make. Whatever choice he settles on may appear stiflingly unfair. But that is the nature of this mechanism that moves against the natural laws of life. We move with its coarse grooves, or we suffer under the weight of its unforgiving cycle.

You may turn away now, scoffing. But my hypothesis is that you are far too intrigued to do so at this point. Get Bradley in front of my body then, and he will know what to do. He is compelled to do it, after all. The stars have already dreamt it, and of you. The diamonds have already sent you, most likely without your knowing, towards my door. And if I understand the movement of this damnable clockwork properly, the circle will do the rest. I have helped forge this machine, this cycle of unlife, and in so starting, it may well run forever.

Perfect.

About the Author

Raven McAllister is a psychotherapist hailing from southwest Louisiana. His stories have been featured on a number of eZine sites such as Dark Energy Speculative Fiction, Macabre Cadaver, and Flashes in the Dark, and in the print anthologies Hindered Souls and Deadman's Tome: The Ancient Ones. His latest story, "The Language of the World," is part of the Frith Books ghost anthology Restless, and his story "Four Turns" will be featured in the upcoming Between the Tracks collection put out by Oz Horror Con.

BETTER HALVES

By KC Grifant

Something wasn't quite right, but Anne couldn't place it. At first, she thought it was the weather, casting a gloomy sheen over their summer beach trip.

"Stupid New England," she said. *An apt belated birthday present*, she thought sourly. A face peered at her through the passenger window: her own reflection, frowning and fragmented against the rain flecks.

"It's a week out of the city," said Derick, ever the optimist. "We can get lobster."

The GPS spoke up and her husband yanked the wheel. A small wooden sign with the inn's name in white script clattered against a post barely lit by the headlights, the first sign of a town they had seen since passing the IHop half an hour back.

"But I wanted to take photos," she said, her heart sinking as the house came into view through the mist. It was, well, *older* than she had expected, with peeling paint and raindrops caught trembling in spider webs along the top of the front door. Flowers on the nearby trellis sagged as if their dark colors were about to stream off like paint.

Inside, a carpet studded with dark roses bloomed at their feet before running up a narrow stairwell. "Welcome! Honeymoon suite top floor in back. Breakfast at 8," read a note on the counter, pinned down by a key on a wooden keychain.

Upstairs, Derick bumped into Anne as she stopped at the room's entrance. "What's wrong?"

"*This* is the honeymoon suite?" she said. The room was dark, the bed high with overstuffed lace pillows that her grandmother would've liked. Small watercolors of boats and colonial houses peppered the floral wallpaper.

"It's not so bad."

"It's not great," Anne said, dropping her bag and stepping over to a vanity desk below an enormous, ornate mirror. "Maybe it's the feng shui."

She leaned down to check her hair and stopped, entirely caught off guard by what she saw. It wasn't the unpleasant but familiar sensation of seeing time tug away at skin and flesh. No, something else was off, something in the way the light peeled away at the edges of the mirror, like several reflections of her lay directly behind the first. The boundaries of those reflections' edges began to blur when—

"Look what they left for us."

Anne's eyes slid away and toward her husband, who raised a wooden board with crackers and cubes of cheddar cheese.

"Nice," she said. Her voice sounded hollow. "Let's go to bed."

The bed was soft and warm despite its old-fashioned look, and she started to feel relaxed for the first time all day until Derick nuzzled her. She turned onto her back. "Stomachache," she breathed and waited until she heard his breath grow slow and long, asleep.

Like clockwork, Anne's surge of resentment faded to a familiar, throbbing guilt. She knew he wanted a family. She did too, in theory. They had agreed to wait until her thirty-fourth birthday, enough time for her to start up an online photography shop and market herself to galleries. But of course, things had gotten in the way and now her time was up.

Maybe during maternity leave, she'd have time to pursue projects that always seemed to be on hold. Her mother's voice floated to her, sentences Anne had heard too many times.

You'll feel different when you have a baby.
Art school isn't a career.
You are so lucky to have Derick.

It had all worked out well enough so far. Derick was sweet and she had a decent career in banking, on a fast track for a promotion. Having a kid would probably be fine too. So why was she on the brink of hyperventilating?

Anne squashed down the stew of panic into a more manageable ball of unease as she sat up, reaching for her water bottle. From the bed, she could make out her silhouette in the mirror to her left, coarsely granular as the curtains sighed, scattering moonlight around the room.

From here, she looked like a nymph who had climbed up the trellis and crept into their room, feral and damp from the outdoors. Or like a mermaid who had just gained legs for the night and ran across the sand and grass, drawn to the glint of the mirror.

I'm tired, Anne thought, and laid back down beside her husband.

***

The inn manager, Betty, served them breakfast, plopping down plates with scrambled eggs and slightly crooked corn muffins.

"Do you like the room?" Betty murmured. She didn't look much older than Anne, but wore an old-fashioned long green skirt, brown apron, and too-thick glasses.

Derick nodded. "Not bad. How old is this place?"

"1750. It used to be a mansion. Survived two fires." Betty gave a pale grin as she refreshed their juice cups with a glass carafe.

"Any ghost stories?" Anne piped up, stuffing a bite of egg into her mouth. She still had an uneasy feeling she couldn't shake. She didn't believe in ghosts per se, but it always seemed like the local hotels and inns all had a tale of a haunting or two they were eager to share. Part of the New England charm.

An awkward tinkle of a laugh erupted from Betty. "People believe all sorts of things, especially up around here," she said. "Sometimes, we are too easily influenced by others, don't you think?" She shot Anne a stern look that reminded Anne all too much of her mother.

Anne nodded, sheepish as she chewed. The dark shadows along the bottom of Betty's irises seemed to give a jump and the faint morning light reflected against the hard curve of her glasses as she topped off their coffees. "Everyone just loves that room. We've had people who've been coming back for years. Something about this place."

***

As they walked along the harbor to the downtown street with shops and a little boardwalk, Anne's phone buzzed. She ignored it, raising her Canonet Rangefinder instead to take a shot of the bobbing sailboats, their clones resting on a muted, equally cloudy sky in the glassy water. The sky was thick and bloated, threatening to rain at any moment.

"I'm gonna take some photos, hon, catch up for lunch at the tavern in a bit?" Anne said as they reached the small epicenter of gift stores and candy shops atop a hill over the boardwalk. Sometimes, if she looked at him from a certain angle, he looked like a stranger. He smiled at her before taking off toward the bookstore.

The clouds and shadows worked well for her black-and-white shots. Anne framed a shot of an arguing couple with a stroller between two old brick buildings, one of which had strutting overhead that cast hard bars of light and shadow. Another of a young woman frowning into a phone in front of an antique store, a beam of light breaking through the clouds just behind her.

Anne was about to snap a shot of an elderly couple on a bench, a small panting dog trapped between them, when a voice close to her ear made her jump.

"Burn."

Anne whirled to see a dazed-eyed older man with a buzz cut and layers of old clothes wavering on his feet.

"*Burned* it," he hissed again. His smell made her nose prickle and she lowered her camera so he wouldn't grab it as she stepped away.

"I tried!" The man screeched suddenly. A few people's heads turned even as the stream of tourists made a wide circle around them. "But they don't let me. Near. It."

Anne took a step back and then another as the man jabbed his finger toward an ice cream sign on the sidewalk. She quickly turned and ducked into a café, relieved to see the man take off in another direction.

The young barista's eyes followed her up to the counter. "Old Iggy," the girl said sympathetically. "Ignore him. Sometimes he's nice enough."

An older man swiping through an iPad snorted in disapproval. "His father was a vandal and so was he. Nearly set the damn town on fire."

"I can't *wait* to get out of here," the barista's smile turned longing as she plopped down the coffee. "You from Boston?"

Anne nodded politely and glanced down at her phone,

which vibrated insistently. A message from her mother, even though they had just talked yesterday. "You really can't wait any longer," her mother had said then, like she always did, in the same tone she used when she dissuaded Anne from majoring in photography, from moving to New York, from doing anything, really.

Anne had protested feebly. "Massachusetts has the—"

"I know, the highest percentage of old moms." A pause. "You   want   to   be   an   old   mom?"

Now, Anne deleted the message without listening to it and stood at the counter facing the street. Across the way, the toy store's perfectly reflecting window showed a figure with splashes of lighter color marking her face and neck and arms.

The reflection was staring at her, because she was staring at it. It took her a moment to realize it was herself. It looked like her, but   somehow   *didn't*.

Get it together, Anne, she scolded herself and sipped her coffee, trying to appreciate the caffeine buzz. She'd have to give it up – wine, sushi, countless other pleasures – if she was going to get pregnant and let something else take over her body.

You've   wasted   your   life,   haven't   you?

Anne stood, tossing away the drink. When she stepped outside, she felt something flutter at her shoulder and whirled around. A yelp stifled in her throat as she saw Derick beaming at her, holding something in his hand. A flyer, for a jazz festival tomorrow. "Rain or shine," he said gleefully.

In the bathroom at the tavern, Anne washed her hands in the faux marble sink and glanced at the mirror for a second, her reflection looking uncertain before she smoothed down her hair and hurried out.

***

Anne had never experienced insomnia before except the night of her wedding. She closed her eyes and waited, but the heavy, dreamy feeling preceding sleep eluded her as she listened to Derick's gentle snores. When she finally did start to drift off, she jerked awake a second later.

She heard a noise.

She laid perfectly still, her heart pounding, waiting to hear it again. *The ghost*, she thought wildly, even though she technically did not believe in such a thing.

There it was. A little click. From the foot of the bed.

She sat up, trying to whisper to Derick to wake up, but her throat was parched and a small squeak came out instead. She peered through the darkness of the room and saw what it was: the minute hand of a wooden clock on the vanity was stuck.

Anne slid into the vanity chair, pushing the clock hand so that it worked again. Her reflection was barely a silhouette in the darkness with no distinction, no features, a brushstroke of calligraphy ink. Nothing really at all.

Anne's fingers ran over the polished wood of the desk,

376

where tiny pockmarks and dents felt like gritty sand. On the desk's single drawer, curled etchings centered around a keyhole.

She tugged the drawer, expecting it to be locked, but found a small red book inside, too thin to be a Bible. "The Science of Dreaming" ran across the binding in faded thin gold script. She opened it to a well-worn crease and could just make out the words from the moonlight that streamed in.

... your shadow, or dream self — the part of you that sails on during sleep. Reports of "out-of-body" experiences, doorways to heaven, alien abductions and angel encounters have all been traced to separations gone awry between the dream self and conscious self. A schism can cause unimaginable...

She flipped again and the pages settled easily, as if they already knew what they wanted to show her:

Spellcasters used enchanted reflections to communicate with their dream selves. Properly positioned along magnetic fields and treated in an ionic formula, the mirrors let the beholder ask the dream selves anything they wished.

What a strange book, Anne thought and turned the pages again, to the back of the very last one—

... saw too much. The visions drove them to hysterics or to act on the countless evils they believed grew in them. Some wrote that those not strong enough had been lost, drawn too far from their bodies into the shadow realm. One wrote of a dream 'parasite'   escaping.

The book ended there. Anne turned it back and forth, trying to see the stitching. She wasn't sure if pages had been ripped out, or   if   there   was   another   volume.

In the mirror, the seams that traced her outline seemed strained, as if her reflection was a one-dimensional dam, holding back a rush of something desperate to seep out. Her eyes blinked, flat   like   the   gaze   of   a   cardboard   cutout.

It   was   the   Face   again,   watching   her.

"Are you a ghost?" Anne whispered, even though it was silly. Nevertheless, she still felt clammy, her body tense, ready to run.   She   whispered   even   quieter: "A   'dream   self'?"

Shadows moved in synch with the fluttering curtains, where something screeched, distant but high-pitched. A blur moved quickly across the mirror, like wings flapping. She looked closer into the mirror's shadows and could see a world within a world, a two-storied building with small figures running around it. "What on earth," Anne whispered and tried to see closer, but the vision   faded.

She put the book back in the drawer and stepped back, her heart rocketing like it would shoot her into space. She shook Derick's shoulder, but he grunted and she took a long, shaky breath.

Nerves. Hormones. She had just gone off her birth control last month and it was messing with her head, obviously. She climbed back into the too-high bed and waited for sunlight.

In the morning, Anne squinted at the mirror. She saw herself, looking groggy and perplexed. It was time to test things out in the clarity of the gray morning.

"Hey babe," Anne said casually. "You have a little something on your chin." She motioned to the mirror but he merely glanced at it, scratched the corner of his beard and adjusted his baseball cap before stepping away.

"It's weird, right?" Anne persisted. She hadn't remembered any of her dreams, but slept uneasily. "This place feels a little off."

"Getting more into the ghost stories this trip, aren't you?" He gave her a look as they left the room.

At breakfast, Anne dug into the banana pancakes as Betty set down a ceramic miniature pitcher with maple syrup. "I found a strange book in our room," Anne said. "Is it from a local library?" Betty smiled blandly. "I'm not sure, we have many books here. The housekeeper cycles them through." She shuffled over to a bookshelf and retrieved a thickly bound tome, placing it carefully between them. "That reminds me. If you enjoy your stay, do consider us for events."

The book was full of groups posing in the sprawling back yard of the inn, mostly wedding parties. A few portraits caught her eye. Anne leaned closer to see one bride, during preparations and in her wedding gown. She recognized the same lost look in the stranger's eyes that she felt. On the opposite page was a magnificent full portrait of the couple with "1 Year Anniversary!!!!!!" scrawled beneath it. Anne squinted. The bride's eyes looked completely different; self-assured, calm as a cat, with something… sinister about them.

"We've had weddings here, reunions, all kinds of things," Betty grinned. "Think about it."

Outside in the drizzling day, Anne roamed the sprawling hill of the inn's yard with her camera while she waited for Derick to grab an umbrella. At the base of the hill, a lofty white trellis framed a pond. Around that, small fountains and streams fed into each other, surrounded by statues of chipped alabaster deer and frogs.

Half a dozen mirrors, some dirty, were propped up along the fountain streams and behind a birdbath and against trees. Tiny seashells studded along the border of one mirror, with globs of glue in spots. Another was encircled by tiny rusted figures of monkeys holding coconuts. The rest were unadorned, blank slabs of smudged reflections.

More feng shui, Anne thought. Mirrors were supposed to deflect bad energy, after all.

"Babe!" Derick waved to her from the sidewalk and they headed downtown.

***

After lunch, Anne continued on to the many stores while Derick headed back for a nap before the evening's festival. She felt stranger each time she glimpsed her face in a store display reflection. It looked more and more like the Face, or like she was forgetting her own features.

A weird mental illness, she thought. *Early Alzheimer's.*

Finally, she found what she had been looking for. Iggy dozed next to the door of a gas station a block from the main street, in the same clothes she had seen him in yesterday. A smattering of rain came down as she approached him. Faces inside the gas station turned and moved.

"Burn what," Anne said, and then louder, "*What*? You're talking about the inn, aren't you?"

His eyes glazed as he looked at her for a long moment. When he slowly nodded, an unexpected relief shot through her. It wasn't just her. There was something wrong.

Anne, you are agreeing with a crazy person.

"Is it…" she swallowed her pinprick of embarrassment at the word. "haunted?"

Iggy gave a half laugh, half cough and closed his eyes.

"I read – or dreamt – something about shadow selves," she whispered. "I think I'm seeing mine. What do I ask it? A wish?" She laughed, it was all so absurd; yet she knew something strange was happening to her. Something had been opened to her and she had to see it through.

Iggy didn't open his eyes or speak, but his head fell forward and his hand opened. In it were five books of matches from the local fusion restaurant with a bright yellow illustration of a parrot. One fell to the ground. She took another from his hand and walked rapidly away.

***

"Ready for some jazzin'?" Derick asked that evening as he came   out   of   the   bathroom.

Anne cleared her throat and shuffled to the vanity. "Check out this book I came across, isn't it—" she opened the drawer, to see   "The   Science   of   Dreaming"   was   gone. *Don't   look,   don't   look,   don't   look.*

Anne glanced at the mirror. Her reflection, the Face, nodded. *My shadow self*, she thought. It was right there, waiting for her to ask whatever she wished. *Now*, its eyes seemed to say.

"I'll stay here," she heard herself say, tearing away her gaze to look at him. "I didn't sleep a wink. You go."

After a few minutes of back and forth, Derick agreed. She waited until the door clicked shut and his footsteps disappeared down the hallway before standing at the window, watching him recede. One of the angled mirrors in the yard glinted, even in the dimming   sunlight.

The mirrors aren't deflecting negative energy away, she thought, and felt a dread creep over her. *They are channeling it.*

Burn it, Iggy's urgency came back to her and she glanced at the lace curtain. She pulled the bright yellow matchbook from her pocket, the logoed Parrot staring up open-mouthed at her.

It would be so easy. Her pit of unease swelled and a sharp thought pierced her. What? Burn a place down because she felt a little off? That was ridiculous.

She struck the candle next to the clock instead. Smoke poured from the wick and her nose prickled at the unusual, salt-water smell.

Anne looked up and her shoulders were bare, her reflection naked. Astonished, her hands touched the fabric of the cardigan that lined her collarbone, watching reflected fingers touch skin.

Her shadow self stared back at her just as curiously, and she sensed a crippled, twisted thing behind the veneer of her face.

"Tell me," Anne whispered. "Tell me how to do what I want."

But what did she want? The reflection seemed to ask.

"I want to be free," she choked.

Darkness crept across her reflection like slowly spreading ink. Anne wiped at her forehead and hair to get it away, slowly at first and then more frantically.

She heard the words form, and imagined they were spoken in the same voice who wrote "The Science of Dreaming."

The shadow self does not care. The shadow self does not compromise.

It was her own mouth, speaking the words in the mirror. Time drummed, cracked, and stopped.

The Face widened its lips and bared its teeth in a mockery

of her smile. Something flapped and landed on her head. A flash like scales in water as chains coiled up from her reflection's mouth along her cheeks. The chains gleamed and dripped like sausage casings. And when Anne's eyes moved up to what held the chains—

She moaned. The *thing*. It looked like a gargoyle or monkey that had crawled out of a sewer. The small creature squatted on her head, with a long, lean jaw and tiny pinpricks of eyes full of an all-too-human spite.

The creature shot her a sidelong grin, goo oozing from its mouth as it gave a jerk of the chains through hooked claws. Her reflection's head turned in response, then smiled with its mouth full of chains, like a horse with a bit.

Anne couldn't scream - her throat had collapsed. She wanted to jerk back, knock over the chair, climb out the window to get away from that *thing*. But she couldn't move.

This is what you wanted to see. While you did nothing there, we've been very busy here.

"Don't show me this!" Anne shrieked, but it came out in a haggard whisper. Her hands frantically patted the top of her hair. Nothing. In her reflection, the hands reached up and caressed the creature.

"What is on my head?" she whispered. She was frozen, the fear short-circuiting any rational thoughts.

A pet. You bred it yourself, in the dark. Feeding it every compromise, every bit of denial. Aren't you proud?

Her hands trembled, clutched in her lap, though they stayed uplifted in the mirror. The creature dropped the chains and became a blur in the background as it flew away. The sound of its leathery wings beating against each other filled the room.

Everyone has them. Little fears. Little denials. But not everyone lets them get so big.

The Face's eyes were completely dark, brimming over with ink as it smiled and leaned forward. Its mouth, now empty of the chains, formed an "o" and tilted down. The candle's flame went out with a soft *pssf*, leaving them in complete darkness.

Anne felt a rush of hot air and couldn't move. *Asleep, a dream of course,* she thought, until the darkness cleared to a monochrome landscape with a gray building straight ahead and more in the far distance. It was, she thought, the inn, the town, the world in a horrible gray scale.

In front of her, figures paced like people, but they had no faces. Eyes and noses and mouths were blurs like smeared charcoal. But the hideous creatures that rode on their backs were sharp and in focus, their knobby legs twisting like bone ridges against the shadow people's backs. The creatures' arms wound around necks or flicked the chains from the figures' mouths, as if directing disobedient horses whenever they strayed too far from the building.

Anne squinted as one figure came closer and saw the smear

of a face morph into something recognizable, but only for an instant. It was Betty, the whites of her eyes rolling around. The winged creature on her shoulders with both its gnarled, clawed hands stretched into her mouth, turned her head sharply back to the building.

On the ground, other creatures - not even creatures, but masses of dark sinews and gleaming tendons - pulled their way over the dust. One rose up near her feet and turned toward her. Through its dripping, slimed mass, she recognized the Face. Her face.

It spoke with a sympathy that made Anne's heart ache. *I'll do all the things you want. You don't have to struggle.* It flowed up and a gaping hole widened in a muted screech.

Anne recoiled and tried to scream but it launched forward, its hole of a mouth aiming right toward her.

The hot dry air churned into Anne's throat and around her, blotting out the landscape until she was facing her reflection again, gasping for breath and gripping the sides of the chair.

Everything looked different, flatter. Her tension slipped away, like bags of sand cut from her back. She tried to remember what she had been worried about.

The door clicked suddenly. "It's raining way too hard—" Derick said, and light flooded the room. "What are you doing in the dark?"

She turned from the mirror to her husband. She couldn't

feel her face. *My shadow self took it*, she thought dully. She couldn't feel anything.

She watched her shadow self say *I don't think it's going to work out. I need to focus on my art. You're a boring distraction.* Her hand, lifting, to take off the wedding band. Anne watched her hand move over *there* but felt it move over *here*, effortlessly, as if being lifted by invisible threads. She tried to turn to look more clearly at her fingers, but everything was heavy, muffled, much too hard.

She heard their voices rise, watched her hand fling out the ring in an arc of prismatic glinting.

A huge face filled the mirror, showing all its teeth. A moment later, once the light was snuffed out, Anne realized the face was her own.

A door closed and everything went dark. Anne was stuck. She tried to move, to strain and see the landscape around her, to will the blacks into grays. But the thing on her head stirred and she felt heavier than was even possible.

At times, she saw glimpses of her outside self, the dream self. Occasionally, it passed by window displays, puddles, things that made the air shimmer slightly around Anne. Strange, gray-ish things came into distorted view: the toy store, an antique store. But only for an instant. Anne tried to move toward them, but couldn't.

When the gray landscape and building materialized, sometime later, she found she could walk a little. *My shadow self is asleep,* Anne realized thickly through her haze. While her body slept in the real world, she was able to roam the gray landscape. She tried to run but the creature atop her head was large and fierce and didn't give her an inch of slack as it yanked her chains.

But it is easier now, Anne thought. She was free from decisions, from guilt, from stifled wanting. For the first time, she didn't have to feel *unhappy.*

Ivy bloomed around her, made of darkness. Soft wings beat overhead. Something rested gently against her neck. Her mouth full and muffled, Anne relaxed into the shadows.

About the Author

A founding co-chair of the Horror Writers Association (HWA) San Diego chapter, **KC Grifant** is a New England-to-SoCal transplant who writes horror, fantasy, science fiction and weird west stories. Her nonfiction science articles on science, medicine and technology have appeared in hundreds of magazines and newspapers while her fiction stories have found homes in magazines, card games and anthologies, most recently the Lovecraft Ezine, Electric Spec magazine, and the Stoker Award-nominated "FRIGHTMARE: Women Who Write Horror." Visit @SciFiWri or www.SciFiWri.com to learn more.

LAST DANCE IN THEATRE D'OBSCURE

By Jaap Boekestein

I wasn't nervous, of course not. My nerves had been reduced to ashes years ago on the battlefields of Flanders. No, I felt a certain... *anticipation* while I waited for the dark door to open, invitation in my hand. Theatre d'Obscure was extremely exclusive. Rumours and mysteries surrounded the club. Whispered stories hinted at strange things going on. Of course, it was all claptrap to lure in punters, but it was done quite skilfully and I appreciated that.

Ever since I'd heard of Theatre d'Obscure, I'd wanted to visit the place. I regard myself as a connoisseur of the London entertainment scene. There are very few clubs, theatres, music halls and cabarets in London I have not visited at least once. Theatre d'Obscure had always been elusive, invitation only. And slipping the doorman a couple of coins wouldn't get you that invitation, only a scornful scowl of the ridge of bone that should have been his eyebrows.

Still, it was more than the prospect of finally visiting some high class girlie show that fuelled my anticipation. The printed invitation I had found in the pocket of my overcoat – who had put it there? – promised "The Spectacular Feather Fan Dance by Renowned Artiste Ruby Moon. One night only!"

Feather Fan Dance? Ruby Moon? Was it all a huge coincidence? Even the picture of the girl, an impish face, flaming hair, long legs and two huge feather fans, rekindled sweet memories. Could it be? No. Ridiculous. That was quite impossible. But I was intrigued, to say the least.

The door opened and I showed my invitation to the dark bulk of the doorman. He let me in with a respectful bow, though for a moment, his shiny black face was lit up by a grin of his large canine teeth. I entered.

I won't bore you with a description of Theatre d'Obscure. All those places are essentially the same: a cloakroom, a hall with a stage, small tables, smiling girls, thick carpets, brass and velvet, lights and mirrors, the smell of cigarettes, the low voices of the "guests" and the high frolicking laughter of the hostesses. I had made this kind of place my home. Call it sad if you must, but I find the fake warmth in these establishments far more appealing than the hypocrisy and squalor of polite society.

I ordered a drink.

I sat through the opening act (a painted, washed up transvestite singer) and the dumb act (a coarse dwarf). The two acrobats were not bad, curling their fake moustaches and shouting their "alley-oops" before balancing on each other's shoulders or walking on their hands. The house comic had some decent material about The Right Honourable Lloyd-George selling honours like tickets to the Zoo. Still, that was not the reason I was there. Oh, one can pretend to go to such places for the songs, the jokes, the jugglers and what not, but we all know what men really come to see: the flesh of a pretty girl. We are butchers, ogling the lamb of the evening, and we pay for the privilege to do so. It is what it is and we are what we are.

Over the years, I have seen hundreds of girls. Singing girls, dancing girls, actresses, *acrobates*. Plain, exotic, foreign. I've loved them in all their shapes and forms; small, tall, blondes, brunettes, gingers and jet-black vamps that would have mesmerized Allan Quatermain himself. I could watch them endlessly doing their routines, singing their songs or delivering their lines. Tantalizing, beautiful, sensual. Men dreamt of those girls. I certainly did. Their faces, their bodies, even their voices fuelled so many fantasies. *Vive la femme!* They are like candles in the night, keeping away the Darkness. At least, for a while.

Finally, my patience was rewarded. Exit comic, *entrez* the Master of Ceremonies.

"Gents and ladies," the man in the top hat announced. "For only one night, this rare jewel has descended down from the Heavens to perform exclusively for you in Theatre d'Obscure! Without more ado, I give you Ruby Moon and her Feather Dance!"

Amidst the applause, all the lights died, except a single spotlight aimed at the stage, sharp and white as a beam of moonlight. It caught two huge feather fans that completely hid a kneeling dancer. The fans were folded together making it look like an egg about to hatch.

Silence for two, three, maybe four seconds.

The music started; a single trombone, nothing more.

The two fans shook slightly, like new-born butterflies drying their wings in the lightest of summer breezes.

Soft brush sticks and a trumpet joined.

She rose, the feathers folded open, just enough to reveal her face.

I choked on a gasp. Her face, her hair, a thousand and one sweet details I suddenly remembered. The dancer on the stage was Emerald Moon, my dear lovely little Emerald. But, she could not be. Emerald was dead.

The fan dance is one of seduction; it is a dance of the senses. Don't feel cheated, but to describe the dance, I would need the eloquence of a poet or a critic, and I am only a creature of habit.

The fans weaved and turned, lured and enticed. Naked legs, naked arms. Naked hips and breasts? In my heated mind, perhaps she wasn't wearing a flesh coloured body stocking but was nude behind the feathers. The quick glimpses offered were too short to be certain.

I knew that dance. I knew every step, every turn, every subtle move. I had seen it being performed dozens of times. The first time I saw that dance was back in the fall of '18. The hospital had discharged me and I was alone and lonely in the Capital. No friends, no family, embittered and with some money to spare. In a moody and self-pitying torpor, I entered a theatre with "Emerald Moon's Fan Dance" on the bill, and there she was: petite, sensual, exciting. She put a spell on me. Emerald saved me from the endless Darkness that was consuming me. Black dreams, gnawing at my sanity, draining my life force. "Shell shock" they called it. Whatever it was, the doctors could not cure me. But Emerald did. Her dance, her energy pulled me back from the Darkness.

In the dark hall of Theatre d'Obscure I sat and watched an impossible girl dance.

Time went by, but I did not notice. She and I were the only beings that existed, the only two sparks in the universe's eternal void. Thousands of thoughts flowed through my mind – thousands of feelings roared. I wanted to jump up, shout, cry, flee, curse. But I just sat in my chair and watched her.

The dance ended, the music stopped, the spotlight died.

Applause broke the spell, but by then, the stage was dark and empty, the girl gone.

The Master of Ceremonies made his entrance and smiled. "The lovely Miss Ruby Moon! Let's hear it again!"

More applause, but the stage remained empty. No encore.

No! I must... It can't... She! I signalled wildly for one of the waiters.

"Sir? Would you care for another drink, sir?"

"Emer... Miss Moon. I would like to know if Miss Moon would care to join me for a glass of champagne."

The pound notes quickly disappeared from the table. "I will see what I can do, sir."

The champagne arrived before the girl, but not by much.

She was... She... She left me speechless for a few moments. Her movements, her looks. She had to be Emerald Moon; my sweet dancer I'd watched for so many nights. But I told myself again, Emerald Moon was dead. A silver flapper dress clung to her body, her flaming upswept hair was caught under a little pearl hairnet. Only her eyes differed. Emerald's eyes had been green, while the eyes of this girl... I think a very light brown would describe it best. In the dim light of the hall they seemed almost red, like rubies. *Emerald Moon, Ruby Moon.* Were their stage names derived from the colour of their eyes? Who was this girl?

In spite of the comfortable heat of the hall, I felt a shiver. She was like a lost dream. A part of the past that I thought was gone forever.

"Emerald," I croaked.

She sat down, smiled like Emerald used to smile. "Good evening dear, I am honoured by your invitation. I do love champagne."

"The honour is all mine," I heard myself reply. Déjà vu. After watching Emerald for weeks and weeks, never missing a performance, I'd finally found the courage to invite her to my table. She loved champagne, she'd told me. I was honoured, I'd replied.

"It is your first time here? I don't think I have seen you before." Her question pulled me back to the here and now. The girl sounded like Emerald, but her voice was slightly deeper. She was not Emerald.

"You look very much like someone I knew. She also danced with feather fans. Her name was Emerald Moon." I blurted out like a hasty confession.

She looked at me with her red eyes. She was still all smile and loveliness, but I could sense some wariness, too. "Did you? Emerald Moon was my sister."

"You are sisters? Twins?"

Ruby Moon shook her head. "Just sisters. We lost contact years ago."

Sisters. Relief and hope poured into my heart. Could it be? Was it possible? Emerald Moon had a sister, and she was sitting at my table? What were the odds? "Emerald was very special to me. I was with her when she died."

The girl looked at me, said nothing for a moment, then: "You were her friend? Her gentleman friend?"

I nodded. Unable to speak. I shivered again. *Her sister.* Deep inside, I felt something stir. Emerald had been very special. I had not realized what she really meant to me until she was gone. Only then did I understand that I needed her. She was the only one who could subdue my recurring nightmares. I searched and searched for the same combination of joy and loveliness – girl after girl – but they were only temporary distractions. None of them could keep the Darkness away. None of them were Emerald.

And now...

Now her sister sat at my table. The exact same body, maybe the same spirit? I could be whole again! I could be... if I did not waste this chance. It was terrifying to think I might fail. *I must not fail.* I looked at her, desperately trying to think of something that would keep her interested in me.

Smouldering coals, hot and deep, those were Ruby's eyes, so different from the soft, innocent eyes of her sister. "I would like to get to know you better," she said and took my hand. Her touch and her words were electric shocks as power surged through me. One moment I was a helpless rabbit, caught between hope and fear, the next moment I was a roaring lion, proud and sure.

My smile came naturally. "I would like that very much, dear Ruby. Do you want to go somewhere with me?" I knew she would say yes.

"There are rooms upstairs." She did not wait for an answer. She rose, looked over her shoulder. "Come with me."

How could I refuse? I did not want to lose her. I followed.

Every club and girlie show had private rooms. It was not very hush-hush. Everyone knew, even the police. As long as they were paid off, they did not care. The room she took me to was private indeed. No windows, a sofa, a side table, and some second-class paintings of nudes on the walls. The basic things a gentleman would require for a tête-à-tête with a young lady.

I felt the hot rush of lust when I followed her into that room. I knew the body under that dress, and yet I knew it not. It would be familiar and all new and exciting at the same time. Would she be the same as Emerald?

No! Not as Emerald. Patience, patience! This time... I would be watching and touching, nothing more. I had to restrain myself. This girl was special, this girl was my redemption. I had to tread carefully. I could not afford to lose her.

The Darkness inside me growled. It wanted other things. It wanted them *now.*

Being patient and careful was my plan, however, it was not hers. She sat me down on the sofa and curled up on my lap, her arms around my neck, face to face.

She smiled. Her pink tongue darted out to lick her red lips. She said, "I know what you want," and kissed my mouth.

Lips, tongues, tastes. My heart raced. Fire in my head and between my legs. It was so wrong. It was so what I did not want. No, I *wanted* it, but I should not. My fingers buried themselves in the sofa. *She... I can not... This girl can save me, if I have the strength!*

Air! Finally, air. I gasped, looked at her, begging: *please stop. Stop before...*

She purred like a pussycat, covered my throat with hot little kisses, her body rubbed against mine.

No! No! I fought myself. If I gave in I would be lost, and so would she. I would never find any rest. Looking down, I caught a glimpse of her breasts. Delicate, lovely. The Darkness howled, wanted to grab, suck, tear the dress from her body and... *No, please! Not this girl!* Emerald Moon had kept the Darkness in check with her dance. Her sister could do the same. As long as the Darkness did not violate her.

I fought. I really did.

She bit me. Right on the neck. Sharp pain, teeth in flesh. She bit me, and I lost it.

The Darkness – always present, strong, close – took over. It was her own fault. I tried to stop it.

Tear her clothes from her body, throw her down on the sofa, let her shriek, let her writhe. Dominate her. The Darkness wanted, demanded, that I squeeze the life from her. Muted sounds, struggling, anxious eyes. The climax and then... peace. Wonderful peace. Broken eyes, broken body, broken beauty. The Darkness satisfied.

I wanted all that, the Darkness wanted it.

I moved to grab her, but found it impossible. My arms, legs, my whole body motionless, as if I was trapped in steel bands.

However, there were no bands, no barriers. The only thing I felt was the warm lithe body of Ruby Moon on my lap.

I tried to shout but no sound came out. I willed my body to move, but found it useless. What was this? *The bitch, what has she done to me?*

She looked at me. Nodded, as if she could read my mind.

Destroy her! Beat her to a bloody pulp! Kill her! the Darkness howled.

But I was helpless.

Kill! Kill! Kill!

Her delicate little hands caressed my cheeks.

"I have no sister," she whispered, without ever taking her eyes off me. "You know who I am."

Through the haze of lust and anger I slowly realized what she meant. *No sister?* I looked at her and knew who she was. *Emerald Moon.* She was dead, but she was here, sitting in my lap. Emerald Moon had come back for me. Again, I threw everything I had against the strange force that restrained me. All my strength, all my anger, the endless power of the Darkness in me.

It was all in vain.

I. Could. Not. Move.

"You killed me," she continued. "For weeks you were there in the audience, watching me. And finally, you asked me out."

It was true. I had watched her for weeks, visited every show. She eased my mind, kept the Darkness away. Until that one fatal... no, glorious night when I asked her to sit with me and drink champagne. The Darkness had been tamed, I thought. I was at peace. I wanted to celebrate. We got drunk, I took her to one of those cheap hotel rooms. And in bed, her warm body against mine, the Darkness returned. Famished, angry, unstoppable.

I raped her. I killed her. My hands closed around her throat and I squeezed until she was dead. It felt so good.

"I was your first, but not your last."

Emerald Moon was my first one, but after her it became easy. They all asked for it. Teasing, seducing, showing their legs and bums and tits. They smiled and laughed and were so stupid. Did they not know the world was full of Darkness and violence? I lured them with cheap presents and sweets, with easy compliments and flowers. The whores sat on my lap or laid in my bed. They undressed themselves and showed me their bodies. I let the Darkness take them. Some screamed, some fought, some begged, some cried. All died. The Darkness in me devoured them. They got what they deserved.

The hands at my throat were no surprise.

She can't do it. Her hands are too small, she is not strong enough.

Her fingers seemed to grow, gaining in strength.

I made one last attempt to break free.

Futile.

Hands around my throat. Squeezing and squeezing.

I kept fighting nonetheless. In my mind, I cursed her a thousand times.

Breath, sweet breath! Please! *Pleasepleasepleaseplease.* I will never do it again. I will change. I will...

No mercy. The filthy bitch.

I felt light-headed. Those red eyes. I knew I was going to die.

My head spun.

Heat.

Red.

My lungs burned, no release.

I don't deserve this! I... I...

Darkness.

***

The being that once was Emerald Moon stepped back from the body. Her killer was dead; justice had been done.

"Thank you," the girl whispered. Silence was the only answer. The ghost of Emerald Moon faded away.

And I?

Yes, I.

I am still here. A whisper, a shadow, now a ghost, too. Damnation. I am bound to this filthy place. I can see, hear, feel, but I can never touch. All those delights, taunting and teasing, always out of reach. All those dumb girls, asking for it. *Take them, use them, give them to me*, the Darkness demands.

I want to give in, but I am unable. It is Hell.

Remember me, dear visitor of Theatre d'Obscure. I will be watching the show with you. I will see the flesh, the lambs, the seduction and the promises.

And I will hate every second of it.

About the Author

Jaap Boekestein (1968) is an award winning Dutch writer of science fiction, fantasy, horror, thrillers and whatever takes his fancy. Five novels and almost three hundred of his stories have been published. He has made his living as a bouncer, working for a detective agency and as editor. He currently works for the Dutch Ministry of Security and Justice. His English publications include stories in: *Cyäegha*, *Nonbianary Review*, *Strange Shifters*, *Lovecraft after Dark*, *Surreal Nightmares*, *Urban Temples of Cthulhu* and *Sirens Call 27*. http://jaapboekestein.com/.

THE ATTIC ROOM

By Sammi Cox

Bryony Thompson pulled into the half-full car park and switched off the ignition, cursing her luck. But she supposed that was the problem with going to visit friends who lived in the middle of nowhere. If you had car trouble, you'd had it.

Looking out her window, she couldn't see anything in the gloom. There seemed to be nothing around this lonely spot for miles, and yet the road sign had indicated that a village – no more than a little hamlet, most likely – was close by.

Still, the isolation and the stillness unnerved her. She was a city girl, used to the hustle and bustle of an urban environment that was always moving, always visible.

She got out of the car and crossed the gravel to where the welcoming golden light was oozing out from all the downstairs windows, doing its best to keep the early winter night at bay. The sign, hanging from a bracket on the wall facing the road proclaiming that this was the Blacksmith's Arms, creaked once as if pushed and then immediately quieted. A shiver ran up Bryony's spine. She hated the country.

Pushing open the door, she stepped under the low doorway – a sign of the age of the inn. The current building probably dated back to the sixteenth or seventeenth century.

In the small hallway, there was an unmanned reception desk, positioned in front of a set of narrow stairs that led to the upper floor of the building. To the right, was a sign that pointed to the restaurant. To the left, one that pointed to the bar.

Thinking the latter would be more populated at this time of day, she opened the door on the left and entered.

It was a typical, traditional old pub. Horse brasses and copper kitchen utensils were everywhere, interspersed with ceramic pitchers of flowers and old iron farm equipment. Hanging from the beamed ceiling could be found corn dollies, plaits and wheels, probably locally made this last harvest past, as they no doubt had been in these parts for generations.

"Good evening, miss," a middle-aged gentleman called out from one of the tables.

With one glance, Bryony could see that the bar, like the reception desk, was currently unattended.

"Hi," she smiled, awkwardly.

"You seem lost."

"No, not lost. Just delayed. I've got a bit of car trouble. I called the nearest garage and they said they couldn't get out to me until tomorrow morning. So they directed me here. Thankfully, the car made it."

"So you'll be wanting a room, then?" another voice said from behind her, making her jump. She hadn't heard them nor felt their presence so close to her.

Bryony turned around to find standing only a few feet away, a woman shorter than herself, around forty-five years of age.

She had a hard face, but a soft smile, that quickly broke out as she realised she had startled her guest.

"Didn't mean to frighten you, there." She put her hands on her hips and sighed. Although her manner was abrupt, the smile was friendly. And yet that sigh - almost a huff - spoke volumes. It told everyone in the room that the woman wasn't happy someone wanted a room for the night in her pub.

Bryony picked up on it and immediately felt uncomfortable. "Sorry, is there a problem?"

"We've only got a few rooms of guest accommodation here. We're not exactly a popular tourist destination, being so far away from everything. But what we do have is already occupied, I'm afraid."

"Oh."

The gentleman at the table stood up and walked to the farthest side of the room, indicating for the landlady to join him. He had probably thought Bryony couldn't hear what he was about to say. He was wrong.

"You do have *one* more room, Jan."

"I can't put a young woman in there all on her own."

"What else is she going to do? Bed down in the stables with the horses? Kip in the bar? You heard her; she's stuck out here until tomorrow and she needs somewhere to stay."

"*Matthew*. You know very well why I can't do that."

"So you're going to turn her out?"

Bryony took a few steps closer to them. "I'm sorry. I didn't mean to overhear, but… why can't I stay in this room you're talking about?"

"Because it's supposedly *haunted*, my dear," Matthew said.

"Ain't no supposedly about it," Jan, the landlady, snapped. Bryony got the feeling this was an argument the pair had had before.

"I don't believe in ghosts and things like that," Bryony countered, waving her hand in the air, as if that somehow explained what "things like that" meant.

"See! She's a sensible girl. Now, stop fretting and get her checked in."

The landlady scowled at Matthew before studying Bryony's face. It was obvious she didn't want to give her the room, but what choice did she have?

"Fine, but don't say I didn't warn you. And at the first sign things don't seem right, you get out of there and come and find me."

Jan marched off through a doorway behind the bar.

"Don't mind her. Jan thinks she's looking out for you. As if sleeping in your car on a night like this would do you any favours."

At that moment, a strong gust of wind rattled a stout tree branch against the window, causing a high-pitched scraping sound to echo round the room. The wind had certainly picked up since she'd left her car.

"She doesn't mind too much if the guests aren't alone, but she tends to get a little overprotective when it's single women."

"Why?"

"Ah... well... that'd be because of-"

Again, the landlady appeared as if from nowhere, elbowing Matthew out of the way. "Let's get you checked in then, and sort you out something to eat. You look like you could do with a proper home-cooked meal. Nothing fancy here, just proper food."

The landlady guided Bryony swiftly out of the bar and back to reception.

"I'll find the key while you go and get your bags from the car. The name's Jan, by the way. You've already met Matthew. It's his night off, but he's either working here or drinking here, causing me trouble one way or another..."

Once Jan ceased her grumbling, Bryony introduced herself. Then the landlady shooed her towards the door so she could get what she needed for her stay.

***

As Bryony stepped out into the cold, she noticed just how low the temperature had dropped. There would be a heavy frost come morning. She couldn't imagine trying to sleep outside in the car in this weather. Grabbing her bags, she trudged back towards the inn, just as the first drops of cold rain - or was it sleet? - began to fall.

Back inside, where it was dry and warm, the landlady led

her up the stairs behind reception, turning right when the first-floor corridor split into two, mirroring the layout of the floor below. At the end of the corridor was a doorway, but unlike Bryony expected, there wasn't a room behind it, but rather a short flight of stairs. Just inside, the landlady flicked a switch and the stairwell and the room above lit up.

At the top of the stairs, Bryony was speechless. She couldn't imagine a more beautiful room, and to think the landlady spent most of her time refusing to use it!

"It's stunning. Magazine-photo-shoot stunning." Bryony didn't bother to hide her surprise.

The room was large, probably the size of two, if not three, of the other rooms on the first floor. The walls that housed the windows sloped towards one another, though they didn't meet. The floorboards had been painted white, just enough to let the grain of the wood come through. The walls were also white, while the furniture was antique dark wood, creating a striking contrast.

"I was expecting something dark and dank, I must confess." Damp, dusty, dirty and full of cobwebs, too, she thought, but didn't want to say that and appear rude.

But the landlady remained silent. She was still not happy about her staying.

"Well, I suppose I had better let you get settled, then," Jan said, after a time. "Here's the key. The restaurant starts serving at six. Like I said earlier, proper home-cooked food. Nothing too fancy, I'm afraid." Jan edged her way towards the stairs. When she reached them, she turned back to face Bryony, her face creased with concern. "And if you should need anything... well... you know where you can find me."

With that, she quickly descended the stairs and shut the door behind her. Bryony was left alone.

In the quiet, she unpacked some things she might need that evening and the following morning, whilst thinking over the strange behaviour of the landlady, and what Matthew had said. Hanging up a few of her tops in the wardrobe, she realised they hadn't claimed that the pub was haunted; only this particular room. But why?

As soon as the question manifested in her mind, she decided she didn't want to know. She didn't believe in ghosts, that was true, but neither did she want to go out of her way to frighten herself into a sleepless night. She still had a fair distance to travel tomorrow, and driving whilst tired was not a great idea. And, she certainly had no intention of allowing another person's superstition to affect her.

Quickly changing out of the clothes she had spent the day driving in, she freshened up and then headed downstairs towards the restaurant and dinner. That, she hoped, would put this nonsense to bed.

***

The restaurant was an almost exact replica of the bar and

crammed full of the same "olde worlde" paraphernalia, alongside which, jostling for space on the walls, were old black and white photos of the pub from bygone eras. For a moment, Bryony saw the pub as the sort of place where the people in the aged photographs could walk straight off the wall and into the room with her, and it made her think of her haunted room. A chill ran up her spine.

Determined to ignore it, she marched over to a table and sat down to peruse the menu. Very quickly, Bryony realised that Jan had not been joking when she said they only served what the older generations tended to term "proper food." There was nothing light, and nothing other than British cuisine, much to Bryony's dismay. When Jan arrived at her table to take her order – sausage and mash with onion gravy – the landlady made one more comment about whether Bryony was sure she wanted to stay.

"Look, I appreciate your concern, but you really don't need to worry. I'm a big girl. I can take care of myself."

Jan huffed, then disappeared into the kitchen.

Dinner was a quiet affair. Only a couple of the other guests chose to eat in the restaurant and they kept to themselves. The others favoured the bar.

Just as she had finished dessert – apple crumble and custard that Jan insisted she give a try – Matthew walked into the restaurant. On spotting Bryony, he headed straight over.

"Don't fret over what Jan said," he said, sitting down. "I

would hate for one slip of the tongue to ruin your stay. It's such a nice inn, this, and we don't get too many new faces here. It would be a shame for this little joke to spoil it."

Bryony sipped her lime and lemonade, choosing to ignore Matthews's inclination towards understatement. "I understand. It's a nice place. I would be interested to hear more about the pub and its history."

"Well, wait one minute." He exited the restaurant only to return thirty seconds later carrying a hardback book. It looked old.

Handing it over to her, he said, "A little light bedtime reading. It was written about forty years ago, but the chapter on the Blacksmith's Arms won't have changed at all. Some chap went round to all the pubs in the county and put together everything he could find about each one; historical records, folk memories, and myths and legends that he thought someone down the line might find interesting. It's not a long chapter."

Bryony thanked Matthew and promised to return the book before she left the following day. Then she headed back to her room, to bed. She could feel Jan's eyes on her all the way to the door. That, if nothing else since her arrival, unnerved her.

***

Getting into bed, she curled up with the book Matthew had lent her. It had been such a long and busy day, however, that she didn't make it past the first paragraph before the book was slipping out of her hands on to the bed covers, and she was falling fast asleep...

***

A loud bang had Bryony sitting bolt upright in the bed, feeling confused and disoriented, in a room that was not her own. In the dim light cast from the bedside lamp, she glanced about and then recalled the events of the day before. Her car had broken down but she had managed to make it to the Blacksmith's Arms, a pub in the middle of nowhere.

Rubbing her face and working to calm her breathing, she tried to work out what had woken her so suddenly, but nothing appeared out of place in the room. Heavy rain splattered loudly against the windowpane, but that wasn't the cause behind her waking. It was a *bang* or a *thud* she had heard.

Leaning over to the bedside table, she grabbed her phone. The display read: *2:33am.* As she put the phone back down, she spotted out of the corner of her eye, half sticking out from under the bed, the book she had been reading. She reached down to pick it up, deciding it must have been the book falling onto the floor that had startled her from sleep. Just as her fingers brushed the cover, something out of sight brushed the top of her hand.

There was something under the bed.

Gasping, she recoiled and moved away from the edge. With her heart beating rapidly, she couldn't remember the last time something had made her jump so.

But what the hell was it?

With a nervous, embarrassed laugh it dawned on her. The bottom of the valance that went around the bed frame must have lightly skimmed over her skin as she made to retrieve the book. There was no monster under the bed, nor some ghost lurking, waiting to terrify her.

Still, it took her a minute or two to feel at ease once more.

When her mind had settled and her breathing had returned to normal, she scolded herself for being so childish, then moved the book to the safety of the bedside table and turned out the light.

Only… in the dark, the room now seemed different. Strange. There was a tension in the air that hadn't been there before. She couldn't help it; she felt afraid. But of what and why, she had no idea.

Bryony rolled over and pulled the covers up to her ears, her eyes shut as tight as they would go. She willed herself to fall asleep. She didn't want to hear any noise in the room, and yet, she found herself straining to catch even the smallest sound, though the space was as silent as the grave.

Then a floorboard creaked over by the stairs. She whimpered and pulled the blankets higher, her heart thundering in her chest. Had she really heard it, or was her imagination playing tricks on her?

Her answer came when she sensed, rather than heard, something to one side of the bed. In the darkness, she knew it was coming closer and closer. But there was no other noise in the room

415

except her quick, shallow breathing that seemed deafening in the silence.

That was, until something climbed on the bed, causing the mattress to squeak. It was only then that Bryony decided this was real and she needed to do something. She couldn't stay hiding in the bed.

But it was too late. The covers were ripped back away from her face, though in the darkness she couldn't see anything. As she made to get up – her intention being to make it to the stairs – something held her down, making it hard to breathe. An invisible weight was on her chest, pinning her to the bed, whilst she could feel something tightening around her neck.

Flailing about in a panic, Bryony's hand struck the book on the bedside table which brought it crashing to the floor with a thump much louder than the one that had roused her. On the way down, it knocked over the lamp, which followed the book to smash upon the floorboards.

Moments later – though to Bryony it felt much, much longer – there was a sound at the door, the light flickered on and Bryony came face to face with her ghostly attacker. And wished she hadn't. Although it was only a glimpse – the brightness of the sudden light in the room caused her to momentarily close her eyes – it was a sight that she knew would stay with her forever. Footsteps hurried up the stairs, and then Bryony saw Jan, wrapped in a flannel dressing gown, charging at the bed.

"You get off o'her!" she screamed, as she cast something – it looked like dust – in the air in their direction. As soon as it struck the ghost, she vanished, growling and hissing as she disappeared.

Holding her throat, Bryony took in great lungfuls of air. She tried not to cry, but a few tears did escape.

Then Jan was there, all motherly, with an arm around her shoulder, patting her on the head and mumbling comforting things. 'There, there. It's all right. You're safe now. She's gone and won't be back in a hurry. There, there.'

When the shock had passed and Jan could tell Bryony had somewhat recovered, she let her go.

"My neck," Bryony whispered. "I could feel her hands around my neck." She lifted her head back for Jan to inspect the skin around her throat.

"I know, I know. There's no mark, no bruising, and there won't be. There never is."

"Would she have killed me?"

"I don't know if she can, truth be told. But it's frightening enough as it is. Come on. Get your things together. You're not staying another moment in this room."

Bryony didn't need telling twice. She jumped out of bed, and started to refill her suitcase. In less than a minute, she was following Jan down the stairs and across the corridor to another room.

"This is my room. You take the bed. I'll take the sofa."

Soon they were both lying down, tucked in, with a low lamp mutedly glowing in the corner of the room. However, neither of them was quite ready for sleep, Bryony especially. She had a thousand questions running through her mind.

"Go on," Jan whispered. "I know you have things you want to ask. I would too in your place."

"Who was she? And what was that you threw at her? It looked like black dust."

"Ashes and salt."

"*Ashes*? As in the cremated remains of a dead person?" Bryony's voice was filled with horror and disgust as she checked to make sure there was none in her hair.

"No," Jan almost laughed. "Ashes from the grates downstairs. Ashes to remind her she's dead. Salt to send her away, though not for good. She still comes back." Jan sighed. "It was my mother who told me about that. And her mother told her. An old woman turned up here, many moons ago, before even my grandmother was born and said to use a mixture of ashes and salt to help with the 'disquiet.' Old Peggy has been causing a stir in this pub for generations."

Old Peggy. So that was her name. Bryony thought over what she had seen between the lights coming on and the ashes and salt hitting... the entity? The ghost? Whatever was on the bed. A grey form tinged with green, dark eyes and black teeth, straggly hair waving around her head like Medusa's snakes. The thing was so *angry*, and that saddened Bryony a little. When you died, you were supposed to rest in peace, *be* at peace. But Old Peggy was the furthest thing from it. She was *enraged*.

"Is there nothing that can be done for her? To help her on her way?"

"We've had priests come in and exorcists, but it's done no good. She refuses to leave and doesn't want to move on. She can't seem to let go of that fury that possesses her."

"Just why is she so mad?"

"It's not a pleasant story."

"I guessed it wouldn't be. Otherwise, I rather doubt she would be spending eternity terrorising people. Please, tell me."

Jan made one of her customary sighs, and then acquiesced. "Well, the story goes, back in the early 1700's, Old Peggy ran this pub with her husband, Billy. She loved him from the moment she first laid eyes on him, but he was more interested in getting his hands on the Blacksmith's Arms, which belonged to her father. Anyway, they married and when the father died, the pub came to them. But it was Peggy that did most of the work, while her husband drank and chased after women. Not that Peggy believed it; it's said that she loved him something fierce. That was until one day she returned home early from going into town – her horse had thrown a shoe, or some such. When she got back, she searched the inn for Billy, from the cellars and stables, to their rooms on the first floor, and couldn't find him anywhere. There was only one place left to look. The attic where the maids slept."

"At the top of the building. Where I was staying."

"Exactly."

"And I can assume she found Billy, and he wasn't alone."

"Yes. Overcome with rage, she grabbed the first thing that came to hand: some say it was a poker and others a knife. Either way, she stabbed him with it a few times. He managed to make it down to the tap room before collapsing and dying. The men drinking downstairs, wanting to know what had happened to the landlord, followed the trail of blood all the way to the attic room, where they found Old Peggy, covered in Billy's blood, leaning over the dead body of the maid.

"Of course, she was hanged for it, but they quickly learnt that Old Peggy was still here, and what she would do if she found a young woman, alone in that attic room.

"Now, I think that's enough ghost stories for one night," Jan concluded, rolling over. "We both need to try and get some sleep."

"Thanks, Jan."

"For what?"

"For rescuing me even though I ignored your warnings. Next time someone tells me I can't sleep in a haunted room, I'll not argue with them."

Jan chuckled lightly. "Somehow, I believe you."

About the Author

Sammi Cox lives in the UK and spends her time writing and making things. Ghost stories, fairy tales, folklore and witchcraft have all played their part in firing up her imagination and inspiring her to write. You can keep up to date with whatever she is scribbling by visiting her blog: https://sammiscribbles.wordpress.com/.

HUSH

By Edmund Stone

Brenda stood on the sidewalk next to the tall shotgun house. A cold wind crept up her back, helping to punctuate the feeling of uncertainty that nagged her. This was her first time on her own, though she seemed to be that way most of her life. Her mother had passed away giving birth to her and her stepmother treated her as a second citizen. Brenda flipped the collar of her coat up to shield herself from the increasingly frigid air. She felt a storm coming on and wanted to be inside, but she would tough it out. The landlord had to show soon.

Clouds were forming in the sky, enhancing the dark façade of the house. The number on the front read 112. She looked up at the street sign. Second and Vine, the address the landlord had mentioned over the phone. The house was reminiscent of a French dwelling, with fleur-de-lis designs adorning a wrought iron railing on the second story. The balcony looked to be closed off. Brenda had arrived a few minutes early, to make sure she had enough time to find the place. But now the owner of the building was late, only adding to Brenda's nervousness. As she stood there, moving around to stay warm, she scanned the street pole and noticed a recent poster of a girl fluttering in the wind. A blonde-haired beauty, smiling as though she hadn't a care in the world. It read:

Missing Person, Sally Freeman.

If you have any information on her whereabouts, please

call.

Brenda peered at the photo for a moment and felt remorse for the girl and her family. She thought the girl to be a victim of the drug trade; another unfortunate teen that ended up on the wrong side of things.

Brenda, young herself, was a sophomore in college. She had lived with her fiancé during her freshmen year, but soon found that the two of them were too young for that to work. Her stepmother had tried to warn her.

"Foolish girl, why do you always let yourself get into situations like that?" she would say. But when did Brenda ever listen to that woman? It was funny that her stepmother should even give a Holy Hell now. She sure hadn't cared during the time Brenda lived in her house.

The disastrous ending to that relationship resulted in the decision to seek out an apartment in town. She also wanted to avoid the high cost of campus living. The dormitories were owned by second party landlords and were only loosely affiliated with the college she attended. So, the rent was exorbitant to say the least. This new place was two blocks from campus. Farther than she would like. She would have to get up earlier to get to class on time, but the savings were worth it.

A car pulled up to the sidewalk and a small lady, who looked to be in her mid-fifties, got out.

"Hi, you must be Brenda?"

"Yes, I'm here to check out the apartment."

"Right. My name is Sadie and I own this lovely house," the lady said. She produced a small key and placed it in the keyhole below the doorknob. She jiggled the key up and down until a low click signaled the lock's release. "These old homes tend to have their own temperament," Sadie explained. "This lock was replaced when the house was renovated, but it's never worked right."

Sadie pushed the door open, and they walked inside. A large foyer greeted them with a stairway off to the side that stretched up to a second floor. A red mahogany stair rail, with wrought iron posts beneath it, adorned the staircase. Swirls worked inward to a fleur-de-lis design in the middle. The architecture was very nineteen twenties. Large crown molding snaked along the top of the walls and pressed tin blocks were patterned across the ceiling. Black and white tiles decorated the floor in diamond shapes that stretched out across the entire room. A black, non-descript door with a glass knob lay behind the stairway.

"The apartment is at the top of the stairs," Sadie said.

"Where does that door go?" Brenda asked. Sadie looked at the door.

"I'm not sure; I've never been able to open it. The locksmith who made the keys for me couldn't figure it out either. Old houses." Sadie shrugged her shoulders.

The stairs were the same red mahogany of the stair rail and they creaked with each step. At the top was a small ledge, no more than a few feet, with more of the same stair rail. At the end was a large door, also mahogany, with a glass knob.

"Is this the only apartment in the building?" Brenda asked.

"Oh, umm, yes. There were several rooms in this building at one time, but some contractor thought it would be a good idea to section off the whole place, make it a sort of duplex, I suppose. I think it just destroyed the charm of the original place. I used to live close by here, but went away for a while. When I came back this section of the building was for sale, so I bought it. I'd like to buy it all back and restore it to its former glory."

Sadie turned the doorknob. The door creaked open with an audible clack. The room inside was small and open, with one window. The twenties architecture continued, with oak hardwood floors in a herringbone design that covered the floor and there was more of the crown molding at the top of the walls. A bed was neatly tucked into the corner and an antique desk sat beside it, with a tiffany style lamp. There was a kitchen area on the other side of the room, complete with a gas stove and four feet of counter space. A small microwave sat on the counter and a refrigerator was at the end. Beside it, an open door revealed a bathroom with a pedestal sink and claw-foot tub, complete with a shower and curtain. The black and white tiles that covered the foyer adorned the bathroom as well.

"What do you think?" Sadie asked.

"It's nice, and I do like that this place is close to the

school."

"Two blocks," Sadie pointed out.

"I think I'll take it," Brenda said.

"Great. The rent is six hundred a month with the first month's rent as the deposit. I make all of my tenants sign a six-month lease, also."

Brenda thought for a moment. This was close and still much cheaper than campus. "How soon can I move in?"

"The apartment is ready. So, as soon as you'd like," Sadie said.

"Okay. I'll call my dad. He said he would pay my deposit if I found something. It shouldn't take more than a couple of days."

"That's wonderful, dear. I think you'll like it here. This place has character and good bones," Sadie said. She looked at her with a disingenuous smile and turned to walk toward the stairs. Brenda followed close behind. When Sadie got to the street, she started for her car, but paused for a moment and looked at Brenda.

"You look as pretty as the last girl who stayed here," she said.

"Why did she move out?"

"I'm not sure. She didn't even tell me she was leaving. I do know she left before her lease was up. She was a nice girl, but did complain at times. I'm sure you won't do that. You seem very well rounded," Sadie said.

Brenda produced a half-smile and said, "No. I'm sure I

won't."

"Ta-ta. See you in a couple of days with the keys." Sadie got into her car and drove away. Brenda called her parents to make arrangements. She looked up at the house one more time and headed for her car.

***

Two days later Brenda moved into the shotgun house on Second and Vine. After she moved her personal belongings into her new room, she decided to look around the place. There wasn't much to see beyond the foyer. The black door at the end of the room stood out like a beacon and Brenda couldn't help herself. She had to investigate. Even though Sadie said it couldn't be opened, Brenda wanted to try.

She turned the knob, but the door was locked and wouldn't budge. Brenda tried the key. It entered the bolt, but wouldn't turn. She wiggled up and down and pulled the key out a little, but still nothing. There was a cold draft on her feet, coming from the bottom of the door. *Must go to a basement*, she thought.

Brenda gave up and went back to her room to make supper. Ramen noodles and leftover pizza were on the menu tonight. She poured a glass of Moscato wine and made a silent toast to her new place. Before Brenda knew it, she had consumed half the bottle and her eyes were heavy from the alcohol. She curled up in bed and pulled the covers up tight around her neck. She fell asleep quickly.

In the middle of the night, a loud clack woke her up. Startled, she rose from the bed. It was too dark to see, so she turned on the lamp to get a better look. Brenda surveyed the room. Nothing seemed out of place. Then she heard a creak from downstairs in the foyer.

Brenda hopped back in bed and pulled the covers over her head. She tried to ignore the noise, but realized that the door to her room didn't lock. Anyone could walk through. She heard the creak again, louder this time, followed by a noise. It sounded like music, but she wasn't sure.

Brenda reached into her backpack and fumbled around until she found a small handgun; a snubbed-nose .38 caliber revolver. The one her daddy taught her to shoot, before she came to the city. She got out of bed and walked toward the door. She cracked it open and looked out into the foyer. She flipped the light switch by the door, but the light didn't work. Brenda awkwardly stumbled for her phone. With shaky hands, she pushed the flashlight app and shined it at the stairs. There was nothing there. She heard the creak again, but this time a voice accompanied it; a female voice.

Hush little baby, don't say a word,

Mama's going to buy you a mockingbird.

Brenda closed the door, but could still hear the muffled sound downstairs. She was shaking so hard, she nearly dropped the phone. *What the Hell am I going to do now? Maybe I should call 911? What would daddy do in this situation? He'd say, "Stick that* gun in their face and watch 'em piss down both legs!" If I'm going to live alone, I must be strong.

She breathed deeply and with gun in hand, eased her way out onto the landing and toward the stairway. With her phone in the other hand, the flashlight app's beam guided her down the stairs.

She heard the creak again and realized the noise wasn't coming from the entrance, it was coming from the door by the stairway. At the bottom of the stairs, she walked into the foyer. She shined the flashlight toward the back of the room. The black door was slightly open.

Brenda held the gun up in front of her and walked toward the door. She heard the song again, coming from just behind the door. A soft, female voice, almost a whisper.

If that mockingbird won't sing,

Mama's going to buy you a diamond ring.

She reached out and grasped the doorknob, but it slipped from her hand and the door slammed shut. She stepped back and over her shoulder heard, *"Hush!"*

Brenda dropped her phone on its back and the room fell dark. She bent down and frantically moved her hands back and forth across the floor until she located the phone. She turned around and aimed the light at the stairway. She pointed the gun into the air of an empty foyer, the phone's light moving in cadence with her shaking hands.

Brenda gathered herself and ran back up the stairs. She closed the door behind her and jumped into bed, pulling the covers tight over her head once more. She cradled the gun to her chest like an infant. *What the Hell just happened?* Whatever it was, Brenda wanted no part of it. She lay there, with goose bumped flesh, until sleep finally took her.

Brenda woke to daylight streaming through the window. She raked the covers from her head and adjusted her eyes to the obtrusive brightness. She squinted to look at the clock on the wall. 10:00 am.

"Damn, I'm late for class!" she cried. The covers flew to the floor as she made her way to the shower. After bathing, she dressed quickly, then grabbed her book bag and headed out the door. She ran down the stairs, but before going out to the street, she looked back at the black door. It was shut, as though nothing had happened. Maybe it hadn't. Maybe she'd been dreaming. She would call Sadie, though, the first chance she got.

After class, Brenda walked the two blocks to her apartment. She pulled her coat around her and tightened the wool scarf at her neck, trying to block the cold. As she walked, she noticed another flyer for the missing girl. This one had extra information on it and a photo of a girl in a sweater and plaid skirt.

Missing: Sally Freeman, age 22. She was last seen at Second and Vine, living in apartment 122. If anyone has any information, please call.

Brenda fumbled for the phone in her coat pocket and called Sadie.

"Sadie?"

"Yes, who is this?"

"It's me, Brenda, your tenant."

"Oh yes, dear. How are you? Is everything all right with the apartment?"

"Yes, the apartment is fine, but I'm calling about the door at the bottom of the stairs. Has it ever opened by itself before?" There was a pause on the other end before Sadie responded.

"No, dear. I told you that door hasn't been opened since I owned the apartment. Did something happen?"

"No, everything is fine," Brenda said. "Sadie? Did the last girl who rented from you hear things?"

"Well, now that you mention it, she did complain of noises in the apartment. But she left so suddenly, I never got the chance to check it out," Sadie said. "She must have been in some trouble, because she left her clothes there and the keys were on the countertop. I never heard from her after that."

"What was her name?"

"It was Sally, I think." Brenda stood, numb and cold, the blood draining from her face .

"Was it Sally Freeman?" Brenda breathed.

"Yes, that was it! Did you know her?"

"No. I just heard her name somewhere, maybe from school.

Thanks Sadie, I'll talk to you later."

"Okay, if you need anything else, don't be afraid to call," Sadie said and hung up the phone. Afraid? Brenda was so afraid, she didn't know if she could go back to the apartment. But she had no choice, she'd signed a lease. She studied the flyer and jotted down the number.

It was dusk when she arrived at the apartment and an eerie dark covered the front of the house. Brenda opened the front door and walked into the foyer. She reached for the light switch to her right. The yellow incandescent bulb glowed brightly, giving her the ability to navigate the stairway safely.

Shadows crept throughout the house, covering everything below the stairway. Brenda didn't want to think about the door, but it invaded her thoughts no matter how hard she tried to ignore it. She tapped on the flashlight app from her phone's home screen, and shined it at the door. Deciding to face her fears, she tried the door again. She wiggled the handle, but it was still locked. Her stomach growled and she realized she hadn't eaten since morning.

Brenda ascended the steps to her apartment. She looked in the cupboard and found some more Ramen noodles and saltine crackers. She boiled the noodles then took her budget meal to the table and pulled the number she jotted down from her pocket. She dialed the number.

"Hello? Who is this?" asked a woman's voice on the other end.

"Hi. You don't know me, but my name is Brenda and I rent an apartment on Second and Vine; the number 122." There was a strange silence on the other end. "Hello? Is anyone there?"

"I'm still here. My daughter was last seen at that apartment. How long have you been renting it?" the woman said.

"Only a couple of days now, but I signed a lease, so I'll be here for a while. Your daughter was Sally Freeman?" Brenda asked.

"Yes. How do you know that?"

"Oh, I'm sorry. I found this number on the flyer outside the apartment. I'm sorry for calling, but I wonder if you can give me any information she had about this place," Brenda said.

"Get out of there. Get out as fast as you can," the woman said.

"Excuse me?"

"That place is toxic. My Sally called me several times before she went missing. Have you heard voices downstairs?" Brenda dropped her spoon into the bowl of noodles. She suddenly felt light headed.

"Uhmm…I'm not sure. What do you mean?"

"The voices, like nursery rhymes. You had to have heard them," Sally's mother said. Brenda's mind began to reel.

"I guess I did hear something. I thought I was dreaming," Brenda said.

"That's what Sally said. I brushed it off as the same, but

now I'm not so sure. No one has called since I put those flyers up, until tonight. Have you seen my Sally? Did you see her in that apartment? For God's sake, she was pregnant! I have to know if she's okay!" the frantic woman cried into the phone.

"I...I don't know. I haven't seen her; she was pregnant? My God, I'm sorry," is all Brenda could manage. "I have to go now."

"No, don't hang up. I have to know if she's still there, please!" Sally's mother continued.

"I have to go, I'm sorry...I'm sorry," Brenda said. She pushed the end call on the screen and hung up. Brenda sat there shaking. She had no idea what to do. The phone screen came to life again, Sally's mother calling back. Brenda ignored it, put the phone on silent and threw it face down on the bed. She buried her face in her hands and wept. The girl was pregnant? Brenda needed to clear her head, maybe a bath would help.

In the bathroom, she filled the deep claw-foot tub to the brim, then immersed herself in the steaming water with only her head showing. She relaxed in the heat, trying to forget what happened. The phone vibrated a few more times on the bed in the other room, but soon stopped. The apartment fell silent and Brenda drifted off to sleep. A sound woke her. Soft, but urgent; a woman's voice whispering.

Hush little, baby. Don't say a word...

Brenda rose from the water and looked around. The room

was empty. She grabbed her towel from the rack near the tub and wrapped it around her. She crept into the bedroom and flipped the light switch on. The overhead light filled the room with soft, white brilliance. Brenda gathered her night clothes and put them on while keeping an eye on the door. She fished the gun from her purse and grabbed her phone. She eased up to the door and opened it just enough to peer out into the foyer. The yellow light above the stairway was still on; the stairs and entrance door lit. The rest of the foyer was dark.

Brenda opened the door as gently as possible but it creaked as it swung out. Brenda cringed, fearful something would hear. She tiptoed out onto the ledge and looked over the railing. She craned her neck to the side and scanned the floor below. A dark blanket covered everything from the bottom of the stairs back to the black door. She heard a clack and a sliver of light invaded the foyer.

She descended the stairs, staying close to the wall. Every step brought a new wave of terror, but she was determined to keep going.

The light from the door created a path for her, like the beacon from a lighthouse. As she moved toward the door, the air began to get colder. Brenda could see her breath in front of her, hovering in the air by the thin tendril of luminescence emitted from the cracked door. The light above the stairway started to blink and make a low buzz. The door slammed shut.

She froze, the gun held in front of her, the barrel so cold it stung her fingers but she held on tight. A creaking noise came from the top of the stairs. Brenda turned toward it, the gun shaking uncontrollably in her hands. The cold had intensified and her teeth chattered.

She looked up to see a lady in a blue dress with a white smock that had a red cross emblazoned on the front. She looked like a nurse, from long ago. She was holding an infant close to her chest. She stroked its hair as the infant cried. As she walked, she sang:

> *Hush little baby, don't say a word*
> *Mama's going to buy you a mockingbird.*
> *If that mockingbird don't sing,*
> *Mama's going to buy you a diamond ring.*

The glowing figure mesmerized Brenda. She had no recourse. She could only watch in amazement as the ethereal being came closer and closer. It turned at the bottom of the railing and continued to saunter toward her. The aura around the nurse glowed brighter as she approached. She continued to sing.

> *If that diamond ring turns brass,*
> *Mama's going to buy you a looking glass*

The door opened wide and a rush of cold air rolled out into the foyer. Brenda felt as though her blood would freeze, as she shook violently from the cold. The nurse continued to move in an apparent path toward the door. But as she walked in front of Brenda, she hesitated. Brenda's knees went weak with fear and she fell to the floor. She scooted herself back against the wall, the gun still firmly grasped before her.

The nurse seemed to consider Brenda. Her head tilted and moved from side to side, as if studying her. Her eyes were white, void of all color. Brenda wasn't sure if the nurse could actually see her, or if she simply felt her presence. Without warning, the nurse opened her mouth and emitted a shrill, ear piercing shriek. The baby began to cry and the combined noises echoed loudly throughout the foyer. The nurse lunged toward Brenda.

Brenda snapped her eyes shut and fired the gun. The bang assaulted her ears, an incessant ringing to replace the nurse and baby's screams. When she opened her eyes, the light above the stairway was back on. There was a bullet hole in the wall, but no nurse. The cold had subsided and she was warm, as though she never experienced any temperature change at all.

Brenda ran back up the stairs and jumped into bed. She pulled the covers over her head and wept. She had never experienced fear like this before. She didn't want to be here alone anymore. Her body convulsed with sobs as she cried herself to sleep.

When next she pulled the covers back, morning light illuminated the room. Brenda was still shaken, but felt more secure, now that the day had arrived. On her way to the bathroom, a wave of nausea overcame her. She ran for the toilet and fell to her knees. She pitched her head over the cold porcelain and heaved into it the contents of her stomach. She continued until nothing was left but dry heaves.

Brenda sat back on her bottom and leaned up against the wall. She was never sick in the morning. Maybe it was from the events of last night? Her head was spinning and she felt dizzy. Then a thought occurred to her: she was late for her period.

She climbed to her feet and tried to think back to when she had lived with her boyfriend; had she missed a pill in the blister pack? Her mind reeled with possibilities. One thing was certain, she would need a test from the drugstore to confirm her suspicions.

Brenda took a quick shower, dressed and grabbed her purse. She ran down the stairs, jumping the last two steps in an attempt to avoid the foyer, and headed straight for the door. It opened with force from her enthusiasm. She was taken aback by the sight of a woman about to knock.

"Hello? Do I know you?" Brenda said.

"I'm Doris; Doris Freeman. I'm Sally Freeman's mother. I think we spoke on the phone last night. You called me," the woman said. Brenda stared, caught off guard.

"Umm…yes I remember you calling. I'm sorry I didn't call back. I had some… things come up," Brenda said. Doris looked at her. Brenda looked away uncomfortably.

"You've seen her," Doris said. "You've seen the nurse."

"I don't know what you're talking about. I have to go, I've got a class to get to," Brenda said. She tried to sidestep Doris but was grabbed by the arm.

"You can't go back in that house. It's too dangerous. Where are your parents? Do they know what's going on? Have you told them?" Brenda pulled away indignantly.

"I have to go! Leave me alone!" She walked fast along the sidewalk, away from Doris.

"Please listen to me. I'm only trying to help!" Doris shouted, but Brenda was already turning the corner.

Brenda had no classes that day, but it was the only thing she could think to say. The drugstore was her objective and little else mattered at that point. Brenda walked another block and crossed the street. She flung open the door to the drugstore with such fury that the other customers all looked at her. She looked down, embarrassed, and noticed a slight tremor in her hands. So much had happened, and the revelation of a pregnancy scare only added to her problems.

Brenda rummaged through the aisles until she found the test she was looking for and went to the counter to pay. Her hands continued to shake as she placed the test on the counter.

"Are you okay? You look pale," the clerk said. He looked down at the pregnancy test and then back up at Brenda. "We sell a lot of these to girls in trouble. There is a free clinic across town. You know...if it's positive." Brenda's eyes flashed indignantly. The thought of anyone suggesting she give up a baby did not sit well with her.

"I'll be fine, thank you," she said, and threw the money toward the clerk.

"Okay, just trying to help," the clerk said, placing the test in a bag and handing it to her. Brenda snatched the bag from his hand and stormed out of the store.

When she got back to the apartment, Doris was gone. Brenda was thankful for that; she couldn't deal with another person trying to be helpful. She opened the large entrance door and looked into the foyer. It was dark, but unassuming. The black door, still locked she supposed, looked as though it were miles away.

Brenda made her way to her bedroom and opened the box to the pregnancy test. The directions said to wait until the morning to get a good sample, but she didn't think that would be possible; she had to know now. After peeing on the little stick, it was time to wait. Brenda sank to the floor with her head in her hands, and silently counted the seconds.

When time was up, she reached for the test, her heart pounding and her forehead beaded with sweat. She looked, and her fears were confirmed. *What now?* She wondered. *Will I be able to live on my own anymore or does this mean I should drop out of school and go home to my parents?*

Brenda walked solemnly to her bed and lay there on her back. She massaged her stomach and looked up at the ceiling. Tears welled in her eyes and once again, she cried herself to sleep.

She was dreaming now; on a beach, the sun beaming down

on her; warming her body. She lay lazily on a blanket, listening to the wash of the waves crashing into the sand. She heard the voice of a child nearby. A voice so familiar; it was her voice. She sat up from the blanket to see the little blond-hair girl playing in the sand with her pail in hand, gathering seashells. The realization hit Brenda that this was *her* little girl. She was so beautiful. Brenda reached out, but a wave rose up from the water to crash over the girl and drag her into the surf.

"No!" Brenda screamed. She ran for the girl, *her* little girl, but the water was too strong. Brenda jumped into the water, searching for the girl, screaming and thrashing her arms. She was gone. Another wave grew in the water and its fury consumed Brenda, pulling her under. She struggled violently as it carried her down within its murky depths.

Her eyes opened with a start and she was in bed. The room was dark. Brenda sat up and looked around. There was someone in the corner, a woman in a dress. As Brenda stared in disbelief, the woman glided toward the bed.. As she neared, Brenda saw that she was holding something. No, someone. It was a baby. Brenda's baby. Just like in the dream, she somehow *knew* that the child belonged to her. The woman stroked its hair and the baby cooed. Brenda blinked and her baby was gone, though the woman remained, hidden in shadow.

Brenda looked down at her midsection. Her stomach was round and swollen, ready to have a baby. She fell back on the bed as the woman advanced from the shadows. Sharp pains seized Brenda's insides and she could feel the baby starting to crown. It felt as though her insides were coming out. She screamed in agonized pain as the woman pressed hard on her abdomen to coax the baby out.

Brenda caught a glimpse of her midwife and realized it was the nurse from the stairs. Her skin was pallid and her eyes were glazed over, a milky white landscape with no expression. Brenda pushed one more time and the baby came forth. The nurse held the blood-soaked infant in her arms and turned to walk away.

"Bring my baby back to me. It's mine, not yours!" Brenda cried. The nurse stopped. She slowly turned to face Brenda. The nurse produced a large knife and raised it up over her head. She brought the blade down with a monstrous chop and severed the infant's head. Blood gushed down the front of the nurse's uniform. Brenda screamed and sobbed.

The nurse threw the lifeless infant in the corner and raised the knife again. She ran toward Brenda, shrieking. Brenda screamed and threw her arms up to shield herself instinctively.

She woke in a pool of sweat. She was alone in the room. It was all a dream; a vivid one, that was for sure, but just a dream. Brenda was still shaking when she heard it.

Hush little baby, don't say a word.

Mama's going to buy you a mockingbird

The singing was coming from downstairs. Brenda

reluctantly got out of bed and eased her way to the door. She opened it and saw the nurse at the bottom of the stairs. She immediately closed the door, unnerved by the sight of the ghost. Brenda gathered her courage and opened the door again. The nurse was hovering at the bottom of the stairs, looking at Brenda.

"What do you want!?" Brenda cried. The nurse looked up at her again and then turned her head in the direction of the black door. The nurse continued to sing, as she walked toward it.

Brenda was terrified, but she needed to put an end to this, no matter what that end may be. She opened the door and stepped out onto the landing. She paused before walking down the stairs. She looked down into the foyer, but the ghost wasn't there. There was a creak and light filled the foyer. Brenda crept down the steps with measured caution, her eyes trained on the floor below. She stopped at the bottom of the stairway and looked back into the foyer. The black door was open and bright yellow light shone from the passageway. The nurse was standing there, her white eyes fixed on Brenda. She turned and disappeared behind the open door.

Brenda crept forward. She was drawn like a moth to a flame. The light grew brighter as she drew closer. She stepped into it and was swallowed. The door slammed behind her.

The brightness blinded her; she could see nothing else. Then suddenly, she was plunged into darkness.. She reached back toward the door and found the handle. She turned it, but the door was locked. She traced the door with her hand and found a wall with a railing attached to it. She held onto it for balance and used her foot to tap the ground in front of her. There was a slight drop-off to indicate she was on steps. They must lead to the basement, she thought.

Brenda cautiously maneuvered her way down the steps until she got to the floor below. She couldn't see, but the smell in the air was repugnant. It was antiseptic, like a hospital emergency room, mixed with decay. She felt along the wall beside her and located a switch. A fluorescent bulb hummed into existence and a dim light illuminated the room. Brenda studied the area before her. There were cabinets the length of one of the walls with surgical tools laid out on the countertop. The floor was wet with a liquid she couldn't make out in the dim lighting.

Near the countertop in the middle of the room was a table covered in a large sheet of plastic. Brenda moved toward the table, but hesitated halfway there. She could see the floor, as the lights were brighter now. There was a thick, red liquid creating a large pool around the table. She could hear a continuous drip, emanating from the thing beneath the plastic.

Brenda had reservations about going any farther. She should just turn around and go back to the door. She could wait for someone to come along and open it and everything would be fine. But her curiosity had gotten the best of her and she was trapped, at least for the time being. What would her parents think if they knew she were here?

"Foolish girl," her stepmother would have said. "Why would you let yourself get into a situation like that?"

"Curiosity killed the cat!" her father would have said. Brenda could see his finger pointing in her mind's eye. No, it was too late to take any sound advice now. She reached for the table with the plastic heap on it.

Brenda pulled back the plastic, but before she could reveal what was underneath, something on the wall caught her eye. There were several news clippings pinned to a corkboard. She saw the picture from the article first; it was the building she was in. The caption read: ***The Slaughter of the Innocents***. Intrigued by the title, she read on.

March 1, 1995,

Nurse Margaret Kline of Second and Vine Street, house 122, was shot and killed, after confronting police. The police were called to the residence after reports of an illegal orphanage and abortion clinic were in operation in Ms. Kline's home. When the police arrived, they found Ms. Kline with an infant in her arms. They asked for her to step away and come with them. Ms. Kline appeared to be surrendering, as she placed the infant in a bassinette. At this point, she brandished a shotgun and the police opened fire; killing the woman in the process. Luckily the infant wasn't harmed. After an investigation of the property, police found boxes strewn throughout the basement, full of the bones of several infants that Ms. Kline had apparently delivered and discarded.

They also found her fifteen-year-old daughter and three other women under the care of Ms. Kline. The three women were near ready to deliver. In the basement, they found the body of a woman, decayed, and cut open, lying on an operating table. It is speculated that she was the victim of an abortion procedure gone wrong. The infant that survived and the teenager are in the protection of child services. The police are still investigating the scene and none of the victims' names have been released at this time.

Brenda stepped back, shocked. She saw another article. It read:

Grand Opening of new apartment building

March 1st, 2010

Sadie Kline is opening a new apartment on Second and Vine. The residence is close to the college campus and would be a great alternative to campus housing. Reasonable rates are offered. Only female applicants will be accepted. No fraternities or sororities or anyone affiliated with such, will be accepted. Only serious applicants need apply.

"Sadie Kline?" she said aloud. There was one more article that read:

Investigations are ongoing for disappearances of young girls

October 5th, 2016

The disappearance of another young college girl baffles police. "This brings the total to three now," police reported. All the girls were college students and all were pregnant at the time of disappearance, as reported by their parents, leaving police to speculate the work of a serial killer. If anyone has any information about the girls or their whereabouts, please contact the police immediately.

Brenda's knees were weak and her stomach churned nauseously. She turned to the table. The heap underneath the plastic wasn't moving. Did she expect it to? Brenda grabbed the edge of the plastic and with one jerk, pulled it off.

The scene was, to her horror, what she expected; a girl, or what was left of her. The decayed body looked as though it had been there for a while. The skin was tight around the face; sunken in, with sinewy striations mapping their way down to the neck and up to the hairline. Her lips were shriveled pieces of leather that made her teeth stand out. Her eyes were glassy and bulged from her head. The hair was blonde, that much was evident, and Brenda immediately knew who she was looking at. The only other evidence that was needed could be seen at the corpse's midsection. The girl's abdomen was separated, as if something was torn from it. Brenda didn't have to speculate what that was. The girl was at least clothed and to make the scene more poignant, it was the same clothing that she was wearing in the missing person's photo; a sweater and plaid skirt. The skirt was ripped due to the violent expulsion of a child, Brenda assumed. She looked at the girl with remorse.

"Rest in peace, Sally Freeman," Brenda whispered. Then a

noise made her jump to attention; the door was opening. Brenda started for the stairs when she heard a familiar voice.

"Hello? Is anybody down here?" Doris Freeman said. Brenda turned toward the corpse to cover it before Doris could see. But it was too late. She had a hand on the plastic, but not enough time to cover anything.

Doris stood frozen, staring at the scene before her. The blonde hair and tattered clothes Sally was wearing, were enough for Doris to understand that this was her daughter.

"Sally? Sally, my God no! Please no!" she cried. She looked at Brenda and her sobs became angry. "What happened, why are you here? Who did this to my Sally?"

Doris grabbed Brenda with both hands. Her strength was surprising for an older lady. She shook Brenda and screamed.

"What have you done!? What have you done to her!?"

"I...I didn't do this. I'm sorry," Brenda said, tears of her own streaming down her face. She closed her eyes, hoping Doris would go away. A loud crack made Brenda open her eyes. Doris was staring at her with a confused expression. Blood ran down her forehead from where the baseball bat had split her skull.

Doris slumped to the floor and Brenda saw a grinning Sadie standing there, bat in one hand and a gas can in the other. She set the gas can down and held the bat with two hands. She continued to hit Doris in the head several times, before looking up at Brenda.

"Now, isn't that better? That woman was getting on my last

nerve," Sadie said. "She always got on my nerves. I wondered why Mother took her in the first place, she was nothing but trouble." Brenda stared at Sadie, her body stiff and unmoving.

"Oh, I suppose you'd like to know what the Hell I'm talking about?" Sadie smirked. Brenda was petrified; frozen to the spot. She could do nothing but gape at Sadie in horrified disbelief.

"Mother always took in the college students. They had nowhere to go, poor things. All they wanted was for Mother to lift their burden; take the child, so they could go on living in sin!"

She looked toward the clippings on the wall, ignoring Brenda. "When the police came to take Mother, I knew she wouldn't go. She was too proud, too righteous. What she was doing here resonated with sainthood! She was the ultimate saint! Those girls were nothing but whores!" Sadie's breathing grew labored as she continued to ramble. "Mother sacrificed herself for them and what did they do? Nothing, they just whined and cried, like they were the victims. My mother paid the price for their transgressions. She paid the price!" Sadie shifted her glance to the table. "That girl and her mother," she tilted her head toward the bludgeoned corpse of Doris. "They were the last to die."

Sadie raised her head up, along with the bat, and looked at Brenda with a cold, calculated stare. "All of those girls deserved to die for the sins of their mothers. They were the unborn trash that littered the beds here. But instead of dying, like they were supposed to, they lived. But the apple doesn't fall far from the tree.

They committed the same sins as their mothers did. So, I brought them here, one by one, to put an end to the cycle. But do you know what the best part is? Now that the girls are dead, the mothers will come looking, just like that one!" Sadie pointed the bat toward Doris. She smiled at Brenda and tightened her grip on the bat.

Brenda felt as though her legs would fall out from underneath her. Her gun was upstairs, oh, how she wished she had it now. She looked down at her feet and watched the fresh blood flow like a newly formed river. She had to get out of here somehow, but Sadie was blocking the exit. *How did you get yourself in this situation?* The words of her stepmother resonated in her mind. Brenda took one cautious step toward the stairs, but Sadie put the bat in front of her like a turnstile.

"Oh, dear, where do you think you're going?"

"Please, I just want to leave," Brenda said. Her voice cracked with fear.

"You can't leave, you can never leave. This is where you started life and this is where it will end," Sadie said.

"What do you mean?" Brenda said.

"Come now, you read the newspaper clipping. The baby that mother laid in the bassinette?" Sadie said with a maniacal glee. "That was you!"

"What, but how?" Brenda cried.

"How? Your mother was a whore and my mother was more than glad to rid her of her problems, so she could go on sinning.

That was her plan anyway, but she met the same fate as the girl over there on the table. You, thanks to the police, lived."

"I was the baby that lived?" Brenda said, still trying to comprehend what she was hearing.

"Yes, dear and I was the teenager. Thankfully, mother taught me her trade before she died. She was a midwife, you know, not a nurse like the article said. Mother would deliver the babies and I was responsible for taking care of them after that. She didn't know I was killing them, at first. But instead of scolding me, she protected me. She was protecting me when the police came. She saved your life too, for reasons I'll never know. She should have let you die, instead of putting you down when the police came. It would have been much easier. But that's okay, I'm taking care of things now. And when I'm through, I'll burn this place to the ground!" Sadie said.

Brenda let this revelation sink in. It did make sense, she was adopted after all. All these years, wondering who her mother was, only now to find she had died, scared and alone, on some crazy lady's operating table. Tears welled in her eyes, but she blinked them back forcefully, as her cold fear turned to hot anger.

"You're crazy, bitch!" she screamed.

Sadie leaned in close to Brenda's face and in a cold, but stern voice said, "I'm crazy? You told that cackling bitch on the floor that you saw a ghost. Now, who's the crazy one?" Sadie raised the bat above her head. Brenda stumbled back and grabbed

452

the first thing on the counter she could find. She was thankful it was a scalpel. Brenda stabbed the instrument into Sadie's arm, forcing her to lower the bat. Brenda ran for the stairs, but Sadie still held the bat and brought it down on Brenda's knee. Brenda cried out in pain and fell to the floor, sliding with hands outstretched in the pooled blood.

She tried to get up, but it was too late, Sadie was on top of her holding her down. The woman was unbelievably strong, stronger than she should be. Sadie pulled Brenda's arms behind her back and cinched a wire tie on Brenda's wrists, binding them together. Brenda tried to crane her neck to prevent her face from touching the blood. Sadie turned her over onto her back with the ease of someone twice her size

"Sit still, little girl, it will all be over soon," Sadie said. Brenda tried to sit upright, but only slid back into the blood. She was a blood-soaked wreck, partially coagulated mats in her hair.

"Please don't," Brenda sobbed. "I just want to…"

"What!? What do you want? To go home and forget your responsibilities? To drop out of school and raise that brat inside of you? The same way you were raised? No! You shouldn't be here and neither should that child!"

Sadie brought the bat high above her head. Brenda looked at the monster standing there, with bat in hand; scalpel stuck in her shoulder. The perfect mix of a nightmare she couldn't wake from. Brenda wished she could bring her arms up, to shield herself from the blow. Maybe she would have a chance, but deep down she knew this was over. She hung her head and thought of the baby she would never hold. Her body shook with deep, sorrowful sobs as she waited for the bat to strike her. But nothing happened. Brenda looked up to find Sadie just standing there, staring at something behind Brenda, dumbfounded.

Brenda stretched to look over her shoulder. There in the corner was a ghost. A ghost that Sadie didn't believe existed. But a ghost that Brenda knew was all too real. It was the ghost of Margaret Kline.

She was more brilliant than before, with her hair flowing in streams, like it was caught in a spring breeze. She floated, wispy, and effortless along the basement floor. She wasn't holding a child this time, Brenda noticed. Her eyes were dark sockets and Brenda watched Sadie stare at her mother's face with an intense disbelief. The ghost came between Brenda and Sadie, paying no attention to either of them. She was focused on the table.

Margaret Kline placed a hand on the face of the deceased girl. She caressed the girl's cheek like a mother would if it were her own child. Then she began to sing.

Hush, little baby, don't say a word,
Mama's gonna buy you a mockingbird.
If that mockingbird don't sing,
Mama's gonna buy you a diamond ring.
If that diamond ring turns to glass…

Margaret Kline stopped singing. She only stared at the corpse; her head in a slight tilt. Then she turned to Sadie. Her ebony eyes held Sadie's attention. The light was still bright around Margaret Kline, she illuminated the room in an ethereal brilliance that was hard to ignore.

"Mother, is that really you?" Sadie whispered. Sadie took a step toward her, but as she did, Margaret Kline turned a different color. She had been white; the blaze of a young star. But as she looked at Sadie she turned to a darker hue of blue-black, almost purple. Her eyes became red, as if they were on fire.

"Enough of this!" Margaret screamed.

Sadie covered her ears. Brenda desperately wanted out of there and she struggled to stand upright using the wall as support. She only managed to get halfway before her feet slipped in the blood on the floor. She landed hard on her backside, unable to do any more. She was to be a front row spectator for the family feud.

"But, Mother, I don't understand. I'm just continuing your work," Sadie said.

"Wicked, child! This was never my intention! This is a perversion, you have destroyed my work!"

Margaret, awash in her blue-black flame, rushed toward Sadie; her eyes glowing a brighter red. She placed her hands on either side of Sadie's face and ripped the flesh from her skull. A river of blood cascaded to the floor, as the ghost of Margaret Kline held her daughter; her eyes an inferno of crimson anger. Sadie's body jerked a few times, then fell still. Margaret let go and Sadie's body fell limp to the floor.

The ghost's light changed back to white and she made her way to Brenda, who was cowering in the corner with her head to her knees, trembling. Brenda noticed the light surrounding her and she slowly raised her head to look at the brilliant apparition before her. Margaret seemed almost angelic at this point, very different from the malevolent being that had just killed Sadie.

"You're safe now, my dear. I saved you so long ago, that was always my intention. I wish I could have saved your mother, but some things aren't always possible. I was never the monster that my daughter was. I knew the police would arrest her, so I tried to protect my child. It's what any mother would do."

Margaret Kline faded away into the darkness and disappeared. Brenda was thankful for Margaret's atonement, but now she had to get herself out of here. She pushed her back against the wall and bent her knees.

"C'mon, girl, you can do it," she said aloud. With a strength she didn't know she had, Brenda crept up the wall. Her hands were still tied behind her back, but she was on her feet. She made her way to the table. Though her wrists were bound, her fingers were useable. She located a pair of scissors, but figured that would be impossible to manage in her current state. She scanned through the rest of the tools and found a small knife that she could maneuver with her fingers. She turned her back toward the counter and picked up the knife.. She fought the urge to wretch, as she could see the dismantled face of Sadie right before her.

Brenda mustered all her strength and moved the small knife blade across the plastic strip that held her wrists. It was tedious work and she dropped the knife several times, but she cut enough of the plastic to break the wire tie. Her wrists were bleeding from the effort, but at least she was free of her binds. Brenda wasted no time getting to the top of the stairs and into the foyer. She left the black door open as she walked toward the main entrance. Brenda stopped cold when she heard the door creak behind her and then slam shut. She turned slowly to see, holding her breath. There was nothing there, only the same non-descript door that she had seen several times. Brenda sighed, exhaling a long breath. She shook her head and felt relieved. *I guess that's to be expected, after all I've seen*, she thought.

Brenda turned toward the entrance and the blood left her face. There in front of her was Sadie; faceless, a blood drenched skull with eyes bulging from the sockets. Sinewy tendrils were the only thing holding them in place. Sadie and Brenda screamed at the same time and Brenda covered her eyes with her hands. Then all was silent. Brenda uncovered her eyes to see that Sadie was gone; just an afterthought of a creature that was bound for Hell.

Brenda flew up the stairs to retrieve her phone then ran outside where she called an Uber driver and waited.

The air outside was calm, as dusk had settled in. Brenda's

mood became stolid, she had nothing left emotionally, she only wanted to get away and hide from the terrors that would indelibly haunt her mind for the near future. She wanted to go home and forget.

The Uber driver pulled up to the curb and Brenda hastily jumped in. The driver looked back at her with surprise. He could see the caked and dried blood on her skin and in her hair.

"What happened to you? Do I need to call the police?" he said.

"No. Just drive. Get me the Hell away from here," Brenda said.

With that, the driver obeyed her wishes and drove. Second and Vine faded from the rearview, like some distant memory. Brenda would never return there. She would have her family hire someone to retrieve her things, but she would never step foot in that house again. When the police asked what happened to Doris and the other victims, Brenda said she wasn't sure. She only saw Doris that one time. When they asked if there was a key to the black door, she said she didn't know. They attempted to batter it down, but were unsuccessful.

The house sat idle for the next year, with police tape across the door. Then out of nowhere, a fire destroyed it. By the time the fire department got there, the house was a total loss. The fire was determined to have come from the basement.

That same year, a baby was born to Brenda. She weighed in

at eight pounds and eleven ounces and had a thick tuft of black hair. After the delivery, Brenda held her baby. As the baby began to cry, she stroked its hair and sang.

"Hush, little baby, don't say a word, Mama's gonna buy you a mockingbird…"

About the Author

Edmund Stone is a writer and poet of horror and fantasy living in a quaint river town in the Ohio Valley. It is a rural and backward area from which he derives a wealth of characters and strange ideas. He writes at night, spinning tales of strange worlds and horrifying encounters with the unknown. He lives with his wife, a son, two dogs and two mischievous cats.

Edmund is an active member of The Write Practice, a member only writer's forum. Edmund's poetry is featured in the Horror Zine, Summer 2017 issue. He has a poem featured in issue #6 of Jitter by Jitter Press. He also has two upcoming short stories, one in a Year's Best Body Horror anthology 2017 by Gehenna & Hinnom and February 2018 in Hell's Talisman by Schreyer Ink Publishing.

Contact: edmundstone69@gmail.com or visit him on Facebook.

About the Editor

Amber M. Simpson has been writing short stories and poetry since the age of ten. Lover of all things horror and fantasy, she writes mainly in these genres, often with a touch of romance thrown in for fun. Amber lives in Kentucky with her husband and their two crazy but loving little boys.

About the Editor

Madeline L. Stout started writing when she was a little girl and completed her first full-length novel at the age of 15. Mostly, she loves creating fantasy worlds filled with beautiful creatures and strong heroines. When her husband insists she takes a break from writing, she enjoys reading and gaming. She started *Fantasia Divinity* to give back to the writing community and to help spread great stories. She is the author of *The Moon Princess* and the children's series, *Once Upon a Unicorn*.

Want to know more? Madeline is featured in an interview by Cathleen Townsend, where she discusses the magazine and her writing.

https://cathleentownsend.com/2016/07/29/theres-a-new-e-zine-in-town-interview-with-madeline-stout/.

SEE THESE TITLES FOR MORE GREAT STORIES!

Waiting for a Kiss:
            A Princess Fairy Tale
Anthology

Available Now

The Evil Within:
            A Fairy Tale Villains
                        Anthology
Available Now

Winter's Grasp:
            A Winter Fantasy
                        Anthology

Available Now

Distressing Damsels:
            A Fairy Tale
                        Anthology

Available Now

Made in the USA
Columbia, SC
05 October 2017